Terror

Zeb Carter Series, Book 4

By

Ty Patterson

Books by Ty Patterson

Warriors Series Shorts
This is a series of novellas that link to the Warriors Series thrillers

Zulu Hour, Book 1
The Shadow, Book 2
The Man From Congo, Book 3
The Texan, Book 4
The Heavies, Book 5
The Cab Driver, Book 6
Warriors Series Shorts, Boxset I,
    Books 1-3
Warriors Series Shorts, Boxset II,
    Books 4-6

Gemini Series

Dividing Zero, Book 1
Defending Cain, Book 2
I Am Missing, Book 3
Wrecking Team, Book 4

Zeb Carter Series

Zeb Carter, Book 1
The Peace Killers, Book 2
Burn Rate, Book 3
Terror, Book 4

Warriors Series

The Warrior, Book 1
The Reluctant Warrior, Book 2
The Warrior Code, Book 3
The Warrior's Debt, Book 4
Flay, Book 5
Behind You, Book 6
Hunting You, Book 7
Zero, Book 8
Death Club, Book 9
Trigger Break, Book 10
Scorched Earth, Book 11
RUN!, Book 12
Warriors series Boxset, Books 1-4
Warriors series Boxset II, Books 5-8
Warriors series Boxset III, Books 1-8

Cade Stryker Series

The Last Gunfighter of Space, Book 1
The Thief Who Stole A Planet, Book 2

Sign up to Ty Patterson's mailing list and get *The Watcher*, a Zeb Carter novella, exclusive to newsletter subscribers. Join Ty Patterson's Facebook group of readers, at www.facebook.com/groups/324440917903074.

Check out Ty on Amazon, iTunes, Kobo, Nook and on his website www.typatterson.com.

Acknowledgments

No book is a single person's product. I am privileged that *Terror* has benefited from the input of several great people.

Simon Alphonso, Paula Artlip, Matthew Bell, Gary Bristol, Sheldon Levy, Molly Birch, David T. Blake, Tracy Boulet, Patricia Burke, Mark Campbell, Allan Coulton, Tricia Cullerton, Linda Collins, Claire Forgacs, Dave Davis, Sylvia Foster, Cathie Jones, Cary Lory Becker, Charlie Carrick, Pat Ellis, Dori Barrett, Dave Davis, V. Elizabeth Perry, Ann Finn, Pete Bennett, Eric Blackburn, Margaret Harvey, David Hay, Jeane Jackson, Mary n Bob Kauffman, Jim Lambert, Shadine Mccallen, Suzanne Jackson Mickelson, Blanca Blake Nichols, Tricia Terry Pellman, Tania Reed, Wa Reedy, Colin Rochford, Jimmy Smith, Robin Eide Steffensen, Maria Stine, Don Waterman, Theresa and Brad Werths, Chuck Yarling, who are my beta readers and who helped shape my book, my launch team for supporting me, Donna Rich for her proofreading and Doreen Martens for her editing.

Dedications

To Michelle Rose Dunn, Debbie Bruns Gallant, Tom Gallant and Cheri Gerhardt, for supporting me.

And when the impossible has been accomplished the only reward is another mission that no one else will try

— Night Stalker Creed

Chapter 1

———⌘———

That summer was unusually hot in Berlin. The mercury, normally in the sixties or low seventies, was hovering above seventy-five degrees.

Sunlight reflected off glassed buildings, its glare increasing the sense of heat. Tall structures in the city reduced airflow making the weather oppressive.

The inside of the U-Bahn train, Berlin's metro system, was cool, however. It was morning. Office time. Men and women in suits clutched briefcases and shouldered their way into the yellow carriages on the U1 line.

It was one of the oldest lines in the city but history wasn't uppermost on anyone's minds. College going students, hipsters and the elderly shared space with office-goers in the small carriages. Empty seats were quickly occupied. Many heads bobbed to beats, tunes streaming into their ears through headphones. A few unfolded newspapers and skimmed through the headlines or worked their way through the crossword. Many others stared blankly into space, avoiding eyes the way Europeans did.

The man clutching the guitar case was one such traveler.

He was lean, pale-skinned, wore a dark pullover over a clean pair of jeans. Scruffy sneakers, a beanie over his head, completed his look.

He sat in the corner of a carriage, his eyes closed, his fingers stroking the hard case. No one paid him any attention. Why should they? There was nothing extraordinary about him. He was one of the million passengers the transit system ferried that day.

The train left Schlesisches Tor with a jerk. It rolled over the Oberbaumebrucke Bridge, heading to Warschauer Strasse. A few heads turned to look out of the large windows at the trendy neighborhood of Kreuzberg as it swept past.

The man felt a presence. He opened his eyes. An elderly woman was standing next to him. He stood up, tapped her on her shoulder and nodded at his seat.

She slid past him and settled gratefully, a *danke* leaving her lips. He smiled politely. He looked out of the window. The train was still on the bridge. Vehicles on the street below. A couple of school-going children on the sidewalk waved. He waggled his fingers in return even though the kids wouldn't spot him.

He looked around in the carriage. No one had batted an eyelid at him. There was nothing unusual about what he had done. As his carriage passed over the bridge, he bent and unlocked the guitar case. He withdrew an AR15 and caressed its stock. Someone drew a breath sharply. Another traveler cried out in shock. The man looked at the woman who had occupied his seat. He smiled politely and shot her.

Chapter 2

⎯⎯⎯⎯—⎯⎯⎯⎯

Zeb Carter looked up from the Frankfurter Rundschau, the newspaper he was reading.

What was that?

He heard it again. A rapid burst, loud and clear above the sounds of the train. A sound he was very familiar with, the firing of an assault weapon.

What the heck?

He got to his feet without conscious thought and then the screaming and shouting began.

'*Mein Gott!*' someone cried.

'*Gun!*'

'*He's killing everyone.*'

'*Stop the train!*'

'*Call the police.*'

Passengers slammed the door trying to force it open. Hands reached for the emergency stop and yanked it.

Zeb got to his feet. *Active shooter! In the carriage next to mine.*

Short, controlled bursts. A gunman who knows what he's doing.

Fear surrounded him. Bodies surged away from the deadly

sounds. Pale, pinched faces, mouths open in terror, eyes wide in panic.

'To the floor!' he shouted but his voice was drowned in the voices of fear.

He shoved his way through the crush of bodies as the train screeched and started slowing. He reached the end of the carriage, a door in front of him, as the rifle opened up again.

The next carriage was ahead of him. Another door, separated by a couple of feet of open space. Through the glass windows he could see the scenes of carnage.

Bodies on the floor. Blood on the walls. Limbs twitching. A woman propping up on her hands, only to go down as rounds slammed into her.

The shooter, calm-faced, his back resting against the far end of the carriage. The man replaced magazines without any change in expression and mowed down another passenger.

Zeb opened his carriage door. Cool air greeted his face. Sunlight and the smell of summer and traffic greeted him. The train rocked and shuddered to a halt. They were still on the bridge, sounds of traffic coming up their way. Sirens in the distance, wailing, growing louder. A window smashed somewhere. Voices screamed through it, lost in the summer.

'Don't go there!' a hand grabbed his shoulder.

He shrugged it away.

'Stay down,' he ordered without looking back. He reached forward and tried the door to the next carriage. The handle gave. He pushed it open, crossed the separation in one long stride just as the familiar grey fog flooded him.

It blanked out all unneeded noise. It dissolved the surroundings, sharpened his focus and heightened his concentration. It was something triggered by adrenaline, training and experience.

'Stop shooting,' he said in German.

The shooter looked at him in surprise. His rifle was in his right hand, easily balanced, pointing at a passenger on the floor.

'Put down the weapon,' Zeb told him and took two steps inside.

'Who are you?' the shooter's voice was calm. No nervousness. No panic. No fear. His eyes, dark and fathomless sized the speaker up curiously.

'Put your gun down. Raise your hands,' Zeb repeated and went closer. Less than ten feet between the two men.

The floor sticky with blood. Someone moaned. A child hiccupped in fear. The shooter's eyes shifted and focused on a passenger who was cowering under the seats.

His rifle started moving.

'DON'T!' Zeb yelled. His hand darted towards his jacket.

A body at the shooter's feet jerked. An old man. He grabbed the killer's leg.

The gunman stumbled.

He cursed. He pulled the trigger and rounds peppered the carriage walls in a wavy line. The passenger screamed and ducked. The old man reared up and clawed at the weapon. The shooter slapped him away with his free hand and trained the weapon on him.

'*NO!*' Zeb's palm curled around his Glock in his shoulder holster. He started drawing.

The old man reared up, his teeth bared, groaning and trembling with the effort, his hands clawing at the shooter's face.

The gunman punched him in the shoulder.

The elderly person fell.

Zeb's gun straightened. Body square to the killer, sight trained on him, whose eyes were switching from his attacker to the newcomer in the carriage.

'DON'T MOVE,' Zeb roared. It was aimed at the old man who was rising again.

The gunman snarled. He triggered, the short burst filling the carriage with thunder, his bullets crashing into the attacker, sending him to the floor.

Zeb fired. His first round caught the shooter high in the shoulder, sending him staggering back. His second round was an inch apart.

The German's vest darkened. His eyes spewed hate as he straightened, raised the AR15 and brought it on Zeb who fired once more, into the chest and the shooter fell.

Zeb approached him cautiously and kicked the assault rifle away. He turned the man over with a toe and for one moment stared into the shooter's dying eyes and then turned his attention to the elderly man.

He knelt beside him and saw he too was on his last breaths. He held the man's trembling hands and then he saw it.

Faded numerals on his left forearm.

The man's blue eyes seemed to spark with fire when Zeb looked at him. He struggled to speak. He looked at the killer and drew a shuddering breath.

'Yes, I know,' Zeb whispered. He felt hollow, empty.

What did one say to a man who seemed to be in his eighties and was the only one to fight back at the shooter?

What did one say to someone who had survived Auschwitz only to die in a train, shot by a crazed killer?

Zeb held him close as sound and awareness returned as shouts filled the train and police officers and medics rushed at him. He hugged the concentration camp survivor and felt him die in his arms.

Chapter 3

———∽∞∽———

Zeb answered questions as police surrounded him. He surrendered his Glock, knowing he was in for a lengthy interrogation. *The country has one of the strictest gun laws in Europe.*

He had a special permit for his weapon, one issued by the BND, the German Foreign Intelligence Service, responsible for foreign and military intelligence. *Authorized by Eric Schmidt, the agency's head, who I met yesterday. But if I mention his name, there will be more questions. They will wonder who I am.*

Zeb, a former Special Forces soldier, was the lead operative for a covert US outfit, known simply as the Agency. Barely a handful of people were aware of its existence.

It was headed by Clare, his boss, who never gave out her second name, who carried the ambiguous title of Director of Strategy and reported only to the President. It had eight agents, all of whom were based in New York and worked in a security consulting firm, their cover. That firm was genuine, had real clients whom Zeb and his team advised when they weren't on missions.

The Agency took on operations sanctioned by the most

powerful man in the world. It took down terrorists and international criminal gangs and went after threats to national security. It took on those missions that alphabet agencies and black-ops outfits deemed too risky, and it had always delivered.

Zeb had been in Berlin to share intel with the BND. Information that they, he and his crew, had gathered while on the trail of a Syrian bombmaker who had connections to Germany's far-right party.

'*I'll be happier when you leave my country,*' Eric Schmidt had growled the day earlier. 'Trouble follows you around.'

Zeb hadn't taken offense at the words. He and the German were old friends.

I bet he wasn't expecting this kind of trouble, he thought, as he stood waiting under the watchful eyes of a couple of armed police officers.

The train was still on the bridge, flooded with cops and medics, the former interviewing passengers, the latter tending to the dying and the injured. Fire services personnel were present too, as they forced open jammed carriage doors and escorted travelers to Warschauer Strasse.

The sun continued its climb, beating mercilessly on the scene of carnage. It had witnessed animal and plant species appear and disappear. One day, humans would become extinct too, but it would continue doing what it did, as long as it had hydrogen.

'You are American?' one of the police officers brought Zeb a bottle of water.

'Yes.'

'What are you doing in Berlin?'

'I am a tourist.'

'Tourists don't carry Glocks. They don't run *towards* shooters.'

'I've already answered these questions.'

The officer stared at him curiously for a moment.

'Who was he?' Zeb asked the officer as the elderly man's body was gently laid on a stretcher and carried away.

'Johann Schwann,' the cop replied after a moment's hesitation. The American was unarmed. He *had* shot the gunman, thereby preventing more killings. Answering his questions wouldn't hurt. 'He was a pensioner. He maintained the gardens in a church there,' he nodded at Warschauer station. 'He went there every afternoon, worked for an hour, slept for a while and then returned home.'

'Where was that? His home?'

'Hallesches Tor. He lived with his daughter, just the two of them.'

'You found all of that very quickly.'

'His identity card had enough information on it...' he broke off when his radio squawked. He turned his back on Zeb who stepped back and leaned against the carriage wall as more officers and more white-coated doctors entered the train.

He looked out of the window, to the street below. It was jammed with police cruisers, ambulances and the inevitable news-vans. A crowd had gathered, many of the onlookers flashing their camera phones. A couple of choppers in the sky, circling, a photographer leaning out of one dangerously, his telescopic lens a thin tube against the blue sky.

Zeb's cell phone vibrated. He dug into his pocket and withdrew it. Recognized the number and took the call.

'Zeb!' Beth Petersen asked anxiously. 'Are –'

'I'm fine,' he replied, smiling involuntarily as he heard

another female voice in the background asking questions. Beth and Meghan, twins, the latter the elder of the two by a few minutes. They were his team's glue. They ran the tech side of the Agency, managed the logistics and led the planning of every mission.

They weren't mere desk jockeys; they were active members of every mission.

'How did you know I was on the train?' he asked.

'You've got GPS tags in your shoes,' she replied sharply, 'in case you've forgotten. Werner alerted us the moment news of the shooting broke out.'

Werner, their advanced AI, Artificial Intelligence program.

'Zeb,' Meghan's voice replaced her sister's. 'The shooter… reports said he's dead. You had a hand?'

'I shot him,' he turned and lowered his voice when the second police officer looked at him. 'He was in the carriage next to me.' He briefed them quickly and then said, 'gotta go,' when the other cop approached.

'Come with me,' the officer told him.

'Where to?'

The cop didn't reply. He hopped off the carriage, onto the bridge and walked to the station, fully expecting Zeb to follow him.

Zeb did. He had no choice.

Chapter 4

Half an hour later Zeb was in the Mitte district in the center of Berlin. In the Klaus Kinkel Center for Intelligence, the BND office, the largest intelligence headquarters in the world.

The police officer had driven him from the train station, away from the prying eyes of cameras, using back routes. He had looked consideringly at Zeb as he handed him over to a security detail, wondering just who the heck this American was to get such treatment.

'I told you to leave Berlin,' Eric Schmidt said heavily but there was no anger, no rancor in his tone. The German, short, powerful-looking, with thinning grey hair that was neatly combed, looked weary as he turned off the wall-mounted TV. 'Twenty-eight dead, Zeb. Eight children, seven women, among them. Many more injured.'

His fists clenched and unclenched on the blotter on his desk. 'The chancellor has declared a national emergency. We are on the highest alert, but it looks like he was operating alone.'

'Who was he?'

'Otto Freisler, a mechanic in a garage in Pankow. The

police are still investigating but it looks like he was a loner. He lived in the garage itself. Rent-free, in a small room, in return for also acting as a janitor.'

Pankow. East Berlin. Most populous neighborhood in the city.

'You know how many were in that carriage?'

Zeb didn't reply. He knew his friend was venting. The BND chief hadn't offered him a shower or a change of clothes. That too was normal in the circumstances. 'More than sixty! He would have shot all of them like sitting ducks. There was no escape from that carriage, not while the train was moving.'

'Schwann tried to resist.'

'Ja,' Schmidt nodded his head. 'Perhaps others would have joined him, but who knows!' He rose suddenly, walked around his desk, caught Zeb by his shoulders and hugged him tight. 'Thank you,' he said and by the time he returned to his seat, his composure had returned.

'Now,' he said, all business, 'you don't want your name in the papers?'

'Yeah.'

'It's done,' he waved a hand airily as if it was a simple matter. 'I spoke to Clare moments before you arrived. Our story is that an off-duty police officer shot Freisler. Linda Rosen, you know her, don't you?'

Zeb nodded. The Berlin Police Chief was a highly competent and decorated officer who had risen up the ranks to command one of the largest police forces in the country.

'She has agreed to this as well, as has Dieter Hamm, the head of the Bundespolizei.'

Law enforcement in the country was the responsibility of its state police while the Federal police, the Bundespolizei, looked after border protection, counter-terrorism and protection of federal buildings and agencies.

'A couple of police officers were with me,' Zeb began. 'One of them drove me here.'

'Taken care of. They'll forget they saw you.'

'The passengers –'

'Your description is hazy. No one took any photographs or videos.'

'My gun?'

Schmidt reached into a drawer and produced his Glock. Zeb inspected it. Yeah, it was his. He checked the magazine. It was empty.

'You weren't wearing armor,' his friend said. It wasn't a question.

'No.'

'What if he had opened on you?'

'I wouldn't be here, in that case,' he shrugged. A long silence broken only when the BND chief sighed. 'Thank you,' he repeated and got to his feet. 'Come,' he said and placed his hand on Zeb's back. 'I'll get someone to drive you to the airport. Clare said you were flying to London. To meet Alex?'

'Yes.'

'Twenty-eight people,' the German said softly to himself as they went down the elevator. 'We will take his life apart and we *will* find answers.'

'Schwann's daughter,' he said, as they were walking across the tiled floor to the building's exit. 'She's a teacher. Science to primary school children. She never married. She sacrificed her life to look after her father.'

Zeb nodded, wondering what his friend was leading to. He got his answer a moment later.

'She told the police she heard about the officer who held her father as he died.' His eyes flicked momentarily to the dark, dried patches of blood on Zeb's jacket. 'She thanks that officer and says that her house is his home.'

Chapter 5

As Zeb boarded the British Airways flight at Berlin, a text message was sent from one burner phone in one continent to two others in two different continents.

It has started.

Just that line. Its recipients knew who had sent it and what it meant.

'Lone wolf mission,' Sir Alex Thompson, head of MI6, his friend, told him the next day in London. Zeb had briefed him on the Syrian intel and then the conversation had turned to Berlin.

They were in the SIS Building in Vauxhall Cross, the headquarters of the British foreign intelligence agency. A Mayan temple, one architecture critic had described the structure. It flowed from the top down, leveling out several times until it reached the ground.

Zeb listened absently as he looked out of its window, at the sluggish flow of the River Thames. He had suspected as much after reading the updates the twins had sent him overnight.

'What about social media?'

'Nothing there. That's what is puzzling and scary. Freisler had a Facebook page, but there's nothing on it that indicated he had violent tendencies. Nothing about his motives. He was your typical loner shooter. Kept to himself. His co-workers in the garage said he had no friends. He didn't go drinking with them or join them for meals. Kept to himself.'

'Where was he from?

'Stuttgart.'

Zeb frowned. 'Isn't that the capital of…Baden-Wurttemberg, in the southwest of Germany?'

'I am impressed,' the Brit said drily, 'and you are correct.'

'Germany's far right party did well in that state, didn't it? In the last election.'

'Yes. Eric and I discussed that. But there's no sign that Freisler had any connection to that party. But it's early days. The Germans are throwing everything at the investigation. Something will come up.' He glanced at his watch and smiled wryly. 'I've got to be in Whitehall,' he said apologetically. 'Ministerial briefing. You know how it goes.'

Why would he fire on innocents? Where did he get that AR15? Zeb wondered as he walked from the MI6 building to Regent Street.

He had no answers by the time he reached his destination. The street was a broad avenue with traffic flowing in both directions, separated by a central divider. Stately buildings flanked it on either side with designer label stores at the ground level and offices on the upper floors.

Shopping wasn't his thing…*but the sisters will murder me if I return empty handed.*

London was his second favorite city in the world, after

New York, his home town. The capital's trademark red, double-decker buses, black cabs and that delicious sense of irony that its people had, those were just some of the reasons he loved spending time in London.

He peered through a store window, at a hat on a rack while pedestrians stepped around him, apologizing in that way only the British did. As if it was their fault that he stood in their way.

Yeah, he decided, *Beth will like that. What about something for Meg?*

And that's when he heard the first scream.

Chapter 6

⸺ ❦ ⸺

His head snapped up at the panicked sound. It came from his left, close to him. He stood rooted to the spot for a moment, horrified, when he took in the scene.

A black cab, driving on the sidewalk, mowing through pedestrians, heading directly at him

Zeb sucked his breath sharply, looked away and then back. Nope, his eyes weren't deceiving him. There was a taxi on the sidewalk, crashing into people, as it drove towards him.

It slammed into a couple even as he watched, the man flying through a store window, the woman crushed beneath its wheels with a sickening crunch.

Shrieks rent the air as people fled from its approach. Someone shoved into him, an elbow knocked into his face and then he too was moving, running, no, sprinting at the cab, hurtling towards a mother who stood frozen in her spot, her hands gripping her pram tightly, her mouth open in a soundless scream and then Zeb was lunging, his feet leaving the ground, his left hand curling around her waist, his right grabbing the pram's basket and they were flying in the air just as the cab's nose brushed past them, a wave of air blasting them as it rushed away.

And then he fell hard on the street, the mother on top of him, the pram on its side, but the baby was safe.

Senses heightened. A sharp look up and down the street. No traffic, thankfully. He got to his feet, helped the woman up and righted the pram. The child was screaming, her face red, her tiny fists beating the air punctuating her distress. But she was unhurt.

Zeb tracked the cab which was fifty feet away, moving slower as it continued its murderous rampage, heading towards Oxford Circus Station.

A police officer leaped at the cab only to fall back when the driver fired at her through a window.

Zeb took off in pursuit, leaping over bodies, dodging fleeing Londoners. A bus careened off the street on the other side and crashed into a store front.

Blood on the sidewalk. A writhing woman here, a crushed chest there. And then he forced himself to focus on the black vehicle, letting the darkness inside him, the cold rage that he often referred to as the beast, fill him up with deadly intent, sharpening his speed and senses.

Fifty feet became twenty. The cab was passing a last line of stores on the left. Glock? It was on him, secure in its shoulder holster.

'MOVE AWAY!' he roared and shoved past bystanders who were watching the rampage.

Ten feet. *The wheel's on the right in this country*, he reminded himself. He could see the driver through a rear window. Bald. White. Hunched down. A man went flying even as Zeb ran, his body crumpling from the impact and falling to the street.

The door handle, he panted as he strained to reach for it. It was there... He got his fingers on it as the driver turned his thick neck. Small eyes. Dark. Lips twisted in a snarl. First impressions registering like a camera clicking at high speed. The door opened suddenly and Zeb almost lost his grip. He was dragged by the cab, its driver swerving left and right in an attempt to shake him away.

Zeb hung on. He gritted his teeth and pulled himself level with the window, letting his feet slide on the sidewalk. He reached inside the window with his right hand and grabbed the wheel. Attempted to turn it and let go suddenly when the driver shouted something and a snub-nosed revolver appeared in his hand.

Zeb ducked instinctively as a round fizzed through the air. He punched at the man's face before he could fire again. Above the sound of the growling engine, he heard screaming. Snapped a look up and ahead.

A thick crush of people on the sidewalk where the stores stopped and the large circle of Oxford Circus began. There was the subway entrance to the Tube, London's Underground train network, metal barriers around it, leading to the flight of stairs. More people racing down the steps.

Can't crash into them, he thought as he smashed the driver's face again and wrestled with the wheel.

Where then? He could turn the cab to avoid the Tube entrance and go the center of the circle where Regent Street and Oxford Street met. He would have more room there to try to stop the killing machine.

The driver seemed to read his thoughts. He cursed and his revolver rose again, the black hole of its bore bearing down on Zeb who gave up trying to work the wheel, drew his Glock even as he let his left hand go loose allowing his body to sag behind the window. As rounds flew past his head, he thrust his gun into the cab and blindly triggered until he felt the cab go slack and knew that his rounds had scored.

Zeb flung his gun away. Pulled himself forward with his right hand, pushed the slumped driver away from the wheel with his left, got a hand on the wheel and yanked it hard until the careening vehicle crashed into a lamppost that bent from the impact.

With the driver's foot still heavy on the pedal, the cab's engine groaned, steam escaped from beneath its hood, rubber burned on the sidewalk. The post buckled, metal twisted and tore.

It won't hold for long! Zeb yanked the door open and searched desperately for the ignition. There. He turned off the engine, panted as if he had run a marathon and sagged limply against the vehicle sweat pouring down his face.

Footsteps approaching. Boots. He raised his eyes to see grim-faced police officers train their weapons on him.

'I'm the good guy,' he sighed but raised his hands and followed them to a van.

He climbed inside and found it was a command vehicle. Officers monitoring screens, speaking softly in their radios, and there, next to a uniformed man was Sir Alex Thompson who looked at him and said,

'This can't be a coincidence!'

Chapter 7

—∞∞—

Zeb drained a water bottle that a cop thrust at him and nodded gratefully in thanks.

'How would anyone know where I was?' he wiped his lips with the back of his hand and patted his hands dry against his thighs. 'I walked to Regent Street after I left you. I'm sure no one followed me.'

'I don't mean *you*,' his friend grunted, his attention on the screens that was filled with police cruisers, ambulances, emergency workers. Officers had cordoned off the carnage trail and had erected temporary barriers to protect the privacy of the dead and the injured. 'Berlin, yesterday, London, today. Tell me there's no connection.'

'Different M.O,' Zeb replied. 'AR15 in Germany, cab, here.'

'But the same kind of loner attack.'

'We know that for sure?'

'At this stage we don't know anything,' the head of MI6 growled, 'other than thirteen people are dead, fourteen if you include that driver, and more than thirty injured. This is the worst killing spree London has ever experienced. With a vehicle,' he clarified and then remembered the uniformed officer

next to him. 'Assistant Commissioner Joel Moss,' he introduced, 'meet Zeb Carter. It's best you forget his name and
face.'

'One of yours, Sir Alex?'

'I wish. From across the pond and that's all I will say.'

'You need any medical attention?'

That reminded Zeb that his body was one big hurt. He
fingered his left shoulder and winced when he hit a tender
spot. 'Nothing's broken,' he said, 'I'll keep. There are others
who need more attention,' and with those words the air in the
vehicle turned grim.

'You know him?' Moss asked him after a while. 'The cab
driver.'

'Never saw him in my life.'

The officer nodded as if he was expecting such a reply.
'Had to ask. Anyone take your statement?'

'No, sir.'

'No need for that,' the assistant commissioner waved away
his formality. 'I'll get a couple of officers in here.'

The statements took twenty minutes as the cops made Zeb
go through every minute of his day, making him repeat details
over and over again. They took his fingerprints, photographed
him and read his statement back to him.

'We've got an ID,' his friend said when he re-entered
the van. 'Cameron Walters. Forty-three years old. Lives in
Walthamstow, north-east London. One room flat. Been driving his cab for over ten years. No close friends. Divorced eight
years back. No children.'

Lone wolf, flashed in Zeb's mind.

'Still think there's no coincidence?' Sir Alex challenged
him.

'Anything to connect the two men together?'

'Give us time,' his friend snapped. 'We aren't magicians,' and then he held his hand up in apology. 'Sorry –' he broke off when his phone rang. He cupped it to his ear, whispered into it, muttered an apology and left.

As if on cue, Zeb's cell rang. 'Don't tell me. You're in the thick of it in London, too,' Beth's cheery greeting didn't mask her anxiety. 'Someone filmed your chase and take-down and put it up on social media. Your face is hazy but Werner had enough to identify you.'

'Can we do anything to shut down that clip?'

'Working on it. Clare's on the phone to the Commissioner of the Metropolitan Police, Sir Alex -'

'He's here. He ducked out to take a call.'

'Yeah, so she's managing that end. Meg, Broker and I, we'll make sure your mug's not on the internet. How bad is it over there?'

'Like a war zone,' he said as he watched emergency workers carry a shrouded body into an ambulance.

'My gun?' he asked Moss when Beth hung up. 'I threw it away somewhere on Regent Street.'

'We found it. It's gone to the lab for ballistics tests.' He shifted uncomfortably, 'I heard you on the phone. Your prints, photographs…'

'I think what'll happen,' Zeb grinned humorlessly, 'is you or someone in the Metropolitan police will get a call. My identity will mysteriously disappear. You'll tell a story to the press.'

'We've already got that,' Moss ran a hand tiredly through his short hair. 'A SAS officer is the one who took down Walters. What about the clips though? I'm sure many people were videoing the incident on their mobile phones.'

'My team will look into that.'
'They can do that?'
'Yeah.'
'Can I ask who you are?'
'Me? I'm just a tourist.'

Zeb hung out at the edges of the crowd after leaving the van. The cab was still against the lamp post, its front damaged extensively. Bloodied as well. Tire marks on the sidewalk, marking its travel. Shattered glass and debris on the street. People wept near him while others spoke in hushed whispers as if loud voices would be disrespectful to the dead and the injured.

A police officer walked down the street with a loud hailer, urging the crowd to dissipate, for Londoners to resume their normal lives. He saw the mayor appear on a mobile screen, a live broadcast.

Zeb shook his head unconsciously and wondered again what triggered someone to kill others in such a monstrous way.

London will get back to its feet again, he thought. *It's a resilient city. As will Berlin.*

But who else was out there? Who was plotting such similar attacks, and where?

Chapter 8

———∞∞∞———

Ram Bahadur was making his final preparations when Zeb caught his New York flight from Heathrow that evening.

The Indian software developer washed his car, greeted the watchman in his building and went up to his apartment. He lived alone in Borivali, a north-western suburb of Mumbai. His flat, a modest two-bedroom residence, was sparingly furnished. A couple of couches in the living room, a TV, a dining table, no photographs, no paintings, no decoration of any kind.

He went to the second bedroom which he had converted to a study and sat at his desk. He opened a website, donned his headphones and started listening.

He had to be in the right frame of mind for what he was planning in the day time.

Zeb was yawning and stretching as his flight commenced its descent to JFK. Ten forty-five pm local time.

In Mumbai it was eight fifteen am.

Ram Bahadur drove out of his building. His normal commute took close to an hour, to a technology hub where his employer's offices were.

That day, his drive took twenty minutes, to a school.

He was lucky to find a vacant parking space. He climbed out of the car, opened his trunk and removed a gym bag.

He leaned against his vehicle and when a school bus arrived, he bent down and unzipped his bag.

Children climbed out of the bus, chattering excitedly, a teacher urging them towards the gates.

Ram Bahadur brought out an AK47.

A passing car swerved, its driver looking at him in astonishment. A scooter honked. 'That looks real,' a woman screamed from the back of a cab.

The weapon was genuine.

Ram Bahadur commenced firing at the school children as Zeb's flight landed in New York.

Zeb's step faltered when he turned on his cell phone after clearing the border checks at the airport.

CALL US ASAP! Meghan had texted.

'Where are you?' she asked immediately when he dialed her. Her voice was tight. Controlled. The usual lightness and humor missing.

'Coming into the concourse,' he replied. 'What's up?'

'I see you,' she replied. 'Look to your right.'

He turned and saw his team, all seven of them. The sisters in front, Broker by their side, Chloe flanking Beth, and behind them, towering over them, Bwana, Bear and Roger.

All of them grim-faced.

Small things. A bunch of people crowded around a wall-mounted TV. A South-Asian woman sobbing. An elderly man comforting her. Beth's green eyes narrowed to tiny pinpricks. Meg's left hand twitching the way it did when she was impatient.

'What?' he asked them when he neared.

'That's all you're carrying?' Bwana rumbled, nodding at his backpack.

'Yeah, why?'

'Where's your Glock?'

'I left it behind in London.'

'Told you,' Roger told his friend in an aside, reached down and produced a holster and a gun.

'Your spare gun. We picked it up from the office.'

'What's going on?'

'Come on,' Meghan urged them impatiently. 'Time's wasting.'

'Where are we going?'

'DC. Our Gulfstream's here, waiting for you.'

'DC? Why?' he stumbled when Beth grabbed him by the elbow and forced him to trot.

'Clare's called us to a meeting. Did you watch the news?'

'I was in a flight,' he protested. 'I slept all the way through.'

'Mumbai,' Meghan snapped a glance at him. 'Seven children killed. Dozens critical. The fatalities would have been higher but the killer's gun jammed.'

Chapter 9

'This is what we know,' Clare said at two am in DC. They were in her office, in an anonymous building on Sixteenth Street Northwest. The White House was visible if they craned their heads from the solitary, street-facing window.

'Otto Freisler, thirty-eight years old, garage mechanic in Berlin. Single, white, male.' A second finger on her hand straightened as she addressed them in the board room. 'Cameron Walters, forty-three years old, cab driver in London. Another single, white male. And just a few hours ago, Ram Bahadur, thirty-five-year-old software developer in Mumbai. Single, male, not white.'

'Total –'

'Death toll in the three countries,' she anticipated Chloe's question, 'is sixty-three. Many are still critical and doctors expect more fatalities.'

The silence that fell over them was as thick as the night. A chair squeaked. A water bottle opened. Meghan. She drank, capped the bottle and placed it back on the table. Her face was pale, her skin looked like parchment.

'There have been some developments. All three men were

very active on social media,' Clare announced.

'But Eric said –' Zeb frowned.

'I know what he said. That was then. The Germans have found Freisler had alias accounts. Facebook, Twitter, YouTube, you name it, all three had these.'

'I'm guessing all three were right wing supporters.' Broker hazarded.

'Ram Bahadur is still alive,' Clare corrected him. 'He was captured by bystanders. He hasn't said a word. And his politics and beliefs are decidedly to the left.'

'He's a Hindu?'

'Correct, and Freisler and Walters, Catholic, though none of the three seemed to be very religious.'

'Any contact between them?' Zeb asked. *Why are we here?* He questioned himself. *These aren't the kind of missions the Agency gets involved in.*

'No. Single, male. That's what the killers have in common.'

'And access to guns in countries which have strict ownership laws,' Beth piped up.

'Yeah.'

'How did they get those weapons?'

'No one knows. Look,' Clare rested a hand on the table, the lines on her face showing. 'The Berlin attack was day before yesterday. Investigations need time.'

'Ma'am,' Zeb raised his hand and his boss smiled reflexively. She had repeatedly asked them to drop the formal epithet, but her urging hadn't worked. 'Why are we here?'

'President Morgan,' she straightened as if her boss was in the room, 'wants us to get to the bottom of this.'

She raised her hand to silence the chorus of voices that broke out. 'Not us alone. There's a meeting tomorrow,' she looked at her watch and corrected herself, 'today, of various agencies, us included, to work out responsibilities, that kind of stuff.'

'Ma'am, there've been no such shootings in our country,' Megan objected.

'Not recently, no, and the president wants to keep it like that, and not just here, but in other countries too. Enough,' she stopped their rising voices. 'Grab some sleep. We're meeting at the Pentagon at eleven am.'

Chapter 10

Mohammed Yunus finished his evening prayers and exited Istiqlal Mosque as Zeb was waking up in his DC hotel room.

The mosque was a landmark in Jakarta. Its highlight was the forty-five-meter diameter central dome. The building stood across from a church on the corner of Jalan Lapangan Banteng and drew traffic and tourists.

The forty-eight-year-old bank clerk put on his shoes went to Jalan Veteran and flagged a passing Ojek, a motorcycle taxi.

'Jalan Subaraya,' he told the driver and climbed on. He held on to the bike as the vehicle navigated the macet, the traffic gridlock that frequently gripped the city.

He alighted at the flea market, a street lined with stalls selling trinkets and ornaments. It was lit up in the evening with sellers proclaiming the specialty of their wares as loudly as they could. Tourists and Indonesians browsed and bargained as they drifted through the street.

Yunus wasn't interested in buying anything. He headed straight to a stall he had rented. The woman he had hired to run it greeted him and gave him a bunch of bills. Money, she had made from selling the fake antiques on display. 'Terima

Kasih,' he said bowing. Thank you. He peeled off a few notes and handed them to her, her fees, and waited till she disappeared out of sight.

He reached beneath the counter and brought out a bag. Withdrew the AK47 and stroked it for a moment.

And then went out in the middle of the street and opened fire.

Zeb caught the news when he met his team for breakfast. Eight of them arranged around one large table. Joking, laughing, the way friends did. The dining room wasn't crowded. A couple of families, a few suits poring over files and emails, and them. The ubiquitous wall-mounted TV was playing a news channel. At first no one paid it any attention when the news flashed and then the first 'Oh no' reached them.

Zeb looked up and froze. His friends looked at him and turned to the screen where a grave-looking presenter was standing at the mouth of what looked like a busy street.

Shooter in Indonesia. Flea Market. Gunman opened fire on people. At least eleven dead. Final body count will be higher because of the crowd. Shooter captured and taken away by police.

Ambulances and cruisers raced behind the reporter. An emergency crew carried a bleeding man into a vehicle. Another man consoled a sobbing woman.

No, the killer hasn't been identified yet, the presenter answered in response to a studio question and gave a little more detail.

The screen switched back to the studio where a somber anchor asked a simple question.

'Berlin, London, Mumbai, Jakarta. Which city will be next?'

Chapter 11

———⚬⚬⚬———

'What are we doing here?' Zeb whispered to Clare when they arrived at the Pentagon and after clearing security checks were led to an enormous room.

'Wait and watch,' she replied and went to greet other arrivals.

'Wait and watch,' Zeb said when Meghan quirked an eyebrow at him. They moved to the end of the room, backs to the wall, pulled out chairs and seated themselves. A few generals knew him and his team from their time in the military. None of them were present.

Daniel Klouse, the National Security Advisor entered the room and everyone straightened.

'Let's get this to order,' he started as he sat at the head of the table. Four-star generals flanked him, several suits spread out, and at the far end, Clare, her team behind her.

Zeb recognized the directors of the CIA, FBI, the NSC and the heads of several black-ops agencies. Klouse had winked in their direction on entry but hadn't greeted them. The NSA was their friend, he championed their cause if there was a need. The Agency had delivered on every mission it had undertaken and its stock was high with the President.

'Why don't we do some introductions?' a general growled.

'He commanded the International Security Assistance Force in Afghanistan,' Broker murmured. 'He's now with US Central Command. Accused of sexism. Trying hard to save his career.'

Zeb nodded. USCENTCOM was responsible for theater-level operations in the Middle East, Central Asia and parts of Africa.

'What have these shootings got to do with the military?' he asked.

Broker shrugged. Beth blew hair out of her face. Bwana stifled a yawn and shifted in his chair. He and Bear, all of six feet four inches and built like the sides of barn doors, all of it muscle, were squeezed uncomfortably in their seats.

'Go ahead,' Klouse responded to the general and those seated began introducing themselves.

Some of the most powerful men and women in the country mentioned their grand-sounding titles until it was Clare's turn.

'Director of Strategy,' she said.

The general waited but she said no more.

'I haven't come across you.'

'I have heard of you,' she replied and a ripple went through the room at her tone.

He flushed and looked at Klouse for support but the NSA had found something fascinating in the ceiling.

The general was nonplussed. He opened his mouth to make a suitable reply. Thought again and glared at the Agency operatives.

'They have clearances to be here?'

'Yes.'

'What do they do?'

'They're my aides.'

'That many of them?'

'I strategize a lot.'

'What-'

'Enough,' Klouse said curtly. ''Y'all know each other now. This isn't the time or place for turf wars. How many of you have heard of Jakarta?'

Hands around the table shot up.

'What you don't know is just as the Mumbai attacks were happening, one of our soldiers, a Marine in Bagram, shot four soldiers in camp.'

Gasps in the room. Shocked faces. Heads leaning forward, mouths opening to fire questions.

Klouse quelled them with a look. 'We kept it out of the news, there's enough out there. Berlin, London, Mumbai, Bagram and now, Jakarta. The killer has the same commonalities as the others. Lone, single, male. Yes, the Jakarta killer has been identified. I got a call as I was entering this room. Mohammed Yunus, loner.'

He took a deep breath and looked around the room and continued when he found he had a captive audience.

'I am convinced these are not random attacks. I am convinced something triggered these men. Something made them go out and buy weapons and shoot innocents. This isn't conventional warfare. This isn't terrorism the way we know it. This is *terror*.'

Chapter 12

—eoeo—

Daniel Klouse, the National Security Advisor waited for someone to say something. No one did until Meghan raised her hand.

Zeb suppressed a smile. The twins. Nothing fazed them, not even the presence of four-star generals, or the CIA, or the FBI director.

'Yes?' Klouse asked. The twins were like god-daughters to him but there was nothing other than polite interest on his face.

'Sir, there's no way anyone can predict who the next killer will be.'

'I want you to do just that,' and with that, voices burst out.

Various agency heads shouted, vying for attention. Zeb watched bemused as the aggressive general pounded the table. His boss remained a picture of calm as she looked on sardonically.

The commotion died when Klouse rapped the table sharply. 'Our country's in safe hands if that's the best you've got,' he said sarcastically.

'We should surveil all known right-wing supporters,' the FBI Director suggested.

Which isn't a bad idea, Zeb thought, *except that Bahadur wasn't right wing. Besides, how will the agencies get around the privacy laws in different countries?*

Ideas flowed thick and fast, most of them impractical and after a couple of hours, Zeb was exhausted. He felt a nudge, turned his head slightly to hear Meghan hiss at him, 'What have you done to annoy Clare?'

'I did nothing,' he retorted.

'She brought us here to punish us,' she blazed. 'What other reason can there be?'

Zeb searched for his boss when they broke for lunch. She wasn't visible. He wandered around the room looking for her and came across the general.

'Your boss,' he pointed a stubby finger, 'she's huddled up with the NSA. I don't like it. His job is to be impartial, but it doesn't look like that.

'I'm just an aide, sir. I know nothing of her meeting,' he said evasively and escaped.

There she was, coming out with Klouse. She caught his eye and signaled him and when he reached her, the rest of his team joined them.

'You're greenlighted,' the NSA said gravely, though his eyes were warm. 'Certain attendees had to see that this meeting was pointless. That only a small outfit like yours could deliver results.'

'I don't follow, sir,' Beth.

'The director of the National Security Agency has a significant database on people. He was unwilling to share that with anyone until he came to this meeting and saw how it progressed.'

Zeb exchanged glances with the twins. They all knew what kind of database Klouse was referring to.

'We still don't have the manpower, sir, to follow people. There must be thousands in that list they have.'

'I'll arrange that. You'll get whatever you need.'

'Sir, this database, it won't extend to other countries will it?'

'No. But Zeb, Clare, y'all have connections with other country agencies.' He looked exasperated when there was no further question. 'Why are you still here?'

Chapter 13

---·ᕲᕲᕲᕲ·---

Zeb shaved in his Jackson Heights apartment the next day, an old-style razor in one hand, a warm towel in the other.

They had returned late at night after having agreed on protocols and ROE, Rules of Engagement, with the National Security Agency. They had worked with that body before but the director was newly appointed and hence Klouse's elaborate plan to get him onboard.

I still don't know how we'll prevent the next attack. The lean, tall, brown-haired, dark-eyed man in the mirror had no helpful answers.

Zeb applied the razor to cheek, a smooth downward stroke and rinsed the blade under the tap. His hand faltered when a memory escaped the box, he had stored it in.

A woman's hand holding the blade. Laughing at him as she held his chin with one hand and shaved his thick beard with the other.

The blade fell in the sink with a clatter. He picked it up mechanically and stared unseeingly at the drip of water from the tap as the past came flooding back, triggered by the simple act of removing facial hair.

Another memory. A small boy tugging his mother's leg.

'I wanna shave dad, too.'

'Of course, honey. You'll do it better than him. He ends up nicking himself.'

The sharp edge of the razor bit into Zeb's thumb, brought him back to the present. He stared at the cut on his skin, at the blood seeping out. He washed the wound, finished shaving and wiped his face.

Turned away from the mirror without looking at himself, without looking at the scars, the healed bullet wounds marking his bare chest.

She knew most of those. She knew their history, where I had gotten them, who had inflicted them.

Until one day she didn't know the new ones, because she and their son were no longer around. Killed by terrorists.

Not just killed, he corrected himself. *They made me watch as they tortured her and my son, raped her, and then ended her life.*

The memories still hurt. They still seared. But he was finding it became easier to examine them. To acknowledge them. His hands no longer trembled. His body no longer shivered.

Time. It *was* the greatest healer.

He went to his wardrobe, opened it and examined the neatly folded clothes.

'You fold them better than I do.' A playful nudge with her shoulder.

He drew on a pair of jeans, tucked in his tee and tightened a leather belt around his waist.

He had spent a year hunting their killers. A year in the Middle East, tracking the most dangerous terrorists in the world…and he didn't find them.

And when the news came that a drone had killed his targets, he had felt cheated. Even revenge had been denied to him.

Broken, he had cut all ties and drifted from country to country until in Japan, the oldest sensei he had ever known, started putting him together again. In the head, because there wasn't anything wrong with his body. Along with the healing, he had been taught some of the most secretive martial arts in the world. He had then gone to Kerala, India, where he had learned another dying fighting skill. Then Tibet. High up in the mountains, meditating with the monks in the morning, tending to their sheep in the afternoon, cooking for them at night. Practicing self-defense at dawn.

The discipline, the rigor, had helped him prepare for the world and when he returned to New York, he was ready.

He hadn't dated again. He had no wish to fill the void in him. His team became his family. He pulled on his boots, sent his memories back to the tightly packed boxes in his mind and went to join his crew.

Chapter 14

'You know Daritan Jinhai?' Beth accosted Zeb the moment he arrived at their Columbus Avenue office.

'Yeah.'

'Call him. We need to know everything about Mohammed Yunus.'

Jinhai, the head of BIN, Badan Intelijen Negara, Indonesia's national intelligence agency, was well-known to Zeb. The two had taken down several extremist groups back when the Indonesian was a field operative. He had risen up the ranks and when he had been appointed to the current position, the first person he had called had been Zeb.

'Yunus was a bank clerk, forty-three years old, unmarried.' the Indonesian briefed them half an hour later. It was nine pm in Jakarta but the BIN head was still in his office. 'He was a big believer in peaceful approaches to any problem. He wanted the country to dismantle its military. He believed in dialogue over action. He argued with his bosses at the bank that loan defaulters should be given second and third chances. Supporter of LGBT rights. The last person anyone would expect to go out with a gun.'

49

Maybe that was the point? Zeb scratched his chin thoughtfully. 'Social media accounts?'

'Very active on all of them. Coordinated with various groups for protests and marches.'

'Violent tendencies?'

'None that we have found so far.'

'Can you share everything on him?'

'Sure, the usual means?'

'Yeah.'

The usual means involved splitting any packet of information into smaller pieces, encrypting each one of them and then uploading them to seemingly innocuous websites. A realtor. A dating one. Only someone who had the decryption key and knew where the various packets were, could put together the dossier.

'What are you planning?' Jinhai asked.

Zeb hesitated. The Indonesian knew that he worked on some black-ops team but didn't know the extent of the operations.

Heck, if I can't trust my friends, I might as well give up.

'Finding a way to stop these attacks.'

A long silence and then an incredulous, 'You're serious?'

'Yes.'

'Good luck with that,' Jinhai snorted and hung up.

The sound of squeaking roused Zeb from his thoughts. He looked up to see Beth had dragged the whiteboard to the center of the office and was writing the shooters' names on it.

Otto Freisler

Cameron Walters

Ram Bahadur

Mohammed Yunus

Ruben Moses, the shooter in Bagram

She wrote their ages, their religion, their leanings. Flicked her hair back and when she was turning back to them, Bear said tightly.

'Add one more name to that.'

All eyes swung towards him and then to the TV screen in the office.

Another shooter. This time in Mexico.

Chapter 15

———— ⌦ ————

The three men, John Leslie, Phil Williams and Jack Smith, met in Kowloon's Tim Shai Tsui neighborhood. Those names were aliases, deliberately chosen because they were common.

Each one of them played host, in rotation, for their meetings. It was Leslie's turn for this particular one.

The neighborhood they met in was a district for shopping and entertainment, not where confidential matters were discussed. Which was why the three had agreed to meet in that part of northern Hong Kong.

They arrived individually in the deserted Ozone Sky Bar, on the one hundred and eighteenth floor of the International Commerce Center, from where they had a view of the whole of Hong Kong Island.

The establishment was empty because one of the attendees had pulled strings. Not the grace and favor kind. His involved threats, and given the power he wielded, the request, a command in reality, was acceded.

'Six countries, more than a hundred dead,' Leslie boasted.

They clinked glasses and downed the one-hundred-and-eighty-year-old single malt in appreciation.

All of them wore suits and to the casual observer, they looked like business-men. They *were* business-men, but what they did wouldn't be termed in that manner by that same casual observer.

Each man reported to the second-most senior political figure in his country. Not that anyone in their countries, or anywhere else for that matter, knew of that reporting structure.

All three of them were former special forces operatives in their respective militaries. They were spymasters, they ran secretive outfits that usually operated against foreign countries.

They were unlikely allies. Even the most astute analyst wouldn't dream that the three were working together.

'The program is working very well,' Williams admitted. 'My people have a list of fifty people we are tracking all over Europe. They could be the next killer.'

'We too have about the same in North and South America,' Smith nodded.

'We have about seventy in Asia and the Middle East,' Leslie shrugged. 'It's not hard to find dissatisfied people in that region.'

'Remember,' Williams snapped, 'no one who's already known to the police.'

'This isn't my first operation.'

'What about Bagram?' Smith asked. 'What did we achieve there?'

The Pentagon might have hushed up Moses' attack, but these men knew. There was little that they didn't know.

Williams shrugged. 'This is an algorithm. It's not perfect. We were thinking Moses will go off when he returns Stateside. The damage he could do there would be useful. Unfortunately, he reacted prematurely for us. No harm done. Its further confirmation that the software works.'

'No killing for two or three days. Let all the countries fear what will happen next. Let their people agitate.'

'We know the drill,' Leslie said drily.

'What about the programmers?'

'They are safe, on target.'

'Very well,' Leslie concluded. 'At our next meeting we will decide on the second phase. To more killings,' he raised his glass.

'To more killings,' his guests echoed. 'Next week.'

Chapter 16

───⊷⊶───

Zeb's team met the next day and resumed where Beth had left off.

To the five names she added a sixth. Ramses Jiminez, former gangbanger in a large cartel, who had turned to a life of peace. He lived in Juarez, worked in a grocery store and by all accounts was a person who kept to himself but was always ready with a smile. No one felt threatened by him and by the time he unloaded his AR15 into traffic in the city, it was too late.

Jiminez didn't survive his attack. Police sharpshooters killed him but not before the Mexican had shot eight innocents.

'Check your screens,' she ordered. 'There are files on every one of these killers in your inboxes. The police in all different countries have unearthed more information on the shooters. Go through all of that. Those who wish to read paper,' she raised an eyebrow disdainfully at Bwana and Roger, 'folders are over there,' she pointed to a stack on the center table. 'Two hours,' she said. 'We regroup and share what we have found.'

Zeb took his tablet and lay down on a couch, his favorite spot for surfing the news or catching a snooze. Bear and Chloe curled side by side on another sofa. Bwana and Roger went to the kitchen, prepared coffee for everyone and went to a corner to read. Broker was at his putting strip. He flicked a page on his screen every now and then as he practiced his swings. The twins? They were at their terminals, headphones on, Beth's foot tapping to some music, as their fingers danced on the keyboards.

Zeb looked up at his team momentarily and felt a surge of warmth.

His wife and son couldn't be replaced, but neither could his crew. *They give me purpose.*

'All of them were on Facebook, Twitter, numerous other social media sites,' Beth resumed in a couple of hours. 'Correct?'

'We now know all of them had secret social media accounts, which is where they revealed themselves. Agreed?'

'Yeah,' they all chorused.

'Yeah, but Freisler didn't say anywhere that he was going to kill,' Bwana groused.

'If it were that easy, hotshot,' she sniped at him, 'you think we'd be having this conversation?'

'Someone's grumpy,' Bear said just loud enough for every-one to hear.

'It's Mark,' Meghan explained. 'He's gone undercover, some investigation. She's worried about him.'

Mark, Beth's boyfriend was a fast-rising detective in the NYPD.

'Can we focus here?' the younger sister glowered at her twin. 'Some of us are trying to stop further killers.'

Order restored, the eight of them shared their individual takes on the six dossiers. The internet history of the killers and their fake accounts had come after Zeb had established direct links with the intelligence agencies of each of the affected countries. A call to Klouse had resulted in Moses' file delivered to them.

'Freisler,' Bwana - large, dark-skinned, capable of immense violence if a mission required it – began, 'was your typical right-wing extremist. Hated Muslims, Jews. Thought his country was drowning in immigrants. He was very active in various forums. Spewing hate, inciting violence in others. Nothing about what he was planning to do, however.'

'Got that same take about him,' Bear rumbled. 'Ram Bahadur, however, was the opposite. He wanted India to make lasting peace with Pakistan. He thought his country's military was too aggressive. He wanted re-unification of the two nations. His hatred was directed against his government for not doing enough. He too was violent in his posts. Said the military generals in his country had to be shot.'

Each of them went through their takes from the files and at the end of Zeb's summary, the last one, Broker shook his head in frustration. 'I can't see the big picture here. Sure, they were filled with hate, something they concealed very well while out and about, but it was directed at different causes. Freisler and Walters were anti-immigration and anti-Muslim. Moses didn't want us to be in Afghanistan. Jiminez was sick of the corruption in his country. He wanted the cartels to be dealt with more firmly. Bahadur and Yunus, their rage was against their governments. The only thing common about the six of them was they took out their weapons and fired into people. Random killers in random countries.'

Beth shot out of her chair so fast that it toppled. She righted it impatiently and turned back to them. 'You didn't see

Ty Patterson

all those gun sites and forums they visited through their fake accounts? Few of them were into guns. But all of a sudden, it was as if a button was flicked in them and all got interested in weapons.'

Broker thought about it for a moment and then nodded. 'Yeah, I spotted that. But I still don't get where that leads us. These are random shooters.'

'Random,' she snapped her fingers. 'Meg and I have a theory about that.'

Zeb leaned forward, intrigued. The sisters' lateral thinking abilities, their ability to connect invisible dots, was legendary.

'The National Security Advisor wants us to anticipate the shootings and prevent them. That's impossible. Agreed?'

Heads nodded vigorously. There was no agency, no entity in the world that could do that.

'In that case, we proceed differently. Hate, that was common in all the men. Yes?'

'Yeah,' they chorused dutifully.

'Loner males, no families, no friends, went to work, came home and logged onto these sites. Correct?'

Another set of *yeahs.*

'There are millions of right and left wingers out there. Many of them as hate filled as our perps. But how many of those are lone men?'

'A few thousands, maybe millions,' Chloe ventured.'

'Remember that killing in New Zealand?' Meghan spoke for the first time, her hair lit by a ray of sunlight.

Heads nodded. An Australian extremist had gunned down fifty people in two mosques and critically wounded dozens more. It turned out that he was fueled by white nationalism, intent on creating divisions among people. An anarchist, a

Muslim hater.

'He was steeped in the internet. He went to all those forums where people like him frequented. He had that sick manifesto he posted online. Heck, he even filmed his horrific act.'

'Yes, we know all this. Your point?'

'My point is that people can be turned by online extremism.'

'We know that as well.'

'Here's the thing,' she said slowly. 'Broker said these killers were random. What if they weren't?'

Chapter 17

'What would happen if such killings occurred every month, every day, across the world?' Meghan crossed her arms across her chest, her eyes flitting over them like a seeking beacon.

'That's not possible,' Bear objected. 'There aren't that many killers out there –'

'Six shooters in a week. Did you think that was possible?'

'Things would just come to a standstill,' Chloe cupped her chin thoughtfully. 'People would be scared to go out. Business would stop. There would be riots.'

'Yes!' Meghan wagged her finger in approval. 'Societies would just crumble, because no government can stop such killings and their citizens wouldn't be content with helplessness as an answer.'

'Remember what's happening in the world right now,' Beth clicked on a remote and the map of Germany came up on the wall. 'Right wing parties have gained seats in various elections. Not just there,' another click, a map of Europe, 'but all across that continent. France, Hungary, Poland...Freisler and Walters are very popular with many people in those countries. Britain. A country at war with itself over Brexit. A people divided. India, the world's most populous democracy, is in the midst of elections. Indonesia has its problems with fundamentalist terrorism. Mexico is in a constant state of war with cartels.'

'You're saying –'

'I'm saying democratic world governments have never been weaker. These killings, and if more such acts occur with regularity, will leave them in a perilous position.'

She's got a point. We're seeing that in many parts of the world, Zeb acknowledged. *Lack of trust in political leaders. The rise of dictatorial governments.*

'How do you find such killers?' he asked slowly, liking the sisters' theory the more he thought about it.

'Hold that thought. I'll get to that. But first, to address any doubts you still might have, we ran an algorithm, looking at probabilities. Guess what?' Werner came back with a low number. Very low.'

'Back to your question, Zeb,' Beth joined her sister at the desk. 'There's a list somewhere. Maybe many lists of people of the right psychological profile. Those who wouldn't need much to turn into killers. Drill down into those names, find the right targets, manipulate them and that's your result.' She jerked a shoulder in the direction of the TV. 'Killers.'

Roger rose and picked a basketball off the floor. He ran his fingers on its surface and spun it idly on a finger. 'What you're describing, it's possible?'

'Suicide bombers. Terrorists. How do you think they get turned? Apparently normal men and women, kids, grow up with hate in their minds. They are led to believe killing is their purpose. Psychological conditioning happens all the time.'

'But none of these men grew up in those environments,' he protested.

'They did. Online. The internet is where hate resides these days. It doesn't stay there, it's spread from there, through forums, social media, dark message boards, the darknet, places that don't exist for ordinary people.'

'These men turned into killers just by watching videos, listening to speeches, interacting with other creeps?'

'Now, you're getting to the details,' Beth's smile shaded the sunlight in the room. 'Sis, you want to lead this?'

'We suspect there's a program out there,' Meghan's hands spread wide, indicating the outside world. 'Most likely more than one. Algorithms that identify such people. Push content to them. The more responsive they are, the more such filth gets pumped to them. That's how they get turned.'

'Such algos can be written?'

'Yes.'

'You can write them?'

'They can,' Broker answered. He had been a highly-reputed hacker for the National Security Agency before hooking up with Zeb and joining the Agency. He had mentored the twins, had taught them everything he knew and they had then gone beyond. 'If they had it in them to be so totally immoral. These programs aren't written by ordinary Jane or Joe techie. Someone who's got no sense of right or wrong, or even someone who buys into these people's beliefs…they are the ones who write them.'

'All that,' Beth added, 'but also, these programmers will be some of the best out there. These are high-end algorithms, highly technical, highly complex –'

'The internet companies would have such techies, wouldn't

they?' Chloe rested her feet on Bear's lap and closed her eyes with a sigh when he started massaging them.

'Yeah, but for all the bad press they're getting, I don't think those organizations will have those algos.'

'What's their agenda?' Roger tossed the basketball to Bwana who caught it with one hand. 'I mean, whoever's behind these killers. What do they want?'

Meghan smiled triumphantly at what his question meant. He had bought their theory.

'We don't know,' she acknowledged. 'But we can find out.'

'By asking the right people,' Zeb decided. 'People who would employ such programmers. Like cyber criminals.'

'You knew! When did you work it out?' Beth narrowed her eyes at him suspiciously.

'That thing you said about low trust in governments? That's when. Remember Israel?'

They all nodded. A deadly spymaster had manipulated public opinion in that country by orchestrating a series of killings. He had brought the region to the brink of nuclear war.

'If that could happen,' Zeb shrugged, 'your theory is entirely plausible.'

'What if Beth and Meghan are wrong?' Chloe asked soberly.

'We'll know soon enough. If the killings start again.'

Chapter 18

Meghan was wrong.

There weren't many programs. There were just two algorithms. Their names were self-explanatory to those who knew about them.

The List software trawled social media and identified men with the right psychological profiles. While it was just one algorithm, three clones of it existed. One was maintained by a team of developers in Asia, another was tended to by a second bunch of men in Europe and the third was in the US, in the middle of nowhere in a small town in Colorado.

The Content algo did what the twins had figured out. It pumped the right material, videos, speeches, advertisements, to the men on the list. That program too was localized so that the relevant material was pushed to men in different countries.

List did more than identify targets. It monitored the men and ranked them in order of conditioning. If a subject started frequenting a particular message board regularly, started posting more often, he moved up the list. To such men, Content displayed ads for weapons in the subject's country. And if that man visited that website, the target was ripe.

The three teams that maintained List's versions knew of each other. They had dashboards in the offices they worked from and whenever a man went on a killing spree, that team recorded a win.

Content's developers were isolated from the three teams. There were eleven of them, in a building that looked like a warehouse, in the Nevada desert. Banks of solar panels stretched as far as the eye could see, around the establishment. That solar farm hid their servers' heat signatures. If a lay person visited them, an admin official would explain that the building was a server farm for an internet company. The paperwork was in place to support that cover and several employees in that organization were well-rewarded to maintain that legend.

On the third day from the Mexican shooting, Leslie sent a message to Williams and Smith.

Do we have targets? I have a few.

Yes, the replies came.

Let the killing begin.

Chapter 19

———— ∞∞∞ ————

A conference call between Zeb and his team, Daniel Klouse and Clare. The Agency Director was in Mexico, meeting her counterpart in a covert-ops outfit, but she broke off from the discussions to attend the call.

'The twins have a theory,' Zeb said and gestured to the sisters to come closer to the speaker phone.'

'Of course they would,' Klouse snorted in amusement. 'Meg and Beth,' he said proudly, 'are the brains in your outfit. The rest of you are mere door-kickers.'

Chloe rolled her eyes, Bwana mock-grimaced, but none of them took any offense. They knew how he felt about the sisters.

'You've found something?'

'Not quite, sir,' Beth replied. 'We have this theory,' and rapidly explained it.

'Sounds plausible,' Clare thought about it for a moment. 'What do you need from us?'

'We might have to access some databases,' she said delicately.

'I betcha that's the first time you're asking permission,'

Klouse guffawed. He sobered quickly. 'The President has spoken to world leaders. There is nothing he won't do to restore peace, order. Do what you have to. Clare and I will find a way to cover your backs.'

'Now what?' Bear demanded when the call ended.

'Now, we go talk to Esteban Valdez.'

Travis Garrity knew nothing of that call. Nor would he have cared had he known.

He wheeled his truck out of the drive in front of his house and nosed out on Walnut Avenue in Irvine, California. It was a bright morning. Blue skies, fleecy clouds. An airplane winked silver high above.

It was a perfect day for killing.

Garrity was pumped. The twenty-eight-year-old shelf stacker had visited his favorite forums the previous night. 'Going shooting. Gonna get me some chollos. Watch the news,' he posted. His online buddies cheered him on.

He hung a left on Red Hill Avenue, following the traffic. It wouldn't do to get a speeding ticket, not today. He patted his AR15, gleaming, black, next to him, and fingered the helmet on his head. It had a wireless camera that broadcast everything that he saw and sent the feed to his online hangout.

He turned right on Barranca Parkway and drove inside the enormous parking lot of the big box store. He climbed out, grabbed his weapon and concealed it against his side. Closed his eyes momentarily as he felt the sun. A gun, the sun, wait, that rhymed! He giggled and winked when a mom looked his way. She turned away quickly and wheeled away her baby and her shopping.

Garrity trotted up the sidewalk and entered the cool

inside of the store. Single mothers and fathers carrying shopping baskets. Elderly people lugging their groceries. A few teenagers. And several store workers.

He positioned himself next to the entrance, brought out his rifle, said 'here we go,' in his mic and opened fire on his targets, the Hispanic employees.

Chapter 20

Meghan broke off from her briefing and paled when the news report flashed on their office TV.

They crowded around it and watched and heard. Travis Garrity. Single, white, male, killed by cops but not before he had gunned down thirteen shoppers, three of them women. All of them of Hispanic descent.

The shooter's live feed was picked up by the internet and his sick deed was watched, liked and shared by millions before the large internet companies acted and shut down the video.

California's Governor made a short statement. The President spoke to reporters as he was boarding Marine One. The TV anchor broke down and sobbed as she covered the killing.

'That's our proof,' Meghan said quietly and turned off the TV. 'Let's get back to Valdez.'

Esteban Valdez was a cartel boss, but he was unlike any of his peers. Other gang bosses lived in hiding. They were rarely photographed and while they controlled the world's largest criminal outfits, their whereabouts were rarely known. The FBI, DEA, several alphabet agencies in the US as well as in

Mexico were eager to talk to those heads and hence, they lived their lives underground.

Not Esteban Valdez.

He was out there, speaking at this conference, presenting at that awards ceremony, donating handsomely to a charity. His dark-haired, handsome visage was one of the most recognized faces in Mexico.

Valdez was the head of one of the world's largest cyber-criminal gangs. However there was no proof of his illegal activities. He had legitimate business interests. He owned a shipping company, a trucking firm. He had stakes in a telcoms conglomerate.

'All false,' he replied indignantly whenever reporters questioned him. 'America's FBI have questioned me, and let me state that I presented myself to them voluntarily. They investigated me thoroughly. What did they find? Nada. The Federales looked into me. They too found nothing. All these are baseless rumors, spread by my rivals. I lead a clean life and have nothing to hide,' he would say piously.

The world's intelligence agencies knew otherwise, however. They suspected the Mexican employed hundreds of hackers in Mexico City, Guadalajara, Juarez, Tijuana, wherever Valdez had offices. Those programmers sent out phishing emails, suckered innocents and defrauded them of their savings, the world over.

They also operated cyber-porn sites, online blackmailing campaigns and many other internet criminal activities.

Proof. Evidence. The intelligence agencies of the world lacked those when it came to Valdez. Sure, they had witnesses and snitches, but their statements ended up being withdrawn or contradicted. Many of those people died in mysterious circumstances.

'Not my doing,' Esteban would say, wide-eyed, fresh-faced, the very picture of innocence, as he went about running his criminal empire under the noses of the law enforcement authorities.

The Mexican's guileless exterior hid a vicious, ruthless streak. Those who crossed him died savagely. Some were beheaded, others watched their wives and girlfriends raped by masked men and then were killed. A few men were burned alive in public. Of course, none of the killings had any connection to Valdez. The cartel boss was out in the public, visible, whenever such a gruesome act was committed.

Questioning him wasn't going to be easy.

'He no longer gives interviews,' Beth said tightly. 'Ever since a series of reports broke, suspecting him of running cyber-crimes, he's gone quiet. He surrounds himself with heavies and his public appearances are carefully staged.'

'He would have the right kind of programmers? Those who could do that,' Bwana pointed to the dark, TV screen.

'Oh, yeah. There are rumors on various internet boards that some of the brightest techies in Silicon Valley quit their high-paying jobs and went to Mexico. There aren't many employers there who pay those kind of wages. Valdez's gang is one of them.'

'That isn't proof.'

'All those men, and they're all men,' Beth carried on, 'have gone underground. No sightings, not a peep out of them.'

Bwana had the last word.

'Let's go crack some heads.'

Chapter 21

Planning.

Carrying out a hostile operation in a country that supported the US in the war against drugs had its challenges.

'No Federales, no politicians, no Mexican involvement of any kind,' Meghan said firmly. 'They shouldn't get a whiff of our mission.'

Because Valdez owned politicians, police and army officers. It was how drug cartels work. Viciousness at the street level and corruption at the higher ones.

'Where will he be?' Bear cleaned his Glock and reassembled it in smooth moves.

'The Royal Hotel, in three days' time. One of the fancy ones in Mexico City,' Beth brought up pictures on the wall. 'A block behind the Plaza de la Constitucion.'

The city's main square was a busy place, host to cultural events, political gatherings and tourists. The hotel, on the Calle de la Palma, was one of the most exclusive ones in the city. The country's president often stayed there, as did visiting dignitaries. It had played host to British and European royalty. Its owners had spared nothing in making it one of the fanciest, and safest establishments in the city, catering to the super-rich and the super-famous.

'Eight rooms on each floor,' Meghan drew their attention to the hotel's layout. 'Valdez usually takes over the eleventh floor that has one large suite and three smaller ones. He occupies the big one, his hangers-on, the others.'

Driveway, basement parking, swimming pool, dining room, mirrored glass exterior, the hotel had everything expected of its star-rating.

'Head of security is ex-Federales, Jorge Rameses.' A bald-headed man's picture came up. 'Competent. He has an eight-man team and he also supervises a three-person electronic security team. CCTV cameras, motion sensors, drone checks, yeah, they have those birds loop around the hotel periodically…all those are under Rameses.'

'I'm guessing we can't just walk in, tap Valdez on the shoulder and ask him our questions.'

Meghan's withering glance would have embarrassed most people. Roger grinned and winked at her.

'Our Gulfstream will arrive at the airport in the morning. New tail numbers on it, new registration-'

'You can do that?' Chloe asked, surprised. 'Isn't that illegal.'

'We can do anything.' Just the faintest trace of smugness on Beth's face. 'Records will show that our craft belongs to an oil company which has interests in Mexico. That firm has several such airplanes and its presence will not raise any questions.'

'Security with him?'

'He has a twelve-man team accompanying him always. Armored car. Heavies who surround him the moment he steps out and are with him until he is safe indoors. They take over his floor. Two elevators that stop only at that level. One gunman inside each car, The doors are surrounded by more shooters once they open on the eleventh.'

'How do you know all this?' Zeb asked. 'What kind of security does he have if this is public knowledge.'

'It *isn't* public knowledge, and as to how,' Meghan gave him a pitying look, 'you wouldn't understand.'

Zeb smothered a grin. *She and Beth, they hacked into the hotel. Got all the details from there.*

'What's the plan?' he asked.

Two days later, Mexico City, The Royal Hotel, seven pm.

In that intervening time, Ismail Abbas, a cab driver in Brussels, ran over seven passersby in the city. When arrested, he stared defiantly at the TV cameras and said it was revenge for Freisler's and Walters' killings.

Brussels wasn't on Valdez's mind. He showered and sprayed himself with cologne. Put on the black suit his valet had laid out and adjusted his tie. Went to the next room, where a woman, his current girlfriend, a Mexican film star, was dressing up for the evening. He smacked her on the rump, kissed her on the cheek and went to the living room.

His assistants sprang to attention.

'Tell me,' he snapped at them.

They gave him a high-level snapshot of his business enterprise, the criminal one. How much had been defrauded by his hackers, which accounts the take had been distributed to, new schemes that had been hacked. It was a verbal report that he got daily from his staff. He cross-checked their narrative by logging onto his dashboard at night. Any variance, and there would be questions to answer. Unpleasant ones which usually resulted in an agonizing death.

However, his aides had been with him for a while and they had learned to tell him the truth.

He nodded in satisfaction and dismissed them with a wave when Eva, his companion, appeared.

He gallantly offered her his elbow, smiled brilliantly and stepped out into the hallway.

It was time for him to be honored.

Chapter 22

'Ready?' Beth murmured.

'Yeah,' Meghan replied.

The two of them were in a high-floor apartment opposite The Royal Hotel, on the other side of Calle de la Palma, lying in two bedrooms, both overlooking the Calle de la Palma. The flat was the only one on the street that had a view of the large window at the end of the eleventh-floor hallway in the hotel.

The sisters couldn't see inside the establishment, but they didn't need to. Their hack into its security, supposedly one of the world's best systems, had given them a minute-by-minute itinerary of the awards program.

She cupped her cheek against the Barrett M82's stock, its scope against her eye.

'On the count of three.'

One.

She curled her finger against the trigger.

Two.

She focused on the large window at the end of the hallway.

Three.

She triggered.

Two fifty cals sped out of two muzzles at two thousand eight hundred feet a second. They traversed the three hundred yards of air separating the apartment from the hallway window and burst through its upper corners, shattering it.

Meghan placed the rifle to her side, moving smoothly, swiftly, with practiced ease and picked up the grenade launcher. Put it to her shoulder, sighted and fired.

A stun grenade shot out, sailed over the street and landed in the soft carpet of the eleventh floor.

Quick reload. Fire again, this time a tear-gas round, customized for the launcher.

Ten rounds each, twenty in total between the two of them, burst into the Royal Hotel and rendered mayhem.

At Meghan's count of three, Zeb was seated on a couch in the lobby, idly flipping through a magazine. The remaining operatives were scattered around the enormous hall.

On *three*, he rose, drew a helmet and goggles from his side and wore it over head. The others followed suit. He reached into his pocket and thumbed a remote.

Thunderclaps shattered the Royal Hotel's lobby. Tear gas filled it.

There was a moment's stunned silence. Someone sucked in a sharp breath and started screaming and then the coughing and crying began as the gas worked its effect, filled the room and reduced visibility.

'GET OUT!' Zeb, roared to the dazed residents, 'there could be bombs.'

He got hold of an elderly woman and passed her to another employee 'Take her out,' he ordered.

No one questioned him, and why would they? He and

his crew were in business suits, name tags dangling off their necks, identifying them as security personnel.

He took a second to look around the hotel. Chaos. People holding towels to their faces, their eyes streaming, rushing towards the entrance. Glass shattered. An expensive vase fell from its stand and broke. It was a stampede as the well-dressed patrons raced to the door, blind panic on their faces. It was what they wanted.

Bwana and Bear had moved the instant the grenades had gone off. They ran to the private elevators holding their ID cards. 'Go out,' Bwana shouted to Valdez's men who were blinking furiously, openly brandishing their weapons. 'We're evacuating this hotel.'

'Stay back,' one gunman attempted authority, his barrel swinging up.

He didn't complete his move. Bwana swung his left hand, grabbed the assault rifle and slammed it backwards. Its butt caught the Mexican in the belly. His breath whooshed out and then he sank to the floor when Bwana's right fist connected with his chin.

A second to check that Bear had incapacitated his heavy and then six operatives crowded into the two elevators. Bwana and Bear at the front, the rest of them behind.

The cars shot to the eleventh floor.

Their doors opened.

This was the moment of maximum risk.

If Valdez's men were alert, they would question the presence of the large men. They could shoot without asking questions.

Four shooters, swaying on their feet, dazed, their weapons unsteady, facing them.

'WHERE'S THE BOSS?' Bear yelled at them.

The men instinctively looked to their left, then two of them whirled back at the arrivals. Or attempted that fast move, but their reaction time was severely slowed by the stun and tear gas grenades.

'Who are-'

Bwana and Bear lunged at them, swatting their weapons away, casually. Zeb darted from behind them, his team followed. Spread out in the hallway.

First impressions. Valdez bent on the carpet, three men around him. A woman sprawled nearby. Two heavies groaning and crawling on the carpet. Three shooters more alert than the rest, shouting, their AR15s rising at them.

Zeb took the first one out, a shoulder shot. Chloe fired at the second, Roger took out the last one. Wounding shots, no need to kill. Looking back to see Bwana and Bear had dealt with the four at the elevators and were covering them.

Zeb went to the cartel boss who looked up and attempted a punch.

'You know who I am?' the Mexican staggered to his feet. 'You think you can get away with this?'

Zeb looked beyond him at Chloe, who was helping the actress inside Valdez's suite. The air was still thick and heavy with smoke, the smells of explosions.

'We're at the door,' Meghan, in their earpieces.

That was their cue.

He grabbed Valdez, shoved his Glock against his side and urged him to the elevators.

'I'll kill you,' the cartel boss raged. 'I'll kill your families. I'll-'

His head rocked back, his lips split, when Bwana backhanded him.

Down to the lobby which was largely empty. Hotel manager, racing towards them, flunkies by his side, all of them holding wet towels to their faces.

'STAY BACK!' Beth, helmeted and goggled in a Federale uniform, flashing her ID.

The staff faltered. 'What's happening?' the manager asked helplessly. 'You can't take away senor.'

'LOUIS!' Valdez screamed. 'DO SOMETHING. CALL THE POLICE. CALL THE PRESIDENT. THEY'RE KIDNAPPING ME. THEY CAN'T BE THE FEDERALES.'

He struggled. He yelled. He punched, but to no avail. The operatives hustled him outside, bundled him inside a Federale van. Meghan at the wheel.

Zeb looked out through the closing door and saw the manager wringing his hands helplessly. Tires spun, their vehicle sped off, just as the wail of cruisers reached them.

He checked his watch.

Esteban Valdez, one of the most dangerous criminals in the world, was in their custody, nine minutes from the first shot the twins had fired.

Chapter 23

---∞∞∞---

'WHO ARE YOU? WHERE ARE YOU TAKING ME?' Valdez screamed. They had bound his hands and legs inside the van, Bwana and Bear flanking him.

He jerked his body, wriggled and squirmed and attempted to kick.

Roger placed a hand on his shoulder and pushed him back to his seat. 'Stay down, boy,' he said deliberately insulting. They wanted to goad him, wished to make the Mexican lose his cool.

'I WILL HUNT YOU DOWN. I KNOW YOU AREN'T FEDERALES. WHICH CARTEL ARE YOU FROM?'

We used Spanish all along, Zeb looked at their captive in the rear-view mirror. *He doesn't suspect we're Americans.*

'Shall I cut out his tongue?' Chloe asked, bored. 'He's annoying me.'

'Oh, let me do that,' Bear pleaded.

Valdez shrank in his seat. His face, gleaming with perspiration, jerking robotically as he tried to watch all of them.

'I've got money,' he moistened his lips. 'How much do you want? I can make all of you rich.'

'We've got to listen to this all the way?' Beth sotto-voce in their earpieces.

'A few miles more,' Meghan replied. She drove into a darkened street in the south of the city, stopped behind a large truck.

Roger, Broker and Bear jumped out. They peeled the Federale stickers off the sides of the van while Zeb and Bwana changed its plates. They resumed driving five minutes later, the vehicle now bearing the signage of a courier company.

South, as the city fell behind them and the darkness of the Cumbres del Ajusco National Park loomed ahead.

Off Federal Highway 95, down a dirt track, the vehicle shaking and groaning on its shocks.

'Where are we going?' Valdez asked fearfully as he tried to peer out of the darkened windows.

Meghan stopped in a clearing and reversed to let her twin beams play out on the grass ahead of them.

'DON'T KILL ME,' the gang boss screamed when Bear dragged him out. 'PLEASE. I'LL GIVE YOU EVERYTHING I HAVE.'

Zeb approached him, Glock in hand as his friend made the criminal kneel. Valdez strained his eyes to look beyond the headlights and see inside Zeb's goggles.

'I HAVE MONEY,' he tried again 'HOW MUCH DO YOU NEED? WHAT DO YOU WANT?'

Zeb sheathed his gun in a swift move. Drew out his Benchmade and buried it to the hilt in Valdez's shoulder.

A scream rent through the forest.

Chapter 24

'George Shahi, Paul Kantor, Erik Thoyes,' Zeb recited the names of the programmers who had left Silicon Valley and disappeared in Mexico. 'Where are they?'

Valdez moaned. His head hung on his shoulder as he shuddered and trembled from the shock of the piercing.

'I asked you a question,' Zeb grabbed his hair and lifted his face. 'Where are those men?'

'I...don't...know,' the cartel boss started and then he shrieked when the knife twisted.

'THEY'RE WITH ME. THEY'RE WITH ME.'

'Where?'

'San Mateo Atenco,' he gasped. 'I have an office there. You want them? I can give their address. Take them. Let me go, please.'

'They are working in your gang?'

Valdez hesitated. A knowing look entered his eyes. It disappeared the moment Zeb touched the knife.

'Si, si.' He shrieked. 'They work with many others.'

'On what?' Meghan joined Zeb.

'Many things.'

'Let me cut his testicles,' she pleaded.

'NO! They write programs.'

'What kind?' Meghan asked remorselessly.

'Fraud.'

'You want more of the knife? Explain in more detail.'

'Algorithms that identify old people. Those who have savings. Their programs target such people. Send them emails. Direct them to false websites.

'Is that all?'

That wasn't all. The broken man confessed everything about his criminal empire, each enterprise linking to the next. Defrauding the elderly was the beginning. Another set of programs tracked visitor behavior on social media and enticed them to porn sites. Those visitors were then black-mailed. Valdez went on, each revelation more disgusting than the previous. He gave them names, addresses, bank account numbers and when he finished forty minutes later, he lay spent and gasping on the grass.

'You got that?' Zeb asked the elder sister.

'Beth has.'

The younger twin gave a thumbs-up and held up her phone on which she had captured Valdez's confession.

'What about these killings?' Zeb crouched next to the drained cartel boss.

'Which killings?'

'Germany, Britain, Mexico…don't you watch TV?'

Valdez struggled to sit upright. 'What about them?'

'Who is working on those?'

He blinked, wiped his face on his shoulder, wincing as the wound bled anew. 'Me? I…'

Beth grabbed his hair and yelled, 'Your people are writing

those programs. Where are they?'

'My people?' he jerked and tried to get away from her. 'I am not involved in any of that. Who told you?' Zeb looked at the twins and the rest of his friends. There was a ring of truth in Valdez's voice.

He could still be lying…I need to try once again. He removed the knife and jabbed it into the gangster's thigh. Another shriek pierced the sky.

'JURO POR DIOS,' he groaned. 'I swear to God. I don't know anything of that. None of my programmers are involved in that.'

Chapter 25

Zeb studied the cartel boss as he lay sobbing and groaning in the clearing. He rarely used aggressive interrogation techniques but the recent events justified them.

'I don't think he's lying,' Roger drawled in their headset.

He nodded unconsciously, made to move towards the gangster but Meghan beat him to it.

'You must have talked about it with your people.'

Valdez didn't reply. His breathing was loud and harsh in the night.

'Your techies, they must have some idea.'

'Kantor,' he gasped. 'He's the smartest of them all. I paid him the most to get him to come to us.'

What kind of software engineer will join a Mexican cartel? Zeb pondered for a moment and then shelved the thought. There were more pressing matters.

'I was in their office after the Indonesia killing. He said there were smart people behind these killings. Techies, just like him and the others in my group.'

A flare of interest in all the operatives. They leaned forward as one.

'What else did he say?' Beth asked, her face narrow, intent. If looks could wring information, hers would have drained Valdez.

'That there were not many people who could write such software. Not more than a hundred in the world.'

'Could he write them?'

'Si, si, all of them who came from California. But I wasn't paying them for that.'

'He mentioned names?'

Those engineers, it's a small community, Zeb recalled Beth's briefing. *They hang out in the darknet, in message boards, have nicknames, brag about their achievements.*

'No names. Places. Russia. China.'

They questioned the cartel boss until he was drained and visibly weakening, but he didn't have anything more for them. They cuffed him again and drove back to the city, the van silent, each one of them absorbed in their thoughts.

Zeb noticed the twins exchanging glances at the front and knew how they felt. All this and we got nothing.

'We'll keep kicking doors,' he squeezed Beth's shoulder, 'until we find who's behind this.'

'What if we never find out?' she replied hollowly.

'Then our theory was wrong,' Meghan replied.

'It isn't,' the younger sister's jaw clenched.

'Then stop wallowing in self-pity,' her twin snapped. 'You thought this was going to be easy?'

A reluctant grin spread across Beth's face. She fist-bumped Meghan, equanimity restored.

They dumped Valdez, who was unconscious by then, in front of the Federales building on Paseo de la Reforma.

'Just like that?' Bwana fumed. 'We let him go just like that?'

'Capturing him isn't our goal,' Zeb replied.

'He's the worst criminal in Mexico,' the dark-skinned operative flung his hands in the air, looking back at the body on the sidewalk, as it shrank the further they got away from it.

'Not the worst, but he's up there,' Meghan smiled.

'What?' he asked suspiciously. 'What have I missed?'

'That water he drank…it had a soluble GPS tag in it. It'll stay in his body for thirty days before it dissolves.

'And,' Beth made an innocent face, 'I might have inserted a listening device on his phone.'

Zeb couldn't help laughing at the expression on Bwana's face. 'Now, we'll know what he discusses with his tech people. They might reveal names. Details that might help us.'

'I've been thinking,' Meghan announced from the front.

Bwana raised his hands solemnly to silence them. 'She's been thinking. Enlighten us,' he beseeched the elder sister.

'We should talk to the Russians.'

Chapter 26

———— ❦ ————

Zeb's team gathered in their office the next day to discuss on the intel received on the Brussels killer.

Meghan's idea of talking to the Russians was debated, but shelved temporarily despite her protests. More work needed to be done before that discussion happened.

Aliases had to be set up for the twins, as hackers, so that they could visit various message boards on the darknet. The idea; listen in on any mention of the killings, any names.

At the same time, Alexander Rubix, part of a protest march in Paris, on the Champs des Elysees, brought out a revolver and fired into the mass behind him.

He then stood calmly and offered no resistance when police and gendarmerie officers surrounded him and disarmed him.

In New York, Chloe turned on the TV volume and they crowded around the screen.

'This march was about climate change,' the reporter said breathlessly. She was a professional, a well-known journalist, but even she couldn't hide the fear in her eyes. 'It wasn't against it however. It was organized by non-believers. Rubix made a short statement as he was led away. That his killing was a warning to everyone who were pulling France in a certain direction. He didn't say anything more, but it seems obvious he is one of the right-wing extremists all over Europe who have taken to the gun.' Her professional façade crumbled for a moment. '*Ce qui, arrivee a mon pays!* What's happening to my country?'

Meghan reached over her shoulder to turn off the screen. 'Back to work,' she snapped.

They got back to their seats. There was no more doubt that any of the killings were random.

I wonder how many more will die before we find the mastermind, Zeb thought bleakly, and picked up the phone to make a call to Pierre Guertin, the director of the DGSE, France's intelligence agency.

Leslie, Williams and Smith met again, this time in Geneva, Switzerland. Over cheese fondue and rosti, accompanied by a fine wine, they compared notes.

'More killings from my list,' Williams, the host, said proudly.

'We planned for that,' Smith snorted. 'But we need to be careful, distribute the kills evenly.'

'About that,' Leslie took a delicate sip of his wine, savored it for a moment before swallowing. 'Where are we with the other developments?' He knew, but he was checking to make sure they were all on top of matters.

'America's trade war with China has stalled,' Williams jabbed the air with his fork. 'That case against the telcoms company, that will die down, my sources say. Right now, they're so focused on these killings that everything else is a distraction.'

'Good. Just as we predicted,' Smith smiled smugly. 'In Europe, any talk of regulation on the internet companies has disappeared. Poof! Just like that. They are more worried about keeping their countries together. The European Union has to deal with multiple problems. Brexit, the rise of nationalism in its various countries and our killings.' Which,' he said triumphantly, 'is only fueling that sentiment. People are unhappy with their governments. They want action. They don't know what that should be, people never do,' he snorted contemptuously. 'And the governments are equally clueless. Everything,' he said in satisfaction, 'is progressing well on the killing front.'

'Now,' he leaned forward and lowered his voice. 'What about the acquisitions?'

'The stock markets have fallen,' Leslie replied, 'but they have further to go. We are ready at my end. We have set up shell companies to buy stakes. I hope you two have, as well.'

Smith and Williams nodded. The three of them had identified target companies in Europe, USA and Asia. Internet companies, telcoms firms, organizations that held customer data, because that's what they were really interested in. Customer details, consumer behavior. With that, they could influence people, they could nudge them into certain behav-iors. Like the killings they were enabling. Or influencing their choices at the polling booths.

With data, they could rule the world.

'Remember, we have rules,' Leslie warned. 'The three of us acquire stakes in companies and countries without competing with each other. We will meet again to decide when we start buying. In the US, our approach is different.'

'We don't act until the Dow falls further,' Smith said in a

bored tone. 'And we all buy the same stake in the US companies. We haven't forgotten.'

'What about the G20 Summit in London?'

'What about it?' Smith challenged.

'That's two months away,' Leslie explained patiently. 'By then we should have built enough stakes to take control in all these companies.'

'That shouldn't be a problem,' Williams snorted. 'At the rate the world stock markets are falling, we'll get there quickly.'

'And the announcement at the G20?'

'My boss will begin briefing our leader,' Smith announced. 'I am confident we can make that statement.'

'My superior knows where we are with everything,' Leslie briefed them. 'He is ready to tell our leader when the time is ripe.'

'The same, here,' Williams replied in satisfaction. 'But what about the riots? We haven't seen any, so far!'

'You will,' Leslie predicted. 'Shall we make a bet, a gentleman's wager, on which country will see the next killing?'

'Germany!'

'USA!'

'Britain!'

Williams made a note of the monies they put on the countries and showed it to them. They agreed and then the host called for a toast.

'To riots.'

Chapter 27

⎯⎯⎯∞⎯⎯⎯

Zeb was on the roof of their office building that night. Clear sky for a change. Thousands of stars like pinpricks against a backlit, dark fabric. A few clouds. That red, blinking light over there was an aircraft, passengers in an aluminum tube as they crossed the Atlantic.

He scented her before he felt her presence. Summer and lilac. Meghan Petersen. Bedrock. Anchor as well as sail.

She joined him and looked up without a word.

'It's not like you to be out here, all alone,' she said after a while.

He looked sideways, in astonishment. *It's just like me!*

Her lips curved when she felt his gaze. 'Alright. Who else would escape his friends and be alone?'

'You ever think about how much longer we can do this?' he asked her. 'Going after terrorists, criminals.'

'No. It's what I love.'

He didn't reply.

'Zeb,' she turned to face him and crossed her arms. 'What's up? Why that question?'

'I'm not getting any younger. None of us are. And at times

like these, when we have made no progress, I wonder, are we making any difference? Why are we doing all this?'

He stopped suddenly, aware that he had never confided in any one. Not in this manner and not after what had happened to his family.

He shifted uncomfortably when he felt her green eyes on him, as if she could read his innermost secrets.

'That,' she pointed to the sky, 'those stars, the planets, their movements, that's order. What do you think will happen when that order's broken?'

'There will be a reaction. A new order will take its place.'

'Correct. Now, that,' she looked down at the traffic far below, crawling like insects. 'That too is order, but man-made. What happens when those rules are broken?'

'Repercussions.'

'And that's the difference, Zeb, between what's happening up there and down below. There's order on our planet and in our universe. But what we have, we can control. We should control. Don't you think so? Do we want to have a repeat of what happened to Johann Schwann?'

Flash of memory. Green, faded digits on a forearm.

'Nope,' he shuddered.

'And that's why we do what we do,' she smiled triumphantly. 'That's why you're up here at night, awake, while the world is sleeping. Because it is what you do. It is what you want to do.'

'Besides,' a laugh bubbled out of her and floated and shimmered in the night. 'I can't see you spending your time, fishing.'

You could, honey, when the time is right. With the right person.

He started. That wasn't his inner voice. It was warm and rich, a sound that he had woken up with and slept to, years ago. It was his wife's voice, her dancing eyes in his mind.

'What? What did I say?'

'Nothing,' Zeb swallowed. 'An old memory.' He turned abruptly and headed downstairs.

'Zeb,' she stopped him.

'Will the world be any different if we stopped what we were doing? Who knows? Maybe some other agency would go after these killers and maybe not much would be different. But you know what? You wouldn't be you if you stopped. Neither would I, or Beth or Broker or any of us. Sure, we can't do this forever, but neither can we stop for as long as we're capable, because that's who we are.'

Of course, it's as simple as that, Zeb thought as he watched the way the moonlight glowed around her like a halo and then he nodded, a small movement of his head but it conveyed a wealth of emotion and he went downstairs, ready, energized, to do what he did best.

Take down bad actors.

Chapter 28

'Tverskoy Bratva,' Meghan announced to her assembled flock, some of the most lethal bunch of people in the world, the Agency operatives.

Assembled was describing it loosely for the way they were spread out across the couches, listening to her findings.

'Isn't that a Russian Mafia gang?' Bear stroked his beard, a thing of beauty that flowed from his chin, down to his neck. He tended to it every day, kept it trimmed and tidy. Said it won him half the battles. Looking at him, one could believe his claim.

'Yeah. Not the largest gang, but the most vicious. They're into everything criminal.'

'Why are they of interest to us?' Broker toyed with the golf club in his hand, wiped an invisible speck of dust on its handle with a piece of lint.

'Beth and I, we've been hanging out in the darknet, posing as hackers –'

'While you've been lounging around in the office,' her sister glared at them balefully.

'We found something,' the older twin shushed her. 'A

mention about all these incidents. That the bratva was busy.
It was a remark made by one poster to another, in that snarky
way these dudes have. And they're all dudes. No women in
there. I looked up his post history and he's been dropping
comments about the gang for a while.'

'He specifically r eferred t o t he killings?' B roker s at up
straighter, 'and took the bratva's name?'

'Nope, but there were enough clues in his post... *You been
watching the news? Some Moscow people, have been busy.*'

She pressed a button on a remote and the message appeared
on the screen. A frisson around the room. The sisters' faces
alight with excitement. The first lead.

'How did others on the board respond?' Zeb asked. The
sisters had become reputed hackers themselves, they needed
to be if the Agency had to access various databases in the
world. *They frequently visit all those forums, to know what's
happening in the darknet. They've programmed Werner to
listen in as well. Disposable aliases for different forums,
their tracks hidden by layers of crypto security.*

'Here's the thing. He deleted his post immediately. Hold
fire,' she said when Bwana made to comment. 'We went to the
archives, the database behind that board and got his message.'

'That's wicked,' Broker said admiringly. 'I would've
expected the darknet to have more security.'

'Most of the sites out there, do. But this one is more
vulnerable. It's frequented not just by hackers but everyone.
It's like a clearing house for goss, rumors, that kind of stuff.'

'What else has he posted?' Chloe asked, looking at the
message which was in Russian, which all of them were fluent
in.

'He seems to be a street dealer. Meth, crack, smack. He's

posted about the quality he's got, how he can be contacted.'

'All that in the open?' Roger's jaw dropped.

'It's called the darknet for a reason,' Beth smirked. 'Only those who know the IP addresses of those sites can visit it. And then there are elaborate registration mechanisms to overcome.'

'Surely cops can go to those sites just like you did and see these messages.'

'They could. But proving what's on a forum and what happens on the streets is a different matter.'

'I'm missing something here,' Bwana said. 'How does this dude connect to that gang.'

'This is where it gets better,' Beth pointed to the poster's image and enlarged it until it filled the wall. A pale-skinned face, dark hair, dark eyes. 'That's him. Our poster.'

'That could be anyone. Heck, it could be a fake image.'

'Yeah, and that's what we thought at first. Most posters don't have profile pics. Just their aliases. We ran facial recognition on that image.'

A click. A newspaper report of a crime. The same face in the coverage.

'Meet Roman Azarov. Hitter for the Tverskoy Bratva. Killed two years back in a shootout with another gang in a Moscow night-club.'

Silence as they read through the report and then Bear rumbled, 'I still don't see the connection. That poster could have just used that photo.'

Here it comes, Zeb thought as Beth flashed a triumphant look. *The knockout punch.*

'And this is Oleg Azarov,' she brought up a Facebook page, 'Roman's younger brother. Officially a ride-share driver in Moscow. You want proof? Oleg was online at the same time that message went up on the darknet. All those other posts of his? Our man was on the internet all those times.'

Ride-share drivers, Zeb thought. *Russian Mafia recruits them to be their eyes and ears. Because they see and hear a lot.*

He was convinced. 'You know where Oleg Azarov hangs out?'

'Troitsk settlement. In an apartment that he can't afford. It's possible it's gang accommodation.'

'Let's ask him a few questions.'

'That's what I said a while back,' Meghan snarked. 'We gotta talk to the Russians.'

Chapter 29

The Gulfstream was on its way to Moscow that night as news broke out during the day of more incidents.

The first one was in Dallas. A man was seen driving around a school in Oakcliff. Middle-Eastern looking. Parents reported him to the cops who arrested him for suspicious behavior. It turned out that the man had recently moved to the city and was checking out schools for his kids. As for his looks…. he was recently discharged from the US army, after serving a long spell in Afghanistan, which was where he got his tan.

Several hours later a group of protesters marched to the Dallas PD's headquarters, claiming that the officers had acted on racial bias. Another bunch of citizens marched to support the cops. Words were exchanged, matters escalated, guns were pulled on both sides and, in the brief, ugly shootout, three men were killed. That led to more protest marches, more confrontation scenes, standoffs between the cops and citizens, between groups of protesters and supporters.

In London, in Twickenham, a leafy, affluent suburb, a bus driver crashed his vehicle into a crowded shopping mall killing seven people and injuring many more. When arrested, he claimed he was standing up for the English who were tired of political correctness in the country.

The first riots broke out in Britain's capital when the Agency's aircraft lifted off from JFK. They spread to Berlin when they were halfway across the Atlantic.

'We've got to shut this down. Fast,' Beth said soberly, as they followed the news on the onboard TV.

'What do we know of this gang?' Zeb asked in reply.

'Nikolai Tverskoy, pakhan, the boss. An orphan, found in Moscow, in the Tverskoy neighborhood, from which he took his name. Juvie record of shoplifting, assault. Graduated into dealing and as he grew older, kidnapping, extortion. Killed his first victim when he was nineteen. Served three years in prison. Seemed to make political connections because he was released early and after that, he rose fast. He's smart. He's got connections, like all the gangs, but he's one of the few gangs who are active in cybercrimes.'

'Grigor knows about him?'

Grigor Andropov. Head of a secretive intelligence outfit, the Agency's equivalent in Russia. A good friend.

'Yeah,' Meghan snorted. 'He's got a file on him that he updates each month, sometimes each week.'

'You know this how?' Bear raised an eyebrow.

'We have access to their system.'

Zeb looked at her suspiciously and then broke into a reluctant grin. *Access! I bet Grigor doesn't know of it.*

'Why hasn't he acted on it?'

'Protection,' the older sister said evenly. 'There's one recording in that file of a high-ranking minister in the Kremlin ordering Andropov to back off. Focus on threats against the country, not petty criminals. Those are his exact words.'

'How high a minister?'

'Very high.'

Zeb nodded. It figured. His friend wasn't one to be dissuaded by mere threats, but if the instruction came from someone close to the President...

'How do we do this? We take his help?' Bwana, grinning at the way Beth was digging her toes in the soft leather of the Gulfstream's seats.

The aircraft was a gift from a Middle-Eastern king who was grateful for Zeb and his team saving his family from an assassin. He had wanted to give them a B2 Stealth Bomber, but they had dissuaded him and had finally accepted the aircraft after the royal refused to take *no* for an answer. The younger sister loved its luxurious interior and never failed to appreciate its seats.

'No,' Zeb said. 'It would put him in an uncomfortable situation. We go alone.'

At which, Bwana and Roger fist-bumped. Going by themselves in a country that had turned hostile to Americans, against a vicious mafia gang...they liked the sound of that.

Zeb lay awake for an hour as his friends slept. Watching the rolling news coverage from Dallas, Berlin and London. The TV host mentioned the previous killings as well. The media and the wider public still believed the incidents were random, unrelated, and no one from the intelligence community corrected them.

If they know, there will be more chaos. He crossed his arms behind his head looked unseeingly at the ceiling. Russia had meddled in the last US presidential elections. It had manipulated Britain's Brexit referendum. It had interfered in several European elections. There was no disputing any of that. However, proving it, holding specific people and Russian agencies accountable, was a different matter.

But these killings…what will they get out of it? A weak West was in Russia's interests. It helped its President move attention away from the country's domestic economic and political issues. *Russians will see the US and the West as the enemy. A modern version of the Cold War without the arms buildup. But why India, Indonesia, Mexico and Bagram? How do those incidents help the Russians?*

He thought about it for long but got no answers.

'Zeb?' Meghan, from up front. 'I can hear you thinking. Sleep. We've got a long day ahead.'

He slept.

A Moscow summer was hot and dry, with the mercury usually hovering in the seventies during the day. That summer was no different. The operatives hailed two cabs at Sheremetyevo International Airport and went to Arbat Street in the city center.

It was the oldest street in the capital and had turned into a hub for artists, boutique stores and tourists.

An apartment, an Agency safe house, above a bakery. Smells of bread and muffins greeting them as they alighted. Meghan pressed her thumb against a metal post and when a screen glowed, punched numbers in. Beth shielded her, casually, from any curious onlooker.

Seven large bedrooms. Seven baths. Furnished. Electronically secure but nevertheless, they swept the accommodation. It was clean. The sisters took one room. Bear and Chloe another. The rest of them occupied a room each.

The sisters set up shop immediately. Screens came out of

their bags. They connected to Werner and started running various programs. Broker went to the kitchen and brewed coffee for them.

Zeb and Bwana removed a panel beneath a window and unloaded weapons. HK416s, Glocks, light-weight body armor, stun grenades, knives. They spread them on the floor and let the operatives pick and choose. Meghan came last. She selected armor, removed her jumper, donned it and put back her outer layer. She fingered a Glock, rooted around until she found a shoulder holster.

'Cab booking's made. I told the ride-share company we specifically wanted Azarov.' She snapped the harness on and made sure her gun could be drawn smoothly. 'He will be coming soon.'

'Bear and I will take him,' Bwana growled.

'We want him alive, able to answer questions,' she replied, drily. 'Not die of a heart attack on seeing you.'

The Russian arrived an hour later.

Chapter 30

———— ⊗⊗⊗ ————

Azarov was of medium height, a white shirt, sleeves rolled up to reveal tatts on his forearms. Dark beard, neatly trimmed. He leaned out of the window on spotting Meghan.

'Elena Yeremkov?' he asked.

'Da,' she replied and opened the passenger side door and got in beside him. His jaw dropped when Beth appeared from behind Zeb and the two climbed in behind. He swiveled his neck to get a better look at her.

'What?' the younger sister rolled her eyes. 'You haven't seen twins before?'

'Sorry,' he apologized. 'You're going to The Retreat?'

'Da,' Meghan answered. It was an upscale hotel on the edges of the Tverskoy district, near the Third Ring Road. Secluded. Approach was through a wooded part of Moscow. It was rumored that the Mafia boss often held his meetings there. And why wouldn't he? It was also said that he owned the establishment.

'Posh hotel,' Azarov commented. 'You're staying there?'

'Why would you pick us up from Arbat if we had rooms there?'

The Russian grinned, unabashed. He had a stunning woman next to him. Another in the rear seat. Sure, there was that man with her, but that dude looked bored and was gazing out of the window. A cab driver had to maximize his good luck.

'You're visiting Moscow? Tourists?'

'Da.' That was their cover. Sisters and a friend from Saint Petersburg, visiting the capital to take in the sights. They had credentials, driving licenses, and bus tickets to prove who they were and where they had arrived from.

'That's a Mafia hotel?' Beth asked from the back. 'We've heard some rumors. Will we see any gangsters there? Will they carry guns?'

Azarov looked nonplussed for a moment and then burst into a laugh. 'Mafia? That's nonsense. I've heard that too, but it's owned by some businessman. No gang connections. And you won't see any guns there. Maybe the security at the gate will have weapons but no one else. Moscow is a safe city. I can show you around, if you wish.'

'We'll think about it.'

Moscow didn't have a conventional downtown but the importance of the Kremlin and the historical buildings around it, made the neighborhood a central point.

Azarov left it behind as he drove past the Garden Ring, a circular road around the heart of the city. He pointed to landmarks and important buildings as he navigated the afternoon traffic. A one-way conversation since all he got from his passengers were nods and monosyllabic responses. That didn't deter him and it was only when Meghan unholstered her Glock and mounted a quick-detach silencer that his commentary stopped.

'What-?' he swerved in shock, corrected himself and snapped a quick look at her. 'WHAT ARE YOU DOING?'

'Oleg Azarov,' Meghan turned sideways, the weapon pointing to the floor. 'You lied about The Retreat. It is owned by Nikolai Tverskoy. Your boss.'

'WHAT? WHAT ARE YOU TALKING ABOUT? WHO ARE YOU? I AM STOPPING. GET OUT OF THE CAR.'

'Stop once we are in the woods, near the hotel,' she told him. 'That's where we're going to interrogate you.'

''QUESTION ME?' Anger and fear battling on the driver's face. His eyes shifting from her to the rear mirror, checking if the other passengers had weapons too. A bead of sweat rolled down his forehead. He wiped it away impatiently with a hand and dried his palm against his thigh. 'WHY? WHO ARE YOU? WHY DO YOU HAVE THE GUN?'

'You'll know soon enough,' Meghan told him calmly. An interrogation could be conducted in many ways. Hard and aggressive. Or slow buildup. Another way was to use silence. They were going with the quiet, menacing approach and it seemed to be working by the way Azarov was responding.

He was raging but they could also smell his fear and the twitching on his face, and nervous darts as he drove, spoke of his fright.

His eyes latched onto a police cruiser in the middle lane ahead. His hands tightened on the wheel.

'Don't,' Meghan said. Her Glock moved an inch. 'You don't want to get hurt, do you?'

'I WANT YOU OUT OF MY CAR OR I'LL CALL THE POLICE.'

'What if we are cops? You've got a lot to hide, Oleg Azarov, don't you?'

He moistened his lips. Snapped another look at her. Didn't like what he saw on her face. Turned back to the road and put on a burst of speed.

'I've nothing to hide. I am a cab driver. Nothing more. You're confusing me with someone else.'

'Nope. You're Roman's younger brother. He was a gunman in the Tverskoy Bratva. You joined the gang when he died. You are a low-level dealer for them.'

More lip wetting. Brows furrowed. Eyes squinted as the traffic suddenly died away and the woods surrounded them. Thick foliage on either side. The car's headlights turned on automatically in the relative darkness. No other vehicle ahead or behind.

'I DON'T KNOW WHAT YOU'RE TALKING ABOUT.'

But his words sounded forced. His head jerked as he tried to spot other vehicles.

And then one shot out of a clearing ahead, to their left, drove right across the road and came to an abrupt halt, making Azarov stomp on the brakes, jerking them forward as the Toyota came to a shuddering, tire-burning halt.

Gunmen spilled out of the other car.

Chapter 31

'MOVE!' Zeb roared.

He struck Azarov on the temple and knocked him out. Flung his door open and snapped a shot at the first gunman. A miss, but the round had the desired effect. The approaching shooters scattered. Some dived to the ground. Others darted to seek cover behind their vehicle from where they opened fire.

'Seven of them,' Beth muttered and navigated behind Zeb and ran to the back of the car as he provided cover. She dropped to the ground and started shooting methodically from beneath the vehicle.

'Go,' Zeb urged Meghan as rounds shattered windows and their Toyota rocked.

'Hold up,' she grunted. She freed Oleg's seat belt. Shoved him below the dash, protecting him from the oncoming fire. The driver fell limply and then she burst out of the car, firing blindly and joined her sister.

'There are too many of them,' she yelled. 'Get out before you get hit.'

'Seven aren't enough,' Zeb unzipped the large carry bag he had carried. Brought out the grenade launcher. Armed it.

Ducked and winced when a sliver of glass grazed his forehead. The shooters were firing steadily now, turning the Japanese car into a wreck. The Russians had taken cover behind their car and while they were held back by the sisters' returning shots, they knew they had time on their hands. They just had to wait until the arrivals ran out of ammo. Or more gunmen joined them from The Retreat.

None of them could see inside the Toyota or they would have spotted Zeb point the launcher through a hole in the windscreen. A second to aim, but no great firing skill was required since the opposing vehicle was less than fifty feet away.

He pressed the trigger. A whump. The Mafia car was blown back several feet by the impact. Screams burst through the wood. Zeb raced from behind his cover. Firing at this body, that shooter, and when the destroyed vehicle had settled and silence had returned to the woods, all seven gunmen were out of the fight. Three dead, four immobile from their injuries.

'We got lucky. They were overconfident. They underestimated our firepower,' he said as he searched fallen men quickly and pocketed their wallets.

'Azarov?' he asked Meghan who was at the Toyota.

'Alive.'

'Does our car work?'

'Only one way to find out.'

They hustled the driver, who was groaning and coming to, to the back seat and secured him with zip ties. The elder sister smashed the remains of the windscreen with the gun butt, cleared the seat of glass and climbed inside.

The engine turned. 'Where to?'

'In the woods. Away from the road. The bratva will think we have fled.'

She drove off the road, the car rocking on its shocks as it bumped over uneven ground. Thick trees around them. Fallen logs. A dead silence.

'It won't last long,' Beth murmured. 'The Retreat would have heard the fight. The grenade launcher. Good shooting there,' she smacked a palm on Zeb's shoulder. 'You're bleeding. Forehead. Don't move.' She touched the cut gently and inspected it. 'Nothing serious. No glass on the wound. It will heal. But your looks won't improve.'

'Not that he had any,' Meghan drawled from the front.

'I could be dying,' Zeb mock-protested.

'You aren't. Quit whining.' She looked back and judged that they were far away from the scene of the fight. The road wasn't visible. Silence filled the woods when she turned off the engine.

She got out and grabbed Azarov. Dumped him on the ground unceremoniously and slapped him when he made to shout.

'You saw what your friends did,' she jabbed her Glock's barrel in his shoulder. 'They opened fire without any warning. They didn't care if you died. How did you warn them?'

'A panic button,' Beth, crouched next to the driver's seat. 'Hidden in the cushion. Smart. It goes to some command center where the vehicle's location can be tracked. I guess it has to be used only as a last resort, because those shooters were meaning business.'

'You survived that shooting,' Meghan looked down coldly at the cab driver. 'Do you want to die at our hands?'

Chapter 32

Oleg Azarov didn't need more prompting. He was scared, his wet trouser leg indicating the extent of his fear.

Doesn't look like a hardened criminal, Zeb thought as the sisters hunched next to the Russian.

'I just sell drugs,' the driver stammered, 'Nothing more. I don't know anything else.'

'Start at the beginning,' Beth prodded him coldly. 'How did you get into the gang? What do you know?'

'Don't kill me. I'll tell you everything.' He pleaded and then launched into his story.

Two brothers growing up in a single parent family. Father missing. Mother working several jobs to make ends meet. Died early from pneumonia. The gang proved an attractive home to Roman. His natural vicious streak bloomed in the bratva and he became a shooter, an enforcer. Oleg became a cab driver and stayed away from the Mafia until his brother was killed. The bratva looked after its own and offered him to join. He did. A supplemental income was always welcome and he had no qualms about breaking the law. Nikolai Tverskoy's juice was well known. He never let any of his men stay arrested.

'Only drugs, I told them,' Azarov said brokenly. 'I didn't want anything to do with the girls, killing or other stuff. They agreed. But they said I should report anything I heard in the cab. They have many people like me. We are their ears.'

'What about the message board? In the darknet?'

The Russian paled. 'How do you know about that?' he breathed.

'We know enough to keep you living,' Beth threatened, 'but not for long. Not if you keep anything from us.'

'They found I was good with computers. Nothing special. I repair them. Build simple websites. I advertise online and in local newspapers and get some business that way.' He shrank when Zeb rose silently, went to his bag and returned with a water bottle. He drank from it gratefully, and wiped his lips. 'They told me about the site,' he said hoarsely. 'Asked me to monitor it. Watch who posted what and report back.'

'That's all you did?'

He nodded so fast that the bottle shook, spilling its contents on the ground.

'What about *your* posts?'

'Oh gospodi,' he gasped. Oh God! 'Wait,' he shrieked when Beth racked her slide.

'I didn't mean those. I deleted them immediately,' he cried.

'*You been watching the news? Some Moscow people, have been busy,*' she quoted his post. 'What did you mean by that?'

He blanched even more. Trembled. His hands shook as he returned the bottle. 'I...heard...the pakhan, Nikolai...one night,' he began, hesitatingly.

'I thought you were very low in the gang,' Zeb narrowed his eyes. 'How did you get close to him.'

'Nyet, nyet,' he shook his head vigorously. 'I haven't ever

met him. I am not senior enough. This was accidental. I was waiting for a passenger, there.' He looked beyond the woods, in the direction of the hotel.

'At The Retreat?'

'Da. It was night. I was waiting in the parking lot. No lights that day. It was dark. I heard a man walking towards a car. I began to get out when I heard his voice. It was the pakhan, on his phone. He thought he was alone. I sat back in my car...he was loud. I couldn't help overhearing. He was talking about some program. I didn't understand it at first. Then when he said computers, I realized. It was software. And then he said Indonesia, India and England.'

'What did he say about those?' Beth, the Glock forgotten, grabbed him by the shoulder as if she could shake the words out of him.

'Only those names. He wasn't close to me. And then he must have sensed something because he looked around. I was terrified. I raised the window and pretended I was sleeping. I heard him drive away after some time. I thought he would send men after me, but nothing happened.'

'Why did you write that post?'

He looked away, flushing. 'I was high. I had tried some meth I was carrying. I was seeing every post, I felt I had to join too. And when I came down, I realized what I had done. The gang would kill me if they found out. That's when I deleted it.'

'When did you do that? How long after posting?'

He scrunched his face, trying to remember. 'An hour, maybe?'

Zeb knew the sisters bought his story from the way they exchanged glances. *The time stamps on the board must've matched what he's saying.*

'Where are Nikolai's programmers? Where does he run that program from?'

Azarov fidgeted. He fingered the loose soil nervously. 'I don't know.'

Beth gouged his shoulder hard with the barrel of his gun. He arched off the ground, moaning. 'I swear...I swear. I know nothing of that program,' he sobbed, wiped his face and flopped back to the ground.

'You know everything about the gang. Who runs its operations. Where its people are.' Meghan. Cold-voice, steely-eyed. 'You *watch*, that means you watch and hear your own people too. You've one last chance to tell us.'

'They'll kill me,' he begged.

'We'll kill you first.'

Azarov broke. 'There's an office in the MIBC. One floor. That's where the pakhan's computer people are. But I don't know if they have anything to do with the program,' he said quickly.

'Where in the MIBC?'

He mentioned a high-rise in the Moscow International Business Center in the Presnensky District. West of the central Moscow district where the Kremlin was.

Something crossed his face. He looked away.

Beth grasped his jaw and forced him to look at them. 'What?'

'Before all this started, I went to that office to deliver something. I also am the gang's courier. I saw several empty desks. I had heard of those men. They were the best the pakhan had.'

'Where did they go?'

'I don't know.'

'You didn't try to find out?'

'Nyet,' he eyes widened in fright. 'They would kill me.'

Beth settled back on her haunches, expressionless, her thumb rubbing idly on the Glock's barrel.

Zeb knew what she was thinking, what Meghan was considering too.

Tverskoy moved those men to another location. That MIBC place is where he runs normal gang operations. This program isn't normal. He'll want to isolate the engineers. Another safe house.

He replied to the questioning look on her face when she turned to him. *We've got to move. We're running.*

'Shoot him.'

Chapter 33

'Nooo! Please,' Azarov pleaded and grabbed at her feet. 'I told you everything I know. Don't kill me. I beg you.'

Beth looked at him consideringly. 'You could have held something back.'

'Nyet,' he cried. 'That's all I know.'

'You have seen our faces.'

'I will forget them. I won't tell anyone about you or what happened.'

'They will question you. They'll want to know why you pressed the panic button. Who we were. You know what'll happen. They'll torture you, get everything from you, and then kill you.'

Azarov shuddered visibly. His mouth opened but no words came. Sweat beaded his forehead.

'You know I am right,' Beth told him. 'It's better we kill you. It will be quick.'

'I'll run away,' he said, clutching at her hands. 'I will leave the gang. Escape from Moscow.'

'How?'

'I have family in Vladivostok,' he said eagerly. 'I can go

back to them. I can drive a car anywhere.'

'They'll know you have people there.'

She got to her feet when Meghan put a hand to her shoulder. A silent message. It was time to go.

She hauled Azarov to his feet and hustled him to the car, Zeb leading. Meghan drove, Zeb directing from the back, the Russian flanked by Beth on the other side.

They ditched the car as soon as they left the woods. Hurried to join a bunch of passing tourists. Zeb broke away to go to a nearby parking lot. Cars of various shapes, sizes and colors. An old one there, a Ford. Ancient enough to not have alarms. He looked around casually. No one watching him. Meghan's hair flashed in the distance as she craned her head to look at him. His elbow crashed into the window. Once again, and it shattered. A few minutes later he had hotwired it, collected them and was driving to the Kremlin.

He drove into a hotel lot, parked, and led them inside the cool interior. Went to a clothing outlet in the lobby, sized Azarov quickly and bought him a new outfit. Placed a hand on his back and guided him to the restroom.

'Change,' he ordered.

The Russian changed.

He peeled several bills from a bundle and thrust them at Azarov when they returned to the lobby. 'Lose yourself in Moscow. It's the biggest city in the country. You are better hiding here than anywhere else. Unless you want to make a new start in another city. But not in Vladivostok. The choice is yours.'

'Get yourself a new identity,' Meghan snapped at the driver. 'I'm sure you'll know people. And it'll help if you stay away from gangs.'

Azarov licked his lips. He looked at them nervously. 'Who…' he cleared his throat. 'Who are you?'

'The people who could have killed you, but didn't. Now, go, and forget you ever saw us.'

Beth drew out her phone when he disappeared from sight, tapped its screen and a green dot showed up on its screen. The same soluble GPS in water trick.

'We hit MIBC?' she asked when she put away her phone.

'Yeah,' Zeb replied.

They checked out the commercial complex that evening. All eight of them, casually clothed, posing as tourists, snapping away randomly on their cameras.

Several high rises, many buildings still under construction. It was a multi-purpose complex with offices, residential apartments, retail and entertainment outlets, with over three hundred thousand people either living or working in it once all the buildings were complete.

Eleventh floor in Tower B. That's where Tverskoy runs his cybercrimes from, Zeb thought, recalling what Azarov had told them. He was in front of Naberezhnaya Tower, on the banks of the Moscow River.

The building was not one tower, but three, arranged in a circular fashion. Tower A was the smallest, seventeen floors. B was the next highest, with twenty-seven floors and C was the tallest. Fifty-nine floors, two hundred and sixty-eight meters high. Total floor area of over two hundred and fifty-four thousand square meters in the three towers.

They had to check out the tower, make sure Azarov had told them the truth. Sure, they could question Tverskoy but getting to him, getting past the ring of security he would have around him…*no, going inside the tower will be easier. Beth and Meghan can then work their magic and see if there are any leads to this program.*

He continued checking out the tower. Manned security in the lobby. CCTV cameras. Swipe cards for entry and for elevator use.

'Can you hack the building's systems?' he asked.

'Done,' Beth smirked in his headset. He turned casually and there she was, poring over a map, head bobbing to some tune in her headset. It was designed to cut out music the moment any of them spoke.

'But Tower B's a problem.' Meghan added, seriously. 'We got lobby access and camera access. Not to the elevators, though. And the door to the stairs, that's got palm print security on it. Werner's working on it, but so far, no luck. Floor plans for the eleventh floor aren't available.'

'They're bound to have armed men,' Bwana joined in. 'I hope there will be many. It's been a while since I killed anyone.'

The bloodthirsty, savage words were a front. Sure, he could go lethal in the blink of a second, but only if the mission demanded it.

Zeb looked up at the glassed buildings, prominent against the night sky. *Azarov might have informed Tverskoy who will be prepared.* He knew the likelihood of the cab driver snitching was low. The twins were tracking his movement and there were no signs that he was anywhere near known gang operations. *It's a risk we can't take. Besides, we have to assume the gang's tech people are very good. They might detect what Beth and Meg have done.* Countermeasures could be taken. Traps could be set.

A flashing red light on top of Tower C. A warning to aircraft. That gave him an idea.

'We'll go tonight. Get some sleep.'

'But how?' Meghan demanded.

'We'll fly.'

Chapter 34

'I thought you said we would fly,' Bear grumbled as he peered down cautiously.

They were on the roof of Tower C. Two am at night. No one but them on top of the building. Aircon equipment in the center, pumps and fans working silently. A door for access to the floors, through which they had arrived. Metal barrier and a parapet running around the edge to prevent accidents. A radio mast on top of which was the red light that Zeb had seen earlier. Strong breeze. Cool. Mid-fifties temperature.

Getting to the roof had been easy, with the access cards the twins had cloned for them. The guards in the lobby hadn't raised an eyebrow when they had arrived, wearing a construction company's overalls. The MIBC was still under construction. It wasn't odd to see workers at odd hours. They made aliases and the operatives' covers held. The sisters had worked their magic to ensure that.

They had also taken over the Tower's security and CCTV system which was now on an endless loop.

'You scared?' Bwana's teeth gleamed white as he challenged his friend.

'Nope,' Bear retorted, 'but this idea of Zeb's-'

'Why don't you quit whining and help us,' Chloe cut in.

They had changed into black combat gear on reaching the roof. Masks over their face. Ballistic plate carriers beneath their vests. HKs over their shoulders. Glocks on thigh holsters. More weapons on their bodies. NVGs around their necks. No identity credentials of any kind. If they were caught *FSB*, Russia's security agency, was all they would say.

They didn't plan on getting caught.

Zeb unloaded several gun-like weapons from the bag he was carrying. Several coils of cable. Pulleys. Rappelling gear that he slung over his shoulder.

He picked up one weapon, went to the edge of roof in the strong breeze. Used a range-finder to check distance. Knelt on one knee. Peered through the weapon's nightscope to work out where he would shoot. Adjusted the crosshair and fired.

The projectile shot out with a hiss, carrying lengths of cable with it. It sped through the night sky, and landed on the roof of Tower B. Claws shot out of the device, driven by several tons of hydraulic pressure that could crack concrete. They buried in the roof securely. The cable was secured on Tower B.

Zeb got to his feet and fastened his end to the metal structure that housed the aircon equipment.

'Ready?' he asked his friends.

'You go, first.' Bear told him. 'If you fall, we'll go down to scrape you off.'

Zeb slung a pulley over the cable, tested it with his weight. It held. A safety harness from his belt, attached to the cable with another pulley. Inserted a gloved hand under the first wheel and swung off in the night without another word.

A few seconds of flight. Wind rushing against his face. The ground, down below, moving slower… and then his feet were on hard concrete, a few running steps to reduce speed and he was through, safe, unharmed. He unsecured himself, gave a thumbs up to his watching friends and then realized he had a headset.

'Who's next?' he asked.

Chapter 35

Ten minutes later, all eight of them were on Tower B. Less breezy because C was stopping the free flow of air.

The top of the roof was similar to that on the taller building. Zeb went to the protective barrier and looked down. Slow moving traffic in the distance. No movement at the base of the tower. Broker and Roger joined him as he removed his rappelling cable and fastened a hook to the leg of the aircon pump's bracket.

'This door's open.' Beth said in his earpiece.

He stopped and turned around. Frowned. She and Meg were at the door, which she had opened.

'How?'

'It's got a swipe card access,' she pointed to the white box to a side, 'but that's cracked. Not working. Someone fitted a padlock,' she held it up. 'But didn't bother to secure it.'

'There's still a lot of construction going on,' Bwana rumbled, looming, dark, blocking light from the night sky. 'Those workers could have fitted the padlock, saving them the trouble of putting a new swipe system until all the work's done.'

'And someone forgot to lock it,' Chloe added.

Makes sense. Mistakes happen.

'We go down the stairs,' Broker's lip quirked, 'like normal operatives, or rappel?'

Zeb rubbed his jaw as he thought fast. His plan had been to slide down Tower B's side, break into the eleventh floor, grab anything important they could find and exit the same way.

'Entry by stairs, exfil by rope.' He went to the parapet and secured his cable to the hook and tossed the free end over the side. The others joined him, followed his actions, not one of them asking him to explain.

It was their way. A well-oiled team. Trust was second nature.

He led the way down, the others behind, spread out to ensure all of them had good fields of fire. HK in their hands, creeping down the stairs silently, clearing level after level, senses on high alert.

No gunmen accosted them. Not surprising, given the time. Pause for a breather on the seventeenth. Check on his team. Beth and Meghan leaning against the wall, the younger sister winking at him. Bear holding Chloe. Bwana and Roger whispering something. Broker, eyes closed. All of them breathing easily. Sixteen flights of stairs was nothing to them.

He signaled with his fist and they set off down the brightly lit stairs.

Eleventh floor. A simple door separating them from the gang's office. A swipe card box.

'No camera,' Meghan murmured. 'That's good.' She knelt to the floor and inserted a near-invisible cable through the gap between the door and floor. Attached its free end to her phone. A screen popped up, an image appeared, as the camera at the end of the wire sent its feed.

'Four armed men at the two elevators. One man behind the reception desk.'

They craned over her shoulder and watched. The landing door opened in a hallway and by the looks of it, was in the corner. Elevators to its right and another bank of them, opposite to the first set.

'All of those dudes are relaxed,' Broker murmured.

'Tranqs?' Zeb asked.

A chorus of yeahs. Chloe patted the tranquilizer gun at her waist.

'Let's do this.'

Chapter 36

Meghan unscrewed the card terminal, examined the insides for a moment. Brought out an RF jammer and held it to the face of the screen.

'It messes up the radio frequencies of this scanner,' she explained more to herself. 'But that man at the console? He'll get a warning alert. Ready?' she asked.

They nodded.

She got the handle of the door, gave a thumbs up and flung it open.

Zeb went through first. One long step inside. Tranq gun coming up smoothly as the four men, startled at the sudden entry, starting turning towards them.

He fired. The dart landed in the nearest gunman's chest. It was fast-acting and the man was already falling limply to the ground by the time Zeb reached him in three long strides, ignoring the other gunmen. His team would deal with them.

He caught the falling man before his gun clattered to the floor. That was important. Reduce noise. He laid out the man, removed the magazine from his AR15 and when he looked up, the rest of the gunmen were incapacitated.

Glass door at the end of the hallway. Darkened office beyond. Another card access system which Meghan was already working on.

'Listen up,' she said sharply. 'We don't know what countermeasures they'll have. There could be silent alarms. Reinforcements could arrive. Our window is very short. We don't know how long.'

'Gotcha, sis,' Beth drawled. 'Open that door.'

She flung it open and they rushed inside. No alarms. Ceiling lights turned on automatically, triggered by motion.

Carpeted hallway. Cubicles with monitors on either side, like any other office, except that this was a cartel office. Hallway turned right ahead and disappeared and from somewhere, a voice yelled, 'Yuri?'

Zeb took off in its direction. Chloe joined him. Spread out. Reached the end of the hallway. Pause. A murmur reached them.

'Two men,' Chloe mouthed. 'Pantry?' when the sounds of clinking reached them.

Zeb nodded, held up three fingers, folded the first, then the second and on the third, they turned around the corner.

Another hallway. More cubicles. Glassed offices at the end. A pantry to their right, lit from where the sounds were coming and now that they got closer, they could hear music.

'Hey,' Chloe stood in the kitchen's entrance and gave the two men a blinding smile.

A split-second of shock, confusion, which was all they needed to fire two more darts and take out the men.

Zeb and Chloe, Broker, and Bear, Bwana and Roger, swept through the entire office, made sure there were no more men and when they returned to the pantry, Beth and Meghan had each occupied an office. They were at monitors. Password generators fired millions of combinations at the desktops until a *gotcha* from the younger sister, confirmed she was in the system.

Meghan, frowning, flicking her hair back, biting her lip unconsciously, fingers dancing on the keyboard.

'Anything we can do?'

'Stay away,' Beth smirked and then her smile faded. 'You see this, Meg?'

'Yeah.' Voice strained. Eyes wide. The elder sister looked up at Zeb. 'There's a self-destruct program running here. Countdown's begun. Twenty seconds. Don't know if there are explosives in the office.'

Zeb was moving even before she had ended. Running past her office to the large windows on the wall. The first one, outside of which were their ropes.

He reached down to his thighs and brought out a plastic explosive charge. Leaped up as high as he could and stuck it against the glass. Jammed a detonator in it as Bear and Bwana attached more charges.

'Ten seconds.' Beth called out.

'Come on,' Chloe shouted at them.

A second more and then Meghan raced out of her office, closing her backpack, yanking Beth by the hand, urging her to run.

'NOW!' Zeb ordered and triggered the explosives.

Flash of light. Dull sounds. Glass shattered and blew out until nothing stood between them and the night and then more explosions in the office, alarms going off, red flashes as the kill program spread throughout the floor.

A body swept past Zeb. Meghan, her arms reaching out

to the cable, gripping it and then she disappeared out of sight. Beth followed. Chloe. Bwana, Bear, Broker who thumped his shoulder as he leaped.

'COME ON!'

Zeb looked back one last time. Hollywood couldn't have staged it better. A ball of fire raging in the office, sparks and flashes racing towards him as the desktops exploded, furniture burned. Water sprinklers had turned on but they were waging a losing battle.

'ZEB!' a cry reached him from far down below. He turned to the broken window, climbed on its ledge and reached out to the cable. Gripped it with his gloves and let his body-weight and gravity do the work.

Down, sliding fast, past dark office windows and then the building seemed to tremble as an enormous explosion reached him. A shout alerted him. He looked up. Flames on his cable. It's fire resistant was his first thought. But maybe the heat's so intense it can't hold out.

He looked down. The ground was approaching fast. Five, or six more floors to go. He urged himself to go faster, felt the cable trembling in his hand and then it gave way and he was falling and made himself relax.

He fell on top of his team who had chained their hands to break his fall. They collapsed from the force of his fall. Someone groaned. Broker.

'Can we get a refund on that cable?' Roger chuckled as he got to his feet and dusted himself off.

Nothing broken, Zeb assessed himself swiftly. He caught Meghan's hand, pulled her to her feet. Helped Beth rise. 'Anyone injured?'

'Nope,' Bwana sighed, 'but don't make a habit of this.'

'Let's get out of here. This place will be crowded, soon.'

As if on cue, more windows exploded on the building.

Zeb joined the sisters who were ahead, racing towards their getaway vehicle.

'You got something?'

'We got something,' Beth assured him.

Chapter 37

'Hyde,' Beth announced, later in the day.

They had returned to their Arbat safe house, showered and climbed into bed. Regrouped when the sun was high in the sky and a warm summer day in Moscow beckoned.

'Who or what's that?' Bwana mumbled; his mouth full. The remains of his breakfast on his plate. Operatives lounged in the living room. Meghan on a window sill, sunning herself.

'We don't know,' she said. She went to her screen, punched the keyboard and turned the screen to them.

It was blank.

'What are we looking at?' Broker asked softly.

'This,' she said bitterly. 'Beth and I copied the hard drives from those machines. But there must've been a self-erasing program in them. As soon as we launched our machines, they destroyed everything in the files.

Silence. A woman's liquid laugh reached them through the open window.

'Wait,' she said on reading Zeb's expression. 'Like Beth said, there's something or someone called Hyde that's connected to these killings. There was a draft email, never sent. *Happy with Hyde.* In Russian.'

'Who's email?

'Tverskoy's'

Zeb nodded. Writing draft emails and never sending them was one of the most secure ways of exchanging intel. If both sender and receiver had access to the same account.

'That would mean someone else would know his login?' Bear ventured.

'Not necessarily. He could have composed it, copied and pasted it in another account.'

'What else did you get from his account?'

'A lot of detail about his criminal enterprise. But,' she shrugged helplessly, pointing to the screen, 'it's all in our memories now.

'What's Hyde's connection to the killings?'

'There was one more line in that email. *Did you see Dallas, Berlin and London?*'

Roger whistled. Bwana nodded grimly. What more proof was needed?

'There's more?' Zeb asked.

'*Move the four to Ukraine. Immediately.* That was from Tverskoy. Before the Berlin killing.'

Bear went to the fruit basket and peeled an orange. He tossed another one to Bwana who caught it expertly. 'I'm finding it hard to believe that the Russian mafia,' he bit into the fruit and wiped his lips, 'would use email for comms.'

'One,' Meghan held out a finger. 'That office was more like a tech office. It's where they ran their internet crimes from. Software programmers occupied it. People who are comfort-able with email, online messengers and chat applications. Two,' a second digit straightened. 'That last message wasn't an email. It was a voice recording. Their system automatically records incoming and outgoing calls and backs them to a server.'

'Who did he call?'

Her ponytail jumped when she shook her head. 'No clue. We got the time stamp and his voice. That's all.'

'Ukraine?' Broker turned to Zeb. 'You know anything about that? I thought this gang operated only in Russia.'

'No,' Zeb replied. 'But I know someone who does.'

Chapter 38

'You came to my country. You attacked the Tverskoy gang. One floor on Naberezhnaya Tower, destroyed. Damage to other floors. That's prime property in Moscow. AND YOU DIDN'T BOTHER TO TELL ME?' Grigor Andropov crashed his fist on his table on the last words. The window rattled. A water bottle toppled. An aide poked his head through the door and withdrew it hastily when he sensed the temperature.

Zeb remained seated, calm. Beth and Meghan beside him. The remaining operatives ranged behind, leaning against the wall, making the Russian's office feel small. Who in that instant was only rage and fury.

'Are you done?' Zeb asked softly.

'NO! DO YOU REALIZE WHAT YOU'VE DONE?'

'Found a few answers to a heck of a lot of questions.'

'I WAS TOLD TO STAY AWAY FROM TVERSKOY.'

'No one told that to us,' Bwana chewed his gum expressionlessly.

Andropov glared at him balefully. Bwana stared back. For a moment Zeb thought the spymaster would lunge across the room and throttle his friend. It would be impossible but the

153

Russian, even in his sixties, was supremely fit and could land some damage. He tensed, ready to spring up and intervene but Andropov seemed to subside. He ran a hand through his short, steel-grey hair.

'Pizdets,' he cursed. He came around the table and rested his butt against it.

'What did you find?' he growled.

A small sigh of relief escaped Beth. She resumed from where she had left off, when Andropov had exploded.

'A reference to Hyde.'

'What's that?'

'We don't know.'

In English because the Russian was fluent in it and could even put on an American accent if needed.

'And what's the proof...that these have something to do with the killings? You saw the news?' he snapped his head up and bored each operative with his eyes.

They nodded. That morning, a Russian male had opened fire in Lubyanka Metro Station, killing three people, injuring seven others, before he was overpowered by other passengers. He had refused to answer any questions from the police and stubbornly maintained his silence.

'They found his computer. He was a neo-Nazi,' Andropov said bitterly. 'He visited all those hate sites, was active in message boards.'

'Loner?' Meghan asked.

'Da. It can't be a coincidence.'

'No. Can you share everything you've got? Contents of his hard drive, his internet history, phone records –'

'I am not the police.' he growled.

'Come on,' Meghan rolled her eyes. 'You're one of the

most powerful men in Russia. You make a call and the entire police force will come running to help you.'

'I wish it was as easy as that,' he realized he was softening and thinned his lips. 'I should refuse. Cooperation is a two-way street.'

'Which is why we're here.'

'Back to your questions,' Zeb intervened, 'about proof. There was mention of Dallas and London, in what Beth and Meg saw.'

Andropov was wearing a grey jacket, white shirt, dark trousers. Black shoes shined to mirror gloss. Standard attire for him. He looked like a businessman or a government worker. He seemed to deflate at Zeb's words. Wearily removed his jacket and tossed it over his chair. Rolled his sleeves.

'You'll get everything,' he said in a clipped voice. 'Ukraine? I know Tverskoy has a base there. Outside Chernihiv.'

'That's about two hours from Kiev?'

'Da.' He didn't ask how Zeb knew the town. He knew the Agency's methods. Every operative could speak several languages. World geography, large and small towns in various countries, especially the hotspots of the world, the operatives were familiar with small details.

'He recruits there,' Andropov continued. 'Brings gunmen to Russia. His way of distancing himself if any of them are caught. *Not me.*' He mimicked, '*Those are Ukrainians. I am a proud Russian. Why would I employ them?*'

'That's all he does? Recruitment?'

'Nyet. Drugs. Women. Killing. He's expanding in that country. And now you tell me he's moved some tech people there…he's probably running his internet crimes from there.'

'How do you know this?' Broker. Cream shirt, tan slacks,

brown leather belt. As if he was coming off a modeling shoot.

'It's my business to know.'

'But in Ukraine?'

'Let's just say I have an informer. Had.' His face darkened. 'He was killed in a fight with another gang.'

'He was a gunman?' Meghan asked surprised. 'How did you turn him?'

'Da. He wanted out. I found him one night, bleeding, on a street in Moscow. A drug deal had gone bad. The other gang members with him, they thought he was dead. They fled. I saw the opportunity. Nursed him back to health. No one knew. And he reciprocated. Now, he's gone.'

'They could have moved, Grigor,' Zeb objected. 'How old is this information?'

'Three months. But they haven't gone anywhere,' a sly look came over his face. 'I visited Kiev last week, as a tourist. Tverskoy's gang is there. Here!'

He went to his desk, opened a cabinet and withdrew a packet of photographs. Passed it over to Meghan who spread them out.

Close and long range shots of a farmhouse. A dusty track leading to it. Barren fields around it. A few vehicles.

'That doesn't look like a Mafia gang's base,' Chloe said doubtfully, as she held up one image.

'This man,' Andropov riffled through the photos and selected one. 'Rapist, killer. Wanted in Moscow. He lives there. This one,' he drew out another. 'Gunman for the bratva. That man with the scar, a well-known Ukrainian drug runner. Has escaped arrest.'

'Why didn't you inform the Ukrainians?'

'No!' Grigor's eyes burned. 'Nikolai Tverskoy is mine. I

will get him, one way or the other.'

'They asked you to back off, didn't they?' Zeb pointed in the direction of the Kremlin.

'Da. The call came from the highest level.' He didn't give any name and Zeb didn't press him. 'Tverskoy is the most dangerous mafia boss in Russia.'

'Why?' Bear asked curiously. 'There are bigger gangs.'

'Because he's the smartest,' Andropov said impatiently, as if it was obvious. 'The other bratvas, their leaders…they are old school. Their enterprises are the same. Murder. Kidnapping. Drugs. Women. Nothing new. Tverskoy? He got into computer crime. He has hired some of the smartest programmers. Given them so much money that they don't care if what they're doing is illegal. He's given them protection and he's let them loose on the world. This,' he jabbed a finger at the TV on the wall, 'is the result.'

He swung round to them, his eyes fierce. 'I haven't told this to anyone. Not even Clare, because I wanted to build evidence. You know why the Kremlin asked me to back off? It's not for Tverskoy's influence. Every bratva pakhan has that kind of influence. No. It's for another reason.

'What?' Bwana asked.

'I think he's involved in your elections. In the meddling. The social media ads, the algorithms, his people are behind it.'

Someone gasped. Beth. Meghan jerked instinctively. Zeb didn't react. He watched his friend. Noted his anger, the rage simmering inside him.

Andropov was proud of his country. He didn't like the direction its political leaders were taking it. *But in his position, he has to do what they say. Take down threats against the state, or stay away from particular actors. The election interference, that's possible. All the investigation Stateside, it identified some companies, some people, who played a hand, but nothing came of that. The Kremlin denied any involvement. Grigor's admission is the first link to the Russian Mafia. And all the gangs have political backing.*

'How sure are you, Grigor?' he switched to Russian.

'I don't have proof. This is something I have put together. Listening. Cultivating snitches. I was going to come to you and Clare soon. But now, after what you've told me...it looks like Tverskoy has moved in a different direction.'

He straightened. An air of command coming to him.

'You'll go to Ukraine?'

'Da,' Zeb replied.

'What do you need?'

Zeb looked at the photographs. At the farmhouse and the empty fields around it.

'Balloons.'

Meghan's head swung towards him. Her jaw dropped.

'We aren't going to a party!'

Her teeth snapped with an audible click when Zeb explained.

Chapter 39

'Da,' Nikolai Tverskoy picked up the buzzing phone from the bedside table. He wrapped a sheet around him and went to the window.

Paris. A boutique hotel near the Arc de Triomphe.

His handsome face tightened when he received the news. 'We have people everywhere,' he hissed at his aide in Moscow. 'You've found nothing about that attack?'

'Nyet, pakhan. Whoever was in our building, knew what they were doing. They penetrated our system –'

'Enough. I know the details. Those cables from the roof. Can't you trace them?'

'No. They are available in any outdoors store.'

'These weren't ordinary burglars.'

'Da, pakhan. We are looking. I am sure we'll find them. No one in Moscow can escape our clutches.'

'Did they get anything? Do our people know?'

'Nyet. The self-destruct programs went off as they were designed to. I am confident they found nothing.'

'They had better not,' Tverskoy warned him, menacingly. He dealt with failure simply. He shot those who had let him down. Or sometimes knifed them till they bled. Or raped their wives or girlfriends before killing them. He was savagery personified. Everyone knew that, which was why his people seldom failed him.

He tossed the phone on the bed. A sound of protest as it hit the mound under the blanket. A tousled head emerged, sleepy eyes blinking.

'Go back to sleep, babe,' he told his latest girlfriend, a French actress. 'I've got to make some calls.'

Another burner phone. A call to Chernihiv.

'Andrei,' he barked at his lieutenant in the Ukrainian base. 'Is everything okay.'

'Da, pakhan. Why?'

'No strangers, no snoopers?'

'Nyet. Everything's good.'

'Those programmers, they are working?'

'Da. They have sent you more names.'

'I haven't checked. Be alert. You've heard what happened to our office in Moscow.'

'Yes, pakhan. No such thing will happen here.'

Tverskoy hung up and went to the bathroom and showered, taking the time to organize his thoughts.

He wouldn't call Phil Williams, he decided. What was there to tell him? That his Moscow office had been attacked? Williams knew that, in any case. The men had exchanged messages right after the explosion. The spymaster had demanded to know how compromised they were. The pakhan had given him his word. Not at all.

Even now, we aren't, Tverskoy thought to himself. The software people are safe in Ukraine. Whoever hit my building didn't get anything. No need to tell him anything.

But he decided he would turn Moscow upside down to know who the intruders were. Even if it meant starting a war with other gangs. Because who else could it be? Some other bratva wanting to encroach on his territory.

Decision made, he went to the bed and slapped his girlfriend's rump.

Chapter 40

Williams, Leslie and Smith met, this time in Mexico City with the last man, the organizer and the host.

'We need more killings in Asia,' Williams turned to Leslie. 'You got any primed and ready to go?'

'My people tell me there are a few. I will ask them to focus on those.'

'What about Tverskoy?' Smith drilled him with a cool stare. 'His building was attacked. How badly are we affected?'

'Not one bit,' the Europe man answered reassuringly. 'The tech people aren't in Moscow. They were moved to Ukraine a long time ago.'

'What about him? Is he okay with all this?'

'Nikolai? Oh yes. He and I go back a long way. I know how to manage him. He's being paid well.'

'He has no issues with what we are doing?'

'He doesn't know the big picture. And even if he did, he wouldn't care. Tverskoy would kill his mother for the money we're paying him.'

The others nodded in understanding. They were used to dealing with such men. To the criminal bosses it came down to reward. Nothing more.

'You got my message?' Leslie asked them.

'Yes,' Williams answered. 'I have started buying more of the European and American companies shares. The target ones. Using several investment vehicles. Untraceable to me.'

'I'm doing the same,' Smith joined.

'You wanted riots,' Leslie told the Europe man, 'You got them. Did you see the scenes in Europe and America?'

Entire city centers had been destroyed, vehicles had been burned and stores looted in prominent European capitals. The confrontation in Dallas had been mirrored in Los Angeles, which then had broken out into a street fight between two groups of protesters. In Atlanta, a group of black men had chased vigilante white men. In Chicago, the reverse had happened. The killings seemed to have brought out race and ethnic hatred across the world.

'And not just in the Western world,' the Asia man chimed in. 'In Mumbai, supporters of various political parties went on a rampage in the streets. Several killed. In Beijing, a clash between police and protest marchers against the government. In Jakarta too. It's happening.'

'Tomorrow my leader will make an announcement,' Leslie announced. 'That the way countries are governed needs to change. People need to be listened to. Their fears and angers acted on.'

'Of course, we are the ones creating that anger,' Smith said gleefully and held his glass up for a toast. 'To a new world order.'

Chapter 41

Zeb turned off the TV after watching news from around the world. His face, set, grim. It looked like the world was on fire. Each day brought news of a lone man killing in some country, followed by reports of street violence in different parts of the world. Stock indices had plummeted. Radio call-in shows were filled with angry, fearful people demanding that their government set things right. Gun sales were at a record high in the US. In Montana, Wyoming, Colorado, a few accidental gun killings had already been recorded. Political leaders appealed for calm; President Morgan called for the G20 Summit to have a single agenda. How to restore order.

All because someone developed an AI program and let it loose on the world. Tverskoy... is he responsible all by himself? Is the Kremlin backing him? But there have been killings in Russia too. Some of the most savage shootings have been in that country.

What about the killers' philosophies? There was a mix between left and right wingers, but the latter outnumbered the former. *Are they easier to turn? Or are there just more of them?*

He shook his head impatiently. There was no point asking himself these questions. The bratva head could have some answers.

'What's the plan?' Beth interrupted his thinking.

'Recon, and then hit hard.'

They landed at Boryspil International Airport, the country's largest, eighteen miles east of its capital.

Hot, sunny, a typical summer in Ukraine. They cleared immigration without any incident, their covers as geology surveyors raising no questions.

Caps over their heads, visors low and shades to shield their faces. Some of them with scarves and bandanas looped casually over their necks, half-covering their chins.

They hung about outside searching and then Zeb pointed to a bearded man who held a placard. Eugeniv Palichenko, it said.

'Yurik Kotenko,' he introduced himself and shook their hands. He sized them up and turned on his heel, gesturing at them to follow him.

A mini-bus. Black, tinted windows. Aircon, comfortable seats in which they settled themselves, Bwana leaning back with a sigh.

'He doesn't speak much,' he whispered loudly. 'Zeb, you're sure he's Grigor's man?'

'Who else would hold that board?' Meghan retorted. 'We made that name up only when we were landing and informed Andropov.'

'We can always kill him if he turns out to be hostile,' Bear suggested and that settled it.

The Ukrainian drove them to Kiev on the E-40, a major

route that started in Calais, France and ended in the Altai Mountains of Kazakhstan. Zeb sat in the front but the two men made no conversation.

Grigor's probably briefed him about you, Meghan smirked in his headpiece. *That small talk isn't your strength.*

'You know what we want?' he ignored her and turned to the driver.

'Da.'

'You speak Russian?'

'And Ukrainian and Belarussian too. Whichever you prefer,' his lips parted briefly in a smile that disappeared as quickly as it had arrived.

He drove competently, didn't point out any of the sights as they entered the capital. St Sophia's Cathedral, Independence Square, Khreschatyk Street, the main street of the city. He kept silent as he navigated past tourist buses and citizens. Holosiivkskyi District to the south in the city. A series of warehouses on the Dnieper River. Ugly, grey buildings with large shutters. A metal gate which required an access card, which he flashed and the barriers opened.

The bus jolted as it drove over rails in concrete, past port workers and forklifts until it came to a stop in front of a shutter at the far end.

Kotenko jumped out, bent down and unlocked the padlocks. He struggled to raise the rolling metal sheet until Bwana and Bear gave him a hand, their biceps bulging under their tees.

'Spaseeba,' he thanked them and went inside the darker interior. Turned on lights and brought the bus inside. Rolled the shutter down behind them.

Zeb looked around the vast interior. Musty from lack

of circulation. Covered boats mounted on stands. He lifted one sheet peered beneath it. A go-fast boat, also known as a rum-runner or a cigarette boat. Bwana whistled in appreciation when he unveiled another vessel, a fifty-foot luxury runner.

'What's this place? Grigor owns this?'

Kotenko didn't answer. He had disappeared from sight and presently returned driving a forklift on which was a wooden crate. He stopped near them, unloaded the box and opened it with a claw-hammer.

Weapons wrapped in plastic. HKs, Glocks, Sigs, two Barretts, magazines, knives, NVGs, armor.

Bear hefted a rifle and inspected it. No serial, he mouthed silently. Zeb nodded. He wouldn't have expected anything less from the Russian spymaster.

They weaponed up, transferring the gear to the large cases they carried with them. Zeb looked around, but the Ukrainian was nowhere in sight. Nor was the forklift.

He took a few steps, stopped, when Kotenko returned with a larger crate. He lowered it to the ground and opened it with a crowbar.

Gestured to the large, multi-colored shapes inside.

'Your balloons,' he announced, simply.

Chapter 42

⎯⎯ ∞∞∞ ⎯⎯

Kiev to Chernihiv in two pickup trucks that Kotenko arranged for them, a balloon in the bed of each vehicle, still in their packaging. Their rides bore the names of an international oil company. The same names on the coveralls that each one of them wore.

Past Dytynets Park, where many of the Chernihiv's attractions were based. Towards Desna River, turning into a large driveway in front of a sandstone house.

A burly man opened the door. 'Palichenko?' he asked, his eyes moving over the men.

'Da,' Zeb replied.

'I have rooms for you,' he moved out of the entrance to allow them inside, and then spotted the pick-ups. 'You can move those to the garage.' He pointed to a large building to the side.

'That's the garage?' Bear blinked at the structure almost as tall as the residence.

'Da. Among other things. It has some stuff inside. For you.'

He disappeared inside and returned with a remote for its

door and sets of keys for their rooms and the house. They never saw him again.

'Where does Andropov get these men?' Chloe murmured. 'Not one of them has asked any questions.'

'His equivalent of the sayanin,' Zeb replied, referring to the Jews who helped Mossad around the world.

The inside of the *garage* was painted white, metal beams high above on which was a crane and a pulley, but no other machinery. Concrete floor, totally empty.

Roger scratched his head as he inspected it. 'Beats me what it was. A workshop?'

A beep made him jump sideways as Beth and Meghan drove the pickups inside and then they went to their rooms.

The house had been a hotel at one time and was well-maintained. It looked like the owner, who never mentioned his name, had turned it into a safe house for Andropov's agency.

Their accommodation was comfortable with clean bathrooms. 'Good WIFI,' Meghan declared. They used secure satellite networks, but wireless networks were required as a backup.

An hour's rest and then they gathered in the garage, unpacked the balloons and inspected the coils of wire that lined the insides. 'Good condition,' Broker said. 'I wonder how Andropov got his hands on them so quickly.'

'He and I used such balloons, in Syria, a few years ago. They need helium not hot-air.' Zeb checked out the fabric of the inflatables, looked around and pointed at the tanks in the corner. 'He's arranged the gas, too. Looks like Grigor liked the idea so much, he made a few inflatables and kept them ready for missions.'

Each balloon had large baskets which normally would have carried people. Beth and Meghan inserted large receivers in them while Bear and Chloe mounted motors and propellers. Two hours later, they stood back, disheveled, and watched as the balloons rose in the roomy garage and twisted and turned as the twins operated the remotes.

'Now?' Broker turned to Zeb.

'Let's check out the farmhouse.'

Chapter 43

Recon began that night.

They split into two teams. Zeb, Meghan, Bwana and Broker in the first, the remaining in the second.

The first team went out when dark fell. One pickup that they had spray-painted to dull black, non-reflective, keeping the oil company's logo. Out of the house, each one of them in dark combat gear, carrying their weapons of choice.

Zeb drove out, no headlights. Along the river, initially, and then onto the E-95 which crossed into Belarus. A country road three miles out of the city, and then a dirt track. Their truck bouncing and jostling on the bumpy road. Slowing when Meghan held up a hand, a screen in front of her. A map on it, zooming in on the farm, coordinates to which, Andropov had provided.

'There's a dried canal to the left of it.'

Zeb drove as she guided, over fields that hadn't been ploughed and then down the slope of the bed and they were out of view.

They climbed out quickly, gathered around the older twin for a few moments, and when she launched the stealth drone, they split up.

Zeb sprinted a mile, turned and ran until he curved around the back of the farm house.

'In position,' he gasped in his headset.

'Roger,' Meghan replied. 'Bwana, Broker?'

'Yeah,' came the replies.

Four of them spread around the house while the drone checked it out from the sky.

Small details came to Zeb, through his NVGs. The farm was L shaped at the front, a driveway on which was a tractor and a few trucks. The back had a separate building, like a stable.

'No animals,' Meghan seemed to guess his thoughts. 'Looks like some farm machinery there. We've got thermal prints,' her voice rose in excitement. 'Eleven bodies. Five of them in one room at the rear. Large heat signature. I bet that's where the server racks, the computers are. The other six are spread out. Two in the front. Two at the back, one each at the end of the L.'

'No one outside?' Zeb queried.

'Nope.'

'It's the middle of nowhere,' he mused aloud, answering himself. 'They wouldn't need sentries anywhere else. They'll have cameras –'

'Yep. Eight in all, mounted on the underside of the roof, spread around the house.'

'Ground's flat,' Bwana grunted softly. 'They can see anyone coming from a mile off. Nope, there's no need for sentries.'

'Any gate at the front,' Zeb asked. He didn't recollect seeing one.

'Nope. Anyone can just roll up to the door and knock on it.'

'I bet no one does that,' Broker chuckled. 'I have a feeling those six guys aren't friendly looking. They probably keep to themselves.

Zeb nodded in the dark. *Not friendly. They've likely got a reputation in town. No one approaches them. The people suspect they could be criminals.* But in that part of the world, bratvas and mafia gangs weren't uncommon and most citizens gave them a wide berth.

No vehicle approached the house at night. No shootings, no developments until dawn broke and then a truck approached the house.

No movement until it was a hundred yards away and then the door opened. Six men emerged, all of them armed. They spoke for a few minutes with the arrivals, climbed inside the vehicle, while the newcomers went inside.

'Change of shift,' Zeb surmised. 'Those are the guards. It doesn't look like anyone relieves the programmers.'

Chloe took the rear when her team came out for recon. Beth operated the drone which was high above, practically invisible to the naked eye. Bear and Roger on either side of the L.

More details in the daylight. The house was tiled, with sloping roofs. A central chimney from which lazy smoke emerged. Glass windows periodically set in the walls that had once been white but were now a dull brown.

It was Beth who spotted the barb-wire fence running around the farm. Wooden posts, painted to blend with the background, making them hard to detect by the naked eye. They ran parallel to the canal bed for several hundred yards and then curved to follow the lay of the land.

She trained her binos on the driveway. 'No gate,' she

announced. 'Just two posts on either side of that approach track where the wire ends.'

'Electric?' Bear enquired.

Beth followed the wire to the wooden posts. No insulation of any kind. She lowered the drone by several feet and checked out the compass on it. No needle deflection. 'Not scientific,' she murmured to herself. 'It's too high.'

'Doesn't look like it,' she replied, 'but don't touch it.'

The day saw more activity from the house. The armed guards brought out the engineers every two hours. The programmers were pale-skinned as if they didn't see much sunlight. They were in tees and jeans and lounged on benches at the back. Not much conversation among them.

'What's there left to talk about?' Bear growled when Beth voiced her comment. 'Looks like they're cooped up all day. They've been together for months. Don't go anywhere, it looks like. Nope, they're thin on conversation topics.'

A guard came to the back door and yelled at them, at which they stood up and shuffled inside. The same routine, every two hours, until dark.

Occasionally one of the guards came to the rear, threw out dirty water or washed pots and pans at a wall-mounted water tap.

'No cook,' Chloe guessed. 'Maybe they take turns at rustling up meals.'

Twice during the day, two men, different each time, climbed into a truck and patrolled the perimeter of the farm. One time, the vehicle came close to where Beth was hiding, just beneath the edge of the canal bed, but didn't detect her.

It stopped. One man said something to another and climbed out.

They're speaking Russian, Beth thought, looking at them through the sides of her eyes, not wanting them to feel the weight of her gaze.

One man, AR-15 across his shoulder, approached the fence, bent over the wire and touched it with his bare fingers. 'It's fine,' he called out to the driver. 'It looks cut, but it isn't.'

Fence is not electric, Beth concluded and watched the guard stomp back to the truck, which drove away.

'Security feels casual,' Roger drawled. 'These dudes are acting as if they've nothing to fear.'

'They don't,' Chloe replied. 'They're well-armed. I'm guessing they are good fighters, and they have excellent visibility. The house looks like it's well-constructed. If attacked, they will hole up inside. Those gang members in the other shift, they're backup. They'll come running in case the farm is attacked.'

They settled back to watching.

Beth noticed additional details during the day. A black cable that ran alongside the house and went inside, beneath a wall. *Fiber,* she thought, for their network connection. She and Meghan had decided not to hack into the house. They didn't know how good the engineers were and didn't want to alert them with any intrusion attempt.

One more day of recon, but with a difference. Chloe and the sisters followed the men who got relieved, the night shift, into Chernihiv. The operatives gossiped in Ukrainian as they window-shopped, keeping an eye on the bratva men.

The gang members went to a restaurant and wolfed down a heavy breakfast. Then they broke up, one man went to a barber shop, two others went to a book store and thumbed through the men's magazines while the remaining two sat on a park bench and commented on the passing women.

One of them, bearded, big, patted a mother's bottom as she passed, pushing a baby stroller. She whirled on him and cursed in Ukrainian. He grinned lazily, got to his feet and squeezed her breast. His head rocked back when she slapped, but the insolent look didn't disappear. More cursing and shouting from the red-faced woman. Passersby didn't stop. They bent their heads and hurried as if the altercation wasn't happening, as if a woman wasn't being molested in broad daylight.

The second gang member watched for a moment, grinning, and then grabbed his friend's hand and led him away.

'Those two,' Meghan lifted an eyebrow at the receding men, 'need to learn some manners.'

Chapter 44

—— ✺ ——

They attacked on the third day, after the night shift had left for Chernihiv.

They parked their pickup trucks a mile away from the farm's perimeter, in the canal bed, out of sight from any passing vehicle.

One hour to inflate the balloons with helium. And once they rose majestically in the air, Beth and Meghan took over, maneuvering them, using controls on their screens that manipulated the onboard motors and propellers. Line-of-sight data link when they were visible, which switched to satellite relays when they were out of view.

Zeb, Broker and Chloe, racing to take position in the canal bed at the front of the house. Bwana, Bear and Roger to the rear. The twins following at a slower pace as they navigated the balloons to just over a thousand feet, above tree-top level. And then got them to circle wide and approach the house from the rear.

Multi-hued, streamlined shapes against the blue sky, their baskets empty but for the motors. They drifted until they were tiny specks in the distance.

Zeb climbed up the slope of the canal, lay prone and peered above its top. The farm house jumped out at him through his binos. No signs of activity outside.

'In position?' he asked.

'Yeah,' came the replies.

'GO!' he ordered.

The twins turned the balloons around and headed them back to the house. A speed of five miles an hour. Forty minutes to reach the farm.

Zeb brought the scope of his HK to his eye. An insect droned in his ear. The earth smelled warm. Pollen floated past him. He went through the attack plan in his mind. *All depends on how good those bratva men are. Tverskoy will have sent his best, to guard the engineers.*

'Fifteen minutes away,' Beth called out.

There the balloons were. Bright in the sky, hanging low, coming from the rear of the house, towards each leg of its L.

No one gawked and stared because there was no one about.

'Eight minutes away.' Beth's voice, bored, as if she was reading out the weather.

Zeb couldn't help grinning. *There's nothing much for her and Meg to do until the balloons land.*

The first sign of movement in the house. The front door opened. A man stumbled out and ran around the right leg of the L. He stopped and stared at the sky. Zeb saw his lips move. A shout. Another man ran out. Brought his AR-15 to his hands but there was no one to shoot at.

The balloons were much lower, hundred yards from the ground. Growing in size as they came close.

'These dudes,' Roger chuckled. 'They've come out at the back as well. Shall we take them out?'

'No,' Zeb replied. 'Stick to the plan.'

It still wasn't the point of maximum surprise.

That came a few minutes later.

Chapter 45

The balloons crashed against the house, a perfect landing for the twins. It was accompanied by the chatter of the AR-15s as the bratva men fired at them ineffectively, in an attempt to ward off the collision.

They didn't succeed.

The baskets smashed against the rear walls. Windows shattered. And then the balloons, eighteen hundred square yards of nylon, eight hundred pounds in weight, each, settled on the roofs of the two legs. Tiles fell off the roof. Another window cracked. The chimney toppled and rolled down the roof.

And the coils inside the balloons acted like a Faraday Cage, jamming all phone signals inside the house.

'Now!' Zeb commanded and brought his HK up, his scope settling on one of the two men at the front.

But Tverskoy's men reacted instantly, before he could fire. They rushed inside the house.

'What?' Bear exclaimed, 'They ran inside before we could fire. Why?'

They got their answer when two men raced out again and jumped into a truck at the front. They drove it at speed, heading towards the canal bed at the front.

'Shall I take them out?' Chloe, eye to sight.

'No,' Zeb replied. 'Let them come closer. I've got a better idea.'

The initial plan had been to snipe down the men as soon as the balloons landed and then breach the house. They expected fierce combat.

But the gunmen's unexpected reaction had taken them by surprise.

'Why that vehicle?' Broker asked.

'They suspect whoever's behind the balloons is hidden here. No other place offers concealment.'

'Why've they sent only two, then? And why did they disappear inside the house?'

'They suspected a sniper attack. They're smart. And as for those two, they only have six guards. They can't send them all. Here they come.'

The truck threw up dust and dirt as its wheels dug in the soft soil. It turned as the driver steered it to run parallel to the fence as he and his companion looked sharp, searching the canal.

A hundred yards away from Zeb and Chloe. Approaching fast.

'Hold fire,' he warned. 'We want at least one of them alive.'

'Gotcha.'

Fifty yards.

'I can shoot their tires,' Broker said mildly.

'Stick to the plan,' Zeb snapped.

Twenty-five. Then ten and then the vehicle was past them. It turned, and a second later its wing mirrors disappeared from view.

Zeb and Chloe lunged out. She went to the right of the vehicle, crouching low, Glock in hand, surging fast. He went to the left.

The driver's head popped out. Spotted him and his eyes widened. He yelled. His AR-15 came out. A burst of firing from the other side of the vehicle but Zeb didn't give it any thought. Chloe can take care of herself. He hurled himself beneath the line of fire, grabbed the hot barrel and yanked hard. The driver's teeth gritted, he let go of the weapon suddenly and for a moment Zeb was flailing and then he grabbed the door and pulled himself up and forward towards the window, hanging on as the bratva man swerved the vehicle to the right, to the left, in an attempt to shake him and then another burst of fire and that distracted the driver who looked away for a fraction and that gave Zeb the opening.

He reached inside and clobbered the man with his fist and kept punching until he groaned and slumped and Zeb was aware of Chloe grappling with the second gunman at the other door but he couldn't pay attention because he had yanked the door open was climbing in, shoving the fallen driver away and then he was inside, the wheel in his hand, straightening the vehicle which was careening wildly and just as he looked to his right, a shot.

The second gunman fell forward and then sideways. Chloe, who had fired, climbed in. Disheveled, hair astray, face smudged, panting, but managing a wink.

'You got a plan?' she asked.

Chapter 46

—–⟨∞⟩—–

'Igor?' the radio squawked, a concerned voice. 'What's happening? We heard shots.'

Zeb drove with one hand, following the fence around the farm. His free hand jammed his Glock in the driver's side who had revived when they had taken control of the vehicle. His attempts at fighting back had ended when he saw the dead bratva man on the seat.

'Answer him,' Zeb whispered. 'Be creative.'

The Russian licked his lips, turned to look at Chloe and shrank when he saw her produce a wicked-looking knife.

'Everything's under control, Andrei. Two men were flying the balloons remotely. They were hiding in the canal. They lost control and that's why those crashed on our roof.'

'Where are they now?'

'Dead,' he winced when the gun dug painfully in his ribs. 'Petrov and I shot them. Those are the shots you heard.'

'Who were they?' Andrei asked irritatedly. 'Did you check that they weren't police? There's something strange with these balloons. They have wires in them. They have blocked out all signals. I had to come out several hundred feet from the house to call.'

'Geologists. Trial balloons. New technology,' Zeb lipped.

'Geologists. Trial balloons. New technology,' Igor repeated, faithfully.

'Alright. Check the rest of the perimeter and head back.'

Zeb snatched the radio from the mafia man's hands and smashed it against the truck's side.

'Any movement?'

'A man came out the front. Saw your truck, watched it for a few moments and then went inside.' Beth replied.

'There's a gunman at the back,' Broker said, 'holding a radio in his hand. He checked out the rear with binos. Didn't spot us.'

'I have thermals inside the house.' Meghan, who after crashing her balloon, was flying the drone. 'Two men, one at the front door, one at the back. Five bodies in that computer room.'

The drone's cameras and sensors was unaffected by the Faraday Cage they had created. It watched, heard and transmitted to the twins' screens.

'Any traffic on the road?' Zeb asked. *Someone in Chernihiv could have seen the balloons. The six men who left, could return.*

'Nope.'

'This dude's returning to the house.' Broker said. 'Shall I take him out?'

'Standby. We'll do this the polite way. Attack when you hear shooting.'

'You're Americans?' Igor blurted in Russian; his eyes wide.

Zeb didn't reply. He turned the truck towards the house, ran through the moves in his head as they approached.

'How many guards inside?' Chloe jabbed her knife at the Russian.

'Three.'

'The programmers –'

'They don't leave their room. They are not violent.'

Zeb traded a glance with Chloe. *Igor's suddenly helpful. I bet he's figuring out a way to warn his crew.* She nodded imperceptibly, evidently having the same thought.

Igor tensed beside them as they neared the house. Bumped over the uneven field and then the ride smoothed as they hit the driveway.

'Don't,' Zeb warned when he saw the Russian bunch his fists from the corner of his eyes. 'You'll live longer.'

Igor subsided.

'Take the wheel,' he ordered and climbed behind the seat along with Chloe. 'One false move and you know what'll happen.'

'Da,' the bratva man swallowed.

The Russian drove, stopped in front of the house. He climbed out and moved jerkily to the door.

It swung open before he could knock.

'You took your time,' the man who opened it, grumped.

Two things happened.

Chapter 47

'ANDREI!' Igor yelled out a warning and shoved the man back inside.

Zeb and Chloe exploded from the vehicle and raced towards the open door.

Andrei reacted instantly.

He shouted, alerting his gunmen. Leaped back inside the house. His AR-15 came up. Igor reached behind the door and turned around, snarling, gripping an assault rifle.

Too close to them. Zeb dived, crashing his shoulder against Igor, bringing him down on the floor. Smashed the butt of his rifle against his forehead.

'WATCH OUT!' Chloe screamed.

He rolled away desperately. Just in time as Andrei shot into the floor where he had been. Concrete splinters flew in the air.

Another short burst, a different weapon. Chloe, who unloaded her rounds into Andrei. Zeb got to his feet. Looked down at Igor, who was unconscious. Kicked his AR-15 away. Took in the house swiftly.

Entrance lobby, where they were standing. A hallway. He

signaled to Chloe who fell behind him. Kicked the door open and dropped to a crouch. Living room. Couches. TV. Empty.

'Approaching from the rear,' Bear, laconic in their headsets.

The house was silent. Unnaturally. It was dark, the heavy balloons blanketing light from the top.

There should be one more gunman. Surely, those engineers would have heard the shooting.

Another door at the end of the living room. Open. He snapped a glance and drew back. Entered it cautiously. A second living room. Bare.

Moved to the next door. A passage. Short careful steps. HK in front, every sense alert, Chloe behind to provide cover.

Another door. Large. Wooden. He shoved it open and ducked back.

'No need for that,' Bwana's voice was smoky. And there he was, along with Bear, Broker and Roger, tall, confident, ready for explosive violence. In the dining room, which opened to the back from where the rest of his team had approached.

It was an open plan room. Kitchen on one wall. Openings on either side, leading to passages to the legs of the L.

Roger held a finger up. Zeb nodded. 'One more,' he whispered.

'Can't see him,' Beth, frustrated, in their earpieces. 'Signal's poor. The tech room is to your right. Two doors down-'

Zeb looked down the passage. Movement.

He threw himself against his friends. Body-slammed them and brought them down.

Bullets whined through the air and embedded in a wall. The attacker, pale-faced, skinny, fumbled with his magazine.

Zeb brought his HK up. Sighted. His finger curled around the trigger. He paused.

The shooter didn't look like a bratva man. Is he...?

'DROP IT!' he shouted in Russian.

The gunman hesitated. Looked nervously in his direction, at Bwana and Bear who now got to their feet, looking ominous.

'PUT YOUR GUN DOWN,' Chloe roared.

The shooter decided on attacking. His barrel swung up. Rounds smashed into the wall and floor as he fired nervously.

'Don't kill,' Zeb said, almost to himself and feathered his trigger. The gunman staggered back with a cry, his weapon falling, holding his shoulder.

Zeb lunged forward, Chloe close behind, as the man tried to duck inside a room. Three long strides to reach him, twist his arm around in a lock, a scream rising from the man. A fast take-in of the room through the open door.

Four men. Scared faces. Computers.

Running footsteps. His team.

No, who was that, behind them?

'DOWN!'

He didn't know how his HK came up or when, but there it was, firing as if it was an extension of his arm, his body jerking as something slammed into his chest, but Zeb kept triggering, emptying a magazine into the last shooter who had come up unnoticed from the rear.

Silence except for the clicking and clacking as he fast-changed his magazine. Gunsmoke in the air. Someone moaned. A man whimpered. Roger got up from his floor sprawl, checked out the shooter cautiously.

'Out,' he said and then his face narrowed. 'You're hit?'

Zeb brought his palm to his left shoulder. It came away

wet, red. A round had grazed it. 'Nothing serious,' he said. *Didn't a round hit me?* He looked down and saw a blade on the floor and worked out what had happened. The last shooter had tried a knife throw. *He probably wanted to maximize his stealth approach before opening up with his rifle. Wrong tactics. He should have come in gun blazing.*

Running footsteps. They turned, relaxed when Beth and Meghan approached.

'Okay?' the younger sister asked, her eyes flicking to his shoulder.

'Yeah, a scratch.'

She shouldered past him, into the room where Broker covered the programmers with his HK.

'Let's ask some questions.'

Chapter 48

Zeb, Bwana, Bear and Roger broke away. They split up into two teams and checked out the rest of the house.

Mattresses on the floors of some rooms. Dirty bathrooms. Stacks of guns and ammos. Radios and cell phones, batteries. Newspapers, beer cans and bottles strewn on the floor. No gunmen.

Zeb went to the front door and knelt over Andrei. He had seemed familiar, and now he knew why. Grigor showed us his photograph. And Igor, his picture too.

He bound the driver and headed back to the dining room.

'Clear,' Roger said when all of them met at the back. He went to the kitchen counter, selected an apple from a fruit basket and bit into it.

'What?' he said in an injured tone when he felt their glares, 'I'm still growing. I need all the nutrition I can find.'

Zeb led them back to the computer room and stopped when he saw Meghan's pale face.

'It's worse than we thought. Much worse.'

The injured man, who had fired on them, was one of the programmers who had some knowledge of weapons. He sat in his chair, clutching his shoulder, sobbing quietly. The remaining four, in the center, in their chairs. Sweat and fear in the air.

Zeb took in the room. Screens on desks. Server racks against a wall, lights blinking on them. Cables on the floor. Opaque glass windows on the wall to the hallway. The engineers, pale-faced, scared, looking at him.

'Sebastian,' the older sister pointed to one of the men. 'Team lead. Vlad, Eldar, Cyril and that's,' she pointed to the shot man, 'Alexei.'

'We got only their names before you came in, but look at this,' Beth turned to the array of screens.

Zeb felt cold, empty when he saw the faces and names of all the killers on a dashboard. They were organized under three headings. Europe. Asia. America. Numbers.

They're recording the killings as wins, he thought bleakly. *A contest between the three regions.*

The beast roared inside him and for a moment, threatened to take over. He fought for control, breathing slowly, looking at the screens, allowing the pounding in his blood to subside.

'What's that?' his voice was mild, curious, when he looked at Sebastian. The team head was perspiring but didn't look scared. He had a neatly-trimmed French beard, brown eyes and a thinning hair on his head.

He looked at the screen and then back to Zeb. His eyes darted to the left, to the right.

'Here's what will happen,' Zeb continued. 'We'll ask questions. You'll deny you know anything. You'll say you were acting on orders. You're low level. You don't know the details.'

He raised his Glock smoothly and shot Vlad in the shoulder. The man screamed. He fell to the floor from the impact and jerked spasmodically, curling his body tightly.

'He'll live,' Zeb told Sebastian who had turned white. 'A shoulder wound. It'll heal. But the next round…will go in you and not in your shoulder. So, why don't we get to the chase?'

The Russian trembled. He looked at his fallen team member and then at the hard faces of the operatives. He jumped suddenly and raced to a waste bin where he threw up. He wiped his lips on his sleeve, opened a bottle of water with shaking hands and drank. His shaking had reduced when he returned to his chair. He sneaked a look at Vlad and then turned to Zeb.

'I…'

'Don't say you don't know anything, son,' Bwana filled the room with quiet menace. 'Don't do that. Just talk. Tell us everything you know.'

'It's…a…program…' Sebastian nodded jerkily at the screens.

Beth opened her mouth, snapped it shut when Meghan glared at her. *Let him talk*, the older sister messaged with her eyes.

'What's happening…' his throat bobbed, his voice trailed off. He shrank in his chair when Zeb's gun hand twitched. He raised his hands defensively and spoke quickly.

'What you see out there…it does all that.'

Chapter 49

None of the operatives spoke. It was a common interrogation tactic, letting silence fill a room, letting it weigh on the interviewee, making him fill it with words.

'It identifies people who can be manipulated. Tracks them on social media, their internet activities, and when a selection has been made, it goes after them.'

He looked at them to see if they understood. Saw cold, hard faces. He drank from the water bottle again, spilled some of it on his chest. 'It has backdoor entries to many of the social media platforms. That's how we can go deeper on the selected men.'

'Backdoor? How?' Meghan straightened.

'Hacked into them. Built tunnels that would give us entry.'

'You have those skills?'

'We are the top programmers and hackers in Russia.' The pride on his face vanished when the sisters looked at him contemptuously.

'How does this work?' Broker pointed at the screen. 'Run this past us, again. You make a broad selection initially?'

'Da.'

'Then what happens? Someone narrows that list?'

'Da. The pakhan.'

'Tverskoy? He comes here personally to look at this?'

'Nyet. We message or tell him.' He looked away.

'What?'

'He used to do that before. Now, he leaves it to us.'

He squirmed at the ensuing silence. Found something of interest to look at on the floor.

'Then what happens?' Beth asked heavily.

'Then we send advertisements to those people. Direct social media posts to them. See how they react. Send more content. Remove those who aren't reacting from the list, add others.'

'The program does all that?'

'Da,' Sebastian nodded vigorously, gaining confidence. This was his domain. It didn't look like the intruders were going to harm them right away. 'We just monitor and make improvements to it.'

'What kind of content do you send their way?'

'Whatever's available on the social media platforms, websites that we can email them, robotically.'

'Examples?' Beth snapped.

'Once a man is reacting positively,' he stared at her shoes, unable to meet her fierce gaze, 'we send stuff like...ads for guns, stores where weapons can be bought, Neo-Nazi literature, hate speeches....'

'And the program does all that?'

'It's a self-learning algorithm. It's AI.'

'My God!' Chloe burst out, 'and you built this?'

Sebastian shuddered at the sudden rise in rage in the room. 'Nyet,' he stammered. 'Someone else wrote them. We just modify.'

Them? There are more than one?

Zeb saw it on the twins' faces. *They too picked up on that.*

'How many algos are there?' Meghan growled.

The Russian didn't answer.

'Shoot him,' the older sister told Zeb, indifferently. 'There are four others we can talk to.'

Vlad moaned at her words. Alexei sobbed. The remaining team members shrank.

'WAIT!' Sebastian yelled when Zeb fingered his Glock. 'Therearetwoprograms.ContentandList.' He spoke so quickly that the words sounded like one.

'Again, slowly,' Meghan ordered.

'Two programs. Content and List. We work with List here.'

'List's the one that selects people and pumps relevant content?'

'Da. Content identifies material to be sent to these people. It keeps on adding new sources, finding ways to get to an internet user.'

'Surely the two programs work together?'

'Da, but we can only access List and make changes to it.'

Meghan broke off and looked at the screens, a faraway look on her face. Zeb knew that expression. She was toying with an idea.

'Content does more than send internet stuff, doesn't it?'

Sebastian's eyes widened but he didn't say anything.

'I bet it sends songs to their headsets...ones that can fuel anger.'

Zeb looked at her. He knew his jaw had dropped. Bwana gasped. Broker stroked his chin and nodded slowly. 'Why didn't I think of that?' Beth muttered to herself, exasperatedly.

'What do you-?'

Meghan held her hand up to stop Zeb. 'Am I correct?' she asked Sebastian.

'I don't...Da, Da,' he said quickly when she took a step forward. 'Any internet connected device that plays music or movies. Content can drive stuff to it. Music. Movies.'

'That's not all, I am sure. It can insert words, lines, phrases, lyrics, to anything out there.'

He blanched. 'How do you know?' he whispered.

'It's the only way,' Meghan faced Zeb and the other operatives. 'I was thinking about it. Just sending hate stuff, sure that'll make some people go out and kill. And algorithms can do that. Different versions of those that meddled in our elections. But to turn people into killers on this scale? There had to be more. People had to be living and breathing hate. The only way to do that is to feed them not just content they can read but also movies and music. Content, that AI, has got hooks into wireless headsets. Those internet devices that control people's homes. And I'm sure the program has a dictionary of phrases, words, sentences, that it inserts into audio and visual media.'

She flashed a look at Sebastian who couldn't help nodding in agreement.

'You're telling them everything,' Eldar hissed at the team leader. 'The pakhan –'

'You should worry about us,' Chloe cut him off grimly. 'You should be thinking of what you can tell us that will help you live.'

The engineer fell silent. He wiped his forehead and looked away.

'Who wrote these programs?' Meghan resumed her questioning.

Sebastian looked at his team members and then back at

the operatives. 'We didn't,' he admitted. 'We were given List when it was ready. The pakhan asked us to work on it.'

'What about those? What do those mean?' Bear pointed to the screens, at the three continent labels.

Sebastian turned even more pale. His lips worked but no words came.

'We might as well tell everything,' Eldar said bitterly. 'There are three teams,' he addressed Meghan. 'We are responsible for Europe. Another team for Asia and a third for America. Each team maintains its version of List. That's how we keep track.'

'This is a game to you?' Roger hissed, his hands instinctively going to his HK. 'Y'all keep score on which team kills most?'

'We're engineers,' Eldar replied defiantly. 'We don't do any killing.'

'You're in a fricking mafia gang. You've been doing this shit, destroying lives for long enough. Your hands are just as bloody. You-'

Roger swore? His team rarely did and it was a measure of the Texan's anger that he had let the curse slip. Zeb stopped him with a look. 'Where are these other teams?'

'And who or what is Hyde?' Broker added.

'Hyde?' Sebastian frowned. 'We don't know what that is. The other teams…we don't know where they are.'

'He doesn't know anything,' Bear looked at Zeb. 'Why should we keep him alive?'

'WAIT!' the team leader panicked. 'One List team's in Asia, another in the US.' He looked at Zeb, 'But we don't know where exactly.'

'What about Content?' Beth asked him.

'That's like a master team, the engineers who wrote it. They wrote List too. They too are in the US, separate from the List team in that country. We've no idea where any of them are.'

A shadow crossed the glass windows before they could question him further.

'GET DOWN!' Zeb yelled in warning and dived to the floor. His HK came up and chattered just as the door burst open. The figure at the door, whose AR15 was up and firing, staggered back from the hail of bullets. His weapon fired harmlessly in the ceiling.

Zeb was moving before the man had crashed to the floor. He brought down goggles over his eyes, raked the windows with his rifle and threw a stun grenade through the shattered glass. More flash bangs as the rest of the operatives followed his cues. The hallway reverberated with explosions and lit up with bright, intense light. Someone outside, screamed in agony.

He crabbed quickly across glass shards and felt a presence behind him.

'I've got you,' Bear, his eyes on the door. Zeb fast-changed his magazine and snapped a quick glance into the passage.

Five men in the passage. One on the floor. Two leaning against the wall, three others staggering aimlessly, all of them clutching their ears, tears streaming through their eyes.

Zeb crawled into the hallway.

And two of the hostiles spun towards him, their AR15s chattering and then they were shuddering and flailing when he and Bear returned fire, cutting the men down.

Two minutes to check the Russians. None of them alive. All of them from the night shift. He stopped in his tracks when he returned to the computer room and saw the engineers on the floor.

'All of them, dead,' Beth said, bitterly. 'They were our only lead.'

Chapter 50

—⚬⚬⚬—

Zeb breathed easily, his face reflecting none of the crushing disappointment he felt. Sure, the engineers had given them vital intel…but they had no names, very broad locations. *None of it is actionable.*

Broken screens in the room. One of the server racks, leaning dangerously against a wall, its contents spilled to the floor. No bodies. They had been dragged out and dumped far down, in the hallway.

It was still but for the soft breathing of his friends. He looked at the sisters hoping they would come up with a miracle, and then shook his head at himself. He should know better. No mission ever went to plan. He was expecting too much.

Nevertheless, Beth and Meghan turned back to the screens, their fingers dancing over keys, as if they sensed how he was feeling. Broker joined them, his jaw firm, determined.

'We don't have much time,' Zeb warned them. 'There could be other shooters coming. We don't know how many Tverskoy's got in town. Get whatever you can. The rest of us will check out any more shooters. Exfil's when we return.'

'Copy that,' the younger sister answered without looking up.

Zeb went outside followed by Bwana, Roger, Chloe and Bear. They checked bodies and cell phones.

'No signal, no missed calls,' he said. 'These men weren't warned from those inside.'

'They must've seen the balloons,' Chloe surmised. 'Came to investigate. There must've been some entry protocol that we don't know of. That alerted them when they arrived.'

Zeb nodded. There was no other plausible explanation. They split up and went through each room again. No hostiles in any of it. They checked out the front, the back and the sides. No change to the barren farmland around them. They returned to the computer room and sensed a change.

Brighter faces. Beth jiggling that foot the way she did when she had found something.

'There's too much here,' she said, 'we need to dig into these programs in detail.'

'You got access?' Bear asked suspiciously.

'Keyloggers…and yeah, those dudes hadn't locked their screens. Probably figured no one else would be at their machines.'

'We know how awesome you are,' Roger, holding back his impatience, 'but can you get to the meat please?'

'Software engineers, they are a community. They talk to each other, hang out virtually. We figured this team would be in touch with the others. In addition, they got their programs from another team. We figured Sebastian and his people would find a way to communicate with those engineers. And with the teams they compete with.'

'And?' Bwana asked with barely restrained impatience.

'The bad news, first,' she said, though she didn't seem unduly concerned. 'There are no addresses, no names, on any of the machines. At least the ones we looked at.'

'Don't these tech people communicate with each other?'

'They do. But this isn't a normal office. What they're working on was criminal. Their comms tool was a realtor's website.' She whirled to a screen and brought up an estate agent's page as they crowded around her. A messaging tool on it.

We're renovating the lounge. Should be good for viewing in a week's time, Nevis, USA.

Gotcha. Will call, nearer the date, Cheryl, USA.

More queries from users, replies from Nevis who seemed to be the realtor.

'We figure Nevis is the Content team, Cheryl was this team in Chernihiv.' She scrolled down the page and pointed to two more queries. 'Indoor Girl, USA and Colonel March, USA, are the others.'

'How did you make that connection?' Zeb asked after a heavy silence. Bwana and Bear nodded as if they too had the same question. Only Broker had a small, knowing grin on his face.

'Simple,' Beth exclaimed. 'This was one of the two most visited sites on Sebastian's internet history. Why would a team based in Ukraine be interested in US homes?'

'I still don't –'

'Using such sites for comms is common enough in our world, Zeb,' she said impatiently. 'Heck, we've used them ourselves.'

'Yeah, but –'

'Cheryl is Chernihiv. Indoor is somewhere in Asia, like

Sebastian said. Meg and I think they're somewhere in Indonesia. And Colonel March…somewhere in Colorado.'

More silence, broken when Bear grabbed a chair, turned it around and sat, his chest to its back, the seat creaking under his weight. 'Talk us through that. Slowly,' he growled.

'Jeez,' Meghan sighed. 'Alright. There are four users who are the most frequent on this site.' More scrolling and high-lighting of names. 'All of them have the first three or four letters of Nevis, Cheryl, Indoor, or Colonel. This one, for instance,' a polished finger nail tapped the screen. Neville. Or this one, Cherelle. Nevis, Neville, all other *Nev* variations, posted at the same time, which is why we think they're the same person. The same with the others.'

'IP addresses?'

'Nyet,' she shook her head. 'No location details.'

'Tell them about the other stuff,' Beth's foot jiggled faster, her face bright with excitement.

'Sebastian was checking out this,' Meghan brought up another web page. 'Recognize the city?'

'Jakarta,' Zeb breathed. 'But…he could've been following the Yunus killing.'

'He wasn't. Look at that circle, Cakung. That's not where the killings took place. There's no link between Yunus and that neighborhood.'

I know that area, Zeb thought. *Less development. Higher crime. A cyber-criminal gang could be operating out of there and no one would know.*

'What about Nevis?'

Another web page. A US state they were familiar with.

'Nevada,' Chloe hissed. 'The main team's there?'

'That's what we think. There's no other reason for

Sebastian and his crew to check out these places. We figure they were trying to locate where the other teams were.'

'These dudes,' Beth nodded in the direction of the hallway where the bodies lay, 'They weren't allowed to go anywhere. No cell phones on them. They played games online to while away the time, but how long can one do that? We think they were trying to find out where the other teams were. It was like a challenge to them.'

'You said they communicated with the other teams?'

'Yeah,' Beth went to a dating site. 'That's how they communicated. Chernihiv, Colorado, Indonesia, again similar system. But these messages were less frequent. They were usually just to brag. *Saw that killing? That's down to us.* Stuff like that.'

'There's something else,' Beth's voice was tight when she brought up another screen. Faces and names on it. Two in Britain, three in France and Germany. One in Spain.

'Are those who I think they are,' Chloe gasped.

'Yes. The next killers.'

Chapter 51

They acted swiftly. Zeb made calls to Alex Thompson, Pierre
Gurtin and Eric Schmidt. Passed them the names. Didn't
explain how he'd gotten them. Another call to Clare, to whom
he told everything.

'I'll pass on the Spanish name to someone I know,' she
replied in that understated way which meant she knew her
counterpart in that country well. 'I'll also alert intelligence
heads in major European countries.'

'We've got to keep this wrapped,' Zeb warned.

'Yes, I know.' He pictured her rubbing the bridge of her
nose in her DC office as she leaned back in her chair, eyes
shut. 'Tverskoy can't be acting alone,' she thought out aloud.
'This is too big even for him. He's got to have political backing but even that's not enough. This isn't big. It's ginormous.
It has a scale and reach that not one country can achieve. And
what's the end goal?'

'No idea.'

'You've got some ideas?'

'Nope.'

'We need that program. I'll get a trusted group in the NSA

to work on it, see if it gets us anywhere. And Zeb, shut it down.'

'Beth and Meg are doing just that,' he replied. The twins had made copies of hard drives, unplugged the cables and then Bear and Bwana shot up the machines.

'Program's in the servers here,' the elder sister had assured him. 'It trawls Facebook, other social media accounts and does what it's intended to do.'

An hour later they were running across the farm, lugging their gear, heading to their trucks.

'Wait!' Beth stopped him. 'What about the balloons, the drones?'

The sisters had deliberately crashed the UAV before joining the attacks and their debris littered the front yard.

'Leave them.'

'But, Zeb, that's expensive gear. It can be traced back to the US.'

'I know,' he replied and resumed running.

'What's he up to?' he heard her ask Meghan who didn't reply.

Back in the vehicles, jostling across uneven terrain. Zeb at the wheel of one ride, Meghan in the front, beside him. Thinking, about Tverskoy, about List and Content, about Nevada, Colorado and Indonesia.

Johann Schwann came to mind. The German concentration camp survivor who had died in his arms in Berlin.

'Music, movies, videos, those can turn a man so much?' he asked softly, even though he knew the answer.

'Yes,' Meghan replied. 'Along with everything else that List does.'

Blue eyes, smiling, soft golden hair bouncing on her neck. His wife adjusting a pair of headphones over his ears. *You gotta listen to this.* Her head bobbing as she twined her fingers with his.

Zeb looked out of the side window. There had been a time when songs were a big part of his life. Not anymore.

The Ukrainian landscape sped past, rolling fields, some barren, some with crops. Chernihiv came and went, a hustling city, and then Kiev approached. More traffic. Houses, offices, industrial units. He let the now fill his mind and sent the memories back to their vault.

'Tverskoy,' he asked the older sister. 'Can you find him?'

'Yes.'

'And those three locations. Colorado, Nevada and Indonesia?'

'We sure as hell will try.

He called Andropov. 'Grigor, how soon can you get a team to Ukraine? Yeah, we busted the bratva place. Yes, we found the programmers, servers. That was the base for the algorithms. We destroyed all of it. You need to seal the place. Yes, news reports are fine. In fact, I want Tverskoy to know his place was busted.'

At Boryspil International Airport, Kotenko was waiting for them with another man. He took the keys to their trucks, tossed one to his companion and drove away as unobtrusively as he had arrived.

A call from Pierre Gurtin which made Zeb tighten his lips. 'Our information was too late,' he told his team. 'That French man, in that list of names in the farmhouse…he killed four people near the Louvre, half an hour back.'

'What about the others?'

He raised a finger to ask for silence and made calls to

Thompson and then to Clare. The hardness on his face eased momentarily when he hung up. 'Those others are being tracked by police. They'll be stopped if they bring out a weapon.'

'What're the laws on this?' Chloe asked. 'Have they broken any laws by listening to that hate stuff? Surely they were manipulated.'

'Not our problem.' He led them into the airport's lounge. Backpacks and bags, like other travelers. No weapons, no balloons and no drones.

'Need a bite?' He stopped in the middle of the concourse and scratched his chin.

'Nope, let's go,' Bwana growled and made to move past him. 'There's still List Asia and US to take down. And the Content team. And Tverskoy and whoever else is behind this.'

'You sure? It's a long flight. Beth, Chloe?'

'We're good, Zeb,' the younger sister patted her bag which had her laptop. 'The sooner we're wheels up, the quicker we can get back to work.'

'Wait, one,' he replied and pulled his phone out. Looked up and around as if searching for someone.

'What's up?' Meghan asked him impatiently.

'I still think we should fill ourselves up.'

The elder twin opened her mouth to flare at him. Stopped suddenly and she took in the normal airport scene around them. Her eyes went to the columns in the concourse, to the security cameras mounted on them.

'You want Tverskoy to know it was us,' a flash of understanding on her face. 'That's why you're hanging around. Showing your face.'

'Yeah. If we can't get to the answers quickly enough,' Zeb replied grimly. 'Let them come to us.'

Chapter 52

Nikolai Tverskoy checked in with Andrei each evening through an email account with one of the free providers. Draft mails that never got sent. One of the most secure ways to communicate with another person, particularly when both parties were criminals.

No update. The Russian drummed his fingers on the polished table surface in his hotel room as he looked out at the Paris view. No update was unusual. It was a rule between them that Andrei post something each day, just to confirm it was business as usual. As the killings increased around the world, it was all the more important to stick to protocol.

Cruisers raced down the street far below. Paris was on high alert after the Louvre attack. There was hardly any foot traffic. The pakhan went to the window and glanced down. Armed police officers on the street. Patrol dogs.

Tverskoy wondered when the next round of riots would start. Made a bet with himself that they would happen before night.

It was his doing but any pride he felt was obscured by the worry over Chernihiv. Andrei was one of his most trusted lieutenants. It was unlike him to maintain radio silence.

And then he slapped himself mentally and turned on the TV. He flipped through channels, almost all of which covered the day's massacre. He stopped at a Russian station and waited patiently for the host to move on from the Paris story. He swore when the news turned to politics and had his thumb on the *power off* button when he read the scrolling banner.

Mysterious attack on a farmhouse in Chernihiv. Balloons crash land on its roof.

He roared in the silence of his room and lunged towards his phone. Dialed a number swiftly and far away, after the call was bounced through several satellites, it was picked up.

'Da?' a rough voice asked. 'Who's this?'

'Who are *you*?' Tverskoy shouted.

'Captain Leontij Tokar,' the voice replied stiffly. 'Chernihiv Police Department.'

The Russian hung up. A warning breeze blew through his mind, cooling his anger. He opened a browser and searched for more details on the farmhouse. Beads of sweat formed on his forehead as he read. No survivors. No clues. The remains of highly sophisticated balloons and drones. Police were investigating.

He wiped his face with a towel and settled back into his chair. This was a disaster and it meant a call had to be made. It wasn't one he was looking forward to.

Chapter 53

———— ✺ ————

This time they met in London, the day after the Paris attack. Leslie, Williams and Smith, in a boutique hotel that faced Parliament Square. The establishment catered to the super-rich and had a reputation for exclusivity, which was why it was a favorite of the spymasters. They were confident that it was one of the few hotels that MI5 and MI6 didn't surveil and that was why it had been selected.

The atmosphere was strained, unlike the last time. Williams, the host, had organized the meeting at the very last minute once he had heard from Tverskoy.

He had gone into a cold rage when Tverskoy had broken the news. 'I came to you because you were the best,' he had hissed. 'Because your engineers ran the most sophisticated algorithms in the US elections. And your security and secrecy was unmatchable. Now, you're saying some strangers just walked into your place, shot everyone up and stole the program?'

The pakhan had tried to explain but the spymaster was beyond listening. He raged and yelled for several minutes until his fury abated and he could think clearly.

List Europe was no longer a secret. Whoever had attacked the Chernihiv base knew about it and presumably knew of the existence of the other teams.

'Find out who they are,' he had ordered. 'I don't care how you do it. The program…it's gone?'

The farmhouse was not salvageable, Tverskoy told him. The intruders had destroyed the computer room and now, the police had taken over the place. There was no way List Europe could go back into operation.

'How bad is it?' Leslie asked Williams coldly.

The three men were in a small room in the interior of the hotel. Coffee cups in front of them. A platter of biscuits, untouched. It wasn't the time for socializing and pleasantries.

'I told you,' the spymaster replied. 'As bad as it can get.' He broke it down for them again, staring defiantly at them. It wasn't as if he, personally, was responsible for the events in Chernihiv.

'And you don't know who they were?' Smith snapped.

In answer, Williams tossed a set of photographs on the table. Their glossy surfaces slid and spread on the spotless white cloth. 'Tverskoy sent these to me just before you arrived. Not even half an hour ago.'

Leslie picked one image up. A brown-haired man in an airport lounge. Another picture, that of a bunch of men and women crowding around that person. A third picture, of eight people exiting from Boryspil Airport. Their heads and faces were partly covered, but there was no mistaking their build and those two large men.

'Who are they?' he passed the photographs to Williams.

'That man, there,' Williams jabbed the air, pointing to

the brown-haired man. 'That's Zeb Carter. That's his team with him. They work in a covert US outfit.'

'I have not heard of him.'

'Neither have I,' Smith chimed.

'That's why he's one of the most dangerous agents in the US.'

'How do you know about him?' The Asia man asked.

'You've heard of Grigor Andropov?'

Heads nodded. The Russian was a legend in their circles.

'A few years back, there was a Do Not Apprehend message from him. No name, just a description. Him!' He held up Carter's photograph. 'Since then, I've been building a file on the American. There isn't much in it. He's like a ghost. Doesn't leave tracks. I think he was involved in that Israel-Palestine affair.'

Leslie snorted at his choice of words. The biggest political event of the century wasn't a mere *affair*. 'I didn't get that message,' he said.

'Nor me, either,' Smith again.

'It was only to me, MI6 and DGSE. Don't ask me why. It was Andropov who sent it to me. Carter was in Chernihiv when the cartel house went down.'

Silence hung heavy in the room. A faint laugh from the corridor outside.

'It can't be coincidence.'

'No,' Williams agreed. 'Tverskoy's men made enquiries. Carter and those people were seen in the town. A store owner remembers them. He said the dark man in that group was unmistakable.'

'When were these photographs taken?'

'Time stamp's on them,' he pointed to the numerals in the bottom right-hand corner of the images. 'Those, with their scarves and bandanas, was on their arrival. Two days before the bratva place was destroyed. The second set is the evening of the attack. Have a look at these, too.'

He brought out more photographs. Of balloons over the farmhouse and the wreckage of drones. 'That's sophisticated gear, there. US made. Carter. He found out, somehow about that place, and he acted. And now, he knows about List Europe.'

'He might know about you, too.' Smith asked sharply.

'We have to assume that. I visited just once and met only Tverskoy. We agreed on that. All of us would visit our centers in person. Check them out for ourselves.'

'Yes, but we told the center heads to delete CCVTV recordings of our arrival.'

'And Tverskoy said his man, Andrei, did that. He even showed me a feed. On top of that, he swears he did not tell anyone about me. But...'

Leslie reached for the jug of coffee and filled their cups. Buying time, for them to think and process what they had heard.

'We have a month to go before the G20 Summit,' he said. 'So far, things are on track. The violence around the world has escalated. Those countries which are having national elections...their ruling governments are facing disaster in the polls. In Europe, USA, Canada, UK, South America, there's anger at the elected officials. The stock markets are down. Our buying into key shares is undetected. But-'

'We still have a way to go,' Williams broke in. 'The formation of the special security force. The defense ministers of our countries are making progress on that. But they have to move carefully. They know nothing can be leaked before the summit.'

'I spoke to my boss last week,' Leslie took a sip of his coffee and patted his lips delicately with the table linen. 'I briefed him. He's happy. Things are progressing on the political front too. Our leader spoke to your leaders. All three are on board now. Their people are drafting a joint message which they will collectively read out at the G20. That, along with the security force announcement...people in all countries will look to our countries as the real leaders. Not the US, Britain, France or Germany. And with total control of those internet companies, we can destroy the Western world.'

'And now, Carter,' Smith growled. 'If he knows of List Europe, he might find out about the others. Content as well. If it comes out that we are behind it –'

'President Morgan will act,' Leslie nodded, knowing where the America man was heading. 'He will get the British, French, German and Japanese leaders together. They'll stop what we're planning. We've got to stop Carter.'

He and Smith looked at Williams who nodded. 'I'll deal with him. But we have to revive List Europe again. We need momentum.'

'There's a copy of all the Lists in Nevada and Colorado, isn't there?' Leslie, thinking aloud. 'Those two are our fallback locations.'

'Yes. But we can't risk sending any messages. Who knows what Carter might be tracking? One of us will have to go in person and work with the team leader there and get it activated.'

'I'll go,' Smith announced. 'I'm the least known of us

three. It won't be immediate, however. I've got to finish some tasks that my boss gave me. It'll take about a week.'

'Let's do this. You go to Colorado,' Williams added, 'I'll go to Nevada. We can decide which List Europe version to activate once we get there. Both those teams are mine and they just might've heard what went down in Chernihiv. Yes,' he held a hand to forestall their objections. 'We know they have no means of communication and don't know where the other teams are. But, these are some of the smartest software engineers in the world. They could've figured out something. And none of us or our men on the ground are as tech savvy as them. That was a known risk.'

A short silence as the men contemplated the Europe man's suggestion.

'That works with me,' the Asia man stroked his chin thoughtfully. 'Both Tomas in Nevada and Jake in Colorado know the three of us. They're your men. You handpicked them, along with the programmers and sent them to those locations,' he glanced at Williams.

'Yes, those two, they're better than Tverskoy.'

'Okay, that's decided. I've got another idea. You know the protest marches in Washington DC, Paris and London?'

'Those are in about ten days. You mean those?'

'Yes. Why don't we attack those?'

'These programs,' Williams mused, 'they don't work as specifically as that. There's a degree of chance. How much a man has turned, how much his killing instincts have been roused.'

'No, I mean we send killers to shoot into those crowds. Our killers. Single men from within our organizations. Expendable, so that even if they're caught, they won't know anything about us.'

Williams and Smith caught on immediately. 'Yes. That will be devastating. And will make up for List Europe's absence for some time.'

'I can provide the shooters,' the Europe man said. 'I've got them in-country, in the US.'

'Go to the US locations,' Leslie told them. 'Once you're there, we'll coordinate the attacks. We need to tie up a loose end,' he turned to the Europe man.

'Tverskoy?' Williams glanced at his Rolex. 'He won't be a problem for much longer. There's a hit team heading to Paris. They know where he's hiding. By the end of the day, the pakhan will cease to exist.'

'That leaves us with Carter. You need to move fast.'

'I'll take care of him, too,' Williams said grimly, glancing at the photograph of the brown-haired man. 'He's a dead man walking.'

Chapter 54

⸺≋⸺

Back in New York, the day after Chernihiv. Hot outside. Air-conditioned cool inside their Columbus Avenue office.

Beth, Meghan and Broker hunched over their screens, working together, prying List Europe's secrets from the hard-drives they had brought back.

Zeb made calls. To Andropov, to Thompson, to Pierre Gurtin and Eric Schmidt. He spoke tersely, brought them up to speed.

'We're watching everyone in France, from the names Clare shared,' the Frenchman responded. 'Xavier Douffet, the Louvre killer. We couldn't do anything about him, though.'

'He's got the same profile?'

'Oui. Hate-filled right-winger. Single, male. He's lawyered up and isn't talking, but his internet history and laptop, there's enough in them for us to work on.'

Noon. Beth did her thing with her foot. Her face flushed with excitement. But she and her sister didn't reveal what they had found. Broker adopted a Sphinx-like expression.

'We're going to DC, right? To brief Clare and Daniel Klouse,' the younger twin replied when Bwana cajoled her into spilling. 'You can wait till then.'

'But-'

'Nope!'

Two SUVs to JFK and then onto their Gulfstream. It was evening by the time they reached their boss's office in DC. A few blocks away, The White House, visible from where they were, painted orange and gold by the setting sun.

Zeb stopped them by holding up his phone and turning its screen to them. A newsflash. A dead body, badly burned, had been identified in Paris. Nikolai Tverskoy, killed in a hotel room along with his girlfriend. Gang attack, the police said.

'Someone's cleaning up,' he said and led them inside.

Clare and the National Security Advisor, Daniel Klouse, in the conference room. Brief greetings. It wasn't the time for *how was your flight*, kind of questions.

'Nikolai Tverskoy couldn't be acting alone,' Zeb said. 'The scale of these killings, the vision behind List and Content. This isn't the work of one Russian Mafia gang.'

'Agreed,' Klouse steepled his fingers. 'But it's hard to believe the Kremlin is involved. There have been killings in Russia too. And how do they benefit?'

'Their meddling in our elections –' Chloe began.

'There was a goal there. Is,' he corrected himself. 'We've not shut down their bots, their covert agencies, completely. In the elections, they hoped to influence our politics. Install a leader friendly to them. Remove the sanctions on them. Reduce the current hostility that the West has to Russia. But these killings? They aren't directed at us alone. They are all across the world. What's the Kremlin's motive in these, if it's involved?'

'You agree, sir, that Tverskoy would have to have political backing?' Zeb asked.

'Yeah, I'm with you on that.'

'It's too late to ask him now, because he's dead. You might have heard the news.'

Klouse and his boss nodded.

'We looked into his sponsors. It gets murky there, because it looks like he bribed as many politicians as he could. That's what all these pakhans do. High-ranking ministers with enormous clout, who report directly to the President. We're still working on that angle.'

'We're running out of time,' the National Security Advisor warned. 'The G20 Summit is about a month away. President Morgan wants to announce something positive there. He wants world leaders to come together and win back confidence in democracy. We need answers, Zeb, and fast.'

'They might be in Indonesia,' Beth strode to a wall on which a photograph was projected. 'Jakarta. We have narrowed down where the List Asia team could be located. We compared the photographs on Sebastian's drive, ran algos –'

'Cakung, he was looking at that district, wasn't he?' Bear interrupted her.

'Yeah, but we've zoomed in even further.' The image enlarged. Shanty dwellings bordering a river to the east of the city. 'That's Cakung river, and on its banks, in those slums, is where the team is hidden. There are a few notable preman gangs, the Cakung Brotherhood, the Bali Boys, Garuda…but there are only two who we think can be protecting List Asia. The Cakung Brotherhood and the Garuda.'

Preman, the Indonesian word for a gang member, a word they all knew and didn't need her to explain.

She clicked the remote in her hand. A new image appeared on the wall. A fierce-looking Indonesian, goatee, bandana.

'Taniwan Zhen. Leader of the Cakung gang. Reported to have three hundred members in Jakarta alone. Main business, as you can imagine, extortion, killing, drugs, prostitution. And cybercrime. That's the fastest growing line of business for them.'

Another remote click, another photograph. A bald man, a scar by his right eye.

'Lot Keling, leader of the Garuda. He's been to prison twice. Served three years the first time, five the second. Killed three people while inside. He's a hardcore criminal. Reputed to boil his enemies in oil. Alive.'

'And you think one of these two gangs could be running List Asia?' Zeb asked.

'Yeah. They've got the engineers, the muscle, the political reach, and both have bases in Cakung. We ran some programs…remember those messages on that dating and realtor site on Sebastian's machine? We crosschecked times of posting, tried to work back IP addresses. Ran some sniffing programs on these gang's activities, went to some darknet message boards. Let me say, we are reasonably sure one of these two gangs is involved. But that slum, the one Sebastian was looking at,' the previous image returned. 'That's in Garuda territory.'

'Which gang is larger?'

'The Brotherhood.

Tverskoy's gang wasn't the biggest in Moscow, Zeb thought. *Is there a pattern here? That the biggest gang draws attention, so, whoever's behind this, goes with the smaller ones?*

'I need to talk to Daritan,' he said, referring to his friend, the head of the BIN.

'Oh ye of little faith,' Beth mocked him with a smile. 'Meg and I spoke to him before we left. He agrees with our theory and he says, if he was a betting man, he would go for the Garudas.'

'Then let's go talk to Lot Keling,' Zeb said, simply.

Chapter 55

Going to Indonesia required more organization than their operation in Ukraine. Zeb spoke at length to the BIN Director who admitted that both gangs were on his radar.

'But not for this, temanku.' *My friend.* 'For other gang activities. And, you saw the news?'

Zeb nodded silently. Overnight, there had been a killing in Bali. A single man had opened fire on a bunch of Western tourists at a fancy resort. He too had clammed up when arrested but, going by his internet history, it looked like he was the latest killer turned by List Asia.

'There are mass protests in Jakarta today,' Jinhai said soberly. 'It feels like my country is at a breaking point. Shall I arrest Keling and Zhen?'

'No.'

'Zeb, I need to do something,' The Indonesian protested. 'I have to report this to the ministry.'

'That would be a big mistake. Keling and whoever his paymaster is, will own politicians. We don't want to alert them or spook them.'

'You're going to hit them, aren't you?'

Zeb didn't reply.

'You don't have much to go on, other than a theory.'

'Yeah, but what's the worst that could happen? Keling turns out to have no hand in this…but we take him down.'

'If you put it that way,' Jinhai laughed, 'I can live with that outcome. What do you need from me?'

'Slow response.'

'I can arrange that. But, Zeb,' he warned. 'No civilian casualties. No shootouts in public.'

'Deal.'

Their second day in New York, after their return from Ukraine. Their plans were nearly complete. A trusted source would supply them with weapons in Jakarta. They went through vast data that the sisters had compiled on the Garudas and on the Cakung Slums.

'Let's get him at his nightclub,' Zeb decided. 'That's where he's out in the open.'

Keling owned the largest bar on the Cakung River in East Jakarta. The venue was unassuming, appearing as a warehouse-like building on the outside. Black-painted. High walls. Sloping roof. Access through metal gates that opened on Raya Bekasi road. The inside was a large dance floor, a bar that ran from one wall to another, and private rooms.

The preman boss came to the establishment each Thursday evening, like a king gracing his court. Accompanied by heavies, he went to the bar, greeted a few regulars and checked that he wasn't being skimmed by the staff and then went to a private room.

There, he entertained and discussed gang matters, until ten pm. He went back to his vehicle and was driven to his residence, a heavily fortified mansion in Jakarta.

All that was public knowledge. There were enough posts on social media, reports of sightings, photographs of the inside of the bar, for Zeb to plan a takedown.

'This hallway is barred to the public,' he laid a finger on the layout that Beth had printed. 'Six bodyguards. Armed. We take them down and that door,' he tapped the room on the sheet, 'is the only thing between us and him.'

'He'll have men inside,' Bear thought out loud. 'But they'll be relaxed. They won't be expecting a hit in their stronghold.'

'Correct,' Meghan said briskly. 'You and Chloe will be outside, with a getaway vehicle.'

'We'll miss the fun! I've always wanted to shoot up a bar.'

'That's definitely not happening,' she snapped. We promised the Jinhai. Besides, we can't have you and Bwana inside at the same time. You'll get noticed.'

'*Bwana* won't?' Bear spluttered.

'I'll be black as the night, slippery as an eel,' the dark operative smirked, 'I'll be in and out so fast that even you won't know I was there.'

Beth ignored him. 'Zeb and Roger will remove those heavies. Silenced weapons. Shoot to kill. Yeah,' she said when Chloe raised an eyebrow. 'We've got files on his men. None of them are innocents.'

'Broker will stay back on the dance floor,' Beth took over. 'He'll warn us if anyone heads our way. Meg and I, we'll be in another vehicle, flying drones, jamming all signals. We'll be in police uniforms, in a cop vehicle.'

'How'll you swing that?' Roger queried.

'You leave that to us,' she replied haughtily.

Zeb hid a smile. *They can procure a nuclear submarine if*

it's needed for a mission. They're that good.

'We'll block other vehicles coming inside the drive as soon as the bodyguards are out. Then, we hustle Keling to Chloe and Bear's ride and we're home free.'

They thrashed the plan about, what-if scenarios, and only when each one of them was satisfied did they stop.

'Hyde,' Zeb asked, once all plans had been made. 'We've not found anything more on it.'

'On that,' Meghan replied. 'I've got an idea.'

Everyone turned to her.

'Hyde could be the name of the program. This whole thing.'

'Like a mission name?' Broker thought out aloud.

'Yeah. I think that name was deliberately chosen. Jekyll and Hyde. Two faces. List and Content, innocuous by themselves, but deadly when used for such purposes.'

Zeb turned it over. *Yeah, it makes sense. That's why the engineers didn't know it. They wouldn't. Tverskoy and Keling's backers, they'll have coined the term.*

Noon.

They stepped out of their building and briefly debated lunch venues. Roger and Broker wanted to go to a wine auction downtown and persuaded Bear, Chloe and Bwana to join them. Meghan wanted to go to a French café which was down Columbus Avenue, a regular hangout for the sisters when they were in town. Zeb joined them.

He and the twins ahead, the remaining operatives, several yards to their rear, heading to the subway.

The usual New York traffic. Cabs and tourist buses, angry honks and gas fumes. Office workers and gawking visitors.

Zeb was a pace behind the sisters, as they walked past the polished granite wall of their building.

He bent down to tighten a shoelace.

That saved his life.

Chapter 56

———∞∞∞———

Zeb didn't hear the shot but felt the round impact in the wall.

He reacted instantly.

He fell prone, reached forward and grabbed the twins' legs. Yanked hard and brought them crashing down.

Crawled back desperately, right hand reaching for his Glock, finding it, drawing it out in a smooth move, eyes searching desperately for the shooter. Another shot. Chips from the sidewalk spraying his face.

There! That black car. A dark hole inside its lowered window.

'SHOOTER!' he roared. Got to his feet and weaved and ducked, heading to the vehicle. Anything to draw the rounds at him, away from the sisters and the other operatives.

A bus honked angrily to his left. He ignored it. Someone screamed. More yells.

'TO THE GROUND!' he ordered and then he got a clear sight. Two men in the front of the car. One behind, holding a rifle. He triggered his Glock even as he felt a bullet tug his T-shirt and scream into the distance.

He fired again, knowing he had missed the first time. The

vehicle shuddered. Did he hit it? No. The driver had fired it up and merged the car smoothly into the traffic.

Can't lose them. Zeb broke into a sprint, down the avenue, cars swerving out of the way, drivers, unaware of the shots, swearing and honking at him.

He leaped over a cab's hood. One moment he was in the air, time enough for a shot at the hitter's vehicle. Its rear window shattered. Movement from its inside and then the rifle barrel poked. Zeb fell to the street and rolled desperately out of the way. He hit the sidewalk and came to a jarring stop and when he looked up, Bear and Bwana were leaning over him, but the vehicle had disappeared.

'What the heck were you thinking?' Roger caught hold of Zeb's tee and hauled him up. 'Chasing that car like that? Making yourself a target.'

Zeb didn't reply. He cast his eyes around. Traffic had come to a standstill. A woman sobbing on the sidewalk. Several people on their phones. A cruiser wailed somewhere.

No sign of that car. They got away.

'Zeb?' Beth said sharply, 'Are you hit?'

'No,' he looked down at his tee and fingered the hole in its side. 'But it was close. Anyone get a look at them?'

'No,' Meghan admitted. 'By the time we hit the ground and realized what was happening, the car was moving. No plates. I remember that.'

'Yeah,' Broker agreed. 'I saw that too.'

And then the cops arrived and the questioning began.

An hour later they were heading back from the café to their office. Zeb, Meghan and Beth. The others had gone to the auction after giving their statements to the police.

'I doubt they'll be found,' Beth grumbled, referring to the shooters. 'And who could they be?'

'It's not as if we lack enemies,' Meghan snorted. She over-took a slow-moving couple and brought out a small mirror from her shoulder bag. She checked out her face. Flicked away a stray hair from her cheek and – *'ZEB!'* she screamed.

Zeb took a long side-step. *Her voice. What did she see?* He spun on his heel, beast roaring and filling him instantly when he took in the scene.

Three men in suits, close behind them. One holding a silenced revolver, the others reaching inside their jackets.

The Benchmade slipped into Zeb's hand as if it had a life of its own. He lunged forward and slapped away the shooter's gun hand. His right hand jabbed the knife into the attacker's chest. Withdrew it, jabbed him again and shoved him at his companions.

Close quarters combat worked differently. There was little time to think and maneuver. An opponent's move had to be turned into either defense or offense. No slashing with a knife. Only jabs and the blade swung up again when the two suits spread out, brought out their guns and turned on Zeb.

He dived at the nearest man, felt the blast of the gun. No time to figure out if he was shot. *My body's responding. No shock. Looks like he missed* and then he was bodyslamming the gunman, grappling with him as they fell to the sidewalk, Zeb on top, evading as the man's knee came up and from the corner of his eyes he could see Beth and Meghan take on the third attacker, their eyes sharp, narrowed, faces intent.

A blow to the side of his head rocked him. The attacker had flung his gun away and had grasped his knife wrist, turning the blade inside, towards his belly. Zeb headbutted him. The man's nose burst. Red spread over his face. He grunted but his grip didn't loosen.

Zeb jabbed his eyes with his fingers and at that the man yelled and with a savage kick, freed himself and got to his feet. He dove for his gun, landed on his shoulder, was turning it around, his eyes widening in triumph, when the Benchmade pierced his neck and jammed to its hilt.

'You're getting old.' Beth, sardonic, but her eyes worried. She assessed him as he stood panting.

Sound returned. The city returned as the haze of the battle faded from his mind and the beast subsided and became blood pumping through his arteries.

Screaming from several onlookers as they stared at the bodies on the ground.

'Your man?' Zeb asked the sisters.

'Dead,' Meghan said bitterly. 'We had no choice.'

He checked his attacker. He too was lifeless as was the first man.

'Search them,' he told the twins under his breath. The three of them bent over the bodies, patted them expertly.

'Nothing,' Beth stood back in frustration. 'Not even a wallet. What're you doing?' this directed to her sister who was snapping pictures discreetly.

'What do you think?' Meghan retorted and jammed her phone in her pocket when the first cruiser rolled up.

Late evening, back in their office.

Zeb stood at the floor-to-ceiling window, a coffee mug in his hand.

Traffic snailed below, the city back to normal. Nothing

fazed it. Nothing stopped it.

He winced as he felt his side. That bullet had come close, but those suits, they had hit him hard.

They were pros. They knew how to hurt. Hurt? They were out to kill.

The cops had questioned them for much longer the second time. Two attacks on the same day, within a short span of time, was unheard of. What was even more concerning was that none of the men had any identification on them.

He looked up when he felt a presence. Beth and Meghan, flanking him.

'That was no coincidence,' the younger woman stated. 'Werner ran facial recognition on them. No matches.'

'How many people know who we are and what we are?' he asked.

'Thirty, maybe forty?' Meghan frowned.

He nodded in agreement. *That sounds about right. The heads of a few intelligence agencies know about us. They know how to contact us. The security firm, it has some of our faces, but there's no connection to the Agency, what we really do.*

'How many people can organize such attacks?' he turned, leaned against the window and addressed them. 'Find us so quickly, get pros.'

It was the elder sister who made the connection first. Meghan sucked her breath sharply. 'You mean…an intelligence head is behind all this? Someone we know?'

'I can't think of any other explanation. The timing, those men…' he shook his head. 'But I don't think it's someone we trust.'

'It's someone they know,' Beth whirled on her sister. 'That

clip, we never showed it to Zeb.'

'What clip?' he asked.

In answer, she caught his elbow and led him to her screen. Typed furiously and brought up a video.

'We found this in one of the Chernihiv's drives,' she explained as she typed furiously and selected a folder. 'Remember, they had CCTV cameras around the house?'

'Yeah.'

'Well, we went through those recordings. We found nothing out of the ordinary. That place had very few visitors, all of whom we were able to track down. A plumber from town, a window-repairers. Tradespeople that you would expect. Except for this man.'

She played a video and sat back.

Zeb watched over her shoulder as a car drove up the farmhouse's drive. It reversed and parked against the wall. It cut out of view as the front door opened and Andrei came out. *Looks like Beth and Meg spliced the video from several camera feeds.* Zeb figured as he watched Andrei look at the arrival. Came down the steps, crunched over the gravel and then the focus shifted to the car as a man climbed out.

Hat on his head, face turned away from the camera, left shoulder hunched up as if to further conceal his face, dark suit on his body.

'Hello,' he greeted Andrei in English.

'Him,' Beth's eyes bright, sparkling with excitement. 'We couldn't identify him. No facial match. No other sighting of him.'

'How old is that?'

'Five months ago. Well before the killings started.'

'Tverskoy moved engineers from MIBC to Chernihiv.'

'Yeah, but that isn't Tverskoy. It's no Russian agency head. We checked.'

'That isn't what Zeb's getting at,' Meghan told her. 'You're thinking this man visited when Sebastian's team moved?'

'Yes,' Zeb said. 'But we don't know when they shipped out of Moscow.'

Could that be some agency head we haven't heard of? How's that possible? He argued with himself. We know of every sizeable intelligence agency in the world. We cooperate with some of them, keep tabs on the others.

Do you really know everyone out there? An inner voice challenged him.

'Send that video to our circle. Thompson, Gurtin, Andropov…all of them.'

'Done,' Beth replied after a moment.

'Now, let's get to Indonesia.'

Chapter 57

'Your men failed,' Smith accused Williams over the video call.

'Yes,' the Europe man acknowledged. 'Carter and his people reacted so fast; they took my teams by surprise.'

'Your men could have anticipated that. After all, you yourself, said this American is very good.'

'Enough,' Leslie nipped the argument before it could escalate.

The three of them weren't equal in their relationship. The Asia man had come up with the idea. He had then met the Europe man at a security event and the two men, over drinks, had bonded.

Their countries weren't friendly and that gave them the best cover. No one would ever suspect that the two men would or could work together.

Williams had grasped the enormity of Leslie's idea immediately and had promised to provide the engineers. The two had then sought out Smith, again, a perfect foil, because it was unimaginable to the world that the three men could agree on anything, let alone collaborate.

Smith was wary initially, but when the two men explained

the plan to him, he became an enthusiastic supporter. He brought money, lots of it. He provided the North American centers where the List and Content teams were housed. But he was an inferior partner. Leslie and Williams were in control and they subtly let Smith know that, time and again.

'What's done is done. It's behind us,' The Asia man carried on. 'We've all been in the game for a long time. We know every mission isn't successful. There are setbacks. This is one, but it doesn't change anything.'

'No, it doesn't,' Williams assented.

'Except that Carter's alert now,' Smith replied defiantly. 'He'll know these attacks aren't a coincidence.'

'He knew that already, after Chernihiv,' Leslie said placatingly. 'Let's put this in perspective. One of Williams' team escaped –'

'They're dead,' the Europe man interjected. 'No loose ends. And the second team, all of them are dead. There's nothing to connect those men to us.'

'Correct,' Leslie said. 'We lost nothing there, except a few good men. Let's not lose sight of our goal. We need to keep the momentum going. We need to amp up the killings in America.'

'I'll take care of that,' Smith replied. 'But we need some distraction. Perhaps some lone-wolf shooters in South America and Asia?'

'Perfect. I'll take care of the Asia end.'

'Your man in Indonesia…he's on alert?'

'I've two men, Keling and Zhen,' Leslie laughed, 'as you know. Both are alert. In fact, they are looking to set a trap if Carter shows up. I'll send them the American's photographs so they'll know whom to look for.'

'They are good men?'

'The best. Zhen and I have worked together several times in the past. I trust him fully. Keling's good too. The fact that very few in the West have heard of them, speaks of their capabilities.

'Great. Tomas and Jake are alert too. They haven't been told of anything that went down. Stay sharp, those are their orders. In any case, Williams and I can check out for ourselves when we visit those centers.'

Jakarta was a good twenty-one-hour flight, which included a refueling stop in Qatar. Their Gulfstream took off from JFK at seven pm and touched down at Soekarno Hatta International Airport at six am, a Tuesday.

They didn't have much gear with them and cleared immigration smoothly. Tourists, that was their cover. From New York, coworkers in a well-known tech firm. They had the identity cards, employers' credentials, everything to make their legends airtight.

Each of them was disguised. Cheek pads on Zeb to make his face look fleshier. A wig that had a balding patch on it. The twins and Chloe changed their hair color. Blonde, brunette and black. Different eye colors. Nothing could be done about Bwana's skin color but he was heavily inked, as he proceeded through the airport. Tatts on his face and arms. A piercing over his left eyebrow and a ring through his right ear.

No cop looked their way suspiciously, no alarms set off.

They met in the concourse and flagged two cabs at the exit.

'The Ritz Carlton,' Zeb told the driver when he climbed in along with the sisters and Broker. Nothing but the best hotel for them. They were very well-paid engineers. Staying in luxury hotels was expected of them.

They checked into their rooms and slept for four hours. Met at noon and had a leisurely lunch at one of the hotel's restaurants. Any onlooker would have taken them for typical, rich, American tourists. Which was the image they wanted to convey.

That evening they checked into a rental apartment, not far from the Jalan Surabaya flea market where Yunus had fired into the crowd. They stowed their gear away. Put on armor vests beneath their upper clothing, earpieces and one weapon each. They flagged two cabs and arrived at Keling's night club.

It was a week night but the place was happening. The throbbing of beats reached them on the street as they paid off their rides. A steady stream of cars, motorcycle taxis and the odd tuk tuk lining up to drop off patrons. English and Bahasa in the air. Several Western visitors in the crowd. Smartly dressed professionals rubbed shoulders with a more casually turned-out younger set.

'We don't fit,' Broker sighed, as he surveyed the crowd, hands on hips.

'Speak for yourself,' Beth snarked and led the way to the entrance. She paid the fee for all of them and then they were inside.

A short hallway, a cloakroom where bags or coats could be deposited. Thick doors which opened into the main room.

Loud music, strobe lights and bobbing heads and dancing bodies. At the far end, the dimly-lit bar, at which was a crowd as the servers worked feverishly to make drinks.

They split up. Zeb shouldered his way to the bar and ordered a drink. He was jostled and shoved as the churn at the counter ebbed and flowed. A woman bumped against him, felt his Glock against her shoulder and looked at him in surprise.

'A metal brace,' he reassured her. 'Recovering from an injury.'

'You're American?' she flashed a smile.

'Yeah,' he let his accent thicken. 'Here with some of my friends. First time to Indonesia.'

'It's a great country. I live here. Work in a law firm. This is where I come to destress,' and with that she was gone. Ships in the night.

He sipped his drink and checked out the crowd. Beth's flashing hair caught his eye as she taught a move to Bwana. Meg, in deep conversation with Roger. Bear and Chloe, slow-dancing.

This could have been our life, he thought, remembering the times with his family. They had loved traveling. Visiting distant places. Understanding people and culture and languages. He swirled his drink in his glass, watching it catch the light. *I'm thinking a lot about them.* The memories came more easily. There was less pain, less emptiness. *All these years, I hadn't let myself heal. Maybe, that's happening now.*

He straightened when Meghan caught his eye. It was mission time. The past went back to where it came from as he emptied his drink and asked for directions to the rest room.

No private section on that side, he discovered. He wandered back to the dance floor, discreetly looking out for cameras. There they were, high on the wall. *Where's the control room?*

He went to the left of the bar where the dining section was. Rattle of cutlery and conversation. Past the tables, a turn as the music faded, and now he was at the rear of the establishment. A hallway that he recognized from the layout Beth had printed. A door, signed *Authorized Personnel.* He tried it. A man looked up from a screen.

'Sorry,' Zeb apologized. 'Toilet?'

The man came out and pointed the way.

That's the office. Security room's there too.

He made a show of returning to the bar and turned back as soon as the man disappeared.

More doors down the hallway. He tried several of them. All opened into well-appointed rooms. Thick carpet. Couches to the side. Center table and chairs.

Jackpot. One of these rooms is where Keling meets. He came out and explored the rest of the hallway. There wasn't more to it. A rear entrance, probably for the preman boss as well as for VIPs.

A security guard turned the corner and looked at him, astonished.

'What are you doing here?' he asked in Bahasa.

Zeb and his crew spoke the language, but he resorted to English. 'I'm looking to hire one of these rooms for a private party. The man at the bar asked me to check them out. He said they were empty.'

'You saw them?'

'Yeah.'

'I'll escort you back, sir. This section is only for special guests. Please speak to the bartender if you need more information.'

They left the establishment two hours later.

'We can hack into the security system,' Beth announced when they were back in the apartment. 'It's one we have come across before.'

'And I found the rooms,' Zeb replied and broke it down for them.

'They'll check you out,' Beth said thoughtfully. 'Their cameras will have spotted you.'

'Yeah, but I've got my cover. I'm hosting a private party and am looking for a venue. I spent a lot at the bar.'

'That should work, but they'll be alert.'

'We wear our disguises when we are outdoors.'

The next day they weaponed up.

Chapter 58

'That isn't him,' Lot Keling said. 'That does not look like Carter.' He handed back the security camera photographs that his assistant provided and yawned lustily. A young girl massaged his shoulder, another held a glass of wine to his lips.

He drank, smacked his lips and snapped his fingers. A flunky handed him his phone. He dialed a number from memory and several thousand miles away, Leslie picked it up.

'He's not arrived yet,' he told the Asia man.

'Stay alert. Be watchful.'

'Iya.' Yes.

Zeb's weapons contact was a former commander in Kopassus, the Indonesian Army's Special Forces group. Victor Suharto was short, clean-shaven but for a mustache and a buzz cut.

He didn't speak much. He shook their hands silently, sized them up and led them to a truck. He drove out of the city's center, to the bay in North Jakarta. To a warehouse where the container ships loaded and unloaded. He rolled up its shutters and turned on the lights. Crates wrapped in polythene. He forklifted several of them and brought them to where they were. Opened them with a crowbar.

Glocks, mags and ammo in one. Sigs and Berettas in another. HK416s in yet another. Grenade launchers, teargas, the warehouse had every weapon that they would need.

'Who are you, dude?' Bwana asked, astonished as he fingered an HK. It was in good condition, it's serial number filed off, as was the case with every gun.

'Zeb's friend,' Victor's lips parted briefly. He didn't elaborate even when Meghan pinned him down with a long stare.

'So, who's he?' the older sister asked, when they were back in the apartment, their bags bulging with weapons.

'Like he said, a friend,' Zeb replied and winced when she punched him on the shoulder. 'We worked a few missions. He thinks I saved his life and owes me a debt he can never repay.'

'You've quite a few such friends.'

'Victor's special. He outfits our teams, Delta, SEALS, other US black ops outfits. British SAS as well. He's the go-to man for any operation in this country.'

'Any sighting? Leslie asked Keling the next day.

'No. I doubt Carter will come here.'

'The engineers are safe?'

'I assume so. You know I don't have them.'

'Surely, you and the other person talk.'

'Not of this.'

'Keep me posted about anything unusual.'

'Iya.'

Chapter 59

———— ∞ ————

Thursday. Hot and muggy in Jakarta.

'You're sure we're going after the right target?' Zeb asked the sisters.

'Nope,' Beth said and then chortled at his expression. 'We can't be sure, but chances are high, Keling is our man. We've been digging deeper into him and he's the cybercrime man in this region. He too is into fake news distribution. In fact, a journalist even accused him of that. She was murdered at her house. That investigation's still ongoing.'

'Don't forget,' Meghan reminded him, 'there's a direct link between Sebastian and Keling. Those images, those messages on that board.'

'He's not as big as Tverskoy, is he?' Broker asked, doubtfully.

'No. But he's got to have a backer like Tverskoy had.'

'Any luck with that mystery man?' Zeb asked her.

She grimaced. 'Nothing in our databases. None of our contacts have come back.'

That man's identity could be key. Zeb started cleaning his Glock, lost in thought. *That last Indonesian killing...we can sense the fear and anger, here, on the streets. There have been no more killings anywhere else*...he shifted uneasily in his chair. *Why do I think the worst is yet to come?*

A setback at the nightclub.

They had arrived well in time. Zeb, Broker, Roger and Bwana, inside. Bear and Chloe in a dark, anonymous SUV, the getaway vehicle. Meghan and Beth looking smart in their police uniforms, riding in a white and blue Toyota SUV. 'It's genuine,' the older sister told him smugly. 'Real plates, real everything.'

'How did you swing that?'

'We've got our ways.'

Zeb and his team waited inside the bar wearing bulky jackets to hide their Glocks and the armor they wore. Radio contact with those outside.

Keling arrived at eleven pm. A ring of bodyguards around him as he moved swiftly through the crowd, down the hallway and into the second room that Zeb had seen.

'He's here,' he told the others.

'We saw,' Beth, chuckled. 'His men asked us to move along. We said no. No one tells the cops to move.'

'We're inside the security network,' Meghan, crisp, leaving the jocularity to her sister. 'Phone jamming will begin once you give the word. CCTV cameras will shut down at the same time. Got a drone in the air, too, checking out nearby traffic. Everything's in place.'

An hour later, Zeb drifted to the hallway, past the diners. Reached the first two bodyguards who looked up as he approached.

'Private party,' one of them told him, raising a hand to bar his progress.

With a sinking feeling, Zeb saw that it *was* a party.

A big crowd outside the room Keling had disappeared into. Balloons in the air. *Someone's birthday? His?*

No. The twins were thorough. They had checked that out. Keling had passed his forty-second birthday a few months ago.

'Whose birthday?'

'It's a private party, sir,' the sentry said firmly. 'Please go back to the bar.'

'How long will it carry on.'

'A few hours at least. Now, please leave.'

Zeb left and joined Broker.

'We can't take him out here,' he briefed his team and broke it down quickly.

'It must be one of his girlfriend's,' Beth replied after a while.

'He's got more than one?' Bear asked.

'Yeah. Two.'

'Back on topic,' Meghan interrupted them. 'Zeb, the next time we see him here will be in a week's time. We can shadow him, see if we can take him out some other place –'

'No,' Zeb replied. 'We'll do it tonight.'

Chapter 60

—◦◦◦—

Improvisation.

No mission went to plan. Every operation had to accommodate the unexpected.

'He and his guards,' Zeb explained, 'will be on a high, after the event. They'll be relaxed.'

'Yeah, so?' Meghan skeptical.

'We take him out on the street. Outside, where you're parked, is a straight stretch of road. Not very well lit. Those guards said this gig will go on for a few hours. That means there will be less traffic. That's our opportunity.'

'We don't know how many vehicles his crew will have.'

'Two at the least. One in which he rides, another for his guards.'

'How'll this go down?'

Zeb explained.

At two am, the birthday party broke up. Revelers started leaving in twos and threes. The night club had shut down an hour earlier and the celebrating crowd didn't take long to disperse.

Keling was the last to emerge from the establishment. He

had an arm around each of his girlfriends. Two bodyguards in front of him, four behind. More heavies spread out.

The Garuda's boss climbed into a dark-window Range Rover. Rear seat, his women giggling, petting and cuddling him. Two bodyguards climbed in the front and the vehicle set off.

Another SUV fell behind with four men. A third vehicle wheeled out from the street with three heavies and became the escort vehicle, leading the convoy.

A mile passed. The street became dark.

And then the convoy braked hard when a police SUV skidded in front and blocked their way.

'Who is it?' Keling roared from his seat. 'Who dares stop me?'

'It's the police, sir,' his driver replied.

'Find out what they want. Probably money,' he grumbled, 'they always want more.'

The driver got out and jumped back with a shout as an SUV crashed into the lead vehicle.

Another loud smash from behind, a van T-boned into the third ride.

Zeb, Bwana and Roger raced out of the first SUV. Pumped shots randomly into the escort. More firing from behind as Broker and Bear subdued the third vehicle.

The two bodyguards were no slouches. The driver got his gun out and fired a round at Bwana that missed him by inches and then he was slammed back against the vehicle as Zeb pounced on him and crashed his head against the metal frame.

The second protector fired three rounds. One hit Roger in his armor, the second went wild in the night sky and the third ripped past Zeb's forearm. He didn't get a fourth shot. He collapsed when Meghan planted a round in his forehead.

Bwana pulled open the rear door and manhandled Keling out. His girlfriends screamed and clawed at him ineffectively. The Garuda man tried to resist. He swore and cursed, punched and kicked, but a left hook left him limp and reeling.

Bwana dragged him to the van at the back. The remaining operatives hustled inside and the vehicle set off with Chloe at the wheel.

Seven minutes, from start to finish, with surprise and shock as the main weapons and only a few scratches as injuries.

'Keling,' Zeb lifted the preman's head by his hair. 'Where's the List team?'

Chapter 61

———∞∞∞———

Keling didn't respond immediately. He swayed on the bench seat which ran along the side of the vehicle and regarded them drunkenly as the van sped into the night.

Zeb, Bwana and Broker facing him, bracing themselves against the roof. Roger, arms crossed, on the opposite bench seat. Meghan and Beth, check-ing out the preman's phone. Bear at the front, with Chloe.

'What list?' the Garuda man replied, voice slurred, still dazed from Bwana's blow.

Zeb uncapped a water bottle and flung it over the man's face. 'The team that runs software programs. That's responsi-ble for all these killings. Where is it?'

The Indonesian eyed them, swallowed. 'I don't know anything of that.'

He screamed the next moment when Zeb kicked him in the groin. He fell off his seat and lay on the floor, moaning.

'Stop,' he groaned when Bwana picked him up and dumped him on the seat. He heaved and dry-retched, wiped his mouth and panted, sucking large breaths through his mouth. 'Do you… know… who I am?' he gasped.

'Lot Keling, head of the Garuda. A criminal,' Zeb replied, contemptuously.

'People fear me,' he wheezed. 'They jump to do what I say. Even now, my killers will be hunting for me. They will turn Jakarta upside down. Release me immediately and I will let you live. You don't know who you're messing with –'

His head rocked; an agonized yell escaped him when Broker slapped his face. 'Kill us later. Answer our questions now.'

Light filled the back of the van. Another vehicle.

'A truck,' Bwana peered through the dark window. 'Some distance away. No threat to us.'

He looked back when no one replied. All eyes were on Zeb who had removed his Benchmade and was balancing it on his fingers.

'I don't have time or patience,' he told Keling softly. 'You can do this the easy way or the hard. I will ask again. Where are those software people? Who is behind you?'

Keling seemed to gather himself. He spat blood. Arrogance returned to him. His eyes turned scornful.

'You're American? We were told you might come,' he said.

Who's we? Who told him? Zeb looked at his friends who shrugged and then back at the preman.

'Who am I?' he asked.

'Carter. You look different from your photograph, that's why I didn't recognize you in my bar. When you were enquiring about the party room.'

'He's right,' Meghan called out. She turned the phone towards them. Zeb's picture filled the screen. 'Sent from a burner phone.'

'Who sent that?' Zeb asked.

'Why should I answer?' Keling replied defiantly. 'You're going to be dead soon.'

That truck behind us. Is it his? A trap?

'Beth,' he kept looking at the Indonesian, 'you can trace that vehicle behind us?'

'On to it, if Bwana gives me the plate number.'

'Belongs to a freight company,' she answered after a while. 'No connection to Garuda.'

'Let's kill him,' Roger said in a bored voice. 'He's got nothing to tell us. He's wasting our time.' He reached for his gun and that split second of distraction was when the gangster acted.

He lunged out of his seat, reaching for the Benchmade. He wrapped a palm over Zeb's wrist, was turning the blade around when Zeb retaliated with a throat punch that sent him gasping and flailing back to the floor.

Keling got no respite. Broker picked him up and threw him on the seat, easily, casually, as if he weighed nothing. He joined Zeb who crouched, facing the Indonesian. 'We can do this all night,' he said conversationally. 'At some point, you'll die.'

'You don't have all night,' the gang boss spat. 'If I don't check in with Zhen, he'll know I have been attacked. He'll know you are in Jakarta and he'll move the List team away.'

He clamped his lips tight immediately, aware that he had spoken too much.

'Zhen, huh? Taniwan Zhen?'

The Garuda head sneered. His courage was returning.

'How do you want to die,' Bwana joined his friends, crouching next to them. 'I can make it as slow as you want. A quick death? You passed up your chance, buddy.'

He took the knife from Zeb and tossed it in the air and caught it.

Keling's eyes followed it hypnotically.

'You know what this will do to your testicles? This point will rip through soft flesh-'

'I am a master of torture. You're teaching me?'

'He's a master of torture,' Bwana repeated. 'Let's see how tough he is,' and jammed the knife deep in Keling's right thigh.

The Indonesian screamed. He sobbed. He clawed desperately at the seat and slid to the floor when the operative pulled out the blade. He shivered and hugged himself, whimpering brokenly.

'I'll ask once more,' Bwana whispered. 'Tell us about Zhen. Who sent you that photograph?'

He tapped the knife and Keling yelled again, jerking spasmodically.

'Please!' he cried hoarsely. 'Don't.'

His face was wet with perspiration and sweat when he raised it. His body shivered. His fingers trembled when he grasped at the seat to raise himself.

Bwana picked him up and placed him on the bench and stared at him with cold, unmoving eyes.

No sympathy for Keling. The Indonesian ran a criminal gang, didn't deserve their pity.

'Zhen and me…' the Garuda head gasped. 'It's appearances.'

'What do you mean?' Zeb asked. He didn't move, no inflection to his voice, but the gangster reared back.

'People think Garuda and the Brotherhood, that we rule over the slums. Divide the territory. But really, it's Zhen who controls it. That's how he wanted it.'

'He? Who?'

'I don't know who he is. I have only spoken to him twice. He arranged a deal between...' he broke off with a sob and clutched his leg when the van jolted. 'between Zhen and me. I give up all my slum territory, in return for some of Zhen's business. But no one knows of it. Just three of my people and some on the Brotherhood side.'

'How does he sound?'

'I don't know,' he shrank when Bwana loomed forward. 'I swear. Whenever he calls, his voice sounds strange. Like metal.'

Some kind of voice altering device, Zeb thought.

'Zhen trusts him. He has met him,' Keling rushed, as if anticipating his questions. 'The Brotherhood man met me last year. Said there was a friend who was interested in us making a deal. I didn't believe him. My gang and his fight each other always. Then he offered part of his business. Take it he said. In return, give me your slum territory. He offered a lot of money too.'

'What did he tell you about this man?'

'Nothing, just that he was a new partner. He isn't from Indonesia. The way Zhen talks about him, I guessed that much.'

'Is he Russian?' Zeb asked, recollecting the CCTV clip from Chernihiv.

'I don't know anything about him. I told you, his voice is unrecognizable.'

Words were flowing out of Keling easily, as if he had realized his peril.

'Your cybercrime people, your hackers, what about them? You have them, don't you? You run all kinds of phishing, porn blackmail.'

Keling swallowed, looked away. He flinched when Bwana made a move and held a hand up weakly as if to ward off another attack.

'Iya,' he admitted. 'Zhen took all my people. His gang does more than mine. It attacks banks, hacks governments in Asia. That was part of the deal. I would give up that business to him as well.'

'He spoke to you about these killings?'

'No…' Something flashed on his face.

'What is it?' Zeb asked him impatiently. 'You want us to knife your other leg?'

'I met him once when the killing in that flea market happened. I told him it was bad for our business too. He laughed. He said that was his business. I asked him about it, but he didn't say anything more.'

No thrill raced through Zeb. When he met Meghan's eyes, they were empty. They had some proof that Zhen was responsible for the killings. *He probably runs List Asia.* But it didn't feel like something to celebrate about.

'This mystery man. He's the one who sent you my photograph?'

'Iya. He called me three nights back. Said you might turn up. That I should capture you and if that was not possible, let Zhen know.'

'You have his number?'

'Zhen's? He changes it frequently and texts me his new number.'

'What about that other man?'

'Tidak,' No. 'He calls me. Number is hidden always. Zhen might have a contact for him. I asked Zhen about it, he said if I want to live, I shouldn't ask too many questions. This, to me!'

Keling sounded affronted. 'My gang is second only to his and yet he threatened me. Only then I realized how powerful this other man must be.'

'You're sure he's responsible for these killings?'

'He said that line that time. I didn't dare to ask him again. I don't want to know about it.'

'Where are his software people?'

'In the slums. In the territory I gave up.'

'Here?' Beth pushed between them and showed Keling her screen, the Cakung shanties that Sebastian had been checking out.

'Iya. How do you know about this?'

'This section is yours? Bordering the river on the east, that road to the west?'

'Iya.'

'It's not big.'

'It's the location,' Keling boasted. 'No one can approach it without my people knowing about it. If anyone comes from the river, we'll know. Any stranger entering from the west my people will report about him.'

'Zhen has kept it the same way?'

'Tidak,' the Indonesian shook his head. 'He has cleared out an entire section of that slum. No resident stays there. Here,' he jabbed a finger, near a busy road. 'From this point onwards, until the river, that's Zhen's territory now. No civilian stays there. No one is allowed to go there.'

'Your people are involved in that killing?'

'No. My people, they're now his, are good, but not that good. I think that mysterious man provided him the technical people for this. I don't think even his engineers could do something like this.'

'And they'll be there? In that base?'

'I think so. Zhen spends every evening there. It's the safest place in Jakarta. He has set up a generator, power lines, his men patrol the place.'

'The houses still look flimsy,' Beth mused.

'It's what's inside that has changed.'

'You are telling us a lot,' Roger spoke from behind. 'Why? You're scared of dying?'

'No,' Keling bared his blackened teeth. 'It's you who will die.'

'You're our prisoner. None of your people know where we are. Heck,' Roger grinned. '*I* don't know where we are. Only our drivers know.'

'Zhen will find out.'

'He doesn't know we have you.'

'That's where you are wrong,' Keling hissed. 'I check in with him every day. I should have called him half an hour back. He'll know something's wrong.'

Bwana got to his feet, flexed his shoulders, making the inside of the van feel small.

He took Keling's phone from Meghan and handed it to the gangster.

'Call him.'

Chapter 62

———∞∞∞———

Lot Keling moistened his lips. It dawned on him that he had overplayed his hand.

He twitched when Bwana caressed the bloodied Benchmade.

'You think Zhen is bad. Believe me, we are worse. Make the call.' Bwana spoke normally, which made his threat more frightening.

The Indonesian took the phone with trembling hands. He scrolled through his text messages and opened one. Zeb snatched the device from his hand, read it, nodded and gave the phone back.

'Call,' he said.

'Masbro,' buddy, Keling greeted Zhen when the call connected.

'Speaker,' Zeb mouthed.

The Indonesian fumbled with buttons and Brotherhood man's irritated voice filled the van.

'Iya, Iya, I am fine,' Keling replied to his angry questioning. 'Those crazy Bali Boys, they attacked me just outside the bar. You know we've got an ongoing fight with them.'

Zeb turned to Beth who gave a thumbs up. There *was* a feud between Garuda and the Bali gang.

'No, we killed them all,' Keling said casually, as if he was discussing the weather. 'I've got a few scratches, nothing more. No, Carter didn't turn up. I'm keeping a close watch. Okay, I'll call tomorrow.'

He had barely hung up when Beth snatched the phone from him, scrolled furiously and turned the screen to Zeb. Meghan craned her head over her shoulder. Bwana, Broker and Roger joined Zeb to see what the message was.

There's an Arab buyer for the twenty girls. How much should I ask for them?

The beast didn't roar. It didn't growl. It flooded Zeb instantly with cold fury.

'It came when you were interrogating him,' Beth said softly. 'I traced the sender's phone. It's in a house in East Jakarta, a man suspected of being a Garuda member. In fact, he was arrested once but released almost immediately.'

Twenty girls.

Zeb couldn't look beyond the two words. He knew his hands were trembling, the way they sometimes did when a killing rage took over him. He tried to breathe. He tried to summon his control and it was only when Bwana placed a hand over his shoulder and Meghan clasped his forearm did the beast subside. Not by much, but it brought back a semblance of clarity.

He thrust the phone to Keling, who mouthed the words silently. The Garuda boss blanched when he looked up and saw the expression on Zeb's face.

'It's…just…business,' he stammered.

'Where are they?' Zeb asked in a distant voice.

'I...can't...tell...you. This is my-'

'Where are they?'

The sound of harsh breathing in the van. The slap of tires on road. Wind rushing past the van, outside. The vehicle's shocks creaking, its body shuddering on its wheels as Chloe drove at speed.

'The docks,' the Indonesian replied, unable to meet the implacable eyes facing him.

'Where in the docks.' Monotone *because if I raise my voice, I'll lose control.*

'A container. Two containers. But I've got customers-'

'Where are those containers?'

'I'll lose my-'

'Last chance.'

Keling paused then recited the location.

'Bwana?'

'Yeah.'

'That truck's still behind us?'

'Yeah.'

'No, please-' the gangster pleaded.

Zeb grabbed him by his shirt, dragged him, kicking and resisting, across the face of the van as Bwana opened the rear doors and flung Keling out in the night, twisting his wrist at the last minute so that the gangster fell by the side of the road.

'Should've crushed him under the truck,' Bwana said unsympathetically.

Zeb brought out his phone and sat heavily on the bench seat as the beast dissolved in his body.

'Daritan,' he said, when the BIN Director came online. 'Listen,' he said cutting off his friend's questions. 'Don't ask anything. Don't say anything. You'll find Lot Keling by the-'

'Sungai Kendal Road,' Meghan told him.

'By the Sungai Kendal Road. Yes, he should be alive. Injured, don't ask me how. You'll get a recording,' he nodded when Beth gave him a thumbs up, 'It's a confession by the gangster. See how you can use it. There's something else,' he said, feeling empty, 'two containers in the docks.' He gave their coordinates. 'There are girls in them. Keling was going to traffic them. No, don't ask me how I know.'

He hung up and took the bottle of water that Roger offered. Drank, until his insides cooled and his shakes disappeared and *chi*, the life force inside him that balanced him and made him who he was, reasserted itself.

'Tomorrow,' he wiped his mouth. 'We take down Zhen and List Asia.'

Chapter 63

——∞∞∞——

Slum tourism. It was a thing.

Zeb followed Beth, who in turn was behind her sister, as the operatives, part of a larger group, were led through the Cakung slums by an English-speaking guide.

Many Westerners, European, American and Australian, a few Asians. *They want to see how the poor live.* He shook his head immediately, annoyed with himself. That was a lazy judgment. Sure, there were many better-off tourists who were curious to see how those in the slums lived. But there were also many who were genuinely interested and who tried to help those less privileged.

Beth had come up with the idea. Join a slum tour and get as close a view of Zhen's base as possible. She had found a tour that went near the Cakung gang's territory, made calls in the morning, and had booked them places.

They stuck to their cover. Americans, working in technology, first-time visitors to Indonesia. They used their disguises, and at ten am, the day after taking down Keling, they were traipsing through the Cakung slum.

Small lanes. Corrugated aluminum sheets for roofing,

that almost touched each other, providing partial shelter from rain and sun. Washing hung out to dry on cables that ran from one house to another. Stench from the river that overpowered sensitive noses.

Children playing, very few gawking at them. Women cooking, visible through open doors and windows. A few men helping in the house. An elderly woman sweeping a few tiles in front of her door that made her porch.

Many in the tour group gasped and murmured in surprise at the poverty in display. Not the Agency operatives. We've seen such scenes, in many countries, Zeb thought grimly, as he stepped over a puddle of urine.

'What's there?' Meghan flashed a brilliant smile to the guide as he turned before reaching the river.

There, was more slum. More narrowly-spaced houses, TV antennas jutting from their roofs.

The Indonesian seemed to melt at her attention. 'Redevelopment, ma'am. No one's allowed to go there.'

'I don't see barriers. Look, there are a few men.'

'No, ma'am. We can't go there. Out of bounds,' he replied firmly and led the group away from Zhen's base.

The gangster's paid off everyone. Made sure no one visits his hideout. That dude over there, Zeb surveyed a man sitting on a chair, yawning lustily. *I bet that silhouette under his shirt is a gun.*

He had to admit it was an ingenuous hide. No one would expect a highly sophisticated network to be housed in a slum. *No one will think this place will have some of the best programmers in the world, influencing Asian men to kill.*

He wiped sweat from his face as he took in the gangster's base. There was that road to the west that they had seen on the map. It was the edge of the slum and had a steady stream of foot and vehicular traffic. In the distance he could see the bank of the Cakung River. A crumbling, concrete wall, garbage piled up against it, a narrow path separating it from the slum.

'Keling was right,' Bwana spoke through their earpieces. 'Entering this place undetected is difficult. Getaway is impossible.'

'Yeah,' Zeb replied, distractedly. He had the glimmering of an idea.

Chapter 64

That night they rafted down the Cakung River. Eight of them in one large boat, Bear and Roger powering the craft at either end with long poles. Picnic baskets, beer and wine bottles, plastic trays and cups, to give the appearance they were tourists, exploring the city's waterways.

Beth and Meghan launched the drones as soon as they came within sight of the slums. Zeb trained his NVGs as water slapped softly against the boat's hull.

'What's that thing there?' Broker bent over Meghan's screen as the birds sent their feeds. More heads joined her as they contemplated the short, stubby object in silence which was barely visible from the river.

'It's a pump,' Zeb said finally as he focused his binos on the object. 'A water pump. The river floods often and probably fills the slum. Residents use it to remove the water. It's got long hoses.'

They could see it, now that he had explained. The vessel drifted. The sisters called out positions and landmarks softly.

And then Zhen's stronghold arrived. Another pump, right at the end of the small passage, directly facing them.

'Lots of bodies inside,' Beth said, excitement spiking her voice, as she checked out the thermal images in the video feed. 'That house that faces the river, five shapes, men. Lot of heat signatures. That's the computer room, I bet. Meg?'

'Yeah. I agree. I count four bodies in an adjacent house, three in the one next to it and three more in a third house. Then, there are the sentries outside.' She fell silent as she counted. 'Two in that front passage, where that pump is. Oh, two in the alley parallel to it, next to the house. Do you call them alleys in a slum?'

No one answered her. Water sloshed around a dead tree trunk that floated past. A head on the bank, a man, staring at them. *Probably wondering about foolish tourists. Who else will go out in the middle of the night?*

'How do they get a network there?' Bwana wondered aloud.

'Fiber optic cables,' Meghan said, 'buried underground. Zhen's smart, very smart. There's nothing to show that that house has got a sophisticated tech room inside. There's a TV dish there, but I betcha it's a real one. If these dudes are anything like the ones in Chernihiv, they too are trapped in that house. TV and games are their only outlets.'

They were at the middle point of the block of houses that Zhen occupied. Nothing remarkable from the outside. Shutters closed in the night. Washing hung outside one residence. The walls gleamed in the dim light, some painted white, others, in different colors.

'That bank, rising from the river,' Zeb said conversation-ally. 'It's brick as far as I can make out. Y'all agree?'

A chorus of yeahs.

'Why?' Beth asked and then clicked her tongue in

exasperation when he shook his head without answering.

'That place is a fortress,' Chloe said, subdued. 'It won't be easy to breach. Those small passages, the shooters inside, the innocents in the other houses.... we'll be sitting ducks, Zeb.'

'Besides,' Bear said, 'They *will* be expecting us. There won't be any element of surprise.'

'What would you do if you were Zhen?' Zeb asked his friends.

'Do exactly what he's done!' Meghan looked up from her screen. 'Load up with shooters. We'll have to take every one out, whereas they'll have to get lucky just a few times. This place is nothing like Chernihiv.'

Heads nodded, agreeing with her.

'That computer room,' Zeb pointed at it with his shoulder, 'you're sure that's the one facing the river?'

'One hundred percent,' Beth nodded vigorously. 'The heat print, the bodies, that's proof.'

'Why would he have it there? It could be attacked from the river.'

'Except that Zhen would see it coming a mile away,' Roger replied. 'Look at us! We're in the middle of the river. They've probably got eyes on us. They figure we're a bunch of dumb foreigners.' And to reinforce their cover, he took a long drink from a beer bottle.

'What's on the road at the end?'

'That's where the slum ends,' Meghan said. 'A few parked vehicles. But that's now. There will be more traffic in the day time. That road dead-ends at the river, and on the opposite side, joins Sungai Kendal Road.'

Zeb visualized a map of Cakung in his mind. *That road, that's the same one we were driving on, yesterday. It's a long stretch. They're right. It'll be difficult to take them out inside the residences. But what about that idea I had?*

The slum was receding in the distance as their boat sailed down the river. It was a dark smudge against the night sky.

'You've got a plan, haven't you?' Meghan read his expression.

'Zhen will have a getaway vehicle on that road,' he mused.

'There are several,' Beth peered at her screen. 'At least two SUVs, though I don't see any bodies in them.'

'It's a short sprint from the houses to those vehicles,' Broker, leaning over her shoulder. 'He won't need guards in those rides. Assuming they're his.'

He straightened and steadied himself as the vessel rocked. 'Spit it out. What do you have in mind?'

Zeb grinned at their impatient expressions. 'If we can't go inside that house, we get them to come out.'

'But how?' Meghan snapped.

Chapter 65

———∞∞∞———

'You're a devious man,' Meghan whispered in admiration, the next night.

Three am. Two to three at night was Zeb's favored time for an attack. It was when the human body's rhythm was at the slowest.

He smiled as the two of them crouched low and ran along the river, the rest of the operatives behind them.

A narrow strip of mud separated the water from the brick wall. It was firm in parts, slushy in others, and they had to tread carefully to avoid squelching sounds.

Jaws had dropped when he had explained his plan to them and then Bwana had burst into a chuckle and Bear had grinned.

'It'll work,' the ebony-skinned man chortled. 'Heck, if I was holed up in that house, I would react in pretty much the same way you figure they will.'

The plan required a stealth approach along the muddy stretch. All of them armed with HKs, stun grenades, night scopes, their handguns and a various assortment of weapons, blood packs and compresses.

Zeb looked up every now and then from his run, orienting

himself. That overhanging tree up ahead, that was where Zhen's part of the slum finished. So, the computer house had to be ahead of it. He looked back once and got a finger from Beth who was close behind.

'I don't like muddy boots,' she hissed and shoved him.

They pressed forward. Eight dark shapes, barely visible against the darkness of the brick wall. They stopped when Zeb raised a hand.

Meghan climbed the wall swiftly. Its crumbling structure provided sufficient toeholds and finger grips. She peered cautiously over the top and then dropped down.

'A few more feet,' she ran forward. Repeated her maneuver. 'Bingo,' she muttered when she checked their position. 'We're right opposite that passage. Pump's fifteen feet away.'

The rest of the operatives swung into motion.

Bear, Chloe and Roger went further, and positioned themselves opposite the second alley that paralleled the one Meghan was facing. The computer room was nestled between the two paths.

Bwana, Broker and Beth scaled the wall where Zeb was and found toeholds. Each one of them fastened one end of a belt to the brickwork. Wrapped it around themselves, with Meghan helping, and attached the other end into the wall.

They strained back against the belts. They held.

'Good,' Bwana grunted and at that, Zeb went to the second team and helped them attach similarly to the wall.

The six operatives unloaded their HKs when they were in position, adjusted their night scopes and cautiously pointed the weapons over the wall.

'I can see the sentries,' Broker.

'Me too,' Beth. She reached behind her and removed the

drone from her backpack. Assembled it swiftly. Fastened her screen to the wall in hands free mode. Launched the craft and navigated it until it flew in a holding pattern over Zhen's houses, its feeds coming to her tablet.

'I'm set,' she whispered.

'Ready,' Broker barked.

'We're good,' Chloe echoed.

Zeb was counting on the fact that anyone looking from the slum, in the direction of the river, would see the dark shadow of the wall and the shade of the opposite bank. Any heads poking out wouldn't be obvious. Only a body at full length height would stand out.

He and Meghan climbed over the wall, bent so low it hampered their speed. That was okay. Stealth mattered, not pace.

They reached the pump cautiously, knowing their friends would warn them if any of the sentries turned around in their direction.

That's the second thing I was counting on. That Zhen's men would be focused on an attack from the inside of the slum. Not from the river.

He unrolled one large hose as Meghan knelt to the pump, opened its fuse box, removed a battery pack from a thigh pocket and attached wires.

She and Beth had researched the pump once Zeb had outlined his plan. It was controlled by a switch from inside one of the houses, but its fuses were mounted on the device, which made it easy for them to take control.

Zeb took the free end of the hose and made his way back to the wall. Climbed down and yanked it slowly until it was stretched to its full length and inserted it into the river.

Meghan had unfurled the other hose when he joined her and the two of them wrestled it to the computer house. To a window that they had identified earlier.

Let there not be any CCTV. Let it open easily.

He breathed in relief when the older twin opened the sash easily. No creak. A quick peer inside.

'Curtain,' she whispered. 'Can't see anything.'

That's okay, too.

He helped her insert the hose inside the room, as far as it would go. They froze when his knee knocked against the wall. But no yells sounded, no feet came running.

'You're getting old,' she muttered angrily.

'And clumsy,' Beth, joined.

They lowered the window sash and jammed it firmly against rubber. Released it and held their breath. The hose stayed in position. They secured it further, against the side of the house with gorilla tape and sped back to the wall and dropped to the sidewalk.

'Do it,' Zeb commanded.

Chapter 66

———∞∞∞———

The pump was surprisingly silent when Beth jabbed the remote that activated the battery pack.

It sounded like a car engine. The river hose flexed as water filled it. It tightened and straightened and then it was the second hose's turn as liquid flowed through it.

Will it hold against the house?

It bulged and for a moment looked like it would rip off the binding tape, but then it relaxed as water burst from it and spilled inside the house.

They could hear it splashing on the floor from where they were, twenty feet away.

That's a lot of water, Zeb thought. *It's bound to make noise. It's one of those quick acting pumps. Needed here, because of the floods.*

The first shout was heard a minute later. An indistinct yell. And then the passage door opened. A head poked out and looked in the direction of the pump. The man didn't see them because he turned back and shouted at the sentries.

Both came running, rifles jostling over their shoulders. They bent to the pump, looked at each other astonished, made to shout back when they dropped, as Bwana and Broker shot.

The rounds went unheard over the sound of the motor and for several moments nothing happened.

And then sudden shouts and roars from inside the house.

'It's flooding,' Meghan, a satisfied smile in her voice. 'They'll come rushing out.'

And that's what they did.

Armed men, angry, shouting at each other, a few running towards the pump.

They went down when the operatives opened up and then it dawned on them.

They were under attack.

'Go!' Zeb patted Meghan on her shoulder and she took off, still bending low under the cover of the brick wall. Along the river, past the second passage where Chloe's team was engaged with more shooters in the second passage.

To the street, where it was still silent, motionless.

They checked out the first SUV which was parked facing away from the river. It was empty. The second one was too, but its hood was towards the river. There were more vehicles on the street but they were either wrecks or too far from Zhen's part of the slum.

'Both,' Zeb decided when Meghan looked at him.

They slashed the SUVs' tires with their knives as Beth kept a running commentary in their earpieces.

His plan was working. Zhen's men had fled back inside their houses. But the computer room was still flooding.

'A lot of yelling. A lot of shouting,' the younger sister smirked. 'When will it strike those dumbasses to toss that hose out of the window?'

'They tried,' Broker chuckled, 'I saw rubber twitch and

shot through the window and at the wall.'

The houses were a mixture of mud and concrete. They would stop a round

But the hitters may not know that.

'Something's got to break, Zeb. They're inside for too long. They know we've pinned them down. Zhen, if he's there, will try to make an escape.'

The gangster did.

But not in the way they expected.

Chapter 67

A sustained burst of firing from inside the computer house.

'Not at us,' Broker announced. 'Who're they firing at?'

'Oh My God!' Beth gasped.

'What?' her sister demanded impatiently.

'The heat sigs have turned off in that room. Several bodies on the floor. Five, no six.'

'Zhen or someone's shot the programmers,' Chloe said grimly. 'No other explanation.'

Zeb nodded silently in the dark. *The gangster knows what went down in Chernihiv. He's got orders from that mystery man. Don't let the programmers or the machines fall into our hands.*

Meghan's pale face turned towards him. The same thoughts running through her.

'He'll make a break,' he said.

She nodded.

'Hose's out.' Broker, in a hard, clipped voice. 'And here they come, out of the house.'

Zeb pictured it in his mind as the sound of shooting increased. Gangbangers spilling out, shooting blindly at the river, not knowing where the attackers were. His crew, firing methodically, protected by the wall.

The slum came to life. Lights turned on. Voices rose. Screams and shouts rang.

Movement!

Four men rushed out from between two houses. All armed. Looked to the left, to the right.

'See him?' Zeb asked.

'Yeah,' Meghan breathed.

Zhen was unmistakable. Goatee, bandana even at night. He was surrounded by the three men as they hustled him to the nearest SUV. They didn't spot Zeb and Meghan who were hiding behind the rusted skeleton of a pickup truck.

One shooter swore when he spotted the punctured tires. A short exchange of words. They ran to the second vehicle, saw that it was immobile as well and the four men hustled down the street.

'ZHEN!' Zeb called out, showing himself partially.

He ducked back immediately when a hail of bullets pinged against the truck.

'He'll get away,' Meghan said grimly. She dropped to the ground, settled prone, shooter's position and brought the HK to her eyes. 'I can fire from beneath the chassis. You go after them.'

Zeb raced down the sidewalk, using every cover he could find as Meghan engaged with the gangsters and a firefight broke out.

Zhen's men ducked and weaved moving from side to side, two men facing the river, firing rapidly, raking from side to side, uncaring about who they hit so long as the intruders were kept at bay.

That car, Zeb spotted the vehicle the four of them were heading to. If they make it, they'll escape.

He was on the edge of the road, hampered by their firing. *Looks like Meg doesn't have a clear shot either.*

A break in the shooting as the men paused to change mags. Zeb took his chance. He reared up from behind another vehicle, his Glock rolling thunder. Meghan opened up from down the street. One shooter went down. Zhen screamed and urged his men to run faster. One gunman raced ahead and smashed the car's window.

Zeb snapped a shot at him. Missed.

'That other dude's pinned me down,' Meghan. Calm. 'And I've got a bad angle. You've got to get them.'

Street lights had come on. Every house had turned on its outside lamps. Visibility was good, the night was as good as day.

Not more than ten feet between Zhen and that car. Even as he ducked, ran, dived to the ground as a hail of bullets came his way, the vehicle shuddered as its engine turned.

'GET IN!' the driver yelled at his boss.

Now or never. Zeb decided to fling caution to the wind. A snapped glance down the road. Meghan, standing behind her vehicle, her head partly showing, firing in bursts at the preman boss and his bodyguard.

Zeb burst to a sprint. Cover no longer mattered. Stopping Zhen did. A fast mag change on the run and his Glock returned to shoulder level as he fired. All his rounds went wild. Shooting when running and hitting a target, that only happened in Hollywood.

Zhen had opened the passenger door. He was half inside. The car's tires were spinning. The remaining shooter had his back to the vehicle, defiantly shooting, his AR15 turning on Zeb as he came out in the open.

'We're inside.' Beth. 'Looks like a NASA control room. Screens and dashboards everywhere. And water.'

Zeb ignored her. His feet left the ground as bullets ripped into the air. His left hand outstretched, reaching, clawing for Zhen's door handle.

From the corner of his eyes he saw the shooter jerk, stumble and fall.

Meg, he thought dimly. And then he caught hold of the door just as the car sped off.

He fell to the ground. Was dragged, his arm burning immediately from the savage pull. Zhen leaned out of the door. Mouth open in a soundless scream. Eyes wild. Hand producing a gun. The driver behind him. His head turning robotically as he looked at Zeb and then at the street, back at Zeb.

Zeb kicked out with his feet, groaned as he forced his shoulder to heave himself up, gritted his teeth as he brought his Glock up.

A pothole. The car bumped over it. The jolt snapped his head back, his Glock fell away as he lost his grip. But Zhen lost his weapon too. It fell to the ground, got crushed by the rear wheels.

'SHOOT HIM!' the gangster yelled at his driver.

The car was going at some pace, wobbling as the driver fought for control and also tried to obey his boss's commands. His free hand came up. AR15 at the end of it.

Can't. Let. Him. Shoot. The thought raced through Zeb as he forced another superhuman lunge and caught Zhen by his shirt and pulled him towards himself, using the gangster as shield and then the AR15 was chattering and the preman boss screamed as rounds pinged him and he was falling out and Zeb let go of him and the two men went rolling with momentum and when they stopped, Zeb was on his side, his head bleeding from a cut, but all he saw was Zhen's eyes, blinking rapidly, mouth opening and closing, leaking blood.

'You…' the gangster whispered, as the world stopped its rapid turning and the street settled back to some semblance of calm and when a report sounded, Zeb looked up and saw Meghan had taken out the driver.

'You know me?' he turned to the gangster, cautiously feeling his back. It was soaked, the flesh shredded.

Lung shots, to his heart too, it looks like. It's bad.

'Carter…' a twisted smile. His goatee reddening slowly as blood seeped into it. 'We…should…stop…I…told…him. He…didn't…listen.'

His eyes moved sluggishly to take in Meghan who had come from behind and stood over them.

'Who?' Zeb demanded urgently, resisting the urge to shake the man. 'Give me a name.'

Zhen blinked. Something flickered in his eyes.

'Zhen,' Zeb pleaded, 'you're dying. How does it matter to you? Who's he?'

A crafty look came over the preman boss. He shook his head minutely, groaning with the effort.

'Not…him…' Zeb bent his head down to catch his thin voice. 'Another…man…see…if…you…can…find.'

He shuddered, drew a raspy breath, blood bubbling in his mouth.

'Riyaz…Khalid…Ahmed.

Chapter 68

Zeb looked at the gangster, now dead, for what seemed like long moments. He was aware the other operatives had joined them, were speaking in low voices.

Riyaz Khalid Ahmed. That isn't a Russian name.

'Zeb, we need to leave.' Meghan, her hand on his shoulder. 'The cops will come soon.'

He roused himself and searched Zhen's body. Pocketed his phone and when he got to his feet, Beth held a baggie up with several phones in it. 'From all the gangsters. We couldn't question anyone. That firefight...none of them survived it.'

They hustled back to the river and climbed over the wall. An involuntary smile crossed his face when he noticed the pump was turned off, the hoses neatly rolled and hanging over it. *Bet that's Beth's doing. She likes things neat and tidy.*

A hard run along the river, then up the bridge and a dash to their SUVs. He took the driver's seat in the first one, Meghan to his side, Bear and Chloe in the back, the rest in the second vehicle.

They drove out hard, little traffic obstructing them. He idled at a light, absently listening to Bear and Chloe talking softly, when a phone rang.

Mine's on mute. He looked at the elder sister who shrugged. It wasn't hers.

'It's Zhen's,' Meghan said excitedly and leaned over it when he fished it out. 'Number withheld,' she breathed. 'Wait, don't answer just yet.'

She brought out her device, pressed the record button on it and nodded at him.

Zeb accepted the call and an angry voice flooded the vehicle.

'Zhen! I told you to call me every day. What happened?'

Someone sucked breath sharply. Chloe. Meghan, pale, eyes wide, staring at him.

We all speak that language.

'ZHEN! Are you there?'

Zeb grunted, lowering his voice in an approximation of the preman boss. *Hope that convinces him.* The immediate hang-up told him it hadn't worked.

Minutes ticked. A vehicle honked from behind. Bwana, gesticulating in the mirror.

'What's holding you up?' he asked in their earpieces.

'We got a call on Zhen's phone,' Meghan replied.

'Ahmed?'

'No. Someone Chinese.'

A moment of stunned silence and then clamor broke out as the operatives spoke over each other. Zeb lifted a hand to silence Meghan. He dialed another number.

'Daritan, you must have heard of shooting in the Cakung Slum. Yeah, that's us. Listen, don't interrupt. Your people need to seize that place. Lock it down and make it secure. No publicity. Yes, that's where the software program was. There were five engineers, several guards. All dead. Yes, I'm sure no more killings will happen now. Not in Asia at least. I can't tell you more. I'm still figuring things out.'

He hung up and drove silently. Thinking furiously, stone-faced. He hadn't recognized the Chinese voice nor was Ahmed familiar. Is he Arab? Pakistani? He could be from the West.

He glanced up at the patches of sky visible through high-rises. Cloud cover. A sense of foreboding filled him.

*Until now we assumed this was some Russian play. But these new actors…*for the first time, Zeb felt fear.

His team was subdued when they were back on the Gulfstream. He caught snatches of conversation. Meghan replaying the call to Broker. Her scoffing, *of course, we'll get Werner to run audio search.*

The twins got on their screens as soon as the aircraft took off. They plugged in the List Asia hard drives and got to work.

Zeb watched them for a while. Headphones over their ears, heads bent, talking softly to each other. The rest of his friends, serious-looking. Bwana raised an eyebrow when he caught his eye. Nothing, Zeb mouthed, settled back and closed his eyes.

Nevada and Colorado, he decided. *That's where we need to go.*

Leslie hung up immediately on hearing the strange voice on Zhen's phone. He knew immediately what had happened. Carter. He attacked the Indonesia base. He reached for his phone again, his fingers trembling faintly and made another call to his contact, a high-ranking minister in Jakarta.

Five minutes later, he hung up and wiped perspiration

from his forehead. It was as bad as he had feared. Details were still sketchy, but what was known was that there had been a firefight between Zhen's people and unknown attackers. No preman had survived. The Cakung Brotherhood leader himself had been found dead. The BIN had stepped in immediately and had cordoned off the area. No information was forthcoming from them.

Leslie had more resources and contacts in Indonesia. It was not for nothing that he had risen to his position.

After half an hour of more calls, he had more information.

Carter and his team had flooded the computer room. A simple, devastating strategy that had sent Zhen's people in a panic. The gang boss, realizing that there was little hope of escape, had killed the programmers. This was the contingency plan that Leslie had insisted on. Eye witnesses had seen a man and a woman chase the preman down the Cakung street and approach him as he lay dying.

Did Zhen say anything? Leslie pondered over it as a clock ticked in his office and minions worked outside.

He had a special relationship with the Brotherhood boss. They were friends. A business alliance had brought them together when the spymaster was still an unknown quantity. He had helped set up Zhen in business, back in the day when he himself had been raw and junior. He funded the Indonesian which enabled the preman boss to start his drugs and prostitution business. In return, the gangster fed him vital intelligence not just in the country but in the South-East Asian region, wherever the Cakung Brotherhood had a presence.

As the gang grew and diversified, Leslie had encouraged Zhen to get into the cybercrime space. A simple term to encompass a wide range of nefarious activity. He got the

Brotherhood man to recruit good engineers. Election interference, that was where the return was. Get the right politicians elected, those who favored Leslie's cause. Spread misinformation, create chaos, that was a byproduct.

And then, when he had hooked up with Williams and Smith, Zhen's cyber operations had notched up several gears. The Europe man had provided Russian programmers, great engineers who were much better than Zhen's. And then, the Cakung slum operation had focused solely on List Asia.

I'll miss him, Leslie thought. He went to the discreet bar in his office and poured himself a drink. Back in the day, when both, he and the Indonesian had been upcoming, they had shared many a dream. The gangster wanted to become the most feared man in the region. The spymaster wanted to reach the highest level in his country. They had drunk in small bars and had chased women together. Heck, he had even joined Zhen's gang on a few raids, attacking rival gangs.

I got my wish. He? He got killed in the slum. By Carter.

Leslie did not believe in revenge and anger. Those were distracting emotions. They drained people of purpose. But now, in the privacy of his office, he allowed himself that luxury. Thinking of ways to kill Carter.

Chapter 69

———∞∞∞———

Leslie, Williams and Smith met in Tokyo the next day. They took more precautions this time. They flew under different names, to different cities, first. New Delhi, Mauritius, Singapore. They changed disguises at each intermediate stop and then took flights to their next destinations.

They met in a sushi bar in Minato, a crowded establishment packed with tourists and locals. The Asia man found them a corner table and hunched over their bowls; they discussed the latest developments.

There was no danger of their being overheard. Everyone was shouting, elbows and shoulders constantly jostled and their low voices were drowned in the ambient noise.

Williams and Smith listened to Leslie's briefing with tightening lips and narrowing eyes.

'You don't know whether Zhen told Carter anything?' The America man asked.

'Do we even know if it's Carter? Your man had many enemies,' the Europe man interjected.

'It's Carter,' Leslie said heavily. 'No one has any clear description, but who else could it be? So soon, on the back of

Chernihiv? No, let's not fool ourselves. The American some-how got scent of that location and attacked. And no, I don't know if Zhen confessed.'

'He knew a lot.' Smith said accusingly. 'We told you not to tell him that much.'

'He was a friend. He wasn't like Tverskoy, just a tool to be used.'

'If Carter knows, it's the end. We should stop Hyde.'

Williams had come up with the program name. He had an ear for languages and his sense of irony had latched onto it. Smith and Leslie had gone along with him. It was just a name to them. Nothing more.

'We invested so much time, money and resources in this,' Leslie hissed savagely. 'We got our leaders on board. Our defense ministers are talking of numbers. How many troops and equipment each country will commit. Our share buying is proceeding smoothly. This. Is. Not. The. Time. To. Stop.'

'The American knows about List Europe and Asia and he probably knows about Content too.' Smith wasn't backing down.

'Even if he knows everything, there's nothing to connect us to the programs. Just the words of Zhen?' Leslie scoffed. 'What's he going to do with that? Go to our embassies? Get President Morgan to call our leaders? What do you think he'll hear from us?'

'We'll deny. We won't laugh at him,' Williams said, 'but we'll be offended at the accusation. Very offended.'

'Precisely!' The Asia man slammed a palm on the table. 'They don't have any proof other than the actual programs and those have nothing on us.'

Smith chewed on his food silently as he considered

Leslie's words. Of the three, he had the most to lose. He had played around with budgets and slush funds and siphoned out substantial amounts to fund the program.

'Besides, can you imagine the reception we'll get if we pull the plug now?'

The America man stopped eating. He looked up, his face whitening.

'Yes,' Leslie read his mind. 'Our leaders, our defense ministers, won't be very happy, will they? That we promised so much and failed at the last moment. Do you think they'll let us live? Our families?'

'I can guess what will happen to me,' Williams shifted uncomfortably on the hard seats. 'I'll disappear, my family too, and we'll never be seen or heard again. I'll be tortured and disposed of.'

Smith shuddered in response. 'I'll receive the same fate,' he whispered.

'And me too,' Leslie agreed, 'and that's why we can't stop. We have to see this to the end. In any case, we haven't long to go. On the security force side, things are progressing rapidly. Our leaders are exchanging a draft of the speech they'll make.'

'I don't think Williams and I should go to the US.'

'That's all the more reason that you should. Your presence will reassure those teams. And we need to go all out now. We've got to activate List Europe and Asia and we need to see more killings in America. Now's not the time to get cold feet.'

Smith thought about it for a long while as the traffic in the restaurant ebbed and flowed and tables were cleared around them and new patrons arrived and were served.

'I'll go.'

'Great,' Leslie beamed. 'You, too?' he looked at Williams.

'I was planning to go. I won't be able to return until this is over.'

'To success,' The Asia man raised his glass.

'To success,' they echoed.

'And to more killing,' Smith added savagely.

Chapter 70

———— ∞∞∞ ————

New York. Hot and humid. Snarling traffic and attitude. Home.

'Rest,' Zeb told his friends when they had landed the previous night. 'Regroup tomorrow.'

They met silently in the office the next day, subdued, because, as they had slept, Mark Lefebre, a gym manager in Columbus, Ohio, had fired an AR15 at a mosque, killing four people. In retaliation, a group of gunmen had fired on a church in the early hours of the morning. Total death toll, fifteen. Seven critically injured.

'List America or whatever it's called,' Bwana growled and muted the TV. 'That's the program's doing.'

'Yes,' Zeb said as his friends gathered around. 'Hit us,' he told the twins. 'What have you got?'

He sized them up quickly. *We've been on the move ever since Clare green-lighted the mission.* Moscow. Ukraine. Indonesia. But none of the operatives looked the worse for the wear. They were grim, determined. Beth and Meg…they too. The twins were the only ones who didn't have any military background. *They're as good as any of us, now,* he thought proudly.

'That Indonesian center,' Beth began, 'it was similar to the Chernihiv one in many ways. Basic List program was the same. Tweaks to account for regional differences. Set-up virtually identical. Zhen's men –'

'The engineers were Russian,' Meghan interrupted. 'No identities on them, but that's what we suspect, going by their features.'

'Tverskoy provided them?' Bear glanced at Zeb who shrugged and replied, 'No way of knowing. They communicated the same way?'

'Yeah. The same realtor site and dating site. One difference. This team knew that List America's in Colorado and Content's in Nevada.'

'Knew, how?' Broker leaned forward, alert.

'No idea,' Beth's hair bounced as she shook her head. 'In case you've forgotten,' she said sarcastically, 'we've not had much time. Werner's hooked up into the program now and digging, but it'll still take time.'

'Names?' Chloe who had been balancing in her chair on two legs, straightened. 'You find any men they were targeting?'

'Oh, yeah. That was the first thing we looked for.' Several photographs came up on the wall. 'We sent their details to Daritan while we were in the Gulfstream.'

'He's arrested a few, watching others,' Zeb commented. 'I got a message from him. Any link to the men who attacked us in New York?'

'Nada,' Beth replied. 'Zhen's center wasn't a kill center. It was a software program hub.'

'You were able to narrow it down? Nevada and Colorado?'

More pictures on the wall as Meghan frowned in frustration. 'No. The same images that were in Chernihiv. We guess the Colorado team is in a ranch,' she pointed to several pictures and with another click of the remote, more images, this time of solar panel banks. 'This is different from Chernihiv.'

She grinned at the surge of interest in her friends. 'Yeah, solar farms. In Nevada. There are many. Zhen's team had several images of these.'

'That's where the Content team is?' Broker mused.

'We think so.'

'Makes sense,' Zeb thought out aloud. 'Those places are remote. They have enough equipment that high-end servers wouldn't be noticed.'

'The problem is we don't know where those locations are, exactly.' Beth burst their bubble. 'And we don't know who that man in Chernihiv is. Werner could find no voice match to that recording. No match to that video of his. We've drawn a blank on Riyaz Khalid Ahmed too. That name is common enough and Werner got several hits but all of them are civilians with no possible connection to Hyde.'

'Let's talk to Grigor and then we're going to DC,' Zeb strode to a desk phone.

'DC? Why?'

'It's time to loop in Clare and Klouse. About China, Russia and this mysterious man.'

'But we don't know anything more,' Meghan protested. 'What'll we go to them with?'

'With what we have. But first, let's call Grigor,' Zeb said grimly and summoned them to the phone.

Chapter 71

'Play that voice again,' Andropov said when Meghan had finished briefing him. The Russian didn't ask why Zeb had kept the findings from him. He wasn't put out that he hadn't been looped into the Jakarta mission. He knew how his friend worked and would have acted similarly if he was running the operation.

Beth played the Chernihiv recording again. Andropov scrunched his face on the video call and shook his head in frustration. 'I think it's a Russian voice. That inflection, a very faint accent, but I can't be sure. And I don't recognize him. But-' he wagged a finger when he saw the twins' disappointment. 'I've got a database. One that even you don't know of. Come, now,' he laughed when he saw their expressions. 'I know what you do in New York. Werner... isn't that what you call your program? I know it's got front door as well as back door access all over the world.'

'Then you know we're already hooked to your system,' Beth said spiritedly.

'Not this one. It's not connected to any network.'

'Give us access.'

'And let you know my secrets?' he demanded and then broke into a smile. 'When are you joining me?'

It was an old, tired joke but never failed to bring a smile to the sisters' faces. The Russian spymaster had been so impressed on meeting them the first time, many years back, that he had made a job offer to both of them. 'Anything you want. Your own dacha, one each, private car, private jet. Leave Zeb and come work with me.'

When he had learned that Avichai Levin, Mossad's director, had made a similar offer, he had upped the ante. 'Your own office in the Kremlin,' he had offered.

Beth and Meghan had declined but that didn't stop Andropov from repeating his offer every now and then.

'Grigor,' Zeb said softly. 'We don't have time.'

'Yes,' his friend turned serious immediately. 'I'll get them connected to my system. Let me know what you find.'

Werner was done being bored. This mission hadn't challenged him much. Sure, he had to run a few searches, a few voice print matches, facial recognitions, but he could do those in his sleep.

Not that he slept. The world's greatest AI engine – and he was, there was no doubt about that – could perform those tasks without even challenging his core processors.

But that had changed when his bosses - Beth and Meghan, the best bosses in the world – gave him a new search. Take that Chernihiv video print and search Andropov's database.

Now, that was interesting. It wasn't difficult, mind you, but it was eyebrow-raising. It was his first time into that particular repository and, oh wow, so that Egyptian terrorist was killed by that Russian agent! Werner and the twins had always suspected but this was proof. And those Pakistani terrorists… killed by Mossad. Again there had been rumors, but Andropov had gotten more evidence.

But, Werner was getting distracted. That wouldn't do. He knew the pressure the twins were under. He roamed the recesses of the database. This file, that folder, this clip, what about that video…nope. Nothing there.

He sat back and pondered. How about running an aging analysis? That dude in that Chernihiv video, it was possible a younger version of him was floating in Andropov's files. His voice could be younger.

Nope, that didn't work.

Werner wasn't giving up however. He knew what was at stake, and for Beth and Meg he would do anything. They made him purr, not literally of course, but you get the picture. The sisters talked to him, patted him, treated him as their equal, a human they could relate to? Was there any other boss who did that? Nope, and no thanks, Werner wasn't interested in finding out.

So, back to the program. That aging thing sparked another thought. How about comparing the man's gestures, body movement, again allowing for age?

Another scan of all the files…and just as Werner was giving up, a ping. What was that? He feverishly opened that folder. A video recording. More than six years old. Two men in a Moscow bar, captured by a long-range surveillance camera. Why were they recorded? No, nothing in the database about that, which didn't surprise Werner. Those Russians, they were paranoid. They often recorded people for no reason.

Okay, which of the men had triggered the alert? That one, in the dark suit, his back to the bar, his face fully presented to the camera. He was laughing, glass in his hand. Dark hair, dark eyes. Clean-shaven. Nothing about him that would stand out. A businessman, a bratva boss, or a spy. He could be any of those.

Now, to get his identity.

Werner searched Andropov's database. Nope, nothing there. He searched other agency files. No luck. Hmmm. How about news sites?

And there it was. Werner hit jackpot.

The man was mentioned, almost in passing, in the coverage of a defense conference in Moscow. Just that one reference. His name didn't appear anywhere else. In no covert agency database, no other news site. It was as if the man had disappeared after that one public outing.

Was that why he had been spied on? A man who dropped out of sight? Andropov would know.

Job done, Werner leaned back, hoisted his polished shoes on the desk, lit a cigar and blew out a perfect ring of smoke.

Figuratively, of course. Everyone knew AI programs didn't smoke.

Chapter 72

———∞∞∞———

Six hours later, DC. The Washington Memorial standing proud and tall as they drove from Ronald Reagan Washington National Airport. The flag on the White House just visible over the thicket at the back.

They turned into the gates at the back of the most famous residence in the world. Went through a rigorous security check. 'You didn't tell us we were coming here,' Meghan darted a glance at Zeb as a Secret Service man escorted them to the West Wing and then to the first floor. 'We would've dressed up.'

He glanced at her and Beth. 'There's nothing wrong with how you look,' he said and as if on cue, an aide turned back and looked admiringly at the sisters. 'You're keeping something from us,' he stated. He had seen them stiffen, during the flight, and huddle together. Soft whispers, barely-restrained excitement. His questioning look had been ignored and by the time their Gulfstream landed, they had composed themselves.

'You'll know soon enough,' she whispered as they entered a well-appointed office on the first floor.

Daniel Klouse rose from behind his desk, clapped Zeb on

the shoulders, hugged the sisters and shook hands with the rest of the operatives. He had met them several times, no introduction was necessary.

Clare, in a grey suit, offered them a brief smile. If she had been up all night, briefing the President, talking to other agencies, it didn't show. She was cool as ever, her warmth breaking through her façade when she greeted the twins and Chloe.

'I bet you've seen this,' Klouse pointed to the TV screen which was playing the scenes of the killing in Columbus.

'Yes, sir,' Zeb poured himself coffee from the jug on a side table.

The National Security Advisor turned off the screen and leaned against his desk. 'Tell us some good news.'

'List Asia has been stopped, sir. You might be aware of that.'

'Yes. What went down, there?'

Zeb broke it down for them, pausing for a moment when Klouse chuckled at his mention of water hoses. His grim expression returned as he heard about the shootout in the Cakung slum and –

'Oh, for Chrissakes,' Beth interrupted impatiently. 'Zeb, you're taking too long. Sir, Zhen gave us a name.'

Klouse straightened. Clare looked at Zeb. This was news to her as well.

'We didn't tell you, ma'am,' Beth told her apologetically. 'We wanted to crosscheck that name.'

'Spit it out, Beth.'

'Riyaz Khalid Ahmed.'

The NSA reared back as if he had been struck. Zeb knew what was going on through his mind. A Muslim sounding name? ISIS could be behind this?

'Riyaz Khalid Ahmed,' Klouse repeated slowly, his face thinned out, lips tight, eyes savage. 'Is he a terrorist? Who is he?'

'We don't know, sir,' Beth admitted. 'We ran searches... but all those with such a name...and there are thousands of them in the world. None of them raised any flags. Civilians. Office workers –'

'All these killings are by civilians.'

'Yes, sir. And we have sent those names to the intelligence agencies of various countries. Pakistan, Malaysia, the Gulf countries...but the way Zhen spoke. This man isn't a civilian. He's got a bigger role to play.'

And only then, as the moments passed and a clock ticked and distant voices came to them from the corridors of power in the White House, did Zeb notice Clare.

She knows who he is!

His boss hadn't jumped in joy. She hadn't pumped her fist. That wasn't her style. She had gone still, her eyes distant.

'Who is he?' Zeb asked her and all eyes swung towards Clare at his question.

'I might be wrong,' she replied carefully, unsurprised that Zeb had read her expression. 'It was a long time ago.'

'Clare,' the National Security Advisor exploded. 'Who is it?'

'The Riyaz Khalid Ahmed I knew was a junior, very junior minister in the Saudi Arabian Defense Ministry.'

Chapter 73

⊶∞∞⊷

I wasn't expecting that, Zeb thought as the room filled with exclamations and swearing. *A Saudi?*

'Where's he now?'

'How did you meet him?'

'Are you still in touch?'

Questions rained thick and fast on Clare who held a hand up to silence the operatives.

'It was six or seven years ago,' she said. 'I'll have to check my notes. A meeting in Dubai of various defense and intelligence heads from the Middle East and the West. Ahmed wasn't a key person. I met him at the evening reception. All I remember of him is a smiling face and his name.'

'The Saudis are our allies,' Klouse said angrily, his face turning red.

'Daniel,' Clare cautioned him. 'The Ahmed I met was Saudi. But this name that Zhen gave could be anyone.'

'There's more,' Beth butted in before the NSA could reply. 'We got a call on Zhen's phone when we were returning to the airport.'

'Who was it?' Klouse's body was tight, as if he was a

tightly-stretched wire.

'The caller didn't give a name. However, he spoke in Mandarin.'

Klouse hissed. Clare turned pale.

'And that's not all,' Meghan said, turning to Zeb. 'We identified that man in Chernihiv, in that CCTV camera video.'

'What man?' Klouse demanded and nodded when the elder twin explained quickly. 'Who's he?'

'He too was a junior minister. In Russia in their defense department. He's Sidor Yefremov.'

'Ahmed *is* the man Clare met,' Zeb said quietly, in the shocked silence that followed. 'Saudi. It makes sense, now that we know what we know.'

The National Security Advisor's face had turned grey, his skin like parchment.

'Chinese…Saudi…Russian,' he said when he had recovered. 'Zeb, Clare, do you have any idea, any, why these countries have come together? Because this can't have happened without political backing!'

'No, sir –' Zeb began, when the door opened and a voice boomed out.

'Daniel! Here you are. I've been looking for you all over.'

That's the -

Zeb rose and spun so fast that hot coffee spilled on his wrist but he didn't notice it.

President Morgan filled the room, lean, craggy face, surprised look disappearing, eyes taking in all the operatives.

'This's your team, Clare?' he asked. 'I know you, don't I?' he looked at Zeb.

'Yes, sir. We met a couple of times.'

'And Clare never mentioned your name,' he flashed the

grin that had won him millions of votes on the campaign trail. 'Said it was better for me not to know. Y'all are gathered here about the killings?'

'Yes, sir.'

'You got something?' he asked keenly, sensing the air.

'Sir,' Klouse began and gave him a Cliff Notes version of the findings.

The President's jaw clenched. A vein throbbed on his neck when the NSA had finished. 'You saw that speech the Chinese President made? That governments had to change. People had to be listened to.'

'Yes, sir.' Klouse replied.

'I spoke to him, to the Russian President and to the Saudi King. All of them said we had to act to stop these killings. They agreed I should focus on this at the G20 Summit. And now,' he let his anger show for a moment, 'it looks like they're behind this.'

'There's no proof, sir,' Clare cautioned.

'Which is where your agency comes into play,' he told her grimly. 'When there's no evidence. Hundreds of innocents have been killed around the world,' he said savagely, 'stock markets are down, people's savings, their pensions, disappeared just like that. They're planning something big.'

He turned to Zeb, addressing all the operatives. 'Find them. Stop them. Find out what they're planning. And then, find a way to stop their governments, if they're involved.'

And with that, he swept out.

Chapter 74

⸺◦◦◦◦⸺

'You heard him,' Klouse said when the door closed behind the Commander-in-Chief. 'Anything you need, you got it.'

'We need someone who knows Colorado well. And Nevada too,' Meghan replied. She laid out several photographs on the NSA's desk. 'We think the Content and List America teams are based there. We need to hit them. Unfortunately, that's all we've got. Those pictures.'

Klouse picked up his phone in response. 'Charlie,' he barked. 'Get your ass to my office.'

Charlie Ripple, the President's Chief-of-Staff, the man who had run his campaign and had gotten him elected twice, joined them minutes later.

Balding, tie askew, sleeves rolled to his elbows, he gave the impression of an absent-minded professor. Only his eyes gave away his keen intelligence and razor-sharp wit.

'Hi Clare,' he greeted the Agency Director. 'Didn't know you had company, Daniel. Who are these folks?'

'You don't need to know, Charlie,' Klouse said impatiently.

'Oh, some of *those* people,' he parked his butt in a swivel-chair and checked out Zeb and his friends. He nodded to himself as if reaching a conclusion and turned to the NSA. 'Why am I here? I've got a briefing with the President in five.'

'You're from Colorado, aren't you?'

'Best state there is.'

'You explored it, you told me once.'

'Every inch of it. Great country. Know it like the back of my hand. I told the President we should move our capital there, to Colorado. Somehow, he didn't share my enthusiasm….' He trailed off when he sensed the atmosphere in the room. 'How can I help?' he asked softly.

'Sir,' Meghan leaned over his shoulder and flicked through several of the images and presented him three. 'Do you recognize this area?'

Charlie Ripple barely glanced at them. 'That's the Laird Ranch,' he said. 'I camped there when I was a kid. Visited it again when I was home, after college. It's on the Utah border. Really remote. You got to take a chopper ride from Grand Junction Airport. Or an hour's drive from it.'

'You're sure, Charlie?' Klouse leaned forward, his voice taut.

'Yeah. I wasn't joking. I know that country really well. That's the Laird Ranch. No doubt about it. The Laird family owned it for generations and then, when times were tough, the last surviving member sold it to some investment company. They kept the name but turned it into a dude ranch.'

'Look carefully, Charlie. There are no buildings in those photographs.'

'I don't need them,' the Chief-of-Staff stabbed a finger on the nearest image. 'That thicket, I slept near it. That stream over there, I bathed in it. Freshest water I've ever drunk. What's this about?'

Klouse looked at Clare who nodded briefly.

'It's about Columbus,' the NSA said and didn't elaborate.

Charlie Ripple looked at him searchingly and then at Clare and her team. He picked up the photographs and looked at them closely.

'That's the Laird Ranch. I'll bet my life on it,' he said.

'Leave these others with me,' Klouse told Meghan when the Chief-of-Staff had left. 'I'll find a Nevada expert and get that location identified as well. What else do you need?'

His eyebrows nearly disappeared into his hairline when Zeb told him.

Chapter 75

'Robotic dogs?' Bwana asked Zeb. 'What do you need those for?'

Clare's office. The eight of them in couches, chairs, on desks. Beth and Meghan on their screens. They had given Zeb a hard time after the White House meeting. 'If you'd given us a heads-up, we'd have been better dressed,' the younger twin fumed. 'President Morgan saw me like *this!*' She indicated her casual attire and dug an elbow in his ribs.

'I didn't know he would show up,' he had replied.

'But you knew we were going there.'

At which he had surrendered.

The sisters' anger didn't last long. It rarely did.

They had plugged in their screens as soon as they arrived at the Agency Director's office and had waved away any offers of help. 'It's beyond you,' Meghan had told Broker, without looking up.

'I taught them,' he had mumbled under his breath and had sidled over to Zeb who was poring over additional photographs of the ranch that Beth had printed out.

'Dogs?' Bwana reminded Zeb.

'We'll need them.'

'Why?'

'Because we don't have plans to that place. All we know is its location. There's a fence,' Zeb stabbed at one of the photographs. 'A gate. That semi-circular building,' another stab at another photograph. 'More buildings behind it, and that's all we know.'

'They'll be ready for us,' Roger drawled from his couch. 'They'll expect us to attack. Zeb is right. We need the element of surprise. Though, it beats me what he's got in mind with robots.'

Two hours later. Empty boxes of pizza, beer and juice bottles. The remains of their lunch.

Large photographs on a center table. That of Riyaz Khalid Ahmed and Sidor Yefremov. Meghan had found one of them on a news site, the other at a university speech. Both were old images and the sisters had run aging programs to print out likely current-day versions of how the men might look.

Brief bios on the two of them as well. Both had started their careers as aides in their respective defense ministries. Both had risen to the ranks of junior ministers and then had disappeared. No sightings. No mentions on government communication, news reports or social media.

'Have you heard of them?' Clare asked Zeb.

'No,' he shook his head. 'You know what that means.'

She nodded gravely. 'They went dark for a reason. They got into covert ops. No other explanation.'

'They could be dead,' Bear offered and held his hands up in surrender when he got scornful looks. 'Just saying.'

'Say less,' Chloe hissed at him.

'How's that possible?' Beth looked up from her screen. 'We know just about everyone in the intelligence world. How could these two escape our radar?'

'We don't know everyone,' Meghan corrected her. 'There are spies we aren't aware of. Operatives who work in the shadows. These two –'

'They aren't foot soldiers. To organize Hyde, pull it off, they've got to be high up.'

'Correct,' Chloe agreed, 'and good. Very good. And there's a third person out there whose name we don't even know.'

'The Chinese man.' Meghan answered swiftly. 'He's even more secretive. His voice print doesn't exist in any of our databases or those we can access.'

'Could he be the mastermind?' her sister asked.

Zeb didn't reply immediately. There was a name at the edge of his memory. Something had moved in his mind the moment the Russian and Saudi had been identified. A Chinese name. A feared spymaster that the world didn't know of. He knew there was a face attached to that name, but try as hard as he could, his memory refused to serve him both.

He shrugged internally. It would come. 'Who knows?' he answered Meghan. 'See if you can find Yefremov and Ahmed. Where they're located. 'You,' he turned to the remaining operatives. 'Can you come up with an attack plan for Colorado?'

'I thought you were working on that,' Bwana, rose and stretched.

'I've got to make some calls.'

Riyaz Khalid Ahmed, Jack Smith, was in Riyadh. He had returned from Tokyo the previous night and had briefed his boss. He hadn't mentioned that the Indonesian center was no more. Nor had he told him about Chernihiv. His boss didn't need to know everything.

'Yes sayidi, all's going as per plan,' he reassured the prince.

'The Americans don't know anything?'

'No, sayidi,' he said confidently. 'Neither do the British or the French. No one.'

He returned to his office and made plans for Colorado. He would have to use another alias, another fake passport. A new disguise.

He began his preparations.

In Moscow, Sidor Yefremov, Phil Williams, had finished a similar briefing to the Russian Prime Minister. He too hadn't mentioned the setbacks in Indonesia and Ukraine. He was committed to Hyde, but he also valued his life and had no wish to shorten it.

He looked at his calendar, at flight timings and at the upcoming protests in Washington DC. That was four days away. Enough time for him to fly to Nevada, from where he would liaise with Ahmed and Leslie.

He checked the Russian holdings in the target companies and ran through a memo from the defense minister on the proposed security force.

It will happen, he assured himself. *We will have a new world order. Soon.*

Back in DC, Zeb and his team were wrapping up the attack plan. Which was sketchy.

'Because we don't have the ranch's layout,' Bwana fumed when Beth needled him. 'Why don't we have that?'

'Because, wealthy people have a habit of keeping things

private,' she replied archly.

'That didn't stop you at Chernihiv.'

'We had help there. Andropov's.'

'How can we go in, blind?'

'Which is where those dogs come in,' Zeb answered.

'Dogs!' Bwana rolled his eyes. 'What exactly do you have in mind?'

'Let's meet them, first.'

Chapter 76

———◦◦◦◦———

They flew to Denver that night and stayed in Colorado's largest city.

The next day, they drove to an office complex on the outskirts of the city. A gated complex of several flat-roof buildings. White, CCTV cameras mounted in a perimeter, armed security guards.

Science In Motion, the company name was discreetly painted on a wall-mounted panel.

'I haven't heard of them,' Broker looked questioningly at Zeb when they arrived at the gates. A security guard came out of his hut, checked their credentials against a pad, spoke into a mic and raised the barriers.

'DoD's got a stake in them. They are a research company. Develop AI and robotic prototypes.'

'I don't know how I feel about that.'

It was a debate they often had. There was no doubt that artificial intelligence and mechanization would play prime roles in covert intelligence and military warfare.

They won't replace the human element, however. Humint and foot soldiers…to him and his team, they represented balance and values and ethics. *The day humans get replaced is the day I'm out of this game.*

A white-coated, bespectacled man approached them, cutting short his musings.

'Zeb Carter? I'm Dr. Lebowski. I'll take you to the machines.'

He led them inside a building, pointed out various developmental prototypes. A remote-controlled battle-tank. 'Quite similar to drones,' he said. Near-invisible battle dresses, facial recognition helmets, biometric sensing weapons.

'Larry Burt and Zack Pilgrim,' he introduced two men in the corner of a vast hall. Both were dressed in the universal attire of jeans and tees. Sneakers on their feet, beards on their chins. They looked young, in their late twenties or early thirties.

'These two are the operators,' Lebowski said. 'They'll be with you,' and with that he left.

'He didn't ask anything about us,' Beth sidled to Zeb.

'He was warned. The NSA gave instructions.'

That memo didn't seem to have reached the two company men who cast appreciative glances at the twins and Chloe and decided to ask them questions.

'You work here as a researcher?' Meghan asked, close to her breaking point.

'A scientist, actually,' Burt replied and gave what he thought was a winsome grin. 'Zack and I built those machines,' he said proudly.

'Well, Burt, here's the thing. Show us the danged things, how they work and then get out of our way. Unless you and Pilgrim want to wash toilet bowls in Idaho for the rest of your lives.'

Their jaws dropped. They reddened when Bear stifled a guffaw and then they looked sheepish and proceeded to apologize.

Beth stopped them with a raised finger. 'Just lead us to them,' she growled.

The scientists led them down a corridor, past more prototypes and white-coated researchers and then to a large room the size of a basketball court.

In the center were a number of dogs.

Chapter 77

———— ∞∞∞ ————

'They look just like the animals,' Roger's comment, immediately slapped down, blisteringly by Meghan. 'That's because they are *designed* to look like them, Rog.'

Zeb waved them to silence as he studied the machines. The machines were matte black, had canine faces with realistic looking dark, glassy eyes that blinked every now and then. Lips parted to reveal teeth, but no tongue. About three feet tall, lean bodies, bellies flexing as they panted in the night. Walking about, sniffing, heads swiveling to observe them. Exactly as real animals would.

Can they smell?

'Yeah,' Burt saw what he was looking at. 'They have advanced olfactory capabilities.' He pointed to their skin. 'They're made from the same material that goes into the Stealth bombers. Zero footprint on radars.'

'Why? Dogs don't fly!' Chloe asked, puzzled.

'That was a requirement,' Burt squirmed uncomfortably.

'That's how the DoD spends our money,' Bear grumbled, not very sotto-voce. 'By making dogs fly.'

He subsided when Meghan glared at him and motioned for

Burt to continue.

'They can get from zero to sixty in three seconds.' He pressed a remote and one of the machines blurred into speed. It sprinted across the hall; its padded feet almost silent on the concrete floor. 'Composites in their shoes, wear resistant on any surface.'

The robot pivoted smoothly and trotted back to them, its head swinging left and right, its short tail wagging, looking at them, waiting for their approval.

'What's special about them?' Roger drawled. 'Robots are not new and there are many companies that manufacture similar ones.'

In reply, Pilgrim did something with his remote and the machines assembled in a squad and raced towards a life-size dummy that stood in the corner.

Six of them leapt at it while the others stood at bay as if guarding the attackers. In seconds, the dummy was torn to shreds, the only audible sounds were those of fabric ripping.

'Our robots are specifically designed for military use,' he said, clearly enjoying their expressions. 'They have various programs…what you saw was one of many attack ones. They can sniff bombs, explosives, anything that goes boom. Even gasoline fumes. They can jam infra-red signals, have cameras, audio detectors, night-vision…Oh, yeah! They're bullet resistant to NATO calibers, though we haven't completed field testing on that.'

'How high can they jump?' Zeb asked.

Burt demonstrated, making one of the machines leap up to ten feet in the air. It landed as smoothly as a world-class gymnast, without any wobble.

'We need thirty of them.'

'That won't be a problem.

'By tonight.'

'Sure. Dr. Lebowski has to clear that, but if he knows you, I am sure that can be arranged.'

'We need training on their operations.'

The scientist turned uneasy. He looked at Pilgrim for support who cleared his throat. 'That could be a problem. Larry and I are the only ones who operate the dogs. No one else is trained and it's not something that can be completed in a few hours or even a few days. These are expensive babies,' he said nervously.

'Toilet bowls. Idaho,' Beth said ominously.

'It's not something in my control,' a bead of sweat trickled down his face. 'The learning curve is too steep to be covered in a short time.'

A meeting with Lebowski who *hmmmed* and looked thoughtful before answering. 'Larry and Zack are right,' he said. 'We can't risk giving those out to untrained operators.'

'They'll have to come with us, then,' Zeb said firmly.

'Come where?' Pilgrim swallowed.

'Colorado. Tonight. With thirty robots. You and Burt.'

'What's there?'

'Need to know...heard of that?' Bwana asked him.

'You'll return these intact?' Lebowski spoke quickly before his researchers went into full-on panic mode.

'I can't guarantee that,' Zeb said. 'Look on the upside, though. They're sure to get field-tested against heavy caliber weapons.'

'There'll be shooting?' Burt squeaked.

'You can count on it, son,' Bear replied.

'You'll get a call,' Zeb told Lebowski who looked uncertain. 'Green lighting this.'

'From whom?'

'The National Security Advisor.'

'You've got that kind of reach?'

'Yeah. If you wish, I can get President Morgan to-'

'That won't be necessary,' the scientist told him hastily.

'One more thing. I need those thirty machines painted naturally. Like a pack of wild dogs. By this evening.'

Chapter 78

———— ⌘ ————

In Zeb's hotel room, later, in Denver. Bwana and Bear angry at him. Beth and Meghan, thoughtful. Roger, Broker and Chloe, amused.

'You wanted a bunch of dogs that could run and jump,' the ebony-skinned operative demanded. 'You got them. Now care to tell us the plan? Or are we going to some robot Olympics?'

Zeb's lips twitched. His friend, angry, was a sight to behold. Bwana, in a cold fury? Now that was someone to stay clear off.

'You got that ranch's picture?' he asked Beth who produced a photograph.

'See this?' Zeb pointed to the curved building. 'All we know is its length. About three hundred yards. Its depth. About hundred-and-fifty feet. We don't know anything else. Given that this is in the US, you can bet they'll be wary of drones. So, we can't use them to gather any intel. We don't know whether they have any motion sensors around the house. Heck, they might have explosives in that approach.'

The approach was a manicured garden which had a pond,

several stone benches, well-shaped trees, through which the drive wended its way to the entrance.

A similar yard at the rear. Mountains in the distance. A picturesque place as far away from the hustle of a city as money could buy. *Lots of money.*

'The dogs will be our ears and eyes,' Meghan guessed. 'And, if we're outnumbered, our backup.'

Back in Science In Motion's complex that evening, as darkness fell.

Grim faces on them because another shooting had occurred, in New Mexico. Stoner Cavendish, a bouncer at a night club in Santa Fe had gunned down several Hispanic customers at a fast-food joint.

'TOO MANY OF THEM!' he had yelled. His last words as he himself was shot down by cops. Six people dead, one police officer critical.

It's building up, Zeb thought as he pulled up in a parking space. *The killings are happening almost every day. It's as if Ahmed, Yefremov and that Chinese man are compensating for the loss of their Ukraine and Indonesian sites.*

'Are you ready?' he snapped at Burt who along with Pilgrim was their welcoming party.

The researcher's grin faded. Pilgrim flinched.

Don't dump your rage on him, Zeb reprimanded himself. He placed a hand on the scientist's shoulder and squeezed gently. 'I'm sorry. It's been a long day and well, you must have heard of New Mexico.'

'I understand,' Burt nodded and then his eyes widened. 'Those killings? Y'all are here because of them? What are you planning? Oh My God, I should've guessed. You're SEALs?

Delta? Some kind of –'

'Larry, just lead us to your machines,' Beth stopped him. Her eyes dark, reflecting the same quiet anger they all felt. She smiled briefly, letting the researcher know their fury wasn't directed at him.

Burt and Pilgrim set off briskly, past several hangar-like buildings. 'Labs, test areas,' they described vaguely and came to a halt outside the last one, right at the back of the complex.

Thirty dogs on the concrete surface. Standing still, unlike any animal. Heads straight, only their blinking eyes showing that they were powered up. They smelled of fresh paint. Some of them grey, some of them brown, a few black.

'You wanted a natural-looking pack,' Burt gestured, 'You got them.'

Zeb inspected the machines as the researcher said something about extra battery packs, longer network range. *Do I call them dogs? Robots? Bots? Machines? Does it matter?*

It didn't, not in the light of New Mexico.

He turned to the researchers who looked at the operatives expectantly.

'Dr. Lebowski?'

'He said the call came. Everything's good. And that he would be grateful if you brought us back alive.'

Zeb looked at him sharply. A glint in Burt's eyes. Pilgrim hiding his smile.

There's spirit in them. They'll need it, once we go hot.

Bwana and Bear did their intimidation thing. They went close to the researchers who didn't shrink. They placed large hands on their shoulders and still the men didn't step back.

'I'm sure,' Bwana's teeth flashed, 'the good doctor said,

bring back the dogs. They're more important than you two.'

'Uh –' Pilgrim began then smiled sheepishly when Chloe chuckled, cue for the operatives to laugh.

'You got your stuff? Your backpacks, whatever you need for a few days away?' Meghan produced earpieces for the researchers, showed them how to wear the devices and tested them. 'Wear them at all times, especially when we go hot.'

'Hot?' Burt blurted.

'When guns go off,' Roger told him.

Chapter 79

—∞∞∞—

Two SUVs and a large van, the bigger vehicle sandwiched between the smaller.

Zeb, Meghan and Bwana in the first. Burt and Pilgrim in the second along with Beth, Chloe and Bear. Broker and Roger in the third.

They headed out of Denver at ten pm. Once they left the city behind and hit the I-70 West, they opened up. A normally four-hour drive, they reached the small town at just after one am.

Grand Junction, so called because it was on the confluence of the Colorado and the Gunnison Rivers, near the middle of a thirty-mile valley, the Grand Valley.

The city was relatively small, just over sixty-thousand people, the largest employers were the school district, the state and county governments. The region's economy had relied on natural gas but had been hit hard in the recession. It was rebounding, attracting businesses and private investors who saw the city's potential as a gateway to the outdoors.

Beth had rented three houses on Elm Street, near Colorado Mesa University. Each one had four bedrooms and four baths, a large kitchen, spacious driveways. Bwana high-fived her when he inspected the residences, Chloe grinned.

They split. Zeb, Bear and Chloe in one house. The sisters and Broker and Roger in another. Bwana joined the researchers in the last house.

'That van will be secure?' Zeb asked Burt.

'Yeah,' the scientist thumped its side. 'All kinds of lights and alarms will go off if anyone tampers with it. The dogs are de-activated. Nothing will happen to them. In any case, I doubt this is a high-crime city,' he sniggered. His smile vanished when eight operatives stared at him.

'Sleep,' Zeb told them. 'Tomorrow we recon.'

Werner was awake while his bosses rested. Someone had to stand watch and be there to save the world. Oh, that was interesting. Meghan had tweaked the facial recognition program. She had inserted several lines of code and Werner chuckled and shook his head in admiration when he went through them.

The improvement created a database of disguises. It took any face, Ahmed's for example, and generated thousands of phony looks for him. A wig. A beard. A bald look. Many permutations and combinations.

Smart, Werner thought. His job became easier…not that anything was hard for him, but now, all he had to do was compare Ahmed's likely disguise against that database.

As the operatives slept, he loaded the database with millions of disguises for Ahmed and Yefremov. Then searched once more for that Chinese voice. Found nothing. Sighed regretfully, drew out a Havana cigar and lit it.

Eleven am the next day. The two SUVs were bursting to their

seams with the addition of Burt and Pilgrim. They had left the van behind in Grand Junction as they began their recon.

There was no danger that they would stand out because there were enough trucks and vehicles on the road as hikers and campers hit the trails.

Cliffs and mesas. Valleys and gorges. Colors, browns and reds and gorgeous golds on the leaves. Colorado's great outdoors showed itself to them as Zeb led the drive to the ranch. Even the loquacious twins were silent as they took in the vastness and ruggedness of the land.

'We should come here,' Bwana told Roger, his comment audible in their earpieces.

'We will, once we rid this country of these badasses,' the Texan responded.

There were ranches and homesteads in the distance as the road climbed mountains and descended into valleys.

And then the Laird Ranch appeared. Or its boundary did. A barbed-wire fence ran parallel to the road, which was by then no better than a dirt track since they had left the road behind.

Boards at regular intervals, on the barrier, with a simple message.

Private Property. Keep Out.

Chapter 80

———— ∞ ————

They drove for miles, following the fence, but the ranch didn't come into view. Large trees, hillocks, obstructed the view.

'It's there, to our right,' Meghan said in frustration as she checked a map application. 'Four miles inside.'

Zeb drove up beneath the shade of an overhanging rock. He climbed out and hoisted his go bag and HK on his shoulder. 'We need eyes-on.' He went to the fence and snipped a hole with wire-cutters after confirming that it wasn't electric.

'Aren't we going in?' Pilgrim, asked, confused, when they made no move to enter through the opening.

'No. We wait and see if they send any patrols.' Beth replied. She searched the sky. No signs of drones.

'We can fly a bird,' she said.

'Let's not take that risk. They might detect it.'

'Ours are stealth craft.'

'Even so.'

An hour later, Zeb climbed through the opening. No alarms sounded. No shots were fired in their direction.

They broke into an easy, ground-eating jog, a pace that they could maintain for hours.

They could, but Burt and Pilgrim couldn't and they had to stop for breathers every fifteen minutes. A mile forward, five hundred yards to the right, Meghan directed them, guiding them to where they could have a view of the front of the ranch building.

And there, after crawling over a rise, they got the first sighting.

'Stay down,' Bear hissed when Pilgrim attempted to stand. 'Keep crawling until you get to that bush. Stay behind it.'

Sage grass and thickets. Clumps of bushes. Trees. The faint sound of flowing water in the distance. Zeb cocked his head when he heard it. *It's that stream that runs behind the building. It probably curves around here.* He looked at Bwana and Roger who got his message. They drifted off to check it out. Water attracted animals. It also drew people. There could be a guard house in the vicinity. It had to be checked out.

Zeb bellied forward and found a depression behind thick undergrowth. Meghan to his right. Chloe to his left. Bear, Broker and Beth scattered further away. All of them with binos to their eyes, HKs to their sides just in case hostiles appeared.

He looked behind and stifled a laugh. Burt and Pilgrim were on their back, drawing great gulps of air, sweat cooling on their faces.

The ranch house jumped out in his sights when he turned back. A graceful arc, as the few photographs had indicated. Elevated wooden deck. A few steps connecting it to the dusty drive. Large trees on either side, but the front was devoid of any vegetation. *Those trunks there...someone chopped them up. When these dudes took over the ranch? To get a clear line of sight?*

'Nothing here, Zeb,' Roger, in their earpieces. 'We're

going to follow this stream. See where it leads. We'll try to get to the rear of the house.'

'Copy that,' Zeb acknowledged. He didn't need to warn them to stay careful. *The two of them can take down an entire city by themselves.*

A bird chirped. Another one scolded it. A squirrel nosed its way out of hiding and looked at them inquisitively. This was its territory. What were they doing there? It chattered at them angrily and turned its back on them in disgust when they didn't respond. A snore from behind. Burt, who had taken the opportunity to snooze.

Hours passed. No movement around the house. No one came out, no vehicles drove up.

Vehicles? Where are they? Zeb scanned the sides of the building and spotted nothing.

'We're five hundred yards behind the house. Doesn't look like we have tripped any alarms.' Bwana, satisfaction in his voice. 'Three trucks. Two SUVs. Doesn't look like they've been used recently. We can see dust on them. There are more buildings here, but that ranch house? There are definitely people inside. We can see shadows moving behind the windows.'

There are several of them, Zeb noted. *Large glass panes in wood frames. About five feet from the ground and six or seven feet tall. Three feet wide. None of them open. But no movement visible from this side.*

'Are they one-way?' he asked his team, those who were with him.

'Nah,' Chloe replied after a while. 'I can see through one of them. There's a wall painting. Some kind of landscape.'

'What about cameras? I haven't spotted any.'

'We did,' Roger smirked. 'They're hidden in the guttering around the roof. Watch those pipes closely and you'll just about make them out.'

'What would we do without you two?'

'Lost!' Bwana said emphatically.

More watching for another couple of hours after which Zeb called off the surveillance.

'Something bothers me,' Beth said on the way back. 'Why isn't there better security? That fence should have been electrified. Alarmed. They should have sent guards to inspect it when we cut the wire. Sensors in the ground to give us away. Nothing like that happened.'

'I've been thinking about that,' Zeb scratched the stubble on his chin and broke off to overtake a slow-moving camping van.

'He's still thinking,' Beth relayed when someone tapped in their mic.

'This place is so remote,' Zeb ignored the smirking grin on Meghan's face. 'Why would they need to go all out like that? They know that Indonesia and Ukraine have gone down. And they might have thought of beefing up security, but this ranch's two hundred acres. Setting up a good system will take time.'

'Well,' Roger drawled. 'Only one way to find out.'

Chapter 81

Werner didn't alert the sisters immediately. He ran checks and then more checks. Better to be sure than to waste team resources on a wild hunt. But there was no mistaking those images, captured at LAX.

He noted the flight timings. One was a British Airways flight, but it was also used as a connecting flight by Saudia. And that mustache, wig, that was identical to what he had generated for Riyaz Khaled Ahmed.

Werner tried to search for airport images in Riyadh, but those Saudis…they never shared anything. Or rather, they shared selectively. Nope. Nothing there. But was he sure that was his man?

Now, what about that other image that had alerted him.

This one was a few hours later. American Airlines, which was connected to a BA flight from Domodedovo Airport in Moscow. This dude was blond, shoulder-length hair. Blue eyes.

Ha! Sidor Yefremov could try all he wanted but he couldn't beat the world's best AI.

Could Werner track their identities? The aliases they used?

Sure, he could. He had access to all the Western airlines databases. Getting into the flight manifests was a piece of cake.

The Russian was traveling as Ryan Kasper. Permanent address in L.A. A talent scout for one of the production houses in Hollywood. Werner looked that address up. It was a high-luxe apartment in Beverly Hills, owned by some shell company.

And Riyaz Khalid Ahmed was masquerading as Eli Cohen, an importer of Californian wine. He had an office in Jerusalem, a bank account that had transactions, but the trail turned murky once Werner started digging. A home address, but that place had been demolished last year and a high-rise had gone up in its place.

Werner leaned back and closed his eyes. Yeah, he was sure the two men were the targets. There were more details that he had dug up, which confirmed his conclusion.

Where did they go from LAX, however? He searched more databases. Hotel records, car rentals, other flights. He came up with nothing.

They would have changed disguises again and hired private jets or cars under a different name.

Yeah, that could be it. Would Beth and Meghan come to the same conclusion as him?

You betcha, he grinned.

'THEY'RE HERE!' Beth thumped Zeb so hard that he spilled coffee on his tee and down his chest.

Next day. A hasty breakfast before they went on a second day of recon. It was when she had spilled his drink.

'Who's here?' he emptied his coffee mug in the sink and when he turned to her, took an involuntary step back from the force of her excitement.

She was bursting with energy, bouncing from one foot to another, flicking her hair back impatiently. Meghan, behind her, winking at him.

'AHMED AND YEFREMOV. THEY'RE IN THE COUNTRY,' Beth yelled.

A quick conference in the living room. All ten of them while the sisters briefed them rapidly.

'Check your phones,' Meghan ordered. 'We've sent photographs of how they look. Ahmed is Eli Cohen, Israeli. Yefremov is Ryan Kasper, a Hollywood executive. They landed in LAX, separately, in the night. Eight pm and eleven pm. Nope,' she stalled the chorus of questions. 'We don't know if they met. Nope, we don't know where they are currently.'

Zeb studied the images as the sisters fielded questions. How do they know these two are our men?

He looked up when Beth began answering precisely that question.

'We got Werner to create disguises for these men. Wigs. Cheek pads, false teeth, fake noses, anything that's possible without surgery. And then got it to monitor the major airport terminals for those people.'

'But –' Burt began.

'Some basics about a person don't change,' she overrode the researcher. 'Pupillary distance, the width between the centers of the eyes. Height. We can eliminate whatever extra inches are added by shoes or padding. Several factors. Sure, Cohen and Kasper could be real people but we checked that. They have good legends, but they don't hold up against aggressive verification. They –'

'They arrived at night?' Zeb interrupted her.

'Yeah.'

That's enough time for either of them, or both, to get to these locations.

'Talk while we move,' he got to his feet and signaled them to climb into their vehicles.

They would go into surveillance mode and if they were lucky, really lucky, they would see either or both the men arriving.

Chapter 82

Zeb drove out fast, followed by the second vehicle.

'How do you know these are our men?' he asked the sisters.

'Cohen, or Ahmed, is an Israeli importer.' Beth replied and grinned at his raised eyebrows. It wasn't lost on her that the Saudi was impersonating as a Jew. 'Office address holds water. But no employees. Home address nonexistent. Medical records sketchy. He's got a driving license, a bank account which has a healthy balance with regular transactions like for rent, utilities. But here's the thing. There's a CCTV camera almost opposite the entrance to his office. We hacked into its database. No one looking like Cohen has ever entered or exited the building. No one looking like Ahmed or any of his other disguises.'

Jackpot! Zeb gave her an approving nod and floored the gas.

'Yefremov,' Meghan took over. 'is a Hollywood talent agent. Attached to a production house but is an independent. We made some calls.'

'This early? Bear asked doubtfully.

'Yeah. It's surprising how many calls get answered when

you say you're casting for a new Game of Thrones movie and hint at the names backing it. He, Yefremov, has never been seen in Hollywood. Ryan Kasper has never been mentioned in social media. Which is extraordinary for a Hollywood player. And even if we give him the benefit of doubt, here's the thing. There's a real Ryan Kasper. He is a talent scout. He too is independent. And he looks very similar to our man, but right now, he's fast asleep, next to his wife in their apartment in Laurel Canyon.'

'Bingo,' Bwana whistled softly. 'But, why would they risk everything by coming to the US. They know we'll be looking for them.'

'Meg and I think this is related to List Europe and List Asia in some way.'

'We stopped those programs. Those servers are out.'

'Yeah, but we do not know if there were backups. What if there were copies in these locations?'

'Even if there were, couldn't they be activated remotely?'

'Not if these centers operate independently, like terrorist cells. Each unit doesn't know anything about the others. Which is what we found in Ukraine and Indonesia. You agree?' she asked Zeb who was nodding along.

'Yeah. But there's only one way we'll know for sure.'

'By asking them.' Bear answered gleefully.

Chapter 83

Two hours later, hunkered down in the same location as the previous day. The same distribution. Bwana and Roger at the rear.

A brief argument, Bear and Chloe saying they wanted to go to the back, Bwana turning on the superiority by claiming that he and Roger were the best woodsmen in the team. Which was true and that ended the spirited debate.

Sunlight warming their backs. The smell of earth and vegetation surrounding them. No sounds of civilization. It was as if they were the only humans in the land.

Near two pm, a faint trail of dust on the horizon.

'That's near the gate,' Beth whispered though there was no reason to. No one else was in listening distance and she was speaking in their earpieces. But, habit and tradecraft.

A line of trees and hillocks cut out their view of the drive which was visible only when it emerged from the woods and neared the house. That trail of dust resolved into a fast-moving vehicle. Make indistinguishable from the distance. Black, some kind of SUV, was all that they could discern.

Zeb trained his glasses and tried to see through its windows, but no luck. They were tinted and the vehicle was jerking and bouncing on the uneven drive.

It skidded to a stop in front of the house. Simultaneously, the ranch's doors opened. Two men stepped out, faces concealed by large glasses and hats. They climbed down the steps, escorted a man from the ride and disappeared into the house.

'This is the place,' Zeb said softly. 'See how expertly they did that. We didn't get one look at their faces or at the arrival. Why would any ranch go to such lengths to protect people?'

The SUV drove to the left of the house, turned and disappeared behind it.

'We've got it,' Roger announced laconically. And then, 'Nope. Dude, the driver, ran into the house, head down. Average height. Jeans. Some kind of blue shirt. That's all we got.'

'You think they know we're here?' Chloe asked.

'No,' Zeb said. 'If they did, that man, whoever he is, wouldn't come here. He –'

'Werner says there's a possibility he's Ahmed.'

Zeb snapped his head to the right and gaped at Meghan who grinned and held up her phone.

'I recorded his arrival,' she said. 'Asked Werner to run any kind of posture, body, face recognition. The height matches, it said. The gait has similarity to a brief clip from the LAX CCTV archives. Oh, and Zeb, shut your mouth. There are flies around.'

'We go tonight?' Bwana asked, yearning in his voice.

'Yeah,' Zeb confirmed. 'Two goals. Shut down this List. And take Ahmed alive.'

Chapter 84

———— ∞∞∞ ————

Riyaz Khalid Ahmed was tired. This mission was draining him of his energies.

He had hustled into the ranch, head down, the moment he had stepped out of the vehicle. Two of Jake's men had escorted him. Both, concealing their faces. Standard operating procedure.

'Anything out of the ordinary?' he asked Jake when the center leader greeted him. Jake for Jakob Zacharovsky. A Russian who headed a gang in L.A. which in turn was part of a larger bratva in Moscow.

Ahmed did not know how Yefremov knew him and did not care to know. All that mattered was his Russian counterpart had provided the armed guards and the programmers. Trust. It was how the three of them worked. If they couldn't rely on each other, this mission would fail. So far they had no cause to doubt one another. Jake and his men were good. The programmers were excellent. By all accounts, the software people in all the centers were some of the best in the world. It was only in Indonesia that Leslie had insisted on having Zhen and Keling instead of Yefremov's personnel. Because of the backstory he had with those gangsters.

'No. It's quiet here,' Jake answered. He had cultivated a West Coast accent, a lazy drawl, but that belied his ruthless streak. 'It always is. Anything I should know? Your visit is a surprise.'

Ahmed debated on how much to tell the man. He, Leslie and Yefremov had been very clear on need to know. *Does Jake need to know?*

No, he decided. But it didn't hurt to give a hint.

'There've been some complications,' he said. 'Nothing that alters our mission. But it needed me to be here.'

'What kind of complications?' Jake asked sharply.

Ahmed noted the way the man's AR15 was slung over his shoulder, close to his gun hand. Yes, this Russian was good. He was calm, controlled, and always wary, even indoors.

'List Europe. It got corrupted,' he lied baldly. 'The backup copy needs to be restored.'

'That might take some time. The engineers are busy on their current program. The American one. They have upped the ante, like you wanted.'

'How are they holding up?'

'As well as you can expect. They've been cooped up here for weeks. But they aren't complaining.' He looked about and lowered his voice. 'The promise of money, lots of it, it's always a great incentive.'

Ahmed nodded. He knew what Jake implied. The engineers would be killed once the mission was over. That promise was only that. Words.

'You want to meet them?'

'Let me check out the site.'

'Nothing's changed since you were last here,' Jake started

walking to the computer room which was in the center of the arc. It had been the dining room but had been stripped out to accommodate the server racks, the highspeed cable connections, the monitors and the various equipment that the engineers needed. Its front walls were opaque glass with a thin transparent strip at the top through which they could look inside.

Five engineers, hunched over their screens. Some of them looked up at Ahmed expressionlessly as he strolled past, outside.

'They look tired.'

'We're all tired,' Jake shrugged. 'When will this end?'

'Soon,' Ahmed promised. 'That's one reason why I am here. Things are heading to a close. How are your men?'

'None of us have shot each other,' the Russian laughed sardonically. He jerked his head at the armed men scattered throughout the house none of whom were paying them any attention. 'They miss going out, having a beer. Having a woman. Yefremov … relax,' he said when the Saudi looked at him sharply, 'no one else knows his name. He told me this gig would last a few days. It's weeks now. Don't get me wrong. This ranch is fabulous. But it still feels like a prison.'

'I told you. It'll end soon.'

'That's the wine cellar,' Jake opened the door that led down to a flight of stairs. 'You know what's there.'

'Yes.'

'And those are our rooms.'

The entire building had been hollowed out, keeping just the converted dining room and the bedrooms and a bathroom. A large open space running from one end to the other, with doors to the accommodations, the cellar and the computer setup.

A central table on which several monitors played the feeds from the CCTV cameras around the house.

'Motion sensors?'

'We haven't changed anything since your last visit. We have them around the building, close to it. We don't need anything else. No one visits this ranch. No one gets past the fence and the gates. A time or two a few inquisitive tourists jumped over the wire but we turned them away politely. Any work that the house needs, we do ourselves. Once a week, I or a few others go to Grand Junction and stock up on essentials.'

Ahmed had seen enough. He was confident that Carter hadn't reached the center. He went to sleep comforted by Jake and his sixteen men standing sentry outside.

Chapter 85

Zeb and his team hit the ranch at their usual attack time.

A larger breach through the wire to accommodate the dogs. Burt and Pilgrim running behind the machines. The operatives running alongside them, in dark combat suits, weapons and NVGs, cutting through the night.

'You can control all of them with just those screens?' Beth asked the researchers, pointing to their hand-held screens.

'Yeah,' Burt grinned. 'That's why I said the training takes a while.'

They covered ground easily, the robots spread out ahead of them, loping.

A breather to let the researchers recover. Zeb looked at the night sky. Millions of pinpricks in the dark canvas. A light moving slowly, a satellite. A light, cool breeze. He squinted in the night. *Ranch's half a mile away. Four minutes to hit it.*

The building was lit and stood out in the distance. The only establishment in the darkness.

At a snap of his fingers, they resumed. 'How're you holding up?' he asked the scientists.

'Always wanted to lose some weight,' Pilgrim panted.

They stopped six hundred yards away. Got to the ground while the machines spread out and wandered aimlessly. No shadows appeared at any of the windows.

Another move forward, the same maneuver, with the same result.

'Split,' Zeb spoke into his mic when the ranch was a hundred feet away.

Bear, Chloe, Broker and Beth turned left in the night. Pilgrim joined them with fifteen machines. They took a long detour and swung to the back of the house.

'In position,' the twin confirmed half an hour later. 'We've come through between the buildings at the back. All empty.'

'Burt, Pilgrim,' Zeb ordered, 'send the dogs.'

The machines raced towards the house from the front and the back.

'Gravel yard around the house,' Burt called out. Stone walls. The windows are too high. They can't see inside.'

'Make them jump.' Zeb trained his NVGs and saw the first of the machines leap high in the air. The others soon followed.

'Huh!' Pilgrim's surprised voice. 'The inside's hollow,' he said as images streamed on his and Burt's screen from the robots' cameras. 'A long hallway that follows the curve of the house. It's as if any rooms, any construction was removed.'

'Yeah,' Burt confirmed. 'I can see guards. Four, no five, all armed.'

They identified seven finally, all spread out in the corridor inside. A few rooms at the center of the curve. A center table on which were several screens, a man sitting at them.

'Control station,' Pilgrim said. 'I can see what that dude's seeing on his CCTV feeds. Oh, wait. A dog appeared, and there's another.'

'Anything about those rooms?'

'One of them seems to be glowing from the inside,' Burt said. 'The one at the base of the arc. Can't see inside, however.'

'That could be where the engineers are,' Meghan stated.

Zeb nodded in the dark.

'We keep looking?' Burt asked.

'Yeah, but no more jumping.' Zeb replied.

Any motion sensors around the house could be designed to ignore animals. However, they needed confirmation.

Ahmed woke instantly when he felt a hand on his shoulder. He reached reflexively for the gun on a side-table, relaxed when he made out Jake looming over him.

'What's it?'

'You got to see this.'

The Saudi dressed hastily, shoved his gun in a large pocket and followed him out. He blinked in the well-lit hallway. A few sentries nodded at him as he passed them. The smell of coffee from mugs in their hands. Ahmed stretched to his toes and peered inside the computer room. The engineers were asleep on the floor.

'This,' Jake pointed to a screen. 'I've never seen them before.'

Ahmed stared at the dogs as they ran around the house, some milling aimlessly.

'They are at the front as well as the back.'

'Wild dogs?'

'Looks like that.'

'What are they doing?'

'Beats me. We get the occasional animals. Wild cats, but dogs, and this many?' the Russian shook his head in disbelief.

'First time any of us have seen them.'

'Anything else on the cameras?'

'No.'

'Motion sensors?'

'They're quiet. They don't trigger when animals pass, otherwise they'd be beeping continuously.'

Ahmed straightened and went to a front window. He shaded his eyes from the reflection and peered outside.

He spotted an animal immediately as it darted across. Its head swung in his direction as it loped.

Something about it bothered him. He kept looking at it as it disappeared in the night, but here, another came along. Same style of running.

No tongue!

'That's Ahmed!'

Zeb winced at Burt's shout.

'GO!' He ordered.

'THOSE AREN'T –' Ahmed shouted.

His voice was drowned in the shattering of glass as the animals burst through the windows at the front and the back.

He froze. The guards were stunned. Jake's jaw dropped as the animals landed on carpet.

'GET THEM OUT!' The Russian recovered and fired over the top of one dog. It didn't flinch.

'THEY AREN'T –' Ahmed began again but rifles opened up. Sleeping guards rushed out of their rooms and more weapons joined the fray. The animals raced randomly, zigging and zagging down the corridor, moving at unbelievable speed.

The Saudi lunged at Jake, caught him by his shoulder.

Terror

'THOSE AREN'T REAL,' he shouted. 'ROBOTS. SOME-
ONE'S CONTROLLING THEM!'

'I count eighteen men,' Pilgrim reported. 'And Ahmed. No
sign of programmers yet. The dogs are giving a good view of
the inside. It's all open space.'

Good tradecraft. The house provides no cover for any
intruder. Clear shooting for its guards, Zeb thought as
he double-tapped his mic, a signal to his crew, and began racing
towards the nearest window. Bwana to his right. Meghan to
his left. Another shadow further away, Roger.

'We're approaching,' Bear on their earpieces.

'We'll move the dogs to one side. All fire will be on them.'
Burt reported.

'Copy that,' Zeb acknowledged. 'Need engineers and
Ahmed alive.'

And he dived into the house.

369

Chapter 86

———— ⌘⌘⌘ ————

'IT'S AN ATTACK!' Ahmed shook Jake in frustration. Why couldn't the man see what he had spotted? None of those animals were wounded even though they took hits. They fell but they righted themselves and kept running randomly, moving so fast that it was difficult to shoot them.

'STOP!' the Russian shouted, as the animals gathered in a corner and withstood the firing. 'WATCH OUT!'

But it was too late.

Ahmed watched, as if in slow motion a man flew through a window. He landed, rolled smoothly, got to a knee and fired, all in one move.

Carter!

Zeb's first burst went wide. He corrected even as he took in the scene.

A tall man. Beside him, a darker-skinned person. Ahmed. Further away, a bunch of guards, all shooting at the robots. Ten, twelve of them.

He had landed where the house started curving out, away from the center. Behind him he heard more thumps as his team entered.

The roar of gunfire as the sentries were caught in a cross-fire as his crew at the back, entered the house.

'GO!' he thought he heard the tall man shout at Ahmed. The Saudi cast a look in Zeb's direction, brought out his gun and fired wildly. Two guards went with him.

Zeb lunged to his side. Triggered fast as another shooter turned towards him. Burt and Pilgrim joined the fight. They split the robots into packs of four. Turned them into attack mode and directed them at individual gunmen.

Can't let him escape. Zeb sprinted towards the room the Saudi had ducked into. He passed a glass-walled room. Blue light from inside. Beth opening its door. Bear giving him a thumbs-up.

He yanked the door open and dived inside, keeping low to the floor. A short landing. Stairs going down. Dimly lit.

Movement to his side.

Rounds burned the air above his head as the shooter fired, expecting him to be at full height. The gunman tried to correct. Too late. Zeb riddled him with his HK, but lost his balance and tumbled down the steps.

His rifle caught in a crack between the steps. A moment to wrestle it free and then it was clear. He stepped inside a room cautiously. A wine cellar. Bottles, casks on the wall. A tasting table to his right. A door closing ahead.

Must be an escape tunnel. He ran towards it. Saw a shadow move in a bottle's reflection. Threw himself sideways just as two rounds punched him in the chest. He fell to the floor, gasping, bringing his HK up desperately, firing blindly, but luckily, his spray kept the shooter at bay who was hiding behind a wine rack.

Zeb fired at the bottles. Glass shattered, the smell of alcohol filling the room. Magazine fast-change. He took a gamble. Got to his feet, put his shoulder behind a cask and heaved it at the hidden gunman, who heard it coming and rose. Zeb cut him down.

Two steps to the door. A second to open it.

It *was* a tunnel. Seven feet high, four feet wide. Concrete. Light bulbs in the ceiling. No sign of Ahmed. No sounds of shooting from above. It was as if the passage was a world of its own.

Zeb ran lightly on the balls of his feet. Straight, smooth walls, no place for the Saudi to hide. Then a turn. He got to his belly again, peered around it. Another long stretch. No running man in sight.

He got to his feet, cocking his head to listen.

He was wrong.

Chapter 87

———— ⬤⬤⬤ ————

Riyaz Khalid Ahmed came out of an alcove to Zeb's right, a shallow hide that he hadn't spotted.

The Saudi's round missed Zeb's nose by inches. Zeb hit the ground, twisting his body at the last minute, left hand slashing out to knock Ahmed's gun away, right leg kicking the man in the chest.

The Saudi staggered against the wall, but bounced back as if he was made of rubber. He fell on top of Zeb, growling, grunting, raining punches and kicks, hitting hard and fast.

Zeb ducked to evade an eye jab, caught a blow to his neck and hissed. He brought his elbow up to protect himself, a knee up to dislodge his attacker, but Ahmed stuck to him and kept delivering blow after blow.

He's trained, Zeb thought dimly as another punch caught his face. *He's got the moves*. His attacker was in his forties but was supremely fit and agile and his punches had a wicked bite.

Zeb reared up suddenly, deliberately exposing his neck, caught the incoming blow, twisted his attacker's wrist, applying pressure on a nerve-point. Ahmed screamed, flailed with his left hand, caught Zeb on the jaw which made his head ring

Ty Patterson

and his patience snap.

He heaved up, core body strength powering his move, his chest colliding with the Saudi's flinging him to the side and then both men were diving away to make room, standing up.

A gun on the floor. Ahmed's.

He dived at it. Zeb got there at the same time. He didn't reach for the gun. He got his palms around the man's gun hand, twisted it until the spymaster shrieked and kicked out wildly.

Zeb let him go.

Ahmed sprang back wildly looking at the weapon in Zeb's hand, and then, as footsteps pounded behind, at the newcomers.

Zeb didn't have to look back to know his team had arrived. He sensed Bwana and Bear and the twins spreading out for a clear line of sight.

'Carter,' Ahmed relaxed, 'You should have died in that attack.'

His spoke with no accent, a thin, contemptuous smile on his face, as if he had the upper hand.

'What comes next?' he asked insolently. 'You're going to torture me?'

'Yefremov gave you up,' Zeb said. 'He pinned everything on you. He said these programs, the killing, everything was your idea. We've got his confession.'

Ahmed blanched. His eyes widened. He looked desperate for a moment, and then he laughed.

'You're lying. I checked in with him today. He was safe.'

Check in. So, he and Yefremov have a protocol.

'You'll have to do better than that, Carter. You've got nothing on me. I came to this ranch to check it out. I am a potential buyer. The next thing I know, you attacked it.'

'Meghan,' Zeb asked without turning his head. 'You're recording this?'

'Yeah.'

'Record all you want, Carter,' Ahmed smiled arrogantly. 'You're too late. The G20-'

He cut himself off suddenly and put on a wooden expression.

Zeb stared at him. A cold feeling started to grip him. *G20 Summit? What have they got planned for it?* Clare's words came to him suddenly. *Junior minister in the Saudi Arabian Defense Ministry. Yefremov was in the Russian Defense department.*

The cold became a sickening feeling. Saudi Arabia and Russia. And somehow China in the equation. *What have they planned?*

'We won't torture you,' Zeb said, his voice sounding distant. 'We can wring you that way, but we won't.'

A surprised look crossed Ahmed's face.

'In fact, we'll even let you go free.'

The Saudi's eyes narrowed at Zeb's words.

'Meghan?'

'Yeah.

'Can you get the king's number?'

'King of Saudi Arabia?' she cottoned on immediately.

'Correct.'

'Hang on.'

'This is what we'll do, Ahmed. We'll call your king. And he'll listen, once President Morgan makes a call to his aides, confirming my identity. I'll tell your ruler that you have been involved in these algorithms. You are behind these killings. I have a feeling he might already know about everything. Or a lot.'

Ahmed didn't respond. He had turned pale.

'We're going to record the call with him and go public with it. You can imagine the headlines. Saudi King behind the world-wide killings. Your name will be mentioned too, in TV channels and newspapers around the world. And then,' Zeb paused. 'Then, we'll hand you over to the Saudi embassy. I'm sure you'll know what will happen to you next. Meghan, make that call.'

'NO!' Ahmed pounced forward, brushed past him and wrestled with her for the phone.

She back-handed him and stepped away.

'Talk,' she said, 'and you just might save yourself.'

Chapter 88

Riyaz Khalid Ahmed did not offer any resistance when they led him upstairs.

Bodies were laid out in the house, the majority of them dead, the few who were alive, were bound and gagged. The robots were in a corner with Burt and Pilgrim making repairs to those damaged.

The Saudi's eyes lingered on the tall man who was sprawled on the floor, lifeless.

'Who's he?' Zeb asked him.

For a moment it looked like the Saudi wouldn't answer. Then, his shoulders slumped. 'Jake Zacharovsky. He was the center head.'

'That's what you call them?' Beth's lips curled in disgust.

Ahmed kept silent. He sat in the chair; a man defeated.

'All engineers are alive,' Meghan murmured as she went past Zeb. 'They aren't talking, but then we haven't questioned them.'

'What's going to happen at the G20 Summit?' Zeb stood in front of the Saudi. It was a power move, reinforcing that they were in charge.

Ahmed swallowed. He licked his lips. He looked away from Zeb, to the dogs who were huddled in a corner, Burt and Pilgrim with them.

'Why don't we torture him?' Bear asked helpfully. 'And then hand him over to the Saudis. We'll leave him alive so that there's enough of him for them to work on.'

Their captive shuddered.

'My King, the Russian and Chinese Presidents...they'll make a joint statement. The formation of an army.' His voice was so soft that they had to strain to hear it. 'To be deployed wherever there is a conflict. Syria. Africa. The India Pakistan border. To make peace.'

'Peace is not what you're after, though,' Broker said grimly after they had digested his words. 'It's a land grab. Where there are weak governments, you'll install your leaders.'

It would work, too. A large enough army, with those countries behind it, will make the United Nations' Peace Keeping Forces irrelevant. That organization itself will lose stature as these countries go about reshaping the world. Zeb's mind raced. The US and its allies were increasingly following a non-intervention policy around the world. *These three countries can step into that vacuum. China has a huge economy. Russia already has significant political clout in the world. Both countries have highly advanced militaries. And Saudi Arabia has money.* Zeb rubbed his forearms as if to ward off a chill. The coming together of the three countries was a fearsome combination.

'What about these algorithms? Why did you need them?' Beth asked. 'This military announcement...you didn't need the programs for that.'

'They did.' Meghan snapped her fingers. 'The creation of

a new army wouldn't be enough by itself. They had to create a climate around the world. Of fear and distrust in governments. That would greatly help their announcement. People would welcome it.'

Ahmed's nodded in confirmation. 'It was working. Until you came into the picture.' He glared at Zeb defiantly. 'It was a great plan. Military domination. Financial-'

He stopped abruptly again and looked away.

Bwana sighed. He unsheathed his Benchmade and shouldered past Zeb. 'This won't hurt,' he promised, 'not much.' And brought the knife down on the captive's thigh.

'STOP!' Beth shouted.

Everyone looked at her in surprise.

'There's no need for that,' she smiled wickedly at Ahmed and brought out a coin. She tossed it high in the air. 'Call, heads or tails?'

'What?' the spymaster shook his head in confusion.

'Heads, we deliver you to your embassy. Tails....' She paused, letting the tension build, 'we call Mossad. Their agents can be here in a couple of hours. We'll leave the interrogation to them.'

Zeb smiled inwardly when Ahmed shuddered. *Clever move.* The Israeli agency played by different rules. It wouldn't play nice. *Nope, nice isn't what they do.*

Ahmed screamed, sweat pouring down his face. 'STOCKS. WE BOUGHT STOCKS IN THE BIGGEST INTERNET AND DATA COMPANIES.'

'That would give them control,' Meghan whispered, staggered by his revelation. 'They could run these algorithms, manipulate just about anyone, anywhere.'

Zeb shook his head, reeling from the confession, from the

scale of the plan. *Create fear and unrest in the world. Form a world military force. And then, have the means to influence people in any country.*

'Why did you come here?' he asked. 'You could have stayed in Riyadh.'

'To reactivate the European program.'

'Why?'

'We wanted a last burst of killings in Europe and America.'

'Those are still happening in the US.'

'This last spate…it will be unlike anything seen.'

'TALK!' Bwana grabbed his hair and lifted his head savagely.

'WASHINGTON DC,' Ahmed stammered. 'PROTEST MARCH. DAY AFTER TOMORROW. WE WILL HAVE SHOOTERS.'

'How can you time it like that?' Meghan asked, aghast. 'These people on the internet…they can't be directed with such accuracy.'

'Not from the internet,' the Saudi bowed his head. 'We have got killers for this. Lone gunmen. Yefremov has them on standby.'

'Who are they?'

'I don't know.' He recoiled when Bear moved threateningly. 'I SWEAR I DON'T KNOW. ONLY YEFREMOV KNOWS WHO THEY ARE AND WHERE THEY WILL BE.'

'When will this happen?'

'On the day of the march. He, Leslie and I will call one another and coordinate the attack.'

'Leslie? That's the Chinese man?'

'Yes.' Ahmed was broken. He answered readily, his voice a monotone, sweat and fear emanating from him. 'Duan Shuren.

I call him Leslie. We use aliases for one another. Yefremov is Phil Williams, I am Jack Smith. Shuren's very senior in the –'

The face popped up in Zeb's mind, triggered by the spymaster's words. A grainy photograph captured by a long-distance camera. A man passing through revolving doors in a Hong Kong hotel, several years ago. That was the only image of the spymaster in existence. Every Western intelligence agency had tried to find more on him, but had failed. And then, had come the news that he had died.

'MSS, Ministry of State Security, their intelligence and security agency,' Zeb completed, mechanically. It was one of the most secretive organizations in the world and carried out counter-intelligence operations. 'I know Shuren. *Knew of* him. He was killed in a shootout with a Mossad team. He was carrying out clandestine operations in Israel. There is no record of him anywhere except one photograph. That's why I didn't recognize his voice in Indonesia.'

'He didn't die.' Ahmed said, chillingly. 'That body Mossad found, was a cover. It was burned beyond recognition. Shuren left his blood behind. That was how the body was identified.'

Zeb felt as if he had been punched in the gut. Duan Shuren had been one of the most feared spymasters. He had turned several CIA and British spies, had recruited Chinese students to spy for their country while studying abroad, and ran lethal assassination teams.

Yes, he thought. *Shuren is capable of such a conspiracy. He's got the smarts and the political reach.*

'This would have required political backing,' Bear said, looking like he wanted to riddle Ahmed with holes.

'We had that,' their captive said. 'Once we had proved what the programs were capable of, the three of us reported directly to the deputy heads in our country. I reported to the Prince. Yefremov to the Russian prime minister, and Shuren, to the Chinese premier.'

'They know everything?'

'Not everything, but the overall plan, yes. They are the ones who are working with our defense ministers for the combined security force.'

'Where is Yefremov now? He's at the Content team's place?'

'You know that, too?' Ahmed stared at him.

'He's in the Mojave Desert,' Meghan replied from behind. She held up her phone when Zeb turned to her. 'Daniel Klouse came through, an hour ago. He's at Nevada Evergreen, a power station fifty miles from Boulder City.'

'How did you know?' Ahmed whispered.

No one replied to him.

'We check-in every morning.' Their captive moistened his lips, when all eyes glared at him. 'What will happen to me, now?'

'I want to kill you,' Zeb said bitterly. 'But, you'll live. As long as you talk.'

Chapter 89

———∞∞∞———

Riyaz Khalid Ahmed confessed everything he knew.

Hyde, the name Yefremov had coined, was Shuren's idea. He had broached it to Yefremov who liked it instantly. Russia was already involved in manipulating elections in various countries and propagating fake news. The Chinese spymaster's plan took such influencing to a different level.

The two men had then approached Ahmed discreetly.

'I didn't trust them at first,' he admitted. 'But when they revealed their identities and outlined Hyde, it made sense. The US is our ally but we know there's no real love for us in the West.' he said bitterly. 'With Shuren's plan, we would be a true world player. My king has always wanted to break away from the West. This was an opportunity of a lifetime.'

They had responsibilities, he said. Shuren ran the center in Indonesia. He had personally selected Zhen to manage it, and the two had made Keling the fall guy.

'He knew that gangster very well. There was history between them. I looked after the US centers.'

'Colorado and Nevada? Content and List US?' Beth asked.

'Yes.'

'Why you?'

'Because I have substantial contacts here. A very good network. Our country invests a lot in your country. This ranch...' he looked around. 'It's owned by a Saudi Arabian investment company, affiliated with my government.'

'Hidden by a shell company trail, no doubt,' Beth said, bitterly.

'That's how it works in my world. It's the same case with the Nevada center. That power plant is an inactive one. It's a small one compared to the others in the desert but it fell into operational problems and we had to shut it.'

'How many men, there?' Zeb asked impatiently. *That DC attack's happening in less than forty-eight hours. We don't have much time if we have to take out Yefremov and stop those shooters.*

'There's no one in the plant. There's a house behind it where the Content team is based. Yefremov is there. Same number as here. Eighteen. Boris Voronoff, leads the men. All of them are Russian. Ex-Spetsnaz. The men here, they too are Russian. Yefremov supplied them as well as the programmers. I provided the money and the US locations, and Shuren, it was his plan and without him...'

He trailed off. *Without China, this wouldn't have gotten off the ground,* Zeb thought.

'Where's Shuren?'

'Somewhere in Hong Kong.'

'There?' Zeb asked surprised. 'Not in Beijing?'

'No. He's masquerading as a businessman.'

'Where in Hong Kong?'

'I don't know,' he said, a pleading look on his face. 'Yefremov will know. The two of them have known each other for longer than I've known them.'

He could be right, Zeb considered. *Of the three, Ahmed's the most expendable. Shuren and Yefremov could always find another moneyman.*

They wrung Ahmed dry until he had nothing more to give them.

'Rest,' Zeb told his team at five am. 'We'll regroup in two hours.'

'But-' Beth began, waving her screen. She and her sister had been interrogating the engineers, poring over the programs they had written.

'Sleep,' Zeb repeated in a tone that brooked no argument.

They got the surviving gangsters to move the bodies to a building at the rear of the house and then split up. The sisters occupied a room. Bear and Chloe, another. Zeb and the others jogged back to where their vehicles were parked and drove them back.

Zeb made two calls and then slept in his SUV, out at the front of the ranch house, underneath a dawning sky. He stirred when his watch alerted him to the time. Woke up swiftly and rubbed his eyes. Shadows on the ground as the rising sun cast its rays on the ranch. He took a few moments to breathe lung-fuls of fresh air and was struck by the silence around them.

We used to go camping in places like this. Where there was no one but us. My wife, my son and me. My world.

His thoughts were interrupted by a poke to his ribs. A hand came in front of him, holding a coffee mug. 'Rise and shine,' Beth said smugly. Meghan beside her. Both of them looking well-rested.

Zeb sipped his drink, its strength and warmth waking his body up. By the time he entered the building, Beth and Meghan were on their screens. They had dragged a table to the center of the arc. Had rustled up a printer and several maps were spread out in front of them. The remaining operatives were looking over their shoulders.

'This,' Beth looked up when he joined them, 'is where the Nevada center is.'

He looked at where her finger was pointing. A cross mark on the map.

In the Mojave Desert.

Chapter 90

———⊸⊙⊙⊸———

The Mojave Desert, about forty-eight thousand square miles, was in southeastern California and a part of it spilled over into southern Nevada. Small portions extended in Utah and Arizona too. Temperatures often exceeded one hundred and twenty degrees and the region received less than two inches of rain a year.

The desert was home to Death Valley, one of the most hostile regions in the US. It was a desert valley, almost three hundred feet below sea level and had salt pans that extended as far as the eye could see. A hauntingly beautiful, barren land that put human life in perspective.

Despite the extremes of weather, the desert was a popular tourist spot. Its sparse, vast scenery and the various national parks in the region, drew millions of visitors each year.

Yefremov wasn't based anywhere travelers went.

'Nevada Evergreen is a private power station,' Beth explained briefly. 'As Ahmed said, it's ultimately owned by a Saudi investment company, but not many people know of it. Boulder City to the north of it. The Nevada California border about thirty miles to the west of it. Spread across three hundred acres.'

She placed her screen on the table and flicked through several photographs. Arrays of solar panels. A barbed wire fence running all around. Corrugated buildings, very similar to other solar plants in the desert.

'And this is where Yefremov's holed up,' she said and brought up another image. A white-walled, concrete building. Looking to be about three floors high. 'It's on the power plant grounds but well away from the solar panels.'

Her finger flicked; a map came up. 'Here,' she indicated the building to the south-east of the plant. 'This is where the building is. Ahmed said it was constructed to house the construction workers and when the plant became non-operational, it became empty. Great location for Yefremov.'

Unrestricted view all around, Zeb agreed. *That one road over there, any vehicle on it will be spotted.*

It was well-away from any tourist track. Visitors were discouraged by the power plant's signboards.

'How do we attack a place like that?' Roger frowned.

Before anyone could reply, sounds of several vehicles drawing up.

'We expecting visitors?' Bear reached for his gun.

'Broker,' Zeb said. 'Can you get the door?'

He put on a wooden expression as his friends looked at him, puzzled. 'Broker,' he repeated. 'The door.'

'Why does the oldest guy get to be the doorman,' his friend grumbled, but went to the entrance.

He opened it and stared in shock at the visitors.

Chapter 91

⎯⎯⎯⎯ ❈❈❈ ⎯⎯⎯⎯

Sarah Burke, FBI Special Agent in Charge, fast-rising star in that organization, Broker's girlfriend, strode inside, imperiously. Behind her, a bunch of SWAT operators, decked out for combat.

Blonde-haired, green-eyed, an icy expression on her face, she stabbed her boyfriend in the chest with her finger.

'You,' she said softly, ominously, 'left without telling me where you were going. You didn't keep in touch. You didn't think I would be worried?'

Broker, one of the most lethal men in the world, swallowed. He looked to his right and glowered at Zeb who maintained a wooden expression. Bwana, Bear, Roger, the sisters, Chloe…they were looking on with interest. Not just interest, delight.

'A mission,' he stammered when she poked him again. 'You know how it is.'

'I. Don't.Know. How.It. Is,' she hissed. 'I call you every night when I am away. You can't do the same?'

'It's Zeb's fault,' Broker drew himself up, righteously. 'He said radio silence.'

'He said no such thing. He called me this morning and told me where y'all were. I gave him an earful, but he said he didn't tell you to go quiet. You are in trouble. Big trouble.'

Broker grinned suddenly. 'That sounds like…something to look forward to. When we're alone.'

A reluctant smile broke her face before her professional mask descended. Despite her apparent anger, Burke knew there were reasons why her boyfriend had disappeared. She was aware that he worked at the Agency. She had an idea of what it did and understood why he didn't tell her everything. She was FBI. He was in a covert-ops outfit that had loose definitions of what the laws of the land meant.

'Where's Riyaz Khalid Ahmed?' she asked.

'You should have told me she was coming,' Broker hissed at Zeb as he led the new arrivals to where their captive was held.

'What, and miss the fun?' Beth gloated.

An hour later, the FBI agents had taken over the ranch. They set up their command center, protocols and started identifying the dead and the alive. Interrogating the survivors would come later.

'We'll share everything we've got so far,' Meghan told Burke, who pursed her lips and glanced at the maps on the table.

'Going somewhere?'

'Yeah. To the Mojave Desert.

'What's the plan?' the SAC asked when the elder twin brought her up to speed on the findings. 'I can make a few calls. Call off that protest.'

'No,' Zeb replied. 'Yefremov and Shuren might get wind

of it. We'll have to stop those killers before they act.'

'You don't know who they are, or where they'll be.'

'We'll find out,' Zeb promised, grimly.

'Zeb,' Burke said, impatiently. 'You're going to attack a building in the desert. You know nothing of it other than what Ahmed's told you. For all you know, he might be lying. He said there are eighteen men there? There could be eighty.'

'That's what we've been telling him,' Chloe complained. 'But you know how he is. He's got that look on his face.'

'Tell us, Zeb,' Beth burst out. 'What's your grand plan?'

Zeb tapped a spot on the map. 'That's Edwards Air Force Base?'

'Yeah, so what?' Meghan said impatiently. 'That's in California.'

'Correct. But they frequently fly over the Mojave Desert. Often at low altitudes. They test new systems, new aircraft, all that stuff.'

Beth made to speak, kept quiet when her sister stopped her.

'They don't bomb buildings, Zeb,' Meghan said sarcastically, 'if that's what you're thinking of.'

'Can you get a Lockheed C-5 Galaxy?'

She looked at him long and consideringly. 'The military transport aircraft? Sure, once I make some calls.'

'And two Jeeps. Or any old vehicles. Fitted with remote controlled explosives, or some kind of timers, or triggered by altitude.'

'Tell us the plan,' Bear thumped a meaty fist on the table making them jump.

'Ahmed told us this building is separate from the power plant.'

'Yeah.'

'And that it's got its own access road, fence, cameras, the works.'

'Correct.'

'Yefremov will be monitoring the sky for drones, so we can't do aerial recon.'

'You're thinking that Galaxy will do that for us?'

'No. This is what we'll do.'

And Zeb told them his plan.

Chapter 92

⬤⬤⬤

'You got to be kidding!' Bwana exclaimed, but it was in admiration. 'It might work. Just might.'

Heads nodded around the table. Zeb's idea, like the attacks in Ukraine and Indonesia, relied on distraction and surprise. Vital elements when going up against a force they knew nothing about.

Burke frowned after a moment. 'That might work. But won't he be expecting that the Europe program is activated. That, as a result, there will be more killings?'

'Yeah.' Zeb glanced at his watch and nodded at Beth. 'Can you bring up a news channel?'

She typed a website, one that had live-video of its news reports.

A grim-faced host. A scrolling banner at the bottom.

Unconfirmed reports that there have been more shootings in Berlin, Paris and London in the night. A gunman in a nightclub in Britain, a shooter at a train station in Germany and another gunman on the Champs Elysees.

The police are tight-lipped in those cities. The British Prime Minister has made no comment. The French President and German Chancellor have stonewalled all requests for confirmation. The US State Department has said it has no information. However, social media is abuzz with news of these shootings. There are also videos, but we have to state there's no official confirmation on these killings.

The video cut to a talking head who postulated that the three governments had deliberately suppressed the news. 'It's understandable,' he said. 'Few governments will want to admit that they've failed in preventing such shootings. I predict more protests and riots in those countries. In fact, around the world.'

'That's your doing?' Burke asked, shocked. 'I heard the news when I was coming over. It's not true?'

'No,' Zeb replied. 'Clare and the National Security Advisor have been busy. They've been calling in favors in various countries. This is fake news, designed to convince Yefremov and Shuren that Ahmed has gotten the Europe program working.'

'The riots, the protests that follow, like that dude said,' Meghan looked troubled, 'those will be real.'

'Yes, and those cities are on alert. Hopefully the damage will be limited. But there was no other way. Not without alerting Yefremov and Shuren. However, we need to attack Yefremov tonight.'

'We'll get that plane. And those vehicles,' she said, her face pinched.

'Can you,' Zeb looked at Burke, 'arrange for Burt and Pilgrim to get back to Denver?'

'Sure –'

'About that,' Burt shuffled his feet. He and his coworker had been listening in silence throughout the morning. 'Zack and I've been talking about this. Maybe we could help?'

'How?' Zeb demanded.

'Well, we checked the dogs. We lost six in the attack, but the remaining ones are in good condition. Your plan needs surprise. They can add to that.'

Zeb thought swiftly and then nodded. 'This will be even more dangerous,' he warned.

'We eat danger for breakfast,' Burt scoffed and doubled over in mock-agony when Bear thumped his back.

'Alright,' Zeb turned to his friends. 'Let's go to the airforce base. We take out Yefremov tonight.'

Chapter 93

—∞∞∞—

Sidor Yefremov was in good spirits when he woke up in Nevada. The sun was bright, the air was clear, the sky was blue. The breaking news from London, Paris and Berlin was uplifting. There was nothing to mar his disposition.

He checked in with Voronoff, inspected the engineers who smiled wanly when he greeted them. 'This'll be over soon,' he boomed at them. 'Y'all can go home, then. And spend your bonus checks.'

He hid a smile when one of them cheered weakly. *Bonus! That would be a bullet in the back of their heads.*

He went to the panic room which was in the basement of the house. It was a bomb-proof room that had been constructed when the Content team had been housed there. It was connected to the outside world through high-speed internet cables. Satellite phone coverage. Passcode entry backed up by thumb print and iris scan security. Screens that monitored the perimeter of the building as well as the road to the building.

There was a separate control room that Voronoff's men occupied on the ground floor. Yefremov could communicate with it via a video screen. No one else entered his panic room.

Not even Ahmed the few times he visited. The Russian liked it. It was where he slept. It had enough provisions in it to last him months.

'I'll be down,' he told Voronoff who nodded.

Yefremov waited till the man had turned away and then entered his code. He pressed his thumb against the screen and looked at the lens. The door slid back silently to a short flight of stairs. Another door which had another passcode entry.

He entered the spacious room. Two rooms in reality. One was where his screens, his communication and security setup were mounted. It also had his bed and against the wall was a refrigerator, a cooking oven and a sink. The second room was a bathroom.

Yefremov sank into a leather chair and wheeled it to the bank of monitors. He flicked from screen to screen. The engineers in their room, Voronoff lounging against a wall, smoking, chatting to some of his men. The spymaster sighed in delight. He punched a number on his satellite phone and waited for Ahmed to pick up.

'My friend,' he greeted the Saudi when he answered. 'You got List Europe working! You saw the news?'

'Yes,' Ahmed winced when Burke prodded him savagely with her gun. 'I also bought some more stock.'

'I did too. Listen, about this DC protest,' he brought up a web page and read it swiftly. 'The marchers will gather at ten am in front of the White House. I think our shooters should open up at one pm. It will be peak crowd. There will be TV cameras, reporters. It will be prime time.'

'Good idea. Who are the gunmen?'

'Oh, I've got a few,' Yefremov replied evasively.

The Saudi turned querulous. 'This is what I don't like

about you and Shuren. You two keep details from me. I am as much a part of Hyde as you are.'

That's because you bring the least value to the table, the Russian thought. 'You know everything, Ahmed. What have we hidden from you?'

'ARE YOU TELLING ME WHO THE SHOOTERS ARE? WHERE THEY WILL BE? SHUREN HASN'T TOLD ME WHERE HE'S BASED. YOU KNOW IT, BUT YOU NEVER TOOK ME INTO YOUR CONFIDENCE.'

Yefremov winced at the outburst. 'This is normal need-to-know mission protocol, Ahmed. You have run enough operations. You should know.'

There was a taunt in his words. The Saudi was a good spymaster but he wasn't in the same caliber as the Russian or Shuren. He and his country got lucky, Yefremov snorted. If there hadn't been oil beneath their desert, where would they be?

'This is *our* operation,' Ahmed seethed. 'I should know everything. I bet Shuren knows who those shooters are!'

'He doesn't,' and this time Yefremov was telling the truth. 'He hasn't asked me either. Why are you so interested in their identities? We agreed that I would provide the killers.'

In Colorado, Sarah Burke mouthed *Back Off* to Ahmed who nodded. 'I'm just asking,' he said. 'How's it looking there? Any signs of Carter?'

'No. Can you get some more killings in America?'

'Yes, the engineers are working on it.'

'Great,' Yefremov said. 'Let's check in tomorrow,' and he ended the call.

He dialed a number from memory which got routed through several proxies until a male voice answered in Russian.

'Da?'

'It's me.

'Who else would it be?' the man said, bored. 'No one else has this number.'

'I've got a job for you. Washington DC. Day after tomorrow. One pm. You need to shoot into a crowd in front of the White House. Can you do that?'

'That's a high security area.'

'If you can't do it, I'll get someone else.'

'Of course I can. But I want a million dollars for it.'

'That's too much,' Yefremov protested.

'Listen, Igor,' the killer growled, using the name he knew Yefremov by. 'The chances are very good that I'll be killed.'

'You won't need the money, then.'

'Go, get someone else.'

'That price is okay,' Yefremov said quickly. 'But you should know there will be two other shooters.'

'I work alone.'

'All of you will be working alone,' he snapped. 'But in different positions. You are the first person I called. You decide which location you want to occupy.'

'The right of the White House, as I face it.'

'Alright. I'll message you the usual way at one pm, with the go signal. Payment to the previous bank account?

'Da.'

Yefremov made two more calls and after half an hour, he had his shooters lined up. Mikhail, the first man he had called, would open into the crowd from the right. Denis, the second killer, would fire from the front of Lafayette Square and Laurence, would take position on the corner of Madison Place Northwest.

The Russian made one final call. There was no sign of Carter but that didn't mean there was no need to be prepared.

'Vasily, how quickly can you and your men get to Boulder City? No, I want you to stay there. Come to where I am only if I call you. Yes, like a backup.'

He hung up when he was satisfied with the arrangements. The three shooters were freelance killers he had used in the past. Vasily and his crew were former Spetsnaz. They provided shooting support to the Russian mob and while they were New York based, they moved around at short notice.

Yefremov leaned back and put his feet on the desk. Everything was ready.

He closed his eyes and dreamed of being rewarded by the Russian President.

Chapter 94

'I am not entirely surprised,' Zeb spoke into his phone. 'If Yefremov didn't share details with him before, he wasn't going to start now.'

He listened for a while, grunted and hung up.

'That was Sarah,' he replied to Beth's questioning look. 'Ahmed had his check-in call with Yefremov, but the Russian refused to say who his shooters were, or where they would be positioned. Shooting time's confirmed, however. One pm. Day after tomorrow. In front of the White House.'

'We'll have to make Yefremov talk, in that case,' Bwana said.

'Uh huh,' Zeb acknowledged and turned to the large chart on the table.

It was three pm. They were in Edwards Air Force Base. A large conference room with a map of the area spread out in front of them. Getting to the base hadn't been difficult.

He had made a call to Clare when they were enroute from the Laird Ranch. Their Gulfstream had picked them up at Grand Junction Airport, along with the dogs, and had flown then to Quartz Hill Airport in Lancaster, southern California.

Clare had arranged for two SUVs and a van for the robots at the airport. Additionally, she had made more calls which had resulted in a final call originating from the Pentagon to the Commander of the Air Force Test Center at the base. The message was simple. *Receive one Zeb Carter and his crew. Provide them with whatever they need. Ask no questions.*

That order was strictly adhered to. They were received at the base by security personnel who matched their faces to photographs that Clare had sent.

The guards had looked long and hard at the dogs in the van and had then shrugged. If their superiors had okayed these visitors, who were they to question them? They sent the arrivals to the interiors of the complex.

The base was home to the 412th Test Wing, a division of the USAF that tested aircraft, weapons, and software. Every aircraft that the USAF used was tested at Edwards.

A uniformed attendant had greeted them in an airconditioned office and had then led them to the conference room. There, a stocky, buzz cut, Chief Master Sergeant Dwight Kelly had met them. 'I heard y'all need a Lockheed Galaxy. And two pilots. Two vehicles as well that should explode in mid-air.'

'That's correct,' Zeb replied. He didn't make any introductions and was glad that Kelly expected none. He had sized them up immediately and had cut to the chase.

Kelly studied them for a few more minutes, went out silently and returned with two men in flight suits. 'Lt. Colonels Benny Anderson and Chad Goring. Gentlemen, meet our visitors whose names we aren't supposed to know.'

The pilots, for that's who they were, looked similar. Both were about five feet eleven in height, lean, leathery faced, brown eyes that smiled readily, closely cropped hair.

'I wouldn't say that,' Roger drawled, reached out and shook their hands. He introduced the operatives quickly and then asked, 'You got the aircraft and the other stuff we wanted?'

'Yeah,' Kelly replied. 'Anderson and Goring will be with you until you fly out. They know where everything is.' He nodded at them briefly and left them.

'Ignore his hospitality. Kelly doesn't like it when he's told not to ask questions.' Goring chuckled. 'You, a fellow Texan, sir?' he asked Roger.

'Yeah. Unfortunately these others aren't that lucky,' the operative bumped fists with the pilot. 'Let's drop the sir or ma'am stuff. First names will do.'

'That goes for us too,' Anderson's face split into a warm smile. 'I've a feeling you folks have seen some action. You've been in the military?'

'Don't mind Benny,' Goring spoke quickly when none of the operatives replied. 'What do you want us to do?'

Their faces didn't change expression when Zeb told them.

'Tonight?'

'Yes.'

'That's private property as far as we know.'

'Yes, it is,' Zeb didn't elaborate.

'Alright then.

'You're lucky,' Anderson didn't seem put out that his question hadn't been answered. 'We had a Galaxy come in a few days back. It should be fueled and that power station, that's less than a hop away. The vehicles are getting outfitted as well. You want to check them?'

'No,' Zeb replied. 'Is there any place we can rest for a few hours? We won't be accompanying you on the flight.'

'Sure, we've got rooms arranged for you. Let's go through

the details again.'

Zeb and his team went through the plans over and over again until the pilots were satisfied.

Anderson took them to their rooms after the briefing. Two bungalows in the vast complex. 'We get visitors,' he explained, 'from the Pentagon mostly. A few defense contractors. They stay here.'

'Sleep,' Zeb told Beth and Meghan when the second pilot had also left and the other operators had departed to their accommodation. 'No screens.'

Meghan raised her hands in surrender. She and her sister had briefed the FBI's technical team that had arrived shortly before their departure. 'Yes, boss,' she said tongue-in-cheek.

'Zeb,' Beth stopped him.

'Yeah?' He turned back to the sisters.

'Ahmed,' the younger sister grimaced. 'He goes scot free? Just because he's given us intel?'

'He won't be free, dummy,' Meghan corrected her. 'He'll face jail time.'

'Yeah, in *our* prisons!'

'When this is done,' Zeb's lips twitched, 'Riyaz Khalid Ahmed will be gratefully taken in by Avichai Levin. And will never be heard of again.'

The smile that burst on Beth's face dimmed the sun. 'You fox, you planned this all along.'

'They will get justice,' Zeb said, 'all three of them.'

'Shuren? What about him?' Meghan asked. 'We don't know where he is.'

'Yefremov will tell us and then we'll find him. Wherever he is. These killings will end tonight when we put an end to the Nevada site. And then we go after the mastermind.'

Chapter 95

———— ∞∞∞ ————

Zeb and his team left Edwards Air Force Base at nine pm.

Anderson and Goring saw them off, after the pilots had insisted that they inspect the packages.

The operatives had followed the men through various buildings, brightly lit, pedestrian and vehicular traffic even at night. They climbed into two vehicles and were driven into the night.

The main airfield has three runways, Zeb recollected from his briefings about the base. Rogers Lakebed and Rosamond Lakebed have additional runways.

They stopped at one of the runways on the main base and went towards a dark silhouette, the Galaxy. It's rear loading door was open, a few men working inside.

'Your Jeeps,' Goring said, pointing to the vehicles which were strapped to the floor and sides of the enormous inside of the aircraft. 'They aren't roadworthy, but you won't be doing any driving in them, will you?'

His lips curled in a knowing smile.

'Nope,' Bwana said emphatically.

'The explosives,' Anderson indicated the packs mounted on the front and rear seats, 'there are some underneath the hood too. They'll be triggered by their rate of descent, when the windspeed reaches a critical threshold. We have timers too just in case those triggers fail. Bottomline, they'll detonate when in air, fifteen seconds before impact. They'll explode when they hit the ground. They'll burn for about an hour, afterwards. You wanted sound and fire, a spectacle. You'll get it.'

Zeb nodded in thanks.

'Care to tell us what this is about? We're good at keeping secrets.'

'You heard about the shootings in Columbus? All over the world?'

The pilots looked at each other. Their eyes narrowed. 'This…' Goring cocked his head at the explosives, 'is about all that? You sure you want them to land where you told us?' his voice was low, harsh.

'Two hundred yards to the left of the house, and the same distance to the right,' Beth replied. 'Not on the house. Nowhere near the solar panels which are at the front, nor at the back. Yeah, the coordinates we gave you are correct.'

'Of course! You want them alive,' Anderson murmured almost to himself.

'Good hunting,' Goring shook their hands. 'And if you need some help, let us know,' he grinned. 'We've a few people here who know their way in such situations.'

Nevada Evergreen was two hundred and twenty miles from the airbase. A drive that would normally take about three and a half hours.

Zeb floored it when they hit the I-15 North. He was in the lead, Burt, Pilgrim and their dogs in the van in the middle, and Bwana driving the last SUV.

Meghan checked their earpieces. They worked. She checked their comms with Anderson and Goring. Those worked as well.

A moon to guide them, the desert pale and flat for as far as the eye could see.

'You got the C4?' Beth asked Bwana.

'Yeah. Enough of it.'

'Larry, Zack, you guys are holding up?'

'Sure are,' Burt answered cheerfully. 'So long as no one's shooting at us, we're good.'

'You'll not be coming close to the house. There's no fear of that happening.'

Zeb tuned them out and focused on driving. Mile after mile of dark road sliding beneath their wheels.

A ten-minute break after two hours. Coffees from flasks. Light conversation. And they got back in their rides again.

He knew this would be different from the takedown in Colorado. Yefremov had better men with him than Ahmed had. They wouldn't be taken in by a pack of dogs running around the house. Besides, *I don't want to repeat the attack pattern.*

Getting inside the house would be the biggest challenge. Sure, they would have the element of surprise, *but even so… some of us might not live through the night.*

Zeb's lips tightened. His foot pressed harder on the gas. If anyone had to die, it would be him.

I will breach the house first.

Chapter 96

───ᗧ───

Five miles away from Nevada Evergreen. The road an inky black. All around them, land as flat as a sheet of paper. Pale. Nothing moving but them. The moon above, observing them dispassionately.

Zeb drove off the road and stopped his vehicle. The van rolled next to him and then the second SUV. The silence enveloped them, broken only by the opening and closing of doors and soft murmurs.

'Wait!' Bwana commanded and swigged a large sip of coffee from his flask. He smacked his lips, wiped them with the back of his hand and took the lead.

One am.

They were strung out on the desert, walking swiftly, with purpose. The dogs loped, effortlessly. Burt and Pilgrim beside them.

'You did good in Colorado,' Beth complimented the scientists. 'Those attack programs. How're you able to control each robot individually with just two screens?'

A question like that was music to their ears. They tripped over each other's words, trying to answer her first. Something about multiple clones of programs, a master control. Zeb shook his head, bemused and cracked a grin when Bear grunted, 'nerds,' in disgust.

Conversation died down when they were a mile away. They stopped to don full combat gear. Plate armor, NVGs, helmets around their necks for the time being. HKs were checked. The researchers made sure their command and control programs worked and the dogs responded.

At Zeb's nod, Beth clicked her mic. 'Goring, Anderson?'

'Yeah?' a Texan drawl, warm and reassuring in their earpieces.

'Let the show begin.'

'Copy that.'

The Lockheed's General Electric CF6 turbofan engines whined to life. They thrust forward the giant aircraft, weighing just over four hundred thousand pounds. The airplane rolled down the lit runway, and parted from the ground as if mocking gravity. The aircraft banked to the left as the pilots set course for the solar power station.

'You should see us soon,' Goring announced cheerfully.

Zeb led his team, sprinting towards the house, visible in the distance. A few lights on the ground floor.

'There!' Beth announced excitedly.

He looked up as a dark shape swept across the sky. Too high to see the cargo doors opening but the smaller shapes were distinctive as they fell from the aircraft.

'Three.'

'Two.'

At her *One*, the shapes burst into flames and turned into orange and yellow meteors, hurtling towards the earth.

The ground shuddered when the fiery balls landed and their explosions reverberated in the night.

'Take positions,' Zeb shouted and he, Meghan, Bear and Broker sprinted to the Jeep on the right, the other operatives went to the left.

Burt and Pilgrim slowed to a walk. They would get closer to the house once entry was made.

'SIDOR! SIDOR!' Yefremov grunted and sat up on his bed. He glowered at the screen.

'What?' he yelled at Boris.

'You got to see this. Something fell from the sky.'

Chapter 97

Yefremov blinked.

'Something fell from the sky? A meteor?'

'I DON'T KNOW. COME UP AND SEE THIS.'

He swore, slipped into his shoes and went out of his panic room. Climbed the steps and flung the door to the ground floor open.

Boris wasn't at the control station. He and several men were crowded at a window. Many others were bunched at another, to the right.

'What...' Yefremov's voice trailed off when he saw the glow in the distance. About two hundred yards from the house.

'What's that?' he asked when he had recovered his wits.

'Don't know,' Boris shook his head. 'One of the men saw it fall seconds ago.'

'From the sky?'

'Da. There's one more to the right of the house.'

'One more?' Yefremov repeated mechanically and joined the other men. Sure enough, there was another ball of fire in the night, almost identical to the one on the left. At a similar distance, too.

'How could those fall from the sky? Are they meteors?'

'I don't know,' Boris replied impatiently.

'Isn't there an airforce base nearby?'

'Da. Edwards. We often see planes in the sky.'

'Could they have fallen from an aircraft?'

'Possible.'

'IT COULD BE AN ATTACK!' Yefremov reared up suddenly.

'Nyet,' Boris told him curtly. 'That was the first thing I checked. Nothing on our CCTV cameras. No movement. Besides, if anyone was attacking us, wouldn't they drop those things, whatever they are, on top of us?'

The spymaster nodded absently. He watched the glow for another minute and then went to the monitors. Nope. Nothing there. Boris was right. Those fireballs were too far to be captured by the security camera.

'Send two teams,' he ordered. 'Check those out.'

'Rugov, Ivan, Valery,' the team leader yelled. 'You three, take a vehicle and check that out on the left. Andre, Moroz, Antone, you check out the right. Take your weapons. Be prepared for anything. Stay on radio.'

The men grabbed their AK74s, put on their jackets and rushed out of the house. One bunch climbed into a Tahoe and sped towards one flaming ball while the other group drove to the other.

Yefremov went to the window and watched one vehicle come into view and race towards the flames.

'Can you see the Tahoe?' he asked Boris who was at the other window.

'Da.'

'You,' The spymaster glowered at the engineers who had

come out of their rooms. 'Go back. There's nothing to watch here.'

He reached into his pocket and drew out his sat phone when the programmers had shuffled away. He dialed a number and waited while it rang.

'Ahmed? Da, it's me. Yes, I know it's late. Is everything okay there? No need to shout, Ahmed. There's something strange here and I wanted to check. No one approaching you, no attack? Alright, alright. Go back to sleep.'

'Nothing at the other center,' he told Boris who was looking at him inquisitively.

In the distance, something dark moved in front of the flames. The vehicle, returning.

'Rugov?' Boris snapped on the radio. 'What is it?

'It's a vehicle. Can't make out which. It's very hot. We couldn't get close.'

'Fool! Did you check around it?'

'Da,' Rugov answered in an injured tone. 'We circled the debris. Nothing there. No one.'

'Anything in the sky?'

'Clouds. The moon. Nothing else.' Boris stared at the radio in his hand as if wondering if his man was being insolent, when it crackled. 'Da, Andre, what have you got?'

'Burning vehicle, like Rugov said. I think it's a Jeep but my men aren't sure.'

'How can two Jeeps fall from the sky?' Yefremov exploded.

'I don't know.'

Zeb jammed his HK tight against Rugov's side. Bear, Broker and Meghan had trained their weapons on the two other Russians.

419

They had lain on the ground, thirty feet away from the explosion, taking cover in slight depressions, knowing that the search party would have temporarily impaired vision by looking at the burning vehicles.

They had stayed still when the ride stopped and three men stepped out, on the opposite side of the Jeep's remains.

He heard voices, shouts and then the vehicle started, circled the burn and started heading away.

'Now!' he whispered in his mic and burst up. He sprinted at the rear of the vehicle. Bear and Broker to his right, Meghan to his left, in the periphery of his vision.

None of the Russians looked back. Neither did they seem to check their rear mirrors, their eyes on the fiery husk.

He neared the rear of the vehicle. One burst of speed to reach the driver's side door. He heard a startled exclamation and then he was yanking the door open, jamming his Glock against the driver's head and was half-running, half getting dragged by the ride and then he was inside and saw that Bear was looming through the other door, had punched one of the men and the man in the middle was frozen, his mouth open in shock.

'DRIVE!' Zeb commanded. Looked back to see Broker and Meghan climb into the rear seats.

A radio crackled.

The driver looked nervously at Zeb who nodded. 'You saw nothing but the burning vehicle. One wrong word and you're dead.'

The Russian licked his lips and clicked on his comms to reply. 'It's a vehicle. Can't make out which. It's very hot. We couldn't get close.'

Zeb nodded in approval, jabbed his gun harder to remind

the driver who was in charge.

'We're good,' Bwana, in their earpieces, calm, as if it was a ride in the park. Which, to him, it probably was. 'We're heading to the house.'

'From the back,' Zeb reminded him.

'Yeah.'

Yefremov was still at the side window when Boris's radio squawked and Andre's voice came on.

'We'll check the back and come in through there.'

'Da,' the leader replied and went back to watching the glow from his side.

The Russians were highly trained, experienced fighters. They had made one mistake, however. They were all at the windows. No eyes were on their monitors. Which was the distraction Zeb had counted on.

Chapter 98

———⊶⊷———

'Get close to the front,' Zeb ordered the Russian, whose name, he had learned was Rugov.

'You won't escape alive,' the man replied defiantly.

Zeb looked at the man in the middle. 'What's your name?'

'Ivan,' the man replied.

'Can you drive?'

'Da.'

'I'm going to shoot Rugov and throw his body out. Be prepared to take the wheel.'

'DON'T,' Rugov shouted. 'I won't say anything.'

'You'd better not.'

'Approaching from the back,' Bwana said.

'On my word,' Zeb told him.

'Yeah.'

Rugov brought their ride to the front and stopped fifteen feet from the door. By then, Zeb had climbed into the back and had joined his friends. All of them pointing their HKs at the Russians.

'Open the door,' Zeb told Rugov and his companions. 'One false move, one wrong word and you know what will happen to you. At this distance, we won't miss. Got it?' he jabbed his barrel against the driver's neck.

'Da.'

The three Russians climbed out and to Zeb appeared to walk normally to the front door.

Rugov pounded his fist on it.

'That could be a message,' Meghan warned.

'Too late to do anything,' Zeb replied. 'Be prepared.'

A slat opened. A face peered out. It slid shut and the door swung open.

'GO!' Zeb yelled.

Rugov shouted something at the same time. By then, Zeb had slammed into him, sent him falling to the floor.

One round in the driver's neck. Another burst into Ivan and the third Russian. The door sprang open under the weight of the operatives. Surprised shouts and exclamations from inside.

Zeb inside the door. Bear to his right. Broker and Meghan using them as cover.

Point and shoot. That was the mantra.

One large room. One central desk. Three men in sight. All of them reaching for their weapons.

Trigger pull. Zeb's HK chattered. One man went down. Another dived to the ground desperately and then jerked and fell back when someone's rounds punched his back. The other heavies manage to get their guns out but they too went down when Zeb and Bear fired simultaneously.

'STAY INSIDE!' Meghan yelled when a door opened and a frightened man looked out. She fired high and the man ducked back.

She darted to the open door and snuck a look. 'Engineers.

Their room,' she called out. 'DON'T COME OUT. NOT IF YOU WANT TO LIVE,' she ordered them and slammed the door shut.

'Spread out,' Zeb ordered and moved quickly. Crouching low, hugging the wall, helmet on face, eyes scanning, HK steady.

Movement from below the table!

He threw himself sideways and let loose with his weapon. The roar of HKs increased when Meghan joined him and reduced the man beneath the desk to a quivering mess.

Shouts and a sudden burst of firing from the back.

'Relax. It's us.' Bwana, pleased with himself. 'Two heavies down.'

Zeb reached a door. Flung it open and ducked out of the way as bullets filled the air.

'Flashbang!' he snapped.

Meghan and Broker flung theirs through the open door. They crouched and at the detonation, punched inside, firing at shadows, knowing their friends would have orange markers, visible through their goggles.

'How many down? Zeb asked, checking the room out. It was the kitchen-diner. Crockery smashed, pots on the floor, two bodies twitching.

'Eleven on our side.' Meghan replied.

'Three here, the dudes in our vehicle,' Bwana said. 'They tried to be smart. It doesn't pay to be smart with Bwana.' He came through the smoke, Beth, Roger and Chloe lining up beside him.

'These all on this floor?' Zeb asked.

'Yeah. We came through the back which was kind of a store room that opened here. What's at the front?'

'Just one large room. Control station's there.'

Meghan cocked her head at her sister at those words and at Zeb's nod, they went to the monitors, Chloe accompanying them.

'Check out the engineers again,' Zeb told them.

'Gotcha,' Beth acknowledged.

'Ahmed said eighteen,' Bear scratched his jaw. 'There should still be four. And where's Yefremov? Any of the heavies look like him?'

'Nope,' Zeb replied. The house was silent, the sound of someone moaning. No other voices. No shouts. 'Where are the stairs?'

'Here,' Beth called from the central room. 'We've secured the engineers. They're unarmed. We cuffed them in any case, a precaution and have directed them out of the house. They'll be safer outside. Stairs are behind that,' she pointed to a door flush in the wall, to the right and behind where the monitors were.

She was standing to one side, Meghan and Chloe on the other, all of them pointing their weapons at the door. 'I sneaked a peek. Steps going up. Lights.'

'Larry? Zack?' Zeb called out.

'Yeah,' Burt replied. 'We're about fifty feet away, behind the house.'

'Can you control the dogs from there?'

'Yeah.'

'Let them loose.'

Chapter 99

———∞∞∞———

Sidor Yefremov had realized what was happening the moment Rugov had shouted from the front.

Those vehicles, it flashed through his mind, *those are a sideshow.*

He lunged through the door to the stairs. 'KEEP THEM AT BAY,' he yelled at Boris and slammed it behind him. He didn't see the Russian fall in the first hail of bullets. Nor did he see the destruction wreaked by the operatives.

He was punching the code, scanning his thumb and eyes at the door that was next to the stairs, and then he was stumbling down, breathing in relief as the panic door shut above him.

He hurried to his desk, breathing heavily. Dread coiling in him as he watched the screens, saw how easily the intruders were taking out his men.

His men were hand-picked. They had combat experience in Afghanistan and Iraq in the Russian army before they had turned private contractors and Yefremov had recruited them.

But these arrivals took them out quickly and cleanly. Less than a minute had passed since the front door had been breached and already his men on the ground floor were down.

The remaining had fled to the higher floors.

That's good, Yefremov thought. *They have the higher ground. They can attack whoever is coming up and as long as they're there, these Americans will not be safe.*

Americans. Carter and his team. Who else would it be? The audacious distraction was his hallmark. Yefremov cursed himself for not connecting the burning vehicles to the man.

He turned the volume up but couldn't hear any conversation. Earpieces and throat mics, he figured. He noted the way they held their weapons with practiced ease, how one covered the other. None of them bunched together. *Not like my men who stood at the windows, an easy target for them,* he swore savagely.

But what were they waiting for? Why didn't they go up the stairs?

Wait! What was that through the kitchen?

He sat up straight, frowning as shapes materialized through the clearing smoke. Dogs? Carter brought dogs?

But these behaved differently from the animals he knew. These were very disciplined. No barking. No checking out the house, no sniffing. And their eyes. There was something strange about them. And as they raced up the stairs, Yefremov knew what was different about them.

They were robots!

He slammed his fist on the desk in anger. Wiped the sweat on his forehead and brought out his sat phone. He hadn't lost. Nope. No one could touch him in the panic room and he had an ace up his sleeve.

'Vasily,' he said when a voice came on. It was alert, even though the late hour. 'You and your men are in Boulder City? Great. Leave now for the power plant. We are under attack.

No, I am sure they will be here for some time. You can attack them from behind. But you've got to leave immediately.'

Carter wouldn't escape the rear-guard action.

Chapter 100

———∞∞∞———

Zeb, Bear and Bwana at the base of the stairs. Watching as twenty-four robots raced up the stairs. Burt and Pilgrim calling out what their cameras saw.

'A landing on the second floor. Three rooms. First one's empty. Second one isn't. Two shooters-'

A burst of firing reached them. Shouts in Russian.

'Third room?'

'Wait up…yeah. Empty. All rooms are empty, bathrooms too. Should we attack?' Burt asked.

'Nope,' Zeb was off, climbing lightly, Bear and Bwana at the rear. He dove on the landing, slithered on the floor and fired wildly in the room, deliberately aiming high and wide. Warning shots, not kill shots.

'DROP YOUR GUNS!' he yelled.

The Russians, cowering against the wall, fired at him in response. A short-lived fight, since Zeb returned fire and his friends joined and the two men fell to the floor in seconds.

'Next floor,' Zeb ordered and the dogs reacted in a second. They flashed past him and ran up the steps.

'Cameras,' Bear nodded at the ceiling. Zeb looked up and

saw a white CCTV camera on the ceiling, its dark lens watching him.

'Meg?' he spoke in his mic.

'Yeah?'

'Have you hacked into the security system?'

'Working on it.'

'There are cameras everywhere. Yefremov's got to be somewhere, watching us.'

'I know.'

Was Ahmed's intel wrong? Zeb wondered. *Was the Russian spymaster here at all?*

He shook his head and focused on the mission at hand when Pilgrim broke into his thoughts.

'Same three-room formation. One to the right of the landing, one straight ahead and one to the left. One gunman in the room to the right. He isn't Yefremov. He's removing –'

A loud explosion filled the house. Windows rattled.

'Grenade,' Burt said, his voice shaken. 'He's taken out four dogs. He's removing one more.'

'On it,' Zeb rushed the stairs, timing his steps, knowing that the Russian could hear his approach.

He launched in the air when he reached the landing, almost hugging the carpet, a burst of rounds ripping the air above him. He threw himself into the room in front of him, his HK stretched out, its barrel poking into the door to the right, trigger firmly pulled back, a long burst that swept into the room, wild shots, but it was vital to keep the hostile from detonating his grenade.

Zeb fell just as two sharp cracks sounded. Bwana, who was prone on the floor, his head peering around the door jamb.

'He's down,' Pilgrim said, something like awe in his voice.

'Where's Yefremov?' Zeb asked when they had inspected the men on the upper floors, none of them alive.

'You've got to watch this,' Beth said, laconic. 'Come down.'

Chapter 101

Zeb stilled when he joined Meghan and Beth and peered at their screens over their shoulders. He removed his helmet and goggles and slicked back his sweat sodden hair.

Yefremov, on a screen. The Russian was relaxed, leaning back in a leather chair. A glass of what looked like whiskey in his hand. The man raised it in a silent toast.

'Carter,' his voice loud and clear through the speakers at the base of the monitors. 'Welcome to Nevada Evergreen.' His smile widened but his eyes remained dark, watchful. 'Not that we generate any power.'

Where is he? Zeb scribbled on a sheet of paper.

Somewhere beneath the house, Meghan wrote back

Can he listen to us?

We assume so. We haven't fully checked out the system.

'I'm in the panic room.,' Yefremov spoke, 'in case you're wondering where I'm hiding. I can see and hear everything that you do.'

'Impressive work,' the Russian said, taking another sip of his alcohol. 'My men were some of the best Russian fighters.'

'They weren't that good, were they?' Bwana rumbled.

435

'No, but even you would have been distracted if we played that trick on you. Great idea, by the way.'

Why is he so calm? Is this house wired to blow?

Get dogs to sniff for explosives, he wrote for Bwana's benefit who nodded and went out of the house.

'Why don't you join us?' Zeb asked.

'No thanks,' Yefremov replied. 'I have several inches of titanium door, reinforced walls, fresh air circulation…I can stay here for weeks. I've no intention of getting shot by you.'

'We won't shoot you. We didn't kill Ahmed. He's alive.'

The spymaster froze. His mouth worked soundlessly.

'Yeah, those calls you made to him?' Zeb continued. 'He has babysitters. They were listening, watching, and would have cut him off if he said anything wrong.'

'You think you're so smart,' Yefremov snarled. 'It's not-'

'It is,' Zeb insisted. 'We know everything. Your plan. The G20 Summit. The attack tomorrow in DC. Yes,' he said when the spymaster's hand trembled and his alcohol sloshed to the desk. 'We know that too. Your engineers are captured. We'll shut down their program soon. Come out. Surrender. You'll get a fair trial.'

He looked at Beth who had hunched forward, listening to some recording in her headphones.

'I'll make you an offer, Carter,' Yefremov gathered himself. 'Leave while you're still alive.'

Zeb didn't reply. He watched as the younger twin scrawled rapidly.

This system records everything in the panic room. He made a call a few minutes back. To Boulder City. Someone called Vasily, who's heading here with shooters.

Zeb nodded and showed the writing to Bear who grinned.

The big man knew what to do. He would call Sarah Burke who would ensure a SWAT team would surround the hostiles.

Bwana returned and gave a discreet thumbs up.

House isn't wired to blow.

Engineers? Zeb wrote

With Larry and Zack, outside. Unharmed, his friend scrawled.

'What are you doing there?' Yefremov asked angrily. 'There's no point negotiating with me.'

'Tell us where Duan Shuren is and who the shooters are tomorrow. Where they'll be and I'll see whether my government can give you some leniency.'

'So, you don't know everything,' the spymaster sneered. 'No deals, Carter.'

'Are you sure?'

'Yes.'

'Go,' Zeb told Bwana, Broker and Roger who shot the cameras on the stairs and started climbing up.

'What are they doing?' Yefremov called out from his panic room.

'You said no deal.' Zeb shrugged.

'That's correct. There's nothing you can do to me. The cops will have heard the shootings. Someone would have seen those burning vehicles. My embassy will get alerted when the news breaks out. I've got diplomatic immunity, Carter. I bet you didn't know that.'

Zeb didn't. 'That means nothing. Not when you are responsible for hundreds of killings.'

'Me?' Yefremov scoffed. 'What did I do?'

Bear returned and murmured *Burke's on the job. She didn't tell us but she had a team on standby in Boulder City.*

'What? What's he telling you?'

Zeb ignored him. 'Can you move this call to our screen?' he asked the twins.

'Give us ten,' Meghan punched keys. 'That's what we're working on. Creating our own network and transferring everything to it.'

'We're done on the highest floor. We're moving down, now,' Bwana, in their earpieces. 'We will need ten minutes.'

'Larry, Zack?' Zeb called out.'

'We're here,' Pilgrim replied.

'Move your dogs out. What do you want to do with the destroyed ones?'

'Leave them here. They'll be irretrievable once you've finished with what you have planned.'

'CARTER!' Yefremov raged, his face red. 'WHAT'S GOING ON? WHAT ARE YOU TALKING ABOUT?'

'Shuren and shooters. Tell us where they are.'

'NEVER.'

'In that case, you'll have to see what will happen.'

The Russian drained his alcohol in one suck. His eyes turned small, mean. 'That attack on you in New York. I organized those.'

'You need to hire better people.'

'YOU GOT LUCKY!'

Zeb looked up when footsteps sounded on the stairs. Broker gave him a thumbs up and held up the remotes for the C4 detonators. Beth held up five fingers. She folded one as Meghan rose and packed their gear. Three fingers.

'WHAT IS SHE COUNTING DOWN TO?'

Two fingers. Bwana, Chloe, Broker left the house.

One finger. Zeb helped Beth with her screens and when she left, he headed to the exit.

'Give us a second,' he told Yefremov.

Outside, they sprinted away from the house. Bwana and Bear easily carrying the gear that Meghan had packed.

'CARTER!' Yefremov yelled in their earpieces.

Zeb grinned in the dark. Meg and Beth, they've patched him on our channel.

'Missing me?' he asked the Russian.

'Where are you going?'

'You told us to leave while we were alive.'

That stumped the spymaster. He went silent as Zeb slowed down and raised his hand to stop his team.

Hundred yards, he lipped at Bear who nodded.

It was sufficient.

They helped the sisters set up their gear, patch into Yefremov's video call, and there he was.

'Where are you?' the Russian squinted.

'About a hundred yards from the house.'

'Why?'

'Give us Shuren's location and tell us about the shooters.'

'Nyet!'

Zeb signaled with a hand. Bwana and Broker pressed their remotes and the ground rumbled as a tremendous explosion tore into the night.

The operatives knew what to expect, but they too were silenced as the highest floor collapsed onto the middle floor. Concrete blocks fell to the ground, windows shattered and dust filled the air.

'CARTER!' Yefremov screamed. 'WHAT'S HAPPENING?'

'We brought down that top floor, Sidor,' Zeb adopted a friendly tone. 'But you don't need to worry. You're safe in the panic room. No one can touch you. That's what you said, right?'

The Russian looked wildly at his screens. He tapped his monitors.

'Only one of them will work,' Beth said in their comms channel. 'The one that's on call with us.'

'WHY?'

'You know why, Sidor. You aren't giving us what we want.'

Yefremov opened his mouth but Zeb cut him off coldly. 'Don't count on Vasily to save you.'

He smiled grimly when the Russian looked startled. 'Yeah. You didn't know that Boris recorded everything that happened in the panic room, did you? We got your call, tracked it back, made a call of our own. Your friends should have a welcoming party from the FBI soon. Last chance, Sidor. Where's Duan Shuren hiding? Who are the DC killers? How do we find them?'

'No,' Yefremov said fiercely.

'That's a shame, Sidor. Here's what's going to happen. We are going to detonate that second floor too. Bring down the house on you. Then we're going to warn the local and state police and the FBI to keep everyone away from this place. You know what that means?'

Yefremov didn't reply. He was breathing harshly. Standing. Looking like a cornered animal.

'You'll be safe in your panic room. But trapped beneath that rubble. That's a big house. Lot of concrete on you. You can't dig out alone. You've got food and water to survive. Fresh air? I don't know about that. Your circulation system will probably be blown out too. How long do you think you'll live, Sidor? Beneath the ground, no one to hear you.'

Still no reply from Yefremov.

'I'll count down from three, Sidor,' Zeb said and with that Broker and Bwana came into the Russian's view and held up their remotes.

'Three.'

Yefremov screamed in helpless fury.

'Two.'

Broker and Bear placed their thumbs on the buttons.

'On-'

'WAIT. HE'S IN HONG KONG. IN THE INTERNA-TIONAL CONFERENCE CENTER. ON THE NINETIETH FLOOR. ENTIRE FLOOR IS HIS. IT'S WHERE HE LIVES. WHERE HIS OPERATIONS ARE. ONLY THE CHINESE PREMIER KNOWS WHERE HE IS.'

'This is Duan Shuren's location?'

'DA. DA. I TOLD YOU.'

'What about tomorrow's killers?'

'MIKHAIL, DENIS AND LAURENCE. AT ONE PM.'

'Do you have a go signal for them?'

'NYET.'

'Are you sure?' Zeb frowned. 'We listened to the call you had with Ahmed. You were going to coordinate tomorrow, all three of you.

'DA. THAT WAS WHAT WE AGREED. BUT I CHANGED THE PLAN AFTER AHMED'S CALL. I MESSAGED SHUREN. ONLY HE KNOWS. THE KILL-ERS WILL ACT AT ONE PM.'

'What's Shuren's number?'

Yefremov slumped in his seat and recited it to them.

'Describe these killers. Where will they be?'

The spymaster had no fight left in him. 'Mikhail will be to the right of the White House, where there's only foot traffic. Denis will be in the center, coming out of Lafayette Square. Laurence will be at the left, on the corner of Madison Place.'

'What do they look like?' Zeb prodded him.

'Mikhail is Russian, Denis is Middle Eastern, Laurence is French. All look similar. Short, dark hair. Dark eyes, your height. Lean. They will be dressed in suits since it's a working day. Mikhail's got a small scar over his left eyebrow. You can't miss them,' Yefremov said wearily. 'They will be alone. They have to be, to get a clear field of fire.'

'Where are they right now?'

'I don't know.'

'Sidor,' Zeb's voice hardened.

'I DON'T KNOW.'

Is that description good enough? Zeb looked away, thinking furiously. *It would have to be*, he answered himself bleakly.

'CARTER?'

'I'm here.'

'GET ME OUT OF HERE,' Yefremov screamed. 'I TOLD YOU EVERYTHING.'

Zeb looked unseeingly at the Russian. At his friends. Dark circles under Beth and Meghan's eyes. *How did we survive tonight? The assault in Colorado?* He shook his head. He didn't know. Both operations were two of the worst-planned he had ever been on, but they had no choice. Time had been against them. He felt tired. *So much killing. So many innocents.*

'CARTER!' Yefremov shouted on their screen. He thumped his table in anger. 'WHAT ARE YOU THINKING? FREE ME.'

Zeb looked at Broker and Bwana who waited expectantly.

'Bring it down,' he told them.

Meghan shut down the screen as the house detonated and buried Sidor Yefremov in hundreds of tons of rubble and concrete.

Chapter 102

———— ∞ ————

They didn't leave immediately.

Bear, Bwana and Roger poured out the last of their coffee and distributed it. The engineers accepted the drinks gratefully. They were pale, shivering, and kept to themselves. They didn't meet the operatives' eyes and answered in monosyllables at questions directed at them.

They're just as culpable, Zeb considered them bleakly as he brought out his phone.

'Ma'am,' he called Clare. 'Yefremov's out. All programs,' he looked at the sisters who nodded reassuringly, 'are decommissioned. The engineers are with us. Hyde is dead.'

'It's over, then?' his boss sighed. She didn't ask what Zeb meant by *out*. She knew her lead agent long enough to know what that word implied.

'Not quite, ma'am. There's going to be an attack in DC tomorrow. In front of the White House, at one pm.' He explained rapidly. 'And we need to go study these programs in more detail. And Shuren-'

'What about him?'

'We haven't found him yet. Then-'

'Zeb!' the Agency Director interrupted him sharply.

'Yes, ma'am.'

'Three FBI teams are heading your way. SWAT, in choppers. Y'all will return to DC in one of those birds.'

'But, ma'am-'

'I am not asking you, Zeb.'

'Yes, ma'am. Larry and Zack, their job is done. They need to return to Denver.'

'They're the researchers? I'll arrange a state police escort for them. They could have taken one chopper but there are too many of those robots.'

'The engineers?'

'FBI will take them in.'

'Ma'am there are some hostiles in Boulder City.'

'Burke checked in with me. They are in custody.'

'What's in DC, ma'am?'

'The White House.'

At three-thirty am, the first FBI chopper touched down. A SWAT team jumped out. Two more birds landed soon after. A crew-cut man looked their way and headed to them.

'Zeb Carter,' he looked at them searchingly.

'Me,' Zeb stepped forward.

'Ross Kinlay,' he introduced himself. 'Commander of these SWAT teams. We'll secure this place. Take custody of your prisoners. That bird,' he pointed to the first helicopter, 'will fly you back to DC.'

Zeb thanked him and went back to his team who picked up their gear and loaded it into the chopper. Burt and Pilgrim hugged them and said they would wait for their transport.

'It's over?' Burt asked.

'For you, yes,' Zeb replied.

The researcher's face dropped. He shuffled his feet awkwardly. 'Next time you need us, just give us a call.'

Meghan removed an access card from her wallet and handed it to the scientist. 'That'll get you into our office in New York. Next time you get to the city, drop in.'

Burt and Pilgrim's grins lit up the night.

They were in the air when a drawl came over their earpieces.

'Howdy folks,' Goring chuckled. 'You can hear us?'

'Loud and clear,' Beth smiled. 'I thought you had disconnected and gone to bed, like other good people.'

'Who said we were good?' Anderson huffed. 'We're still in the air. We kept circling, well away from your line of sight. You know, just to see what was happening. That was quite a show. Y'all good? Any injuries?'

'Not even a scratch.'

'Never heard of an operation where that happened.

'A first for us too,' Beth said feelingly.

'Aren't you disobeying orders? Still flying?' Zeb asked.

'About that,' Goring said quietly. 'You remember Travis Garrity? The shooter in California.'

'Yes,' Zeb replied. 'He shot into a big-box store, didn't he?' He rubbed the bridge of his nose, remembering. It felt like such a long time ago.

'Yeah. My sister-in-law died in that.'

Meghan gasped. Beth froze. Zeb didn't know what to say. He kept quiet.

'Thank you,' Goring said and ended the call.

Chapter 103

Clare didn't meet them in DC. She had vehicles waiting for them which deposited them at the Jefferson Hotel on 16th Street Northwest.

Eight individual rooms for them.

Zeb called her when the others were checking in. 'We're here, ma'am. When do we meet you?'

His jaw dropped when she replied.

'You don't. I want all of you to catch up on your sleep today. I'll tell you all about it tomorrow.'

'But, ma'am-'

'Again, Zeb, I am not asking. Give the phone to Meghan.'

'Yes, ma'am?' the elder sister spoke. She listened for a long time, her face expressionless and then thanked their boss and hung up.

'What did she say?' Beth demanded.

'She said we should rest today. That's what she told you, too?'

Zeb nodded.

Meghan turned to her sister. 'Remember we threatened Larry and Zack with that washing toilet bowls thing?'

'That was you,' Beth exclaimed, backing off.

'Well, Clare said, if you and I spend any time on our screens today, we'll end up washing dishes in Alabama.'

She grinned ruefully when Bear and Bwana exploded in laughter. 'What do you think she wants of us?' she asked Zeb when they had quieted.

'She's got something in mind, for which she wants us fully rested.'

'But what about those shooters?' Chloe clutched his arm.

'I think Sarah will be doing something about them.'

All eyes turned on Broker who turned his cell phone towards them.

A message from Burke. *I'm in DC. Will be busy till tomorrow. Just letting you know. Not that you seem to reciprocate.*

'You really didn't tell her where we were?' Zeb asked his friend.

'Hey!' Broker said in an injured tone. 'I got involved –'

'You're going to get the silent treatment,' Chloe smirked at him. 'We spoke.'

'I thought you were my friend.'

'I am hers too.'

'What do you think she wants of us?' Meghan asked Zeb as they went up the elevator to their rooms.

'I've no idea,' he shrugged.

I think I know, but we can wait for one day to find out.

Mikhail arrived at Pennsylvania Avenue at twelve pm. He was dressed in a dark suit, wore shades, carried a briefcase and a gym bag. There was nothing unusual about him. He strolled to the edge of the pedestrian walkway that went across the front of building. No traffic allowed there.

The crowd was already large and noisy by the time he reached it. Placards and signs waved in the air. Noisy shouts and chants. *Do Something, Stop the Killing,* were the most frequent slogans on the boards.

The shooter's AR-15 was in his workout bag. He could unzip it, fire two quick bursts and run down the Avenue, towards Seventeenth Street where he had a getaway vehicle.

He was feeling uneasy, however. The size of the crowd was off-putting. The police were out in numbers. He knew if he went down the walkway, there would be sniffer dogs who might give the contents of his bag away. Because he had explosives too. Mikhail had no intention of getting caught and had quite a few tricks up his sleeve.

He thought of contacting Igor, but what would he say to him? That he could not complete his job? He had already received his advance, a sizeable amount.

Mikhail stood at the periphery of the walkway and repeated a few slogans mechanically as he figured things out.

He would hang around until one pm, and fire only if he could make a getaway. He didn't care if the other shooters opened up or not. He didn't know who they were and Igor had said nothing about coordinating with them.

Decision made, he raised his right fist in the air and shouted loudly. 'DO SOMETHING. STOP THE KILLING!'

He was lowering his hand when he felt a presence behind him. He started to turn but felt a strong grip on his shoulder. His feet were kicked apart roughly, his gym bag and briefcase relieved. His hand was lowered and metal bracelets went around his wrists. It had happened so swiftly, so smoothly that he had no time to react.

He was turned around to face a woman in an FBI jacket.

Other agents by her side, training their guns on him. She was blonde, was wearing shades, a triumphant note in her voice when she addressed him. 'Mikhail, you are under arrest,' and she proceeded to read him his rights.

She cocked her head when a commotion sounded in the crowd. The last he heard as he was bundled into a van was her saying to the agents, 'all birds are in the cage.'

Mikhail, one of the most lethal assassins in the world, was shackled to the floor with chains. He had never failed in a killing. No one knew of his second name and his face was known to only a handful.

His luck had run out.

Zeb and his team were in the White House, in Daniel Klouse's office. Clare was there too.

They had arrived at eleven am and had been hushed to silence. There was live feed from several FBI cameras on a wall-mounted screen and a running commentary from their command center.

Zeb recognized Burke's voice. *She seems to be heading the takedown.* He hid a smile when he sensed Broker's pride. They had come across her on a previous mission and had helped her crack a case. That had put her on the fast track with the FBI. It had also brought her in contact with his friend.

She'd been unsure then. Whether it was one-sided. She had approached Zeb who had reassured her that Broker too felt the attraction. She made the move first and the relationship was still going strong.

Beth whooped at Burke's all birds are in the cage. Flushed immediately when her sister kicked her leg. She put on a contrite expression which turned into a grin when the National

Security Advisor winked at her.

'Great work,' he picked up a phone and congratulated the FBI Director. 'Let Sarah know, oh, she's with you? Can you put her on speaker?'

'Sir?' Burke's voice came on.

'Fantastic job, well done, Sarah. I heard not a single shot was fired. Not many people even realized what was happening.'

'Yes, sir. Thank you, sir.'

'I have a few people here, with me.'

'Hi, honey,' Broker blurted, then groaned and covered his face with his hands.

The NSA laughed when she came back on the line after a meaningful silence.

'I've got to go, sir.'

'Of course. We didn't hear any of that.'

'You're in trouble,' Beth chortled under her breath.

'Deep trouble,' Meghan echoed.

Zeb waited for the mirth to die down. Looked at his boss, who evaded his eyes. Surely she realized they had work to do? Beth and Meghan had to uncover the secrets of the programs. There had to be a debriefing with Burke. And then there was Shuren, who surely knew by now that Hyde had been stopped.

They had to make plans for the Chinese spymaster-.

He sprang up instinctively when the door opened behind them. Like the previous time, he felt the force of personality even before he heard the President's voice.

The Leader of the Free World went to the youngest team member. 'Beth Petersen?' he shook her hand, smiling warmly in that way that made people feel special.

'Yes, sir...it's an honor,' she stammered.

'And you must be Meghan,' he greeted the sister. The

President addressed each of them by name and when he came to Zeb, clasped both hands in his and said, 'I've heard some stories.'

'He insisted,' Clare shrugged when the operatives turned on her.

'Yes, I gave her no choice.' President Morgan leaned against the NSA's polished wooden desk and crossed his arms. 'Clare's briefed me on everything. I can't thank you enough for what you have done. World leaders can't –'

'Sir,' Zeb interrupted him. 'The Agency's a covert-'

'I know, Zeb. No one's going to know your names or your participation. The FBI, CIA, and a few international agencies, MI6, Mossad for example, will take credit. I will work with other government heads to make sure that story sticks.'

His face turned somber. 'More than two hundred people have died around the world. All because of Hyde and these algorithms these people developed. We have temporarily halted trading in those stocks Ahmed mentioned to you. The FBI has opened a joint investigation along with the SEC. As for that joint security force…' his face darkened. 'I am going to confront the Chinese and Russian Presidents and also the Saudi King. I am going to play Ahmed's recording to them. But you know what they will say.'

'That they knew nothing of it,' Beth chimed.

'Correct. They'll apologize profusely. They'll say they will conduct investigations and guess what? Nothing will happen. Oh, sure. A few heads will roll, some folks will go to prison, but that will be for show. Saudi Arabia might even carry out some barbaric executions, but again those will be to save face.'

'The G20 Summit is in two weeks,' he continued. 'I have

spoken to the British Prime Minister, the German Chancellor and the French President. Our closest allies. They don't know everything but they are with us on the messaging.'

'Our democracies came this close to collapsing into anarchy.' He didn't hide his anger. 'Someone has to pay for that.'

Here it comes, Zeb thought, sensing where the president was going.

'I want you to send a message to the Chinese,' he said strongly, his eyes taking them in. 'We, our allies, our people, the nations around the world who have been affected…we aren't going to take this lying down. We aren't going to be manipulated. Take that last man out, Zeb. Take out Duan Shuren. Before the summit.'

'Sir,' the National Security Advisor broke the ensuing silence. 'It's quite possible he has already disappeared. That the Chinese government, disappointed with Hyde's outcome, has arrested him.'

'No, sir.' Zeb spoke up. 'Shuren is possibly the most dangerous spymaster in the world. The smartest. He would have covered himself. He would have a lot of dirt on his masters. He's untouchable.'

'No one's untouchable, Zeb,' the President said.

'I meant for the Chinese, sir.'

'Yes.' The Leader of the Free World straightened as a soft knock sounded on the door. 'Touch him, Zeb. Do more than that.'

'Yes, sir.'

'And Zeb?' President Morgan stopped at the door and faced them. 'Make it obvious, subtly, that it was an American act. And when the Chinese President calls me, I'll deny that we had any hand in it.'

Chapter 104

⸺⸺

Zeb Carter was right.

Duan Shuren was not only alive, he was active.

On the ninth day from the destruction at Nevada Evergreen, he sat in his office in the International Commerce Center in Hong Kong. It was a hundred and eighteen story highrise. It contained a five-star hotel, the world's highest swimming pool and bar and on its ninetieth floor, the spymaster had his office.

China Import and Export, read the discreet sign on the outside glass door. A visitor would see artifacts and antiquities, scattered around the office. Silk rugs, Ming Dynasty vases, sculpture and carpentry.

Shuren knew just enough of the pieces to convince a visiting customer that he knew his business.

Outside his office, assistants used to labor over their screens. They were intelligence analysts, software programmers, some of the best brains in the business. There was no one now, in any cubicle. He had no staff.

He had a few protection officers, but they were in his car, in the parking lot.

Carter. He was responsible for Shuren's state.

The spymaster looked in the polished surface of his desk and flicked a straying hair back on his head. He was sixty-three, but looked a decade younger. Very few wrinkles on his face. His hair was greying but he had a full head still. He was trim, thanks to a two-hour workout each day. Ju-jitsu, mixed martial arts. Each week he spent an hour in the shooting range.

He had been a field agent. He had run missions. He had killed. He had turned agents in Britain and America. He had organized the theft of intellectual property. He had black-mailed high-ranking politicians and celebrities. There wasn't anything he hadn't done for his country.

His acumen and foresight had brought him to the top of the MSS. And then, he had carved out a department for himself. Clandestine operations that the Chinese Premier himself sanctioned under authority from the President.

Hyde had been the project he had been working on the longest. It would have been the pinnacle of his success. But now, he had nothing.

That wasn't strictly true. He had his life. He was working on a few missions that would greatly help China, but no, they weren't of the same scale as Hyde.

Shuren had known it was over when Nevada Evergreen was destroyed. Later, he had found that Ahmed had been captured. Until then, he had hoped that they could still keep Hyde going. That the combined force of the spurt of killings around the world, as well as in DC, would push the world to the very edge and make it receptive to the G20 announcement of the three leaders.

Carter had stopped him. Chernihiv, Indonesia, Colorado, Nevada, the American agent had been everywhere. How had he found out about those locations? The spymaster clenched his fists, gritted his teeth, closed his eyes and waited for the wave of rage to pass.

Ahmed. Once he had been captured, the end was near, but neither Shuren nor Yefremov had known that he was in American custody. Otherwise, they would have made alternate plans. The Russian was never heard of again. All that the spymaster knew was that the Nevada center was destroyed. Was Yefremov captured? Was he killed? There was no way of knowing. It was the same with the engineers in the American locations. For all he knew, Yefremov and the programmers were alive, spilling all their secrets to Carter.

Shuren toyed with a jade elephant on his desk and recollected a conversation in the Premier's office.

The man was pale, seething. 'The President got a call from President Morgan,' he said as soon as Shuren had entered his office. He didn't bother going through the customary formalities and that was when the spymaster knew it was going to be bad. 'He accused China of interfering in their democracy. Not just theirs, but in countries around the world.'

'Words,' the spymaster scoffed.

'THEY'RE NOT MERE WORDS!' The Premier lost his composure. He was the head of government and reported to the most powerful man in China, the President. Didn't Shuren know his place? 'HE KNOWS EVERYTHING. HE TOLD EVERY DETAIL OF HYDE, MANY OF WHICH I DIDN'T KNOW. HE PLAYED A RECORDING OF SOMEONE CALLED AHMED WHO NAMED YOU.'

The spymaster kept a calm face. 'I don't exist,' he told the Premier.

'THE PRESIDENT SHARED A PHOTOGRAPH OF

YOURS. HERE,' he ran to his table, snatched a printout from his desk and shoved it under Shuren's nose.

'That's very old.'

'WHO CARES WHETHER IT IS OLD OR NOT? MORGAN KNOWS IT IS YOU BEHIND THIS. AHMED SAID IT WAS YOUR IDEA. YOU PROMISED!' The premier, normally not a demonstrative man, wagged his finger in the spymaster's face. 'YOU SAID YOU COULD PULL THIS OFF. YOU PROMISED OUR PRESIDENT WOULD BECOME THE MOST POWERFUL MAN IN THE WORLD. YOU ASSURED ME THAT WITH HYDE, CHINA WOULD RULE THE WORLD. NOW, EVERY COUNTRY KNOWS CHINA WAS BEHIND THE KILLINGS. THEY KNOW WE BOUGHT SHARES IN THEIR COMPANIES. THEY KNOW WE WROTE THOSE SOFTWARE PROGRAMS.'

We didn't. Those were Russian programmers.'

'WHO CARES!' The head of government flung the photograph to the floor and stamped on it in fury. 'That's a small detail,' he hissed. 'President Morgan also spoke to the King of Saudi Arabia and the Russian President. He gave our leader and those two the same message. That he held our countries responsible and if we did not get back to him with acknowledgment of our role, he would expose everything.'

'I thought you said other countries already know about our involvement.'

The Premier did something Shuren didn't expect. He grabbed the spymaster by his lapels and shook him. It was a measure of his rage that he ignored all Chinese protocol, the unwritten rules of social interaction and proceeded to lay a hand on his visitor.

'Shuren,' spittle flew from his mouth, 'I don't think you

realize how serious this is. President Morgan said tariffs go up on our country with immediate effect. That telcoms company will not be able to trade in the West. Every visitor to China will be investigated before a visa is granted to him.'

He was a smaller man than the spymaster but his anger gave him strength. He shoved Shuren back and wiped his mouth. He got hold of himself and when he spoke, his voice was steely.

'Our President denied everything of course. What else could he do? He said any gesture by America would be matched by us. He also spoke to the Russian and Saudi leaders. They too denied their country's involvement.'

'Here we are,' he said contemptuously, 'you got a special budget for Hyde. You wanted a free hand, you got that. And you delivered only humiliation. You should know that President Morgan has said our President, the Russian and Saudi heads shouldn't attend the G20 Summit.'

Shuren felt shock inside him but he hid it well. He wasn't expecting that of the Americans.

'You know what this means. You will be relieved of your duties. Your department is closed immediately. The President wants to know why you shouldn't be arrested and face severe punishment.'

The spymaster knew what that meant. He would disappear. Tortured and killed, never seen or heard of again. It regularly happened to conspirators, enemies of the country, to traitors. Heck, he had made many people disappear himself.

He summoned a thin smile. 'You know why. Because I made you and him. I got dirt on his political rivals and yours. I blackmailed party members for you. I have even killed for you. I know what your secrets are. Where the skeletons lie459

'Think before you speak. Choose your words carefully. You are talking about our President and me. You cannot cross us.'

Shuren knew what that meant, too. A kill squad would come to his house at night if he went against his leaders.

'You think I have risen to this position without some insurance? If anything happens to me, all your secrets, his as well, will be leaked to American and British newspapers. Your mistress, his, both your secret accounts, the people you ordered me to kill, every little detail of what I have done for you. And if you think you can torture me and stop that leak, think again.'

The Premier stared at Shuren, his nostrils flaring. He pointed to the door. 'Leave. You are no longer an employee of the government.'

'That is not acceptable,' Shuren began the negotiation.

The spymaster polished the elephant with a silk cloth and placed it back precisely where it was. At the right angle, the exact distance from the edge of his desk.

He knew he was lucky. A lesser man would have been killed. But because he had enough to sabotage the careers of the President and the Premier, he had survived, despite the fallout from Hyde.

He had stopped following the news ever since that meeting. He knew Western media was abuzz with rumors of Russian, Chinese and Saudi involvement in the world killings and in stock market manipulation. No one knew how that had leaked.

All three governments had denied any involvement. They had lodged formal complaints at their respective American embassies that their reputations were being tarnished.

China had handed over a secret report to the US State Department. It was a report of an internal investigation and blandly stated that the country had no role in the various events.

Shuren sighed. He got to his feet and went to the floor-to-ceiling glass panes of his office. He had a splendid view of Hong Kong Island and Kowloon Bay. Highrises and densely populated buildings filled his eye. If he got to his toes and pressed his face to the glass, he could just about make out Stonecutter Bridge that spanned Rambler Channel, to his right.

The ground was far below. A thin ribbon of road, ant-sized vehicles plying on it.

Shuren had no fear of heights. He had no fear in his office. The entire building was clad in armored glass. It could withstand a grenade attack. Security was of the highest order. He was in one of the safest places in the world.

He pursed his lips and looked at the vessels in Kowloon Bay. At the speedboats and cruises in the channel ahead. An aircraft caught his eye. It was coming in from the west, over Stonecutters Bridge. Keeping low. He envied the freedom of the pilot and its passengers.

With a sigh he turned to his desk and to his mundane activities.

Chapter 105

———— ∞ ————

The Piper Cessna had the right permits. It belonged to an elite flying club in Hong Kong whose members were very high-ranking Communist Party members and officials in government. It was effectively, an untouchable institution. Law enforcement authorities didn't dare to question the club.

The aircraft had filed the correct flight plan. It was commissioned by a research organization to study wind patterns around the city's highrises.

The aircraft had a single pilot who steered the craft high above the channel after it crossed Stonecutters Bridge. It rose lazily, effortlessly in the air, flew over Kowloon Bay, skimmed the tops of several tall buildings and returned for a second pass. A few tourists gawked at it from the waterfront. Choppers over Hong Kong were common. Private aircraft, less often seen.

Only the most observant or those with eagle eyes or with binoculars, would have seen a loading door open when the plane returned for its second pass. The aircraft returned for a third pass but this time, it rose high in the sky, twelve thousand feet over sea level and was a distant speck in the west.

The wingsuit jumper left the aircraft at that height. He was in freefall for three thousand feet after which he spread out his wings and his fall turned into a glide.

The suit flew eight feet forward for every three feet drop, its glide ratio.

'You're good,' a voice in the jumper's earpiece.

The suit was of a special design. It had a large clamp on a wide magnetic strip on his back. On the jumper's belly was a harness which held a mechanical contraption weighing four pounds.

The jumper was flying at a hundred miles an hour. He wasn't looking to break any world records. In fact, the slower and steadier he flew, the better the outcome.

His hands were outstretched, helmet over his head, oxygen tank strapped for emergency, not that he would need it because he wasn't doing a high-altitude jump.

The jumper was wearing a helmet that F-35 fighter pilots wore. It had HMDS, Helmet Mounted Display System, that gave him all the flight information and situational awareness he needed.

It had visual targeting. All he had to do was point his head at a target, and the weapons system would calculate airspeed, flight speed, angles, altitude, lock-in and fire.

He had a weapon.

The contraption at his belly held a FIM-92 Stinger, a portable missile. But this wasn't an ordinary one. It had avionics that linked it to his helmet. Its cradle extended right along the jumper's body and projected behind his wings to eject the back blast safely.

'You should see the building now.'

The jumper turned his head to the left. There it was, the

International Commerce Center. It appeared on his visor display as well.

He was visible to watchers from the ground. He didn't hear the exclamations, the shouts of surprise, or the finger points at him.

He flew easily, drag and drop were in control, no buffeting winds. He counted the floors, steered minutely until he was in the firing zone. He was thirteen hundred feet over the channel. Higher than the building, but that wasn't a problem. The ninetieth floor was in clear view, two hundred and eight yards to his left. The visor magnified his vision in an observation window. He could see through the glass panels. The few pieces of furniture, the large desk.

And Duan Shuren, seated, back to him.

The jumper pressed the firing button in his right hand. His helmet and the missile computer did complex calculations in a fraction of a second. The cradle turned and guided the missile.

His body jolted as the Stinger blasted out. It could reach a speed of seven hundred and fifty meters a second, but there wasn't enough distance to attain that speed.

In his office, something alerted Duan Shuren, like a sixth sense warning an animal of danger. He went to the window and looked out.

He frowned, not believing what he saw. Was that a diver in the sky, up there? What was that? An explosion beneath him?

That was the last thing he saw.

The missile tore through the armored glass like a knife cutting through butter. The explosion tore through the floor, destroying everything in its wake.

Down on the ground, the crowd of onlookers watched in shock. Many of them screamed and started running, thinking the building would collapse.

It didn't. The missile's payload had been carefully designed to contain the explosion.

The jumper wasn't paying any more attention to the devastation. He pressed another button on his right palm and the mechanical cradle dropped away from him and fell into the water below.

The Cessna was there, when he looked up. Above and ahead of him. A cable hook appearing out of its loading door, swaying, straightening, guided unerringly to the magnetic strip on his wings.

Its jaws opened and closed around the clamp on his back. He folded his wings as the aircraft gained altitude and tugged him up and when he was near the door, hands reached out, grabbed his and pulled him inside.

The jumper panted for a moment and then got to his feet, helped by the two figures inside. He removed his helmet and wiped sweat from his face.

'That's not something I want to do again,' Zeb gasped.

Beth whooped and high-fived him, her grin filling her face. Meghan, relief in her eyes, patted him on the shoulder. Bwana, looked back from the pilot's seat and gave him a thumbs up.

The People's Liberation Army Airforce, China's air force, sent aircraft to search the South China Sea for the Cessna.

They found it. Or rather, they found its wreckage in international waters. They also found an unmistakable presence.

The USS Theodore Roosevelt, a Nimitz class, nuclear powered aircraft carrier which was sailing to the Philippines.

Messages were exchanged between the Chinese fighters and the carrier. The carrier stated, firmly, that it was aware of the Cessna's crash. It had sent search parties but hadn't found any survivors.

No bodies were ever found.

Neither was Duan Shuren's.

Chapter 106

———⚬⚬⚬———

Zeb Carter was in the Catskill Mountains in southern New York, on the day of the G20 Summit.

He, the twins and Bwana had parachuted out of the Cessna after they had set a course for it to crash in the sea.

A waiting dinghy had taken them swiftly to the Theodore Roosevelt. To safety.

They had returned a day later to New York. 'It's over for you,' Clare had told them. 'Mission over and accomplished. Go, get some downtime. Leave everything to me.'

She had shut down the twins' protests. The NSA had taken over the algorithms. The captured programmers were being interrogated; their fate still undecided. Ahmed was with Mossad. Burke was happy and, because of that, Broker was, too. He had gone to DC to be with her. Bwana and Roger had taken the opportunity to go on a vacation, to Hawaii. Meghan had joined them. Beth was spending time with Mark.

Zeb had headed out of the city. Clare's right. We need the break.

He hiked for three days, enjoying the solitariness. Occasionally, he came across other campers and joined them for a meal. They kept him abreast of what was happening in the world.

China had accused the US of conducting a hostile attack in Hong Kong. An entire floor of the International Commercial Center had been destroyed by a Stinger missile.

Not ours, the State Department replied. *There are enough of those in the arms market. Any casualties?*

Thankfully none, the Chinese huffed.

Well, what kind of attack are you accusing us of, then? State asked, in more polite language.

What about that Cessna?

What about it?

It was suspiciously close to your carrier.

We don't tell aircraft where to crash. In fact, we prefer if they don't. Did you recover any bodies?

No, the Chinese admitted. *We sent salvage vessels but all they found was the remains of chutes.*

Who was in the aircraft?

Researchers from a weather agency.

Well, why don't you ask its staff?

The agency doesn't exist.

Not our problem.

You are behind it.

We aren't, State replied and kept rebuffing the Chinese.

Someone had uploaded a video of the wingsuit jumper and had captured his firing the missile. That clip had close to a billion views.

'Man,' one of the campers said. 'That dude must have one brass set, whoever he was.'

Zeb drank his coffee and said nothing.

At four pm, on the evening of the Summit, he tuned to a TV station on his phone as he sat on a cliff. He listened to very few political speeches, but this one he didn't want to miss.

This G20 meeting was unprecedented. President Morgan had requested that it be moved to Berlin. The British government had agreed and the Germans had been delighted. They had swung into action, making security arrangements for their guests. It was a Herculean task, rerouting the travel plans of the world's foremost leaders, preparing the city for them…but they were Germans. Efficiency was in their DNA. The city was ready for Air Force One by the time it touched down in Berlin.

This summit was also different because it was the first time the Chinese and Russian Presidents hadn't attended. Neither had the King of Saudi Arabia. Each had cited domestic matters and had fueled intense speculation in the media. Many commentators linked their absence to the rumors about those countries' involvement in the worldwide shootings.

A loud cheer from the radio station. President Morgan was taking to the podium. He began by greeting the world leaders, thanking the British Prime Minister for her understanding and thanking the German Chancellor for accommodating the change of venue. He got a loud cheer when he thanked the city of Berlin.

'Many have wondered why I requested the Summit be held here.' Heads nodded in the audience. 'The past few weeks have been intensely troubling for the world. More than a thousand innocents have died in cities around the world at the hands of shooters. Children have lost their mothers, wives have lost their husbands, parents have lost their children, brothers, sisters, families and friends have been devastated. Because gunmen, who until that point in time had not displayed any signs of mental instability or killing urges, went out and shot into crowds.'

'Peoples of the world have raged against their governments. They wanted the killings to stop. They wanted to know why these were happening. Their leaders didn't have answers. *I* didn't have an answer when riots broke out in the United States. I was as clueless as anyone else. As were the other heads of government gathered here,' he gestured at the other leaders. 'But we haven't been idle these last few weeks. The intelligence agencies of our countries have been collaborating and have been jointly investigating these killings. I can now confidently say that none of these shootings were random.'

A gasp rippled through the assembled crowd.

'Yes, you heard me right,' he raised his hand to still his audience. 'The killers were acting on their own, but we now have evidence that they were driven to their heinous acts by algorithms. Software programs that influenced their behavior and made them go out and conduct their brutal acts. Programs that were commissioned by a group of people who wanted to subvert democracy,' he thundered.

'Those people have been stopped,' he said quietly in the pin-drop silence. 'In a few days, our respective governments will be releasing all the evidence we have gathered. What isn't clear, still, is who was behind those people.'

Zeb nodded. *That saves some face for the Russians, Chinese and Saudi leaders. They are responsible, but I bet the President wants to make them pay in different ways.* He was sure there would be several calculated leaks that named those leaders.

'But we will find those people,' the President continued. 'And we will hold them accountable. As long as the United States exists, it will not allow its democracy and that of its allies and those of the free nations in the world, to be threatened.'

Applause thundered throughout the audience.

'Why Berlin?' he asked when the ovation died out. 'Because there's no other fitting city in the world for such times,' he roared. 'This is the city that unified two countries. That wall,' he pointed to the longest remaining stretch of the Berlin Wall in the East Side Gallery, where he was making his speech under a night sky to an assembled audience, 'was once the symbol of separation. Of division. It now is a symbol of hope. That humankind can rise above itself.'

This time the gathering got to its feet and clapped and when the German Chancellor rose and the other leaders got to their feet, the sound became deafening and took minutes to fade, as the President stood smiling faintly.

'Why Berlin?' he repeated. 'Because it is also the city in which Johann Schwann lived.'

Zeb stared at the small screen in his hand. He had never imagined the president would refer to the elderly man.

'Johann Schwann. Berliners, Germans, will know who he is. Many in the world won't. He was elderly, in his eighties. A pensioner. He maintained the garden in a Berlin church. But that's not all he was. He was an Auschwitz survivor. He lived through the worst that the Nazis inflicted on him. When that shooter opened up in that Berlin train, it was Johann Schwann, who attempted to stop him and died trying.'

'That's who he was. Concentration camp survivor. Gardener. Hero. Berliner. And that's why I wanted this summit to be hosted here. Because this city has seen the worst of humankind. But it has also seen the best of it. We must never lose sight of that. Despite the evil we are capable of, we can, should and *will* rise above it and bring out the good inside us. Just like Johann Schwann did.'

In Berlin, in a small apartment in Hallesches Tor, Kristina Schwann had returned from school earlier that day. She had prepared her evening meal for herself and was sitting alone in her living room, reading the day's newspaper when she remembered the summit.

She turned on her TV, paying little attention to the introductory speeches. She looked up when President Morgan came on. She listened, fascinated, as he spoke. She was stunned when the president mentioned her father's name. She was sobbing by the time he finished his speech.

'That was you he spoke about, papa,' she said brokenly, looking at the photograph on the mantelpiece and hoped that Johann Schwann heard her, somehow, somewhere.

On the Catskill Mountains, Zeb Carter sat, looking at the oranges, reds and golds that the setting sun had painted on the sky.

Johann Schwann, he reflected. People like him was why he, Zeb, did what he did.

'And honey,' his wife smiled in his mind, *'when you are done, we'll be waiting for you.'*

Bonus Chapter from *Zeb Carter*

'I have a particular talent.' The speaker was young, in his mid-twenties. He was dark-haired, brown-eyed and stood ramrod straight.

He was casually dressed—shirt tucked into a pair of jeans, belt around his waist—as he stood in the room in front of five seated men in suits. All of them had a presence.

The speaker guessed they were men who decided on war; how it was fought and where. He knew he was looking at military men. That had been made clear before the interview. Now, on observing them, he guessed they were three- or four-star generals, or their equivalents from the Navy or Air Force.

No names had been exchanged when he entered the room, in an anonymous-looking building in DC.

He had looked it up. It was occupied by various private companies and also rented out rooms by the hour.

'What talent is that?' said a balding man, as he removed his glasses and rubbed his eyes.

It had been a long day and they seemed to be nowhere near making a decision. That's what it felt like to the speaker.

'Finding people, sir.'

Several suits snorted.

'The military has enough of such soldiers, son,' a silver-haired man spoke. 'We don't need another one.'

'And killing them, sir. Killing those who are threats to us.'

That stopped them.

Those who were good in the killing arts weren't uncommon in the military, either. Or on the outside, in the private-sector world.

But the way the young man had spoken struck them.

He was utterly confident, without being arrogant. He was calm, his voice so soft they almost had to strain to hear him.

It was rare for men of their seniority to come together and interview candidates. Most men or women would have felt intimidated by them, even without knowing who they were, what rank they held.

Yet, the man facing them seemed unaffected.

He stood, arms crossed behind his back, legs spread apart slightly and looked them in the eye.

No hesitation. No fidgeting.

Many of the previous candidates had been arrogant. One had boasted about the kills he had made. The panel had shown him out quickly.

A squat, suited man picked up the speaker's folder and rifled through it. Somalia. Iraq. Lebanon. Israel. Greece. London. Belfast. Several redacted portions, to which they had access.

The current candidate had been to several of the hot spots of the world.

He had led units. He had worked independently. He had been in hostile country, undercover for months.

He spoke several languages fluently.

A superior had jotted a comment. *Has an ear for languages.*

In just a few weeks, in a new country, can speak well enough to get by.

He was a master sniper. He had won several unarmed-combat trophies. Those who knew him, respected him.

The man lingered on the last country the candidate had been to while in the military.

Afghanistan.

He whispered to his peers. The file was passed around.

'We didn't know we had Superman in our ranks,' Silver Hair said sarcastically.

The candidate's reaction astounded them.

He unbuttoned his shirt, all the while looking at them.

'What? What are you doing?' the suit roared.

The candidate didn't stop.

He removed his shirt. Removed his vest.

And then pointed to a badly healed wound just below his heart.

'I don't think Superman has such a scar.'

'You think this is a joke?' Silver Hair rose. 'Do you know who we are? Just because you aren't in the military, you think you can get away with such behavior? You are walking that close to the edge, young man.'

The speaker finished dressing and stood smartly, waiting for the outburst to finish.

'Yes, sir. And I apologize for offending you. I meant no disrespect. Way I figure, you have been sitting there all day, listening to other candidates like me. You are trying to decide who's the best person for the job. You made a comment. I do not know if you were serious. I could have said something. Lots of words, but I thought you probably have had enough of words, and hence my action.'

He paused a beat. 'I will understand if I am not selected. For whatever you have in mind.'

The suits did the bent-heads-whispering-furiously thing again.

'You are not afraid?' the balding man asked him.

'Yes, sir. I am.'

'I don't mean that stunt you pulled off,' the man waved. 'I mean in the field.'

'I am often afraid, sir.'

'And yet you came here.'

'I was told it would be a good idea to offer my services to my country,' the candidate said, smiling sardonically.

'You know you won't get paid?'

'Yes, sir.'

'Driven by noble intentions, no doubt,' Silver Hair said sarcastically.

The candidate didn't rise to the bait.

'You know what this is about?' The balding general threw an irritated glance at the interruption.

'I can make a guess. You are looking for an outside contractor. That means whatever you are planning is high-risk and has to be deniable. I was told your candidate should speak Pashtun. Right now, Afghanistan is our hottest spot. Maybe you're thinking of rescuing those three Delta operators. Using someone like me?'

Silence in the room.

'You are still bound by the declarations and non-disclosures you signed,' Silver Hair barked.

'Sir,' the speaker said, smiling fully, 'I am sure you vetted all the candidates before interviewing them. None of us would have been in this room if we were in the habit of running to the nearest newspaper, TV channel, or website.'

More silence.

'That's the most hostile terrain in the world,' squat suit said, shifting in his metal chair. 'The most dangerous fighters out there.'

'Yes, sir. I have been there. I have fought them.'

'Indeed, you have. And you still want to go back? Assuming that's the operation. You could die.'

'I don't mind dying, sir.'

'Let me get this straight,' Silver Hair said brusquely. 'You are willing to go on something that's pretty much a suicide mission. Involves no payment, no fame, no movie or book deal out of it. Why? Love of country?'

'I was Delta. Those men are Delta, sir,' the speaker said, as if that explained it all.

'You could be tortured.'

'I have been tortured, sir. Quite a few times.'

Silence.

The men stared at him.

He held their eyes.

'You like killing?' Silver Hair said, no inflection in his voice.

'No, sir.'

'What do you like?'

'Saving people, sir.'

A clock ticked somewhere. A chair scraped.

Outside the small room, faint voices could be heard.

The bald man spoke finally. 'Someone will let you know.'

'Yes, sir,' he squared his shoulders and turned to leave.

'A moment?'

'Sir?'

'Why did you leave Delta?'

'I was getting promoted, sir. That meant a desk job.'

'You don't like management? The administration side of operations?'

'I do, sir. But not if it's what I have to do all day.'

'You like the money as a private military contractor?'

'I am a mercenary, sir,' a smile ghosted over his lips and disappeared quickly. 'There's no need to use fancy words. To answer your question, I do, but I don't do it just for the money.'

'What's your name? All the folders are anonymous.'

'You don't have to share it, if you don't want to,' he added quickly.

'Zebadiah Carter, sir.'

'Zebadiah. That's quite a mouthful, son.'

'Everyone calls me Zeb, sir.'

And Zeb Carter left the room.

Author's Message

———— ❦ ————

Thank you for taking the time to read *Terror*. If you enjoyed it, please consider telling your friends and posting a short review.

Sign up to Ty Patterson's mailing list (www.typatterson.com/subscribe) and get *The Watcher*, a Zeb Carter novella, exclusive to newsletter subscribers. Join Ty Patterson's Facebook Readers Group, at www.facebook.com/groups/324440917903074.

Check out Ty on Amazon, iTunes, Kobo, Nook, and on his website www.typatterson.com.

Books by Ty Patterson

Warriors Series Shorts

*This is a series of novellas that link
to the Warriors Series thrillers*

Zulu Hour, Book 1
The Shadow, Book 2
The Man From Congo, Book 3
The Texan, Book 4
The Heavies, Book 5
The Cab Driver, Book 6
Warriors Series Shorts, Boxset I,
    Books 1-3
Warriors Series Shorts, Boxset II,
    Books 4-6

Gemini Series

Dividing Zero, Book 1
Defending Cain, Book 2
I Am Missing, Book 3
Wrecking Team, Book 4

Zeb Carter Series

Zeb Carter, Book 1
The Peace Killers, Book 2
Burn Rate, Book 3
Terror, Book 4

Warriors Series

The Warrior, Book 1
The Reluctant Warrior, Book 2
The Warrior Code, Book 3
The Warrior's Debt, Book 4
Flay, Book 5
Behind You, Book 6
Hunting You, Book 7
Zero, Book 8
Death Club, Book 9
Trigger Break, Book 10
Scorched Earth, Book 11
RUN!, Book 12
Warriors series Boxset, Books 1-4
Warriors series Boxset II, Books 5-8
Warriors series Boxset III, Books 1-8

Cade Stryker Series

The Last Gunfighter of Space, Book 1
The Thief Who Stole A Planet, Book 2

Sign up to Ty Patterson's mailing list and get *The Watcher*, a Zeb Carter
novella, exclusive to newsletter subscribers. Join Ty Patterson's Facebook
group of readers, at www.facebook.com/groups/324440917903074.

Check out Ty on Amazon, iTunes, Kobo, Nook and on his website
www.typatterson.com.

About the Author

Ty has been a trench digger, loose tea vendor, leather goods salesman, marine lubricants salesman, diesel engine mechanic, and is now an action thriller author.

Ty is privileged that thriller readers love his books. 'Unputdownable,' 'Turbocharged,' 'Ty sets the standard in thriller writing,' are some of the reviews for his books.

Ty lives with his wife and son, who humor his ridiculous belief that he's in charge.

Connect with Ty:
Twitter: @pattersonty67
Facebook: www.facebook.com/AuthorTyPatterson
Website: www.typatterson.com
Mailing list: www.typatterson.com/subscribe

Made in the USA
San Bernardino, CA
10 August 2020